MEASURE FOR MURDER

Also by Clifford Witting

MEASURE
FOR MURDER

CLIFFORD WITTING

Galileo Publishers, Cambridge

Galileo Publishers
16 Woodlands Road, Great Shelford,
Cambridge
CB22 5LW UK

www.galileopublishing.co.uk

Distributed in the USA by SCB Distributors
15608 S. New Century Drive
Gardena, CA 90248-2129, USA

Australia: Peribo Pty Limited
58 Beaumont Road
Mount Kuring-Gai NSW 2080
Australia

ISBN 978-1-912916-52-8

First published in 1941
This edition © 2021

Printed in the EU

In May, 1939, I was present at a performance of "Measure For Measure" at the Bromley Little Theatre in Kent. From that visit, this story has been evolved; but although the Lulverton Little Theatre has many things in common with the Bromley Little Theatre, especially in being fashioned from an old bakery loft by amateur hands, it must not be supposed that the members of my L.A.D.S. have any relation to the players I watched on that tiny stage at Bromley.

My thanks are due to C. F. Greatbach for drawing the masks behind which Melpomene and Thalia hide their real feelings, and the dagger, which is a faithful copy of the stage weapon lent to me by Charles H. Fox, Ltd., the famous costumiers, who also gave me their kind advice on other theatrical matters.

C.W.

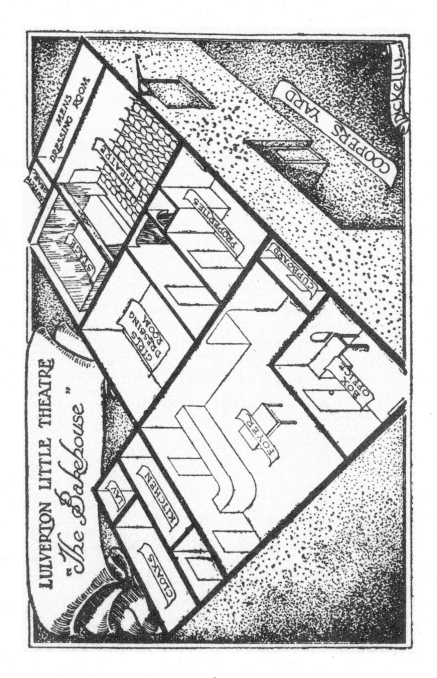

LULVERTON LITTLE THEATRE
"The Bakehouse"

COOPERS YARD

(Dickeleys)

MENS DRESSING ROOM

STAIRS

STAGE

THEATRE

PROPERTIES

GIRLS DRESSING ROOM

CUPBOARD

BOX OFFICE

FOYER

LAV.

KITCHEN

CLOAKS

PROLOGUE

Death is a fearful thing.
Measure for Measure Act III, Sc. 1.

As if she ran on invisible wheels, Mrs. Mudge, with her
string bag on her arm, swept serenely along Harpur Street,
turned without slackening her pace into Cooper's Yard, swung
to the left under the central archway of the old Bakehouse
and, disregarding the door over which some amateur hand
had painted "Stage Door," stopped dead at the door marked
"Entrance."

Humming gently to herself, she fumbled in her bag,
produced a shabby purse, extracted a Yale key and—awkwardly,
for her hands were stiff with the cold—slipped it in the lock.

Mrs. Mudge, as was to be expected in a woman of her size,
had no liking for stairs and it was like a breathless seal that she
flapped up the narrow flight leading to the Lulverton Little
Theatre. Even after she had laid down her string bag, hung
her outdoor clothes on a hook in the cloakroom, donned
her flowered apron and got out the vacuum-cleaner from the
cupboard, she was still breathing heavily.

It was early in the morning of the first Thursday in 1940
and, although the ugly, bustling town of Lulverton was
already going about the day's affairs, the Little Theatre was
silent and still—too silent and still for Mrs. Mudge, who had
been known to admit over a milk stout that, even in broad
daylight, the emptiness of the Little Theatre unnerved her. The
low-ceilinged passage and rooms, the rows of seats in the tiny
auditorium, the grim etchings and Grand Guignol photographs on the walls of the foyer, the Comedy and Tragedy
masks above the stage—all gave her, she would confess over
her second milk stout, the perishin' creeps, so that every
moment she expected to see the livid ghost of Maria Martin
or have the dead white face of Sweeney Todd leering out at

7

her from some shadowy corner. So now, when her breathing was more under control, Mrs. Mudge kept the spooks at bay by breaking into song and set about her work to the tune of "Roll Out the Barrel," accompanied by the thin whine of the vacuum-cleaner.

There had been a dress-rehearsal on the previous evening and, if the whole place was to be spick and span for the first public performance that Thursday evening, there was much for Mrs. Mudge to do, particularly in the foyer, where the buffet, tables and window-sills were littered with empty coffee cups and ash-trays heaped with cigarette-ends—some of them tipped with cork, but most of them with lip-stick. But it was not long before she finished the foyer and turned her attention to the box-office.

With the still whining vacuum-cleaner dragging behind her like an unhappy dog on a lead, she went in and switched on the light. Then at the sight of the seated figure, fallen forward so that the arms hung down, with a dagger driven cruelly up to its ornamented hilt between the shoulder-blades, she screamed and ran from the place.

The vacuum-cleaner whined on.

The gods looked down.
"There!" said Melpomene, the muse of tragedy. "What did I tell you?"
Thalia, the goddess of comedy, had a startled expression on her usually joyous countenance.
"I should never have thought it!" she said at last.

PART ONE

THIRSTY EVIL

> *Our natures do pursue.*
> *Like rats that ravin down their proper bane,*
> *A thirsty evil...*

Act I, Sc. 2.

1

> *We shall employ thee in a worthier place.*

Act V, Sc. 1.

When Ballantyne and Henty supplied most of my reading needs, I had a particular fondness for stories that opened with the young hero giving a few details about his birth—that, for instance, he had come into the world one tempestuous night in '89 on the restless bosom of the broad Atlantic—and finished with the pleasurable, yet a little sad, description of the same young man perched on the taffrail of the good ship *Dolphin,* as they said farewell to Tahiti (or Labrador, as the case might have been) and set a course for England, Home and Mr. Gladstone. And now that I am embarking on a story of my own—a story not of coral islands or the Far North, but of a plain man's doings and sudden death—I see no reason why I should not begin in much the same fashion as did those adventurous lads.

I was born, then, at Lee, at that time in the County of Kent, but now in the County of London, on the 9th November, 1905. My father, John Tudor, was a chartered accountant, having offices in Bucklersbury, near the Mansion House in the City of London; and it was by his decree—against the wishes of my mother, who would have liked me to be named Percival Herbert after her brother, who had distinguished himself at Spion Kop—that I was christened Walter Vaughan, in commemoration of the fact that I came into the world on the same day as Mr. Walter Vaughan Morgan was made Lord

Mayor of London.

With the name of Walter, one thing seems inevitable, yet I never had to answer to "Wally" or the even more horrible "Wal." My parents always used my second name and when I went to school I was known by my surname until some bright form-mate was struck by the significance of my birthday and thereupon dubbed me "Turtle"Tudor.

Of my years as a day-boy at a school in Sidcup, which is still in the County of Kent, I have jumbled memories. It is strange, but I cannot be sure that many of the things I recall did actually happen to me or to some other boy or even to a character in a book.Yet there are pictures that stand out very clearly. For example, during my first term, a skin disease spread amongst the boarders; and while we uninfected ones were at our desks, they roamed the school grounds with their shaven heads covered by tight-fitting, black skull-caps. I vividly remember with what envy I watched them through the classroom windows, climbing the trees in the Grove or kicking a rugger pill about Big Field. How willingly then would I have fallen victim to ringworm!

There are other pictures: a boy fainting in the school chapel during the Armistice Day silence, the English master reading aloud from *The Last Days of Pompeii* on a sulky summer's afternoon, a boy killing a frog by throwing it against a wall....

Then there are smells and tastes: a single whiff of floor polish and I am transported to those school corridors; of linseed oil, to the cricket-pavilion; of ammonia, to the chemmy lab.; of freshly sharpened pencils, to the class-rooms. One bite at a banana and I am carried back to the sandwiches that my mother prepared for my lunch and stowed away in my satchel before I left home in the morning.

At games my achievements were few. I played cricket and rugger because I was forced to, and under the same compulsion, entered every year for the school sports. The peak of my athletic career was reached in 1921, when I was second in the cross-country run and second again in the half-mile, both times being beaten by a boy called Ridpath.

It was curious about Ridpath. As I have said, I was a dayboy—or day-bug, as we used to be called. Ridpath was a boarder, his parents being abroad, and he and I were friends. That may not seem unusual, but at our school it was. There was a clearly defined barrier between day-boys and boarders, hence the scornful name of day-bug. Outside the classrooms, the boarders kept to themselves—and the day-bugs were expected to do the same. Of course, at that time the boarders were in the majority. Nowadays, at the same school, with the day-boys far outnumbering the boarders, there is a very different state of affairs.

Yet Ridpath and I were firm friends, not because he was out of sympathy with his fellow boarders, for no boy in the school was better liked than he, but because each of us found fellowship in the other. On Sundays during term-time, he sometimes came to tea with us at Lee and was a great favourite with my mother, who was accustomed to make cakes for him and slip them in my satchel with my books and banana-sandwiches. Once, as an alternative to spending his summer holidays in the lonely, empty school, he came away with us to Walton-on-the-Naze.

Just as I was called Turtle, so was he known to us as Tiddler 2. Tiddler 1 was his much senior brother, who left before my time and was killed on Messines Ridge. His initials were T. W., from which it was a natural step to Tiddler, and as at our school a nickname was a fraternal monopoly, young Peter Ridpath became Tiddler 2.

I have mentioned that Ridpath beat me in the cross-country and the half-mile, but that was not symptomatic of our association. Tiddler was not brilliant in all things while I struggled along behind. In fact, neither of us showed much distinction in work or play. I was a little better at French, English and cricket; he a little better at history, geography and fives. There was nothing to choose between us at arithmetic, algebra or geometry—we were both hopeless. Nor were we always vieing with each other, like the two William Wilsons in Poe's story. We were too indolent for rivalry.

His only real advantage was that he could play the piano by ear, whilst I could not play it at all.

As for our looks, he was tall, with fair curly hair, delicate features and a thin, sensitive nose; and I was dark, of normal height and with nothing noteworthy about my face, except that, in later years, it tempted people to borrow money from me.

In 1922 we both failed to matriculate, but managed to scrape home with General Schools; and at the end of the same year we left school, he to join his parents in Corfu and I to enter business. Oddly enough, my father did not belong to the keep-the-old-firm-in-the-family school, and was in no mind to have me in the office. I think he was right. Nothing disorganises a concern so much—except, of course, the introduction of System—as the boss's son beginning in a junior position, with the object of picking the brains of those who are later to be his employees. I wanted to be a motor-engineer, but notwithstanding all my expostulations, my father put me into a bank.

It was one of the Big Five and I had not been there a week before my preconceived idea that all bank clerks stand behind counters, languidly paying out and receiving money, suffered a radical change. I was assigned to what was known as the Clearing Dept. at the Head Office of the bank, in which I spent my days sorting thousands of cheques into alphabetical branch-order and casting totals on an adding-machine. The work was easy, but deadly monotonous and, for an absent-minded fellow like me, full of pitfalls. Ryde so much resembles Rye when time is short, and Shaftesbury looks so very like Shrewsbury in a poor light, so that hardly a day passed without my generous contribution of "mis-sorts," all bringing with them the danger of loss to the bank by delayed clearance.

There were sixty-five of us in one enormous room and it was almost impossible to make oneself heard for the continuous, deafening clatter of the adding-machines. Before I got accustomed to it, I went home in a state of nervous exhaustion. I have a few memories of those years. Hot midsummer balances, when the work was heavy. . . . Jackets and waistcoats discarded, sleeves rolled up. . . . Yards of paper jerking from dozens of machines. . . . Most of us carrying on shouted conversations with our neighbours.. . . . We banged down the keys and pulled the handles automatically, yet we were not galley-slaves. Provided we got the work done, there was no strict control. Sometimes one of us would start a song.

Then, on the stroke of half-past three, there was a lull. The banks were closed at that time, and although the public never saw us, we were forbidden to smoke before then. With our pipes and cigarettes going, we settled down again to our machining. It grew nearer to five o'clock, when everything had to be ready for the postmen, who made a special call for our many bulky sacks. One by one, we finished our machining, slipped an elastic band round each branch's consignment of cleared cheques, pushed them into the envelopes and stuck down the flaps with a "slosh" brush. Then one of the tardy ones would discover that the paper in his machine had long since been turned off the spool and that, for half an hour, he had been uselessly machining "on the wood." He would glance at the clock and send out a distress signal, which would be answered by a general "muck-in," half a dozen of his colleagues splitting the balance of his work up between them. *Esprit de corps* was strong in the Country Clearing in those days.

It has always been a mystery to me how I managed to get my father to allow me to leave the bank. Suffice it to say that I did. As I have said, I was interested in cars; and in the early autumn of 1926, when I was nearly twenty-one, what I then thought to be a fine opportunity presented itself. Eighteen months before, two old school friends of mine had opened a garage at Chislehurst and had made quite a success of it. I had, at that time, one of those exhilaratingly suicidal machines known as motor-cycles and, as a friendly gesture, I used to go to their place for petrol, oil and the spare parts that seem a daily necessity for a motor-cycle. One evening, they broached the question of my going into partnership with them.

At first it appeared that all they wanted was my active assistance, but later it emerged that their more important need was more capital, not to keep the business running, for it was already a paying concern, but to enable them to buy some adjoining land and erect lock-up garages. I laughed at them at first, yet they managed to persuade me. It took me two days to pluck up enough courage to mention the matter to my father and even then I might still have faltered, had he not given me an opening.

The time was propitious. Dinner had been to my father's liking and we were sitting together in the garden, I with a cigarette and he with the cigar that was his strict daily allowance. After a silence of some minutes, during which I discarded various introductory remarks, he said:

"How are things at the bank, Vaughan?"

I took the cue. "Not very good. I'm getting awfully fed up with it."

"We all get fed up with our jobs, Vaughan. There's not much entertainment in earning your bread and butter, but you've got to stick at it."

"But I'm getting nowhere!" I protested. "I've been in the bank nearly four years and if they hadn't brought in a couple of new juniors this year I should still be just where I started."

"You're rather young yet for a general manager," murmured my father.

"And what will happen if I ask for a transfer to a branch? They'll send me to Shadwell or Wapping Old Stairs!"

I paused for effect.

"The other day," I went on, "I was talking to Jack Harvey and Phil Pearson. They run a garage at Chislehurst, you know, and they were telling me ..."

There is no need to repeat the whole conversation. I went

on to paint in glowing colours a picture of myself as owner of a chain of garages, repair shops and transport depots, with fleets of plump and luxurious motor-coaches; master of my fate, captain of my soul, a prosperous son, who would keep his parents in comfort in their old age. I cannot believe that my father was convinced by my flummery, yet he agreed, not only to my leaving the bank, but also to himself putting up the necessary capital.

It must have been the cigar.

For the first few months all went well with the garage. I soon discovered two things. Firstly, that the hours I had worked at the bank were trifling compared with the time I was forced to put in at the garage. I used to arrive home at all hours of the night, bone weary and black with grease from head to toe; and had to be up again at six o'clock the next morning. And secondly, that the garage owed its prosperity to Jack Harvey. Pearson was competent enough, but he had neither Harvey's business instincts nor his magic touch with internal-combustion engines. I was on a par with Pearson. I knew something about magnetos and back-axles, and had enough talent to keep the firm's books in order, but to Jack Harvey were due the recommendations of delighted car-owners and the gratifying figures in the credit columns. Harvey led; Pearson and I followed.

On the 1st May, 1927, disaster overtook us.

Harvey and I, after a long and heavy day, closed up the garage just after eleven o'clock. He also had a motor-cycle, but that same afternoon the engine had been taken to pieces for overhaul and other matters had prevented its reassembly. So as he lived not very far from my own home, I offered him a lift on the pillion of my machine.

That I was wearied to the point of collapse was the principal reason for what happened, although the feeble ray from a nearly exhausted acetylene lamp was a contributory cause. I was anxious to get home before the lamp failed and did not loiter on the way. At Mottingham village I turned to the right and, a couple of hundred yards further along, swung to the left into the new arterial road, where I wrenched round my twist-grip throttle-control as far as it would go.

For something like half a mile the arterial road runs parallel with the railway, then it turns to pass under the line. As we roared along the straight, Harvey shouted over my shoulder:

"We're knocking up the parasangs!"

At a dangerous speed, I threw the machine into the curve—and everything seemed to happen at once. A swiftly moving car shot out from under the bridge. I swerved to the left to avoid it. In front of me, under the bridge, a shape sprang out of the shadows—a cyclist with no rear lamp.

It must have been a ghastly crash, but I do not remember it. I came out of it with no more hurt than a broken leg. The cyclist and Jack Harvey were killed.

That was the end of the garage. During the many weeks that I was out of action, Phil Pearson tried to carry on alone and, when I was fit again, I was there to help him; but Harvey's inspired touch was lacking. Our profits dropped away, until we lost money every week; and on the 29th September, 1927, we closed down for good, sold the business and got out with ten pounds apiece.

So ended another chapter of my life—a chapter that left its mark on me, for before the accident, though I had decided views, I hardly knew what it was to lose my temper; yet afterwards I was too often like Jacques' soldier: "Jealous in honour, sudden and quick in quarrel." And though many years have since passed, there are moments when I go suddenly cold at the thought of that collision, and recall with a deep remorse the last tired, happy shout: "We're knocking up the parasangs!"

II

Peace here; grace and good company!
Act III, Sc. I

What next? was the question that occupied my mind in the autumn of 1927. Phil Pearson took up journalism and to the surprise of everyone, including himself, made a great success of it; but I was not to fall on my feet so easily. My father said very little about the failure of the garage enterprise, merely suggesting that I should look round for a steady job with some well-established firm. I offered him the tenner saved from the wreck, but he refused to take even a part of it. As for a new job, on one point I was adamant: I would not seek reappointment with the bank.

I bought the *Telegraph* every day and studied the Situations Vacant. Nothing appealed to me. I had no wish to be a lift-boy, a funeral furnisher or a door-to-door canvasser. Then on the next Old Boys' Day, I fell in with a former classmate, who reported considerable achievement in the estate agency world.

Here was employment after my own heart—or so I thought. It did not fetter one to a desk or a calculating-machine, offering instead a good deal of personal freedom. There was scope for a young man of initiative, and the ever-present chance of pulling off a big transaction. My friend was with a large London firm, and my first ardour was rather damped when he told me that, although he was, by then, a junior negotiator, he had, for the past three years, been an articled pupil, receiving five shillings a week, for which period of apprenticeship his father had laid out the sum of three hundred pounds.

That seemed to put the kibosh on it. The patience of my own parent could hardly be further tried in that direction. But my friend went on to explain the alternative: employment determinable by seven days' notice, with a flat weekly wage of one pound and no commission, but with the chance of appointment as junior negotiator at the end of three years.

This was more to my taste. Surely, I asked my friend, one could learn enough in three years to ensure thenceforward a steady flow of shekels into the privy purse? Being, as he was, on the point of concluding a sizeable deal, he gave me an enthusiastic affirmative. I heard afterwards that the sale fell through and he gained nothing save experience, but by then I had taken service with Messrs. Littlesmiths of Maddox Street, W.

I was four years with Littlesmiths. Towards the end of 1930 I was made a junior negotiator and was entrusted with such minor affairs as the letting of small houses and flats. I learnt a lot during those four years—and all of it was not in the syllabi for the professional examinations. It is in *Ecclesiastes,* I believe, that one is assured that the race is not to the swift, nor the battle to the strong. My own impression was that if one was not swift and strong, both the race and the battle were to the senior negotiator. Many a nice little slice of commission slipped through my fingers because a colleague took a telephone-call intended for me.

For all that, I did fairly well and gained some reputation for alertness in and around Maddox Street. In November, 1931, just after my twenty-sixth birthday, I received from a rival firm an offer tempting enough to be accepted forthwith. By that time I had passed the associate examinations and was entitled to put a modicum of letters after my name. In my new post I deserted small houses and flats and concentrated on more important subjects. After another year I changed my employers again, this time becoming a senior negotiator; and in June, 1934, with a useful little balance in the bank, reached a momentous decision—to start in business on my own.

Although by birth a Londoner, I had always hankered for country life. There was now the opportunity to gratify that wish. On more than one occasion I had heard that Down-shire offered innumerable openings for a go-ahead young estate agent such as I fancied myself to be, and that Lulverton, its third largest town, on the main road to the coast, would be an admirable centre.

At that time I was running a Baby Austin, and on the first Sunday in July, accompanied by my mother and, in spite of his protests, my father, I turned southward. Lulverton lies about three miles inland from Southmouth-by-the-Sea, in the middle of the sea-plain between the South Downs and the English Channel. It is an unlovely town, dominated not by the spire of a beautiful church, but by the chimney of a hideous rubber-heel factory. Its only claim to fame is that it was the birthplace of William Rycraft, the eminent nineteenth-century philosopher and mathematician, whose many works on the inductive sciences and moral philosophy earned him a tablet in the parish church and the high disfavour of John Stuart Mill.

Yet, for all its architectural shortcomings, there is much to be said for Lulverton. Its twenty thousand inhabitants are industrious, its death rate and unemployment are low, its civic consciousness high and, in 1934, it was ripe for development.

We parked the car, had some lunch at the Bunch of Grapes, a fine old hostelry, and afterwards went on a tour of inspection. As it was Sunday there was not much afoot, but I saw enough to make up my mind. My father was more sceptical and my mother not at all keen; he because this would be the second time I had thrown my bonnet over the windmill; she because it would force me to live away from home.

When we got back to Lee the whole thing was thrashed out and it was I who eventually prevailed. Several more trips during the ensuing weeks enabled me to settle matters to my satisfaction. I took a tenancy of some premises at the bottom of Beastmarket Hill, right in the business centre of the town and, at some expense, fitted them up. I engaged the services of a shorthand typist and an office boy; and arranged board residence with Mrs. Doubleday at Eagle House in Friday Street.

On the 30th July I opened my doors to the public, but I knew enough not to wait for them to arrive. Business does not come to an estate agent: he has to go out after it. So I put on my hat—and luck was with me right from the start. I concentrated on the development of shop properties and sites, by which I do not mean that it was I who did the developing. I was just the go-between, introducing the wishful seller to the would-be purchaser. Sometimes, of course, nothing came of laborious negotiations, but my first year showed a very handsome profit, allowing me to buy a larger car and give the staff a rise. 1936 was a bonanza year, for during it I managed to interest one of the big multiple stores in some ramshackle old premises in the High Street. My commission on that transaction alone made my annual salary as a senior negotiator look like a schoolgirl's pin-money.

The social life of Lulverton was pleasant enough. I have always been of a gregarious turn of mind and it did not take me long to enter into most of the local activities: golf, tennis, bowls and the rest. When other recreation was lacking, there were always the South Downs; and, during the winter evenings, bridge, billiards or snooker under Mrs. Doubleday's hospitable roof, or darts in the public bar of the Bunch of Grapes.

Mrs. Doubleday, of whom I shall later have more to say, called her establishment a Guest House. Although casual visitors came and went, there were six permanent residents besides myself. Some description of them will not be out of place, for they all play their part in my life story.

First there was old Mrs. Stoneham, presumed to be a widow. She was tireless at crochet-work, a wily cribbage player, an inveterate gossip, the terror of the servants and undisputed ruler of the roost. She drank Vichy water with her meals and sent most of the food back to the kitchen. In the winter she occupied the easy chair to the left of the fireplace in the lounge, and in the summer the one to the right: and woe betide the presumptuous fellow who forestalled her! As summer or winter approached, we others ran a sweep, the winner being the one to forecast the exact date upon which Mrs. Stoneham switched from one side of the fireplace to the other.

The second most important resident was Mr. James Henry Garnett, a retired hardware manufacturer from Wolverhampton. He was a widower and had come from the Black Country to Lulverton in order to be near his daughter, who was the wife of a departmental manager at the rubber-heel factory. Somewhere in the middle sixties, he was solidly made, dour of manner, fond of his glass of stout, and a regular reader of the *Midland Counties Express,* the *Hardware Trade Journal* and the *Ironmonger.* Preferring quantity to quality, his taste in food was primitive. I believe he would have dined off cold cabbage, so long as there was enough of it. Rumour had it that he was very well-to-do and had money invested in house property in the district. The only game in which he consented to join was solo, and then called only on a certainty. His hobby appeared to be cycling, for he frequently set out soon after breakfast in Norfolk jacket, knickerbockers and cap, and returned at dusk, to spend the rest of the evening with a fat, red leather-covered notebook, in which he made numerous entries. Bad weather did not curtail these excursions; when it rained he wore a waterproof cape and leggings of a poisonous yellow.

Mr. Garnett was the only one of us to challenge Mrs. Stone-ham's autocracy, although he never gained a conclusive victory, his invariable technique being to stand athwart the middle of the room, with his arms hanging down and his great hairy hands half clenched, his heavy grey brows drawn over his eyes and his big lower lip protruding towards Mrs. Stoneham, who would serenely continue her crochet and say in a clear, incontrovertible tone:

"I prefer the wireless *off,* Mr. Garnett."

The radio was not the only bone of contention, of course, but whatever the trouble had been, Mr. Garnett would stand glowering for some moments, then swing round, lumber across the room, close the door gently behind him—oddly enough, he never slammed it—and march upstairs to the lavatory, where he would vent his rage on the apparatus known in plumbing circles as a water waste preventer.

Then there was Miss Tearle, a middle-aged cripple with both legs in irons—a woman of sweet disposition, a crossword addict, yet as diligent with her needles as Mrs. Stoneham with her crochet hooks. I was told that her private income was very small, but I heard, too, of the good she did by stealth in Lulverton. The servants adored her, and if I had a criticism to voice, it was that she was far too prone to play yes-woman to old Mrs. Stoneham.

Fourth in order was Mr. Mortimer Robinson, a grey-haired bachelor of fifty, who was chief clerk of the valuation and rating department of the Urban District Council. He was a reserved, modest little man, but, when in the mood, a good conversationalist; always well and quietly dressed in black jacket and striped trousers, a wing collar, a pearl pin in his dark tie, grey spats and a white slip under his waistcoat. He always carried a pocketful of pencils of various colours, was secretary of the bowls club and a doughty exponent of end-game play at chess.

Next there was Jack Gough, who was in the local branch of the Southern Counties Bank. I want to describe him with clemency, for he was a dear fellow and became a close friend of mine, yet I cannot, with justice, call him anything but coarse-featured. If I needed a kinder word, I should say Gothic, but I do not wish it to be thought that his ugliness was the ugliness of Bulldog Drummond—the ugliness that women fall for in swooning droves. Poor Jack had the face of a—well, of a ruffian. His sandy hair was always untidy, he wore rough tweeds, brightly coloured shirts and heavy brown shoes whenever he got the chance; his flannel trousers were baggy and always seemed on the point of parting company with him: and for months after his advent to Mrs. Doubleday's, Miss Tearle looked at him affrightedly and refused all his courteous offers of help in winding her knitting-wool. He had been educated at a good school, his voice was pleasantly cultured and he wrote poetry for his Bank magazine under the name of "Gregory Gaunt." He was in the late twenties and invariably short of money. If he had any counterpart in English literature, it was Caliban—Caliban before that preposterous old humbug Prospero got hold of him.

I ought to have mentioned the sixth guest before Jack. She was Myrna Ashwin, a junior mistress at the Lulverton High School for Girls. She came to live at the Guest House in 1937 and was then not much more than twenty-one: a pretty, vivacious, dark-haired little thing, with the merest suggestion of freckles, a musical voice—and a will of her own. Before she had been with us very long, Jack Gough fell for her with a resounding bump, but she thought less of him than Miranda of Caliban and Gregory Gaunt had much to say about unrequited passion in the Southern Counties Bank magazine.

The summer of 1938 saw the beginning of the Little Theatre, and the Lulverton Amateur Dramatic Society—or LADS, as we came to call it. I was there at the inception, which took place at South Down Tennis Club on Saturday, the 13th August, just after I had got back from an ill-conceived and rather too eventful holiday in the Bavarian Alps. Like many another great enterprise, the Little Theatre was started by a casual remark—and it was I who made it.

It had grown too dark to play and ten or twelve of us, some from the adjoining bowling-greens, were sitting about in deck-chairs, smoking, drinking lemonade, shooing off the gnats and lazily making conversation. Of those whom I have already mentioned, three were there that evening: Myrna Ashwin, Jack Gough and Mr. Mortimer Robinson who was, as usual, faultlessly clad, but, as a concession to the sultry weather, had discarded his sober black for a white linen suit and a Panama hat.

The talk drifted from one subject to another, lingered over the Czecho-Slovakian crisis that was then looming on the international horizon, turned to happier things like cricket, and eventually lapsed into a comfortable and unembarrassed silence. It was broken—or is that too harsh a word?—by the tuneful voice of Myrna Ashwin.

"It's funny," she said, "that there's no amateur dramatic society in Lulverton."

Mr. Mortimer Robinson answered her: "We had one some years ago, but it petered out, largely through lack of funds."

"Well," said Myrna firmly, "I think there ought to be one. The Whitchester Society have given some jolly good shows. Last year they did 'The Pirates of Penzance' and 'Twelfth Night' and the place was packed at every performance. Why can't Lulverton do the same? There must be plenty of talent."

Jack Gough's deck-chair was on its lowest notches and his clasped hands were behind his head.

"Catch me on the stage," he said drowsily.

"I said *talent,*" retorted Myrna witheringly, and Jack squirmed even further down in his chair.

"As I just suggested," remarked Mr. Mortimer Robinson, "it is more a question of money than dramatic ability. Even an amateur society, in which all services are given free, must have financial backing."

Myrna replied: "That's easy. All you have to do is ask the richest man in the district to be president, the next richest to be vice-president and all the other money-bagses to be patrons. Then you could be secretary, Mr. Mortimer Robinson, and soak them."

He smiled at her. "The secretaryship of the bowls club is quite enough for me."

Myrna turned in my direction.

"Then you, Mr. Tudor? You'd make a ducky secretary."

I shook my head and trod a cigarette-end into the grass.

"Anything," I said, "but that. Prompter, stage-carpenter—call-boy, even. But secretary, no. He's the man who gets all the brickbats." I paused before adding: "Why can't a secretary be chosen from the other six, Miss Ashwin?"

"Only because you men always like to run the show," she retorted. "I'd take it on like a shot. What do I have to do first?"

"Call a meeting," Mr. Mortimer Robinson told her.

"Get into touch with everybody likely to be interested and—"

"Soak 'em," murmured Jack next to me.

Myrna elected not to hear him.

"I see," she said. "It shouldn't be difficult. There must be hundreds of people in Lulverton who are keen on the drama." She swung round in her chair to address a shadowy, recumbent figure. "Mr. Manhow, you've got to help."

As yet, I have made no mention of Paul Manhow. By profession an architect, he lived with his widowed mother, whom he had to support. He was a stocky young man, still on the sunnier side of thirty, with a large white, rather flabby face. Fond of bodily comforts, idleness and the fierce black briar that seldom got far from between his teeth, he was much given to Left Wing arguments, fervent and prolonged, but delivered in a slow drawling voice. He always wore a bow-tie.

How can I best depict Paul Manhow's character? By inclination, he was a sluggard. He liked indolence for its own sake; yet once roused, he was dynamite. There is a short story by the late Stacy Aumonier. It is called "An Adventure in Bed" and concerns a man called George, who spends most of his life between the sheets. "It was sheer laziness," the author says. "But not laziness of a negative kind, mark you, but the outcome of a calm and studied policy." Then, on one of his brief expeditions into the outside world, he meets a girl—"a daughter of sunshine and fresh air, and frocks, and theatres and social life." Slowly she changes his mode of living; drags him more often from his bed. They marry. He begins to work, to get restless, to use the energy stored up during his years of sloth. He gets worse. Like Frankenstein, his wife has created a monster that she cannot control. He works feverishly all day and seeks pleasure well into the night. His vitality exhausts her, till finally, she cuts the Gordian knot and leaves him. And George goes back to bed.

Paul Manhow was like George. It took a lot to stimulate him, but, when fully awake, no wire was more alive than he. Up to the time of our talk on that summers-evening,

I had no knowledge of this charactertistic of his, thinking him merely turgid and dull. Myrna knew better. Now at her direct appeal, he grunted.

"Game's not worth the candle," he said. "Too little to show for it."

After which pronouncement, he grunted again, replaced his pipe in his mouth and spread consternation among the gnats with a great cloud of smoke.

"Well," asserted Myrna, "I think it's a grand idea."

"The former dramatic society," observed Mr. Mortimer Robinson, "gave their performances in Holy Trinity Hall."

"Then no wonder they failed!" laughed Jack Gough. "It is an awful dump. Poky, draughty and darned uncomfortable."

"Yet," Mr. Mortimer Robinson reminded us, "there are very few alternatives. And the Holy Trinity charges are very reasonable."

It was then that I made my casual remark, little knowing where it was going to lead us. _

"Wouldn't it be quite good fun," I suggested, "to fit up our own theatre?"

The silence that followed was not of awe or surprise, but rather of indifference, as if I had idly alluded to the sport to be had in jumping over the moon. Then there was creaking and heavy movement in the dusk, as Paul Manhow sat upright in his deck-chair.

"Tudor," he said portentiously, "I see something there."

"*You know, my dear,*" *said Melpomene, with a note of intense satis-faction in her voice.* "*I'm not too easy in my mind about all this.*"

Thalia raised her eyebrows in pretty amazement.

"*Why, darling? Things seem to be going along very pleasantly indeed.*"

"*Quite likely,*" *replied the sad goddess,* "*but it is always calmest—*"

"*I know the rest,*" *Thalia told her hurriedly.*

III

> *. . . all difficulties are but easy when they are known.*
> Act IV, Sc. 3

The sleeper had been roused. From the enkindling spark, the flames caught and spread. Paul, at that time, was not interested in the drama as such, but the Lulverton Little Theatre became his ruling passion. He thought of very little else, was for ever planning and scheming, and carried us all along on the flood-tide of his enthusiasm.

The first step was to procure suitable premises, which was where I, as an estate agent, came in. All I could find, however, were the disused store-rooms over an old bakehouse in Cooper's Yard, just off Harpur Street. They were in a very dilapidated condition, but the great advantage was that we were offered them rent free. Dickson, Parrish, Willmott & Lister, who were my own solicitors, represented the owner, whose only stipulations were that he or she should remain anonymous and that our occupation should be entirely at his or her will and determinable at any time.

I took Myrna and Paul along to see the place. The ground floor had long since ceased to be used for bread-making and was now devoted to the manufacture of small dynamos and other electrical apparatus. The store-rooms were reached by two narrow stairways and, when we first saw them, were in a truly dreadful plight. Dirt, cobwebs and piles of refuse were everywhere; and there were numerous indications that the rats had held many a *fête champêtre* on the crazily sloping floors. Myrna was repelled; Paul delighted. He had brought with him a flexible steel rule and, regardless of his clothes, or of mine, scrabbled about taking measurements and jotting them down on the back of an envelope, which he afterwards lost.

We submitted a full report to our newly-formed committee. They were dubious, ready rather to bear the ills of Holy Trinity Hall than fly to others that they knew not of. Myrna, still shuddering, subscribed to their opinion and so, to a lesser degree, did I; yet Paul, his lax white features animated, his dull eyes ablaze, embarked on a magnificent oration that, within ten minutes, won us all over to his side. Even Myrna capitulated.

"After all," she said, "we're getting it free."

The next day I settled matters with Dickson, Parrish, Willmott & Lister and wrote a little letter of acknowledgment and thanks, for them to pass on to our benefactor.

The committee had no cause to regret their decision. The metamorphosis wrought by Paul on that derelict loft was little short of magical. The committee wanted to employ a builder to carry out the necessary alterations, but Paul would have none of it. Ruthlessly he set us all to work. At first there were demurs, but it was not long before we were all as keen as he; and it was surprising how much unsuspected ability was brought to light. Hands that had never touched a tool soon displayed real craftsmanship. We found we had amongst us carpenters, decorators, scene-painters—and even a competent electrician in the person of Archibald Hobson, who was Mrs. Doubleday's handyman and soon attached himself loyally to the society.

The only thing beyond us was the plumbing, which Paul, by some gerrymandering, got done at the cost of a pint of beer. From time to time, he would go off on mysterious missions, returning with rich booty, all bought for a song from market stalls, junk-shops and dealers in that branch of commerce known as miscellaneous disposals. Paul's finest achievement in that sphere was the acquisition of seventy-two tip-up seats from a demolished London theatre. Their plush was shabby and they complained rather lustily, but they were a great advance on the bentwood chairs in Holy Trinity Hall. To disclose the amount Paul paid for the whole six dozen would be to invite ridicule and disbelief.

By the end of the second month after Munich, the Little Theatre—or the Bakehouse, as we all came to call it—was complete. It will be as well, at this point, to give a short description of it.

As one turned from Harpur Street into Cooper's Yard, the Bakehouse lay to the left. To the right was the side wall of Mr. Aaron Sugarman's pawnbroking establishment. At the further end of Cooper's Yard was a high brick wall, so it was a *cul-de-sac,* only giving access to the Bakehouse and Mr. Sugarman's side door. The Bakehouse was rectangular in shape. The ground floor was in two sections, divided by a cobbled way that led to the courtyard at the rear of the building and was spanned by the upper floor. Of the two stairways already mentioned, the first was to the right of the archway. It was not an integral part of the main building, but was cased with matchboarding and attached to the wall. The entrance at the foot faced Cooper's Yard; and Paul made it the stage-door. The second was on the other side of the archway, towards the rear of the building, with its door flush with the wall, and would be used—or so we hoped—by the playgoers.

As one ascended this main staircase, the kitchen was immediately above. To the right of the kitchen was the general cloak-room—we had no space for nice distinctions—and to the left, the foyer. One stepped from the landing into the cloak-room, deposited one's overcoat, and then went back across the landing into the foyer. With beaver board, stained battens and cream distemper, Paul had made a delightful room of this. Its floor, like all the others, had a noticeable list, but that only added to the charm of it. Just to the side of the landing was the buffet, where coffee, tea and sandwiches would be sold. A door at the back of the bar led into the kitchen. Not at first, but later, we had in the middle of the foyer a table with a glass top, under which there were photographs of the society's previous productions. On the walls were other pictures, some grim, others gay, and framed cuttings from newspapers, for our home-made theatre soon attracted the attention of the Press.

At the far end of the foyer was the box-office, with its little ticket-window almost facing the passage leading to the auditorium—if so grand a word can be used for so diminutive a place! To the left of this passage was the girls' dressing-room and, to the right, the properties room. The stairs down to the stage-door were between the properties room and the auditorium. As one entered the auditorium from the passage, the stage was to the left and the seats for the audience to the right. On the other side of the auditorium were the men's dressing-room and the complicated hook-up that constituted Hobson's lighting switchboard.

The general lay-out of the Little Theatre, which was not nearly so big as it may sound from my description, can be best understood by imagining oneself in Cooper's Yard. Over the central archway were the properties room in front and the girls' dressing-room to the rear. Between them ran the passage, linking up the booking-office and foyer on the left with the auditorium on the right. The audience would sit with their backs to Cooper's Yard.

It must not be imagined that meanwhile the acting side of the society had been neglected. Far from it. Before the end of September, we had chosen a play and started rehearsals. Since the August evening when Myrna Ashwin had set the ball rolling, she had altered her mind about being secretary and, despite my spirited protests, the job had fallen to me. She became ticket secretary. Mr. Mortimer Robinson took on the duties of treasurer and Paul Manhow, because of his aptitude for driving hard bargains, was appointed business and publicity manager. Jack Gough had no official status, but acted as liegeman to the ticket secretary.

There remain to be introduced two other functionaries: the producer and the stage manager. Our producer was Patrick Collingwood, a soft-spoken giant of a fellow, who gave us no peace until he obtained the effect he wanted and never got nearer to losing his temper than whistling "Good King Wenceslas" (whatever the season of the year) through clenched teeth. Most amateur dramatic societies prefer to enlist the services of an outside producer, but as Pat Collingwood had had wide experience in repertory and was, as it were, home-grown, we welcomed him as an active participator. His daughter, Felicity, was also a member.

Our stage-manager was Frederick Cheesewright, a dapper, bustling, bald little man of forty-five, who strutted the stage as if on the quarter-deck, waved his arms about and gave his instructions crisply. It was his normal habit to say everything twice in swift succession, but his orders to the company were given three times just as rapidly, as if with the foreknowledge that nobody would heed a thing said only twice. He was a prosperous draper in the Shambles and once, when I went in to buy some socks, I noticed that he brisked his assistants in the same manner. In both spheres, his methods met with great success.

The play we selected was J. B. Priestley's "Eden End" and we hoped to open the theatre with it on Thursday, the 1st December, 1938. Under the guidance of Pat Collingwood, rehearsals went well. Unfortunately, the small cast of seven left most of the members with nothing more to do than act as stewards, programme-sellers or prompter; but they were promised that their turn would come next and cheerfully complied. In those early days, a pleasant spirit of co-operation and give-and-take prevailed. It is with me a matter for regret that into that first harmony, there afterwards too often crept a jarring note.

But that is going too far ahead.

"Eden End" was presented on the due date and was so great a success that, instead of running for three nights, as originally planned, it was, as the Press notices usually put it, "retained for another week, the definitely last performance being on Saturday, the 10th December." With all our private cares and responsibilities, it was too great a strain; and we never tried to break that record run.

A cutting from a London evening paper was the first to be framed and hung in the foyer. For this distinguished recognition, we were indebted to my old garage partner, Phil Pearson, who paid us a special visit and wrote the review himself. I give it below:

"The Lulverton Little Theatre fully deserves the epithet, 'Little,' for it has accommodation for an audience of only seventy-two. The receipts for each performance, on the assumption that it plays to capacity, which should not be difficult, amount to £6 8s. 0d.

"The first performance given by the new society was on Thursday last, when Mr. J. B. Priestley's 'Eden End' was presented to what can safely be described as a packed house. The production, which was in the capable hands of Mr. Patrick Collingwood, who has done good work in repertory, left nothing to be desired, the manifold disadvantages of a tiny stage being cleverly overcome.

"For the cast, there is much commendation and little blame, although one must not forget how much they owed to the brilliance of Mr. Priestley. 'Eden End' is a beautiful play, a play of laughter and tears, a play that would succeed even if acted by a cast, given the gift of speech, of performing seals.

"The outstanding performance was that by Mr. Paul Manhow, who played Charles Appleby, the ne'er-do-well inebriate actor, the part taken by Mr. Ralph Richardson in the original production at the Duchess Theatre. In the famous drunken scene, Mr. Manhow, ably supported by Mr. Basil

F. Northcott as young Wilfred Kirby, the doctor's son, was excellent, even if a trifle reminiscent, in appearance, if not in manner, of the late John Tilley. He imitated Mr. Richardson's heavy, tottering walk to a nicety.

"Miss Hilary Boyson was a lovely and gracious Stella Kirby. When this young actress has had more experience, she should do very well in parts a little less exacting than the high-spirited, temperamental prodigal daughter of the old Yorkshire doctor."

Phil went on to praise the other players and concluded:

"Altogether, a very satisfying performance. Carry on, Lulverton!"

We did not let the grass grow under our feet, but at the beginning of the New Year, started rehearsals on another play—or rather, on several plays by Noel Coward under the title, "To-night at 8.30." These would give more opportunities for our would-be actors and actresses than had "Eden End." We also arranged a series of lectures on production, stage management, make-up, speech, movement and gestures, and fencing classes under the instruction of the Southmouth School of Fencing. At this last graceful art, Jack Gough was a surprisingly apt pupil.

And we found a new leading lady.

Her name was Elizabeth Faggott, a dreadful handicap about which nothing could be done, although Jack Gough did suggest that two small f's would lend the name distinction. She was tall and dark-haired and we discovered her to be a very talented actress, able to adapt herself to any kind of part. Another of her accomplishments was mimicry, not the impersonations of Greta Garbo, Gracie Fields and Marlene Dietrich with which interminable B.B.C. artists have jaded us, but others with more elusive characteristics. Sometimes at rehearsals Elizabeth's impromptu imitations were very near home, the only person not usually impressed being the victim, who was sometimes masculine, for Elizabeth's range was remarkable.

When the casting committee were occupied with "Eden End," she was overlooked, otherwise Phil Pearson might have been more appreciative of Stella Kirby. With "To-night at 8.30," the committee would have repeated their mistake had I not intervened. They were anxious not to hurt the feelings of Hilary Boyson, but I managed to persuade them that her susceptibilities were less to be considered than the general welfare of the society. In rather reluctant response to my appeal, they cast Elizabeth for Lily Peppers in "Red Peppers" and Jane Featherways in "Family Album."

It was a pity that Phil Pearson was not there to see "To-night at 8.30."

With the Little Theatre a *fait accompli,* Paul Manhow lost all his ardour and, figuratively speaking, went back to bed. He consented to play Charles Appleby in "Eden End," only because nobody else was fitted for the part. Even then, strong pressure had to be applied. But Phil Pearson's encomiums whipped up his flagging interest and transformed him into the keenest amateur that ever missed a cue. As Burrows, the old retainer and *deus ex machina,* he was great.

It was to be expected that the novelty of our theatre would not retain its freshness, as far as the public was concerned, yet every seat was sold for the four performances of "To-night at 8.30" and we could have disposed of twice that number.

The last show was on the 4th March.

We rested for a month; then, on the 3rd April, started rehearsing a new play. This time it was "The Likes of Her" by Charles McEvoy. The selection was not made without much heated discussion, the chief argument of the opposition being that a play about the war would be not only old-fashioned, but also unpopular with our public. The critics, however, were finally over-ridden on the grounds that, in the part of Sally Winch, the coster girl who waited for her war-shattered lover, there was wide scope for the talents of Elizabeth Faggott. That, of course, was after I had induced them to retain her as leading lady.

Elizabeth herself was not much taken with the project. She would have preferred Shakespeare, she declared. It had always been her ambition to play Ophelia, Portia, Juliet, Cordelia, Desdemona, Lady Macbeth or any, or all, of the others. I, who had stampeded the committee into selecting her for the chief part, had then to work hard to steer her away from the fair Ophelia and towards Sally Winch. Next time, I assured her recklessly, we would do Shakespeare, but this time let it be "The Likes of Her."

And so, in due season, it was. Finely produced by Pat Collingwood, who had been my only supporter in my championship of Elizabeth, the play was a great success. From the time that slatternly Mrs. Small announced that she would "'ave 'er narsty eyes art," to the moment when Sally Winch murmured to her returned lover, "It's the likes *of you* what matters. Which is the arm you can put round me?" the audience was enthralled. Elizabeth was a Downshire girl, the daughter of a Lulverton doctor, yet as Sally Winch, she might have had no other home than 5, Bridewell Court, Stepney and known no other surroundings than those to the immediate east of Aldgate Pump.

We gave the last performance on Saturday, the 27th May. I was not in the play, but stood in the wings, to the annoyance and discomfort of the company, watching and listening to Elizabeth. It may seem a ridiculous admission, but I could have sat enraptured while she read out the times of departure of trains from Paddington.

All that summer we lay fallow, while war clouds chased each other across the sky. Towards the end of August, the committee met to discuss the programme for the winter. Most of us still clung to the belief that European conflict could still be avoided, if only after another Munich, and it was unanimously decided that the international situation should not affect our plans. Having in mind my promise to Elizabeth, I attended the meeting with some trepidation. I need not have been anxious, for the others appeared to have accepted the eclipse of Hilary Boyson. I told them of Elizabeth's wish and without demur they settled on Shakespeare.

The problem was, which play? With "English and French armies engage," and "The King enters with his Power," the histories were rather too ambitious for us. On our tiny stage, there would not have been much opportunity for the derring-do of Stanley and Chester, and "soldiers with scaling ladders" would have degenerated into screaming farce. Macbeth presented the same difficulties; a couple of gawky men-at-arms carrying twigs in their hands would not have persuaded even an idiot boy that Birnam Wood was on the move towards Dunsinane. We had no actor good enough for Hamlet; and we found one drawback or another to "The Tempest," "A Midsummer Night's Dream," "Othello," "The Merchant of Venice" and a dozen more.

I was the first to mention "Measure for Measure," but when asked what it was about, had to admit that I knew no more than that it was one of the comedies. I had merely come across it while glancing through the copy of the Complete Works with which I had come provided. A quick dip into it told me very little and, as all the others shared my ignorance and none of the remaining plays appealed to us, the meeting was adjourned, to give us all an opportunity to read "Measure for Measure."

We met again the following week, under the chairmanship of Mr. Maurice Scott-Brown, M.C. He was manager of the local branch of the Southern Counties Bank—or "the Bank," as everyone called it, utterly ignoring the other five in Lulverton—chairman of the Chamber of Commerce and an extremely useful man to have on our committee. Massive, hearty of manner, he had a deep, resonant voice and, when amused (which was often), sounded like an amiable ogre laughing in a cave. When speaking, he discarded all trimmings, employing only the strictly essential words. Jack Gough, who was one of his underlings at the Bank, was not wildly delighted about his participation in the affairs of the society.

After opening the proceedings, Mr. Scott-Brown said: "All read it?" There was general assent and he asked:

"Reactions?"

Four of the committee answered at once.

"Most objectionable," said Mrs. Cheesewright.

"We couldn't possibly do it," said her husband. "We couldn't possibly do it."

"Just what we're looking for," said Paul Manhow. "I don't think Angelo should get away with it," said Myrna Ashwin.

The remainder, Pat Collingwood, Mr. Mortimer Robinson, Miss Lark and I, held our peace. Mr. Scott-Brown chuckled deeply.

"One at a time, please! Find it objectionable, Mrs. Cheesewright?"

"Most definitely," was her sharp retort. "Some of the remarks of the character called Pompey should not be allowed in print—and as for uttering them on the stage. . . ."

"Living in broad-minded times," rumbled our chairman with a shrug of his heavy shoulders. "Your views, Collingwood?"

"You find that sort of thing in most of the plays," answered the producer. "Shakespeare was a business man and gave his public what it wanted. I dare say after we've used the blue pencil—"

Mrs. Cheesewright cut him short. "No amount of censoring would make the play suitable for a Lulverton audience. It is fundamentally unpleasant and corrupt."

This good lady, Mrs. Cheesewright, was the wife of our stage manager and a great nuisance on the committee, but nothing less than brute force would have kept her off it. Her husband, five years her junior, was under her domination and, when with her, seldom had the opportunity to say anything once, let alone twice. She was the society's guardian of the proprieties and a militant Mrs. Grundy, though causing more mischief by vicious tittle-tattle than the most ribald wanton. As a district visitor, it was her invariable custom to call at meal-times and then accuse the exasperated working-classes of ingratitude. She had angular features, big feet and five children. Her hair style would have been severe had it been grey.

Now she went on:

"Last Monday afternoon, I bought a copy of the play. I have it here and am going to read to you from the editor's preface, which quotes the opinion of Samuel Taylor Coleridge."

Over her shoulder, I made wild signals to Mr. Scott-Brown.

He got as far as, "Hardly think" but she had risen to her feet and, with the little red book held in both gloved hands at almost arm's length, genteely cleared her throat. Paul Manhow next to me murmured in my ear:

"You can tell the old *Hausfrau* used to be a school-teacher."

Reading clearly and precisely, Mrs. Cheesewright began:

" 'This play, which is Shakespeare's throughout, is to me the most painful—say rather, the only painful—part of his genuine works. The comic and tragic parts equally border on the'—the next word, I fear, is Greek, which I do not understand—'the one disgusting, the other horrible; and the pardon and marriage of Angelo not merely baffles the strong and indignant claim of justice (for cruelty, with lust and damnable baseness, cannot be forgiven, because he cannot conceive them as being morally repented of), but it is likewise degrading to the character of woman.' "

Mrs. Cheesewright fixed us all in turn with an accusing eye.

" 'Degrading,' " she repeated sternly, " 'to the character of woman.' "

"Well, don't look at *me*" protested Paul Manhow.

"In another place," she continued, "Coleridge wrote ' "Measure for Measure" is the single exception to the delightfulness of Shakespeare's plays. It is a hateful work, although Shakespearian throughout. Our feelings of justice are grossly wounded in Angelo's escape".

"Just what I said," threw in Myrna.

" 'Isabella herself contrives to be unamiable, and Claudio

is detestable.' Those are the opinions of Coleridge. When we remember that he wrote 'The Rime of the Ancient Mariner,' we can safely accept his judgment."

With which triumphant *non sequitur,* Mrs. Cheesewright closed the book and sat down. For a space, we were silent, then Paul Manhow drawled:

"And he killed himself with opium."

"Who did?" asked Myrna.

"Coleridge. And Charles Lamb said he was an archangel a little damaged."

"That has nothing to do with our present discussion."

Mrs. Cheesewright was annoyed, probably at Paul's casual assumption of pedagogy.

"Neither has the Ancient Mariner," was his languid reply. "Or the albatross. My own opinion is that no play is any the worse for a bit of rude."

The remark was made simply to rile her. They disliked each other intensely.

"I take exception to that!" snapped Mrs. Cheesewright. "Mr. Chairman, I appeal to you!"

Mr. Scott-Brown shifted heavily in his chair.

"Getting away from the point, aren't we?" he asked. "Any others against 'Measure for Measure'?"

"Father!" said Mrs. Cheesewright sharply.

"I agree with my wife," said the dutiful little man. "The play is not at all pleasant. Not at all pleasant. We should lower the whole tone of the society by presenting it. The whole tone. The young people—"

"Poppycock," said a calm, unequivocal voice.

Miss Lark was a very valued member of our company. A trim little woman of fifty-five, smartly turned out, with beautifully shingled grey hair. Quietly efficient, keen-witted, the fierce opponent of humbug and pretension, she acted as a very potent antidote to Mrs. Cheesewright. And there was— how can I put it?—a certain *awareness* about her. I once made the acquaintance of an old green parrot. Its conversational range was limited, yet when it tilted its head and cocked a wicked beady eye at you, you got the feeling that, if it only chose, it could tell you a thing or two; that, as the French put it, *il connut le dessous des cartes.* Miss Lark in no way resembled a parrot, but sometimes there was the same tilt of the head and the same cock of the eye.

Frederick Cheesewright subsided abruptly. The chairman, mastering a smile, looked towards the interrupter. "Not in agreement, Miss Lark?"

"No," she answered, "I'm not. Angelo certainly ought to have been rapped over the knuckles more severely, but to suggest that we shouldn't do it because it's not suitable for children is ridiculous. How many plays are? Is a pantomime—I mean a modern pantomime? Nowadays, instead of strings of sausages, they have strings of double meanings. I'd rather take a child to see 'Measure for Measure' than 'Puss in Boots'—and if we *must* do Shakespeare, I don't see any reason for not doing 'Measure for Measure.' "

Mr. Mortimer Robinson, sitting opposite me at the table, got his word in before Mrs. Cheesewright could counter-attack.

"If I may express an opinion," he said, "it is in favour of that particular play, because there is very little action in it—a great advantage on a small stage like ours. Another thing is that the play is not in the hands of a few main characters and provides many good opportunities for minor players. Pompey, for instance, Lucio, and Elbow, the fatheaded constable. Paul here would be lifelike as rascally Pompey."

"Thanks very much," said Paul.

"Those are two good points," approved Pat Collingwood, "and a still more important thing is that Isabella will be a grand chance for Elizabeth Faggott. If only we can find an Angelo with sufficient . . ."

It was at this stage of the meeting that the disputation really began. The Cheesewrights were almost literally thrust aside, while the rest of the committee embarked on a number of simultaneous arguments. The chief item on the agenda—the suitability of "Measure for Measure"—yielded place to Other Business, and even the chairman, who should have known better, freely and resoundingly expressed his own views about this or that player for this or that part. The discussion went on so long that finally I had to call the meeting to order.

"Just a moment, everybody!" I shouted above the din. "It's getting very late and we haven't reached a decision. Is it to be 'Measure for Measure'?"

Mr. Scott-Brown coughed *basso* and looked guilty.

"Quite so," he said. "All agreed?"

We looked dubiously at Mrs. Cheesewright, but she, in military parlance, had made a strategic withdrawal to a previously prepared position, and did no more than purse her lips in disapproval.

"Carried *nem. con.*" announced the chairman hurriedly.

"Whatever else happens," announced little Miss Lark with decision, as the meeting broke up, "I am going to be Mistress Overdone."

"Don't be too sure," I reminded her. "We may be at war before the week's out."

"Nonsense!" she protested. "Something will be done at the eleventh hour. It always is."

"I myself gravely doubt it," said Mr. Mortimer Robinson.

The next day Germany invaded Poland.

IV

... 'twas in the Bunch of Grapes ...

Act II, Sc. 1.

With my preoccupations with the doings of the dramatic society, I have failed to record events in chronological order, so must now hark back to the end of the previous May. I have already said that my business affairs were in a very prosperous condition, although 1937 and 1938 did not quite come up to 1936, my bonanza year. My staff comprised a typist, Miss Muriel Jones, and an office boy, or rather, a series of office boys, so alike in appearance and incompetence that I called them all Hindenburg, to save myself the bother of remembering their depressing surnames.

Miss Jones had a moustache and, like most women with moustaches, was most efficient. She could deal with telephone calls, keep the letter-files in good order, type accurately (never remarking primly, "That's what you said") and make a good cup of tea. But I began to find that, with all her merits, she could not give me all the help I needed. I had to be out and about so much. Apart from ordinary estate negotiation, auctioneering and valuation for probate, there was the agricultural side of the business, which entailed frequent visits to outlying farmsteads. So I decided to engage an assistant. Local enquiries produced no suitable applicant and on the last Saturday in May I inserted an advertisement in the *Estates Gazette* for a competent negotiator.

The first response I received was from my old schoolfellow, Tiddler Ridpath.

Of course, I had him down from London to see me. I shall not forget his look of amazement when the current Hindenburg showed him into my office.

"By all that's wonderful!" he said, a slow smile spreading over his face. "It's the celebrated Turtle!"

I found it strange to hear the old name again. Hindenburg withdrew, closing the door violently behind him. I made a mental note to sack him.

"Sit down," I said.

Tiddler was sadly changed. It was eleven years since we had last met. Then he had been a slim young man with delicately chiselled features and fair, curly hair; athletic, full of natural vitality, gay of manner and always elegant. Now he was not merely slim, but as thin as a rake. His face was fine-drawn to the point of emaciation; his clothes had the pathetic neatness of a much-darned tablecloth: and his fibre suitcase was shabby and battered. Even his cheery greeting lacked the old spirit.

There was something else I noticed as he pulled forward a chair; something I had not often seen in my well-nourished life; something that made me say, though it was scarcely noon:

"No, I've had enough of this place this morning. Let's go and chat over some lunch. Or is it," I added, as if in doubt, "a bit too early?"

"Not for me," answered Tiddler.

I took him round to the Bunch of Grapes, which is famous for its food, settled him at a table and went across for a few confidential words with old Charley, who, as impervious to heat as a salamander, stood ready by his blazing grill. Charley listened attentively, touched his tall white hat and replied:

"Leave it to me, sir."

This I knew I could safely do and went back to our table by the window, where Tiddler was staring down at the passers-by and jabbing at the cloth with a fork. He turned as I sat down opposite him.

"About that advertisement—" he began.

"It can wait," I pulled him up. "Food first, business afterwards. I hope you're hungry, because I've just ordered a couple of hefty steaks. A bit substantial for an early lunch, but they're the only things worth eating in this place."

Which was doing the Bunch of Grapes a grave injustice.

In his own good time, Charley forsook his furnace and hobbled across the room with a tilted plate hanging from each hand. Why the steaks did not slide off on to the floor was Charley's secret. Ada, the adenoidal waitress, arrived at the same time with what she described as our "pertyters and groids" and three pint tankards of beer, the third of them for Charley, who disdained tips, but accepted a drink as a gift from the gods.

I passed the cruet to Tiddler, but he had already started on his steak.

We followed with apple tart and lovingly ripened Stilton.

With a black coffee in front of him and a cigarette; pointing towards the ceiling, Tiddler leant back in his chair, pushed his hands into his trouser pockets and murmured blissfully:

"That was good."

Lulverton usually lunched at one o'clock and we had the place to ourselves, except for a solitary man at the other end of the room, with a newspaper propped against the water-jug, who chewed his food with the stolid concentration of a ruminating cow, and held his knife and fork as if he was riding a bicycle.

I stirred my coffee, letting Tiddler take his time.

"Now," he said at length, "about this job."

"Yes, of course," I answered as briskly as pleasant repletion allowed. "The job."

"You advertised for a competent negotiator."

"And are you?"

"No."

He finished his coffee at a gulp, pushed the cup and saucer aside and leant across the table towards me.

"Look here, Turtle, I came down here with the fullest intention of blurring some doddering old country estate agent into taking me on. 'Vaughan Tudor' didn't mean a thing to me till I saw that amiable old phiz of yours. I don't propose to try any funny stuff with you. We've had a very jolly lunch, so now let's forget you need an assistant in your nefarious calling and have a chat about old times. How's the world been—"

"As far as I'm concerned," I coolly interrupted him, " 'competent negotiator' does not necessarily mean a fully trained man. What I need—and what I'm still anxiously searching for is a fellow with a certain amount of *nous*, who can relieve me of some of the donkey-work. I thought, when you turned up, that I'd found him. Of course, if you want to leave me in the cart . . ."

There was some of the old gaiety in his laugh.

"Walter Vaughan Turtle Tudor," he said, "you're an infernal old liar."

"That's not the way to treat your future employer," I rebuked him. "Tell me, Tiddler, when did you last have a decent square meal?"

He turned his head to stare out of the window, and it was some time before he swung back to me. "It's been hell," he said.

"Things not going too well?"

His voice was harsh when he answered:

"That's one way of putting it."

I gave him another cigarette and helped myself.

"Any good telling me about it?"

"No. . . . Just another hard-luck story. You've heard it all before, I expect."

I did not press the point, bur sat quietly drawing at my cigarette. After a few moments' silence, Tiddler went on:

"Do you remember how we both left school at the end of the same term, way back in—when was it?—1922? You were going into business and I went out to my people in Corfu. Mother had always been a bit of an invalid and the governor got himself pensioned off to get her out of England. The pension wasn't princely, but the cost of living wasn't very high in Corfu and they got along pretty comfortably."

He flicked the ash off his cigarette.

"And so did I—far too comfortably. I only went out there to please mother, and life was one big holiday—at any rate, for some months. There wasn't much to do there, except enjoy yourself. I was a lazy young devil and fancied I'd found my niche. Living on the governor's annuity didn't worry me a great deal and I'd have gone on doing it indefinitely if some bloke hadn't been silly enough to get himself murdered.

"Corfu, you know, has been in the hands of a good many different nations in its time, but since eighteen sixty-something it's belonged to Greece. In August, 1923, the Italian delegate at a local fun-and-games society known as the Albanian Boundary Commission was bumped off on Greek territory. This rather annoyed the Italians and, as a sort of sharp lesson, they sent a fleet to bombard Corfu. It was far from being a major engagement, and only a handful of people were killed. My mother and father were amongst them."

I grunted sympathetically and Tiddler continued:

"I was enjoying myself elsewhere and missed the party. It was the end of my island paradise. Our little villa was blown to bits. I soon found that life wasn't quite so jolly without the poor old governor's pension. The only relation I could call to mind was my mother's brother, who lived in Shrewsbury—still does, for all I know. I sent out an S O S and he responded to the tune of a tenner, with a polite postscript to the effect that he was no widow's cruse. With the help of the tenner, I hung on for a couple of months, then worked my passage to Naples.

"Tourists flock to Naples in herds and there was quite a chance of picking up a few pounds as a guide. Not a particularly exalted career, but I couldn't afford to be fussy. As a matter of fact, I did surprisingly well at it and was soon word perfect in the patter."

The tone of his voice altered as he went on: "Now, sir, a delightful motor drive? First the world famous excavations at Pompeii and then on to Vesuvius. What a memory to take home with you! No, sir? Well, then, a drive round the magnificent Bay to the semi-extinct volcano of Solfatara and the celebrated Dog Grotto and Pozzuli, where the Apostle Paul—"

"All right, all *right*! I interrupted him. "We'll take all that as read. How did you manage with the language?"

"Italian, you mean? Quite well. I'd picked up a certain amount in Corfu, besides a smattering of Greek, and the months in Naples made me fairly fluent. Italian's not very difficult to learn."

"So you didn't stop there long?"

"No. Six months, more or less; and I might still be there if it hadn't been for Mrs. Salveter. She was a disgustingly rich American—widow of a Baked Beans Baron of Boston, Mass.

and doing Europe in a car with her niece. She'd brought her own chauffeur with her from the States, but at Naples there was a bit of a shindy that resulted in his getting the first ship back to New York. I happened to be showing the women round at the time, and Mrs. Salveter offered me a princely wage to take his place. By then, I was fed up with Naples and snapped at the chance. I wish I hadn't. It didn't take me long to find out why the other fellow had turned in the job. The niece was a snorter, but the old woman was poison. A nagger. It was 'Ridpath, this' and 'Ridpath, that' the whole time. All over Italy, Switzerland, Germany and France, she was back-seat driving in a high, complaining, nasal whine. Ugh! I can still feel that voice corkscrewing into the back of my neck! She paid well, though.

"When we reached Le Touquet, I got the bullet."

I pushed the cigarette packet across the table.

"Why?" I asked.

He shrugged his shoulders. "Bit of unpleasantness with her ladyship."

"Anything in particular?"

With a cigarette half out of the packet, he paused and looked at me.

"Why do you ask that?" he said abruptly.

"Idle curiosity," I smiled.

"Mrs. Salveter," he said, transferring the cigarette to his mouth, "was one of the most self-centred women I have ever met. She never gave a thought for anyone else and was only concerned about her own comfort. I wasn't really sorry when she gave me the push. When I found myself out of a shop, it was a toss-up whether I should work my passage back to Naples or come to London. I had several pounds in my pocket. London called me—and London won. I was still only a kid of nineteen and quite certain that, when I reached London, all would be well. The old streets-paved-with-gold idea, you know. As usual, it was a flop. Everything went wrong. I drifted from job to job, never managing to keep one more than a few weeks. Didn't seem to have the trick, somehow. Always late in the morning—not more than ten minutes, but late. Never able to do a thing in quite the way they wanted. Not a square peg in a round hole, but a round peg not quite big enough to stop falling right through.

"God knows, Turtle, how many jobs I've been in and out of since I parted company with Mrs. Salveter. I've been a clerk in the London office of a Canadian Bank, a door-to-door canvasser of soap and floor-polish, a lorry-driver, the pianist in a fourth-rate dance band, barman in a West End pub...."

I did not speak when he paused.

"You know those toys," he continued after a long silence; "little grey, woolly dogs that *yap-yap* when you press a bulb at the end of a rubber tube? Last week I was peddling those outside the Lewisham Hippodrome. I sold three in two days. It was in the Public Library at Ladywell that I saw your advertisement in the *Estates Gazette*. What the devil prompted me to hitch-hike fifty miles to answer it, I don't know."

"Providence," I told him. "There's a post to be filled—and you're the man to fill it. Now, to-day's Friday—"

"Look here, Turtle—" he expostulated.

"And," I proceeded, as if he had not spoken, "it's not worth while your coming in to-morrow. Our hours of business are nine to five, so come along at nine sharp on Monday."

"But I don't know the first thing about —"

"I can't offer you much in the way of salary, but may be able to increase it when we've seen how you shape. You'll want a decent suit for the office and probably other odds and ends, so I'd better lend you enough to set you up, and we can deduct something from your salary every week."

My brisk manner struck the right note, for Tiddler ceased to protest. I was pleased that he did, yet the business man in me cried out against engaging a man who had failed in every enterprise he had undertaken. Tiddler himself seemed to agree.

"You'll live to regret this," he said with a half laugh, as I beckoned Ada for the bill.

"We shall see," I smiled.

Nobody ever called Eagle House anything but "Mrs. Double-day's." It was a large residence standing by itself on rising ground and was the biggest architectural mess I have ever seen. Over a period of years succeeding owners had added and altered, without any regard for form. To the original four-storeyed building, which had pretensions to Georgian, one with a taste for the unconventional had added two tile-hung wings with ground-floor garages. Another, a supporter of Classic Revival, had built a pillared porch that always made me feel, as I passed under it, that I was entering Euston Station. The extensive, terraced garden put me in mind of Shanty Town. Reached by a covered way from the conservatory that abutted on to the house was a solid timber building devoted to billiards. Linked to it by another covered way was a second wooden structure that was given over to table-tennis and darts; and beyond that were less handsome outbuildings —the tool-shed, the coal-bunker and the workshop. To one side of the lawn was an imposing summer-house, transported, so I was given to understand, from Hyde Park after the Great Exhibition; and away at the bottom of the garden—or perhaps I should say the top—past the vegetable section, were the chicken houses.

The establishment was reached from Friday Street through a gateway on the summits of whose pillars crouched stone eagles, one of which had lost its head. The gravelled drive split and ran round a circular lawn, in the middle of which was a Chilean pine, known more familiarly as a monkey-puzzle.

The interior of the house, though simple in its main design, held its surprises. Because of the slope on which the building stood, the first floor at the front became the ground floor at the back. And there were far too many doors. My own bedroom had two, one leading to the main staircase and the other, down a couple of steps, into one of the wings, which were slightly below the level of the main floors.

That, then, was Mrs. Doubleday's.

The bill I received at the end of every week announced shyly that Mrs. Doubleday's christian name was Celia. She was a dear soul, but no beauty. Short and dumpy, with a neck so thick that it seemed a continuation of her chin, she resembled a seal. She wore steel-framed spectacles and was always dressed in black. Although close on sixty, she darted about the house as nimbly as a schoolgirl, so that she frequently gave the impression of being in two places at once. For instance, after assuring her that I had everything I required, I would leave her at one end of a passage—and, on reaching the other end, would find her waiting round the corner with the remark:

"Because you've only got to *ask,* Mr. Tudor."

Often I wondered whether the place was full of false panels.

She was a perfect hostess. Nothing ever went wrong—at least, as far as we guests knew. Meals were beautifully cooked and served to the tick. There were no restrictions: we could go in and out whenever we liked. There were plenty of ashtrays in the bedrooms. The bells worked. There was hot water in the taps. And there were no notices beginning "Visitors are requested . . ."

The amazing thing was that Mrs. Doubleday never seemed to sleep. If we came in at two o'clock in the morning—not that we often did—there was hot milk and even bacon and eggs, if we were hungry. Her helpers were few: a couple of maids, a charwoman—and Hobson.

Archibald Hobson deserves a paragraph to himself. It is difficult to define his exact position in the household. "Handyman" suggests too limited a field of activity, for besides more than average knowledge of gardening, radio, carpentry, electricity and motor-cars, Hobson had a natural gift that is best summed up in the words that old Charley used to me in the grillroom of the Bunch of Grapes: "Leave it to me, sir." Whatever you wanted done, however unusual, Hobson could do it; whatever you needed, however uncommon, Hobson could get it. When not a ticket for the Southmouth Hippodrome was to be had through ordinary channels, Hobson could wangle four stalls; when gales had blown down miles of telegraph-poles, Hobson could get you a call to Scotland. Jack Gough once said that if you were to ask Hobson for a Chinese dictionary or a set of corkscrew knitting-needles, he would produce them within ten minutes. Hobson was small, wiry and sharp-featured. He made his own untidy cigarettes and always wore a cap (it was conjectured at Mrs. Doubleday's that he even slept in it). Year in and year out, he wore the same brown suit with an ancient Alexandra rose in the buttonhole. His pockets were full of string, electric-light flex, tools, nails, screws, nuts and bolts. His wife was in a mental home, yet I never saw him with a gloomy face.

It was natural that Tiddler should come to live with us at Mrs. Doubleday's. A room was found for him on the floor above mine. Mrs. Doubleday cast one glance at him, gauged his symptoms and embarked forthwith on a task that she herself described as "building him up." I have made reference to the abundance of her hospitality, but her treatment of us others was nothing to her petting of Tiddler. His attractive appearance and gay manner entirely won her affection, and he could do no wrong. As Jack Gough put it some weeks later, with a fierce scowl on his ugly face, yet, I am sure, no malice in his generous heart: "For Tiddler, as you know, is Celia's angel."

That evening, just before dinner, I introduced Tiddler to the others.

The dining-room at Mrs. Doubleday's was two rooms thrown into one and ran the whole depth of the house. Both sections were set out with tables, but usually only the front was used, the other—depressing because it was virtually underground and overlooked only the back area—being cut off by curtains. Mrs. Stoneham and her yes-woman, Miss Tearle, shared a small table, while Mr. Garnett consumed his silent repast (silent, that is, as far as conversation went) at a table by himself. By common consent, the rest of us—Myrna Ashwin, Jack Gough, Mr. Mortimer Robinson and I—all sat together at a large table by the window. A place was laid for Tiddler next to Myrna. Mr. Mortimer Robinson sat at one end, I at the other, and Jack Gough, with his back to the window, enjoyed under the new arrangement a whole side to himself. Perhaps "enjoyed" is the wrong word.

The conversation turned, as it usually does in these troubled times, to international affairs. Their Majesties the King and Queen were in Canada; and Myrna expressed the fervent hope that they would get safely back.

"Yes," agreed Mr. Mortimer Robinson gravely, "before the storm breaks."

"Do you think there'll be war?" she asked.

Jack grunted scornfully. "Of course there won't!"

"I'm afraid I differ with you," said Mr. Mortimer Robinson. "Hitler won't stop at Memel. I'm sure in my own mind that his aim is the conquest of all Europe and ultimately the domination of the world."

"That's a bit sweeping," I protested mildly.

"Perhaps it is, but everything points that way. He was quite prepared to go to war against us last August. The Munich agreement has only deferred the conflict. He *must* fight us eventually, to get what he wants. The military alliance with Italy at the beginning of last month was most significant. I myself would not be at all surprised to see him patch up some sort of non-aggression agreement with Russia."

"*Russia!*" scoffed Jack. "They're daggers drawn with the Russians. What about the Anti-Commintern Pact with Japan, Italy and Spain?"

"And what about the Naval Agreement with Great Britain?" retorted Mr. Mortimer Robinson. "One is as easy to denounce as the other. With Russia holding back, Germany could then launch an attack on Dantzig and Poland; and afterwards, with the help of Italy—"

I interrupted him. "She won't get much help from that quarter. Italy's got enough on her hands already. Besides, we know from experience that she's no great shakes as an ally.

Ridpath here can probably tell you something about the Italians."

Since the discussion began Tiddler had been unnaturally silent. I made the last remark to bring him into the conversation.

"They're poor soldiers," he said, "but first-rate engineers. When I was in Naples I saw one of their destroyers. It was tearing along like a motor-boat."

Jack said dryly: "A turn of speed will come in useful."

"Not that I've any cause to love or admire the Italians," continued Tiddler. "They killed my parents."

He told them about the bombardment of Corfu, and went on to relate some of his experiences during his travels across Europe with Mrs. Salveter. I could not help noticing that he made no reference to his precise position in the touring party. A wicked little devil in me tempted me to mention it myself, but at the sight of Myrna's entranced expression as she listened to Tiddler, I forbore.

V

Heaven grant us its peace,
but not the King of Hungary's!
Act I, Sc. 2.

Life went on in Lulverton. Tiddler lost his haggard look and settled down amongst us, carrying out his work for me with reasonable competence. Muriel Jones continued to make good tea. Two more Hindenburgs came, lingered awhile and went. I watched and worshipped Elizabeth from afar, but played Faintheart. Their Majesties the King and Queen returned safely from Canada. Lord Halifax gave a solemn warning to Germany. America gained all five championships at Wimbledon. Ciano, Hitler and Ribbentrop conferred. Myrna and Tiddler carried off the mixed doubles at South Down. Russia signed a non-intervention pact with Germany.

Jack Gough's sonnet, "Solitude," appeared in *Poems of the Day*. King Leopold of the Belgians appealed for peace. The Lulverton Amateur Dramatic Society held their first meeting of the season. President Roosevelt and the Pope appealed for peace. Lady Shawford gave her annual garden party at the Grange, and Tiddler and Myrna won the prizes for the three-legged race and the spot waltz. Slovakia was occupied by German troops. The Lulverton Amateur Dramatic Society held their second meeting and decided on "Measure for Measure." Germany invaded Poland. Parliament met. At ten o'clock on the morning of September 3rd we were asked by the B.B.C. to await an important announcement at a quarter-past eleven.

Paul Manhow had come round early to see me and we were all assembled in the lounge. The weather was beautiful and winter a long way off, so Mrs. Stoneham had her chair to the right of the fireplace. In front of her was a green baize-covered table on which were spread her Patience cards, for although she frowned on Sunday bridge or whist—or even her beloved crib—Patience was permissible. By her side, with her poor ironed legs stretched out, sat Miss Tearle, dividing her attention between the cards and a table-centre that she was embroidering. Now and then Miss Tearle ventured such timely reminders as, "Now the six," only to have Mrs. Stoneham answer sharply. "Don't *rush* me. I was just going to do it."

Mr. Garnett, the retired manufacturer from the Black Country, with his big pipe bubbling like a witch's cauldron, was seated in the middle of the room, his knees well apart, stolidly working his way through the *Hardware Trade Journal*. Jack Gough, coatless, with a green shirt, a yellow tie and a blue pullover, was sitting at the writing-table with a carefully sharpened pencil and nothing more to show on the pad before him than a steadily spreading patchwork of shaded squares and triangles.

Paul Manhow, Mr. Mortimer Robinson and I were in easy

chairs, discussing the new production without much attention. Myrna and Tiddler Ridpath, sharing a settee, chattered gay absurdities. Frequently Myrna, with her hands clasped round her knee, threw back her pretty little head and laughed.

We had some strangers that week-end at Mrs. Doubleday's: a young married couple who had arrived the night before by motor-cycle combination. They were touring Downshire and the south-western counties, and had intended to be off and away soon after breakfast; but the machine had turned mulish and refused to start. The husband was outside in the drive with it then, patiently kicking at the starter. The wife sat with us in a leather coat, blue trousers, high-heeled shoes and a bright red beret with a brooch pinned to the front of it. She was reading a women's threepenny magazine and smoked a large number of the small cigarettes that sell at ten for fourpence, scattering the ash all round her, like the good seed on the land. From time to time she looked at the flashy watch on her wrist and then viciously jabbed out a red-smirched cigarette-end in the ashtray by her side. I pitied the perspiring fellow outside, for hers was the worst kind of bad temper that which goes with lack of intelligence.

I leant across to Paul.

"How would you like to be married to that?" I muttered. He shuddered so grotesquely that Mr. Mortimer Robinson enquired the reason. I told him and he smiled.

She reminds me," he said, "of a magnetic mine. Attractive but very dangerous."

So there were ten of us.

I wonder," said Paul, "how many millions of people are sitting about like we are—just waiting."

We've had war· on our doorstep for years," I said, "but somehow it seems a long way off this morning. Perhaps it won't come to it."

Paul made a wry face and said in his slow voice:

"Optimist! They say that if we'd made our intentions clearer to Germany in 1914 they wouldn't have marched into

Belgium. God knows we've made it clear enough this time, but it hasn't kept them out of Poland. The unrepentant Hun. Since 1918 it's only been a breathing space for them.

They're still fixed on the *Drang nach Osten*, and dreams of their confounded *Tag* are as vivid as they were in 1914."

Mr. Mortimer Robinson said: "Paul is right. The Germans arc stubborn people. They are the *Herrenvolk*, the overlords, and must have their own way. Sir Nevile Henderson is wasting his time. The word 'compromise' has no counterpart in the German language."

Over by the fireplace Mrs. Stoneham ejaculated impatiently and swept the cards together.

"The doctrine of brute force," agreed Paul, "as preached by that colossal old humbug, Nietzsche. The Will to Power, the Master Morality, the Transvaluation of Values—*that's* the German mentality. Society is a trade union of the inefficient. It must be smashed, says Nietzsche. Cesar, Napoleon, Alexander, men to recognize no law but their own wills—they were the ones who mattered. Pity and charity preserve the unfit at the expense of the fit, so there must be no pity and no charity. All things yield to power. That's what we're up against, my boy."

The woman in the red beret lighted another cigarette. Outside, her husband still kicked at an unresponsive engine. Myrna laughed happily and said: "Don't be ridiculous." Tiddler's bantering voice answered: "I mean it,"

"Nietzsche," I said, "may be the pet philosopher of the Nazis, but not all Germans are pro-Nazi, and therefore not pro-Nietzsche. Chamberlain has made it clear that our quarrel is not with the German people."

Paul snorted. "As Miss Lark would say, Vaughan, that's poppycock. They may not all care much for him, but the Huns are solid behind Hitler. If he wasn't head man, they'd find somebody else—somebody to lead them to the promised land, where it will be all beer and sausage, and every good German will be able to put his feet on some *Englisch Schweinhund's* mantelpiece."

"For all that," I smiled, "I still pin my faith to the eleventh hour."

"In other words, said Paul, "a second Munich. We don't want that. If he tells us that we've given way again, I shall begin to believe that we're decadent. What, in heaven's name, Vaughan, are we waiting for? Greenwood said in the House yesterday that he was gravely disturbed that we hadn't taken action—and he's not the only one."

Mr. Mortimer Robinson turned to glance at the clock.

"We shall soon know," he said. "Another ten minutes."

Tiddler rose to his feet.

"Does anyone mind if I play the piano?" he asked.

"Of course they don't, Peter," said Myrna from the settee.

I was not so sure that I agreed. Tiddler's hot music seemed out of place at that zero hour. But Mrs. Stoneham's game promised to come out and as she, the arbitress, was too engrossed to oppose him, he crossed to the piano.

"Good old Nero," muttered Paul, then added with a flash of wit: "Tiddling while Rome burns."

Mrs. Stoneham met with a setback and dealt out a fresh thirteen. Mr. Garnett and Red Beret still read their papers, he with his spread wide at arm's length, she with hers close to her eyes and folded down the middle like an urchin's blood-and-thunder. Jack Gough had stopped drawing squares and triangles, and had both elbows on the writing-table, with his fingers deep in his untidy sandy hair. Mr. Mortimer Robinson had got up and was roving softly round the room, picking up ashtrays and small ornaments, with his mind clearly far away.

There was nothing strident about Tiddler's choice. Quietly he began to play "One Day When We Were Young," a lilting little waltz tune very popular at that time. Paul pulled a packet from his pocket, took out a cigarette, then remembered to offer one to me. Myrna rose from the settee, smoothed down her dress and walked over to stand by the piano at Tiddler's side. He went on playing. Myrna began to sing the words.

> "One day when we were young,
>   One wonderful morning in May,
> You told me you loved me,
>   When we were young one day."

He turned to look up at her and smiled.

> "Sweet songs of spring were sung
>   And music was never so gay,
> You told me you loved me,
>   When we were young one day."

She placed a hand lightly on his shoulder.

> "You told me you loved me
>   And held me close to your heart,
> We laughed then, we cried then,
>   Then came—"

Jack Gough's chair clattered backwards on to the floor. With his ugly face flaming red, he lurched across the room, lifted the top of the piano and let it fall with a crash that brought Tiddler up dead and set every wire humming in discord.

"You capering fool!" he shouted. "This is not the time for drivelling!"

With a furious scowl that took in both of them, he turned and made for the door, which he slammed behind him.

"Well, well, well!" laughed Tiddler lightly. "What's bitten *him?*"

"Play something else, Peter," Myrna hurriedly urged him. Her face was flushed.

"It's almost time for the Prime Minister," reminded Mr. Mortimer Robinson. Myrna ran over and switched on the radio.

We knew, at his first words, what the Prime Minister's message was to be.

"This morning the British Ambassador in Berlin handed the German Government a final Note stating that, unless we heard from them by eleven o'clock that they were prepared at once to withdraw their troops from Poland, a state of war would exist between us.

"I have to tell you now that no such undertaking has been received, and that consequently this country is at war with Germany."

A little cry came from Miss Tearle. Mrs. Stoneham was sitting very straight in her chair. Mr. Mortimer Robinson stood with his back to the room, gazing out of the window, Mr. Garnett was looking at his paper, but he was not reading it.

"You can imagine what a bitter blow it is to me that all my long struggle to win peace has failed. Yet I cannot believe that there is anything more or anything different that I could have done. . . ."

"Poor, dear man!" Myrna's eyes were glistening with tears.

"Up to the very last it would have been quite possible to have arranged a peaceful and honourable settlement between Germany and Poland, but Hitler would not have—"

A deafening roar drowned the radio. Red Beret's husband had started the motor-cycle. Four times it rose to a crescendo as be opened the throttle, then settled down to a steady *chug-a-chug*.

"... no chance of expecting that this man will ever give up his practice of using force to gain his will. He can only be stopped by force.

"We and France are to-day, in fulfilment of our obligations, going to the aid of Poland, who is so bravely resisting—"

The door that Jack Gough had slammed behind him was thrown open and the hot, breathless young husband burst in.

"I've got it to go!" he cried.

"About time, too," drawled his wife and, stuffing her magazine in a pocket of her leather coat, sauntered across the room, implying with every indolent step that she was as good as we were.

"And now that we have resolved to finish it, I know that you will all play your part with calmness and courage. It is the evil things that we shall be fighting against—brute force, bad faith, injustice, oppression and persecution—and against them I am certain—"

We missed the rest of it, for the engine again gave tongue. We stood for the National Anthem as they shot down the drive. I have often wondered since whether those two knew there was a war on.

The last notes of the Anthem died. Then:

"Well, that's that," said Paul Manhow.

"Poor Mr. Chamberlain," said Myrna. "It's worse for him than for any of us."

"He sounded so sad," agreed Miss Tearle, "yet so terribly firm."

It was seldom on Sunday mornings that Mrs. Doubleday strayed far from the kitchen, yet she came in now in a large white apron.

"Has it come?" she asked, and we told her. "There, now," she said, and serenely returned to her cooking.

"This is the end of everything," decided Mrs. Stoneham, reshuffling the pack.

Mr. Mortimer Robinson had not stirred from the window, but now he turned. There was an unusual air about the quiet little man; a light in his soft grey eyes.

"No, Mrs. Stoneham," he told her, "it is not the end. It's the beginning. There's been too much shuffling—too much so-called appeasement. I have never been a soldier. I am, like Mr. Chamberlain, a man of peace; but now that war has come, I'm glad." He paused before adding: "And proud."

"Hear, hear," said Paul. "The English have stood about far too long, behaving like little gentlemen."

We caught a sound that stiffened every one of us. The tall new siren at the top of Beastmarket Hill was sending out its warning.

"*They're coming!*" whispered Miss Tearle.

Old Mr. Garnett broke one of his long silences.

"What did you expect 'em to do?" he growled, and reapplied himself to the *Hardware Trade Journal.*

"Who's for the cellars?" asked Tiddler.

"If they want me," came the decided voice of Mrs. Stoneham, "they will find me here."

Myrna said: "I've never been down to the cellars."

Tiddler bowed with mock gallantry.

"Then allow me to escort you," he suggested, and offered her his arm.

They went off together, but the rest of us stayed where we were. One was enough to show Myrna the cellars.

"I'm no killjoy," grinned Paul, after they had gone.

"Such an excellent match," mused Mrs. Stoneham. "I caught sight of them out in the garden last night. A very pretty picture."

Just as the siren was trumpeting out the "Raiders Passed" Jack Gough came back. He looked shamefaced.

"Sorry for my outburst," he told the room in general, "but I was a bit worked up. It didn't"—he stumbled a little—"it didn't seem the moment for dance music with—with vocal refrains."

"I myself thought it slightly—inappropriate," Mr. Mortimer Robinson agreed.

"Rubbish!" was Mrs. Stoneham's sharp rejoinder. "It was a very attractive little song—and Miss Ashwin sang it charmingly."

It was not really Myrna she defended, but Tiddler. He seemed to have that curious effect on women, whatever their age. Mrs. Doubleday, Mrs. Stoneham, Miss Tearle—all were devoted to him. Whether it was thwarted motherlove or something else, I do not profess to know. The only woman he ever antagonised—at any rate, to my knowledge—was Mrs. Salveter, the Baked Bean King's relict.

"Anyway," said Jack awkwardly, "I apologise ... I hope I haven't damaged the piano."

He was walking across to it when Miss Tearle said:

"It's a great pity you missed Mr. Chamberlain's speech. It will become historic."

He stopped short. "Oh, yes. What did he have to say?"

Miss Tearle's voice was portentous.

"We've declared war on Germany."

"Really?" Jack said absently. "Where are Myrna and Ridpath?"

I answered: "Probably on their way up from the cellar. They went down to inspect the air-raid shelter."

"The modern version of 'Come Into the Garden, Maud,'" he replied with a bitterness that was foreign to him, and turned his attention to the abused piano.

The war was going to have immediate repercussions on my business and I wanted to talk to Tiddler after lunch. But he was nowhere to be found. Then I remembered that, the day before, he had asked to take my car for the afternoon. I was reading the *Sunday Times* in the garden, when Jack Gough dropped into the deck-chair next to mine. From the house came the sound of single, halting notes of a piano. Somebody was trying to play "One Day When We Were Young" with one finger, and not being very successful.

"Who's the Paderewski?" I asked Jack as he sat down.

"Myrna."

He lighted a cigarette.

"Doing anything this afternoon, Vaughan?"

"Only waiting for the war to start. Why?"

"Thought you might like a spin with me in Bluebell. I tuned her up yesterday and want to try her out on Cowhanger."

"A suicide pact, eh?" I laughed. "All right. I'll come."

Bluebell was Jack's heart's delight—or one of them. She had started out by being an Austin-Seven open two-seater, but had had so much added and so much taken away, that she deserved Jack's description of her pedigree: by Hispano Suiza out of Soap Box. She was most uncomfortable to travel in and, like many of her sex, exceedingly captious.

With Jack at the wheel, we left Mrs. Doubleday's like a travelling machine-gun and made inland for Cowhanger Hill. The real test was not Cowhanger itself, which avoided a steep ascent by wriggling between the South Downs, but a lane that led off it and climbed up between the beech trees at an average gradient of one in five. It was a popular rendezvous on Sunday afternoons, not only for car-owners, but also for those who liked to see others in trouble.

Jack turned out of the main road and set Bluebell at the climb. She responded finely until we got to a corner—the *pons asinorum* of the hill—where, war or no war, quite a crowd was stationed. With Bluebell's little engine roaring magnificently, Jack swung her round the corner—and there, across our bows, was a small cheap saloon, sliding, in a series of jerks, slowly backwards to the right, with its radiator belching steam like a kettle. A fat, red-faced man in a bowler hat was fighting desperately with the controls, and three large, dismayed women looked anxiously over their shoulders. The spectators were cheering derisively; that was why they had come.

"Blast it!" shouted Jack savagely.

He wrenched at the steering-wheel, to slip between the other car and the grass bank, but there was scarcely room. Bluebell's near-side front wing dug into the bank and her engine stalled.

"Blast it!" swore Jack again, and pulled on the hand-brake. The other car, with its mass-produced engine imprudently switched off, cleared us and ran backwards down the hill, to the noisy delight of the assembly. As it passed us the women were squeaking like frightened mice, while the man assured them that everything was under control. Jack restarted Bluebell's engine and accelerated, synchronising the action of hand-brake and clutch. But Bluebell had been baulked and could not do it. She screamed defiance, then burst her mighty heart.

"All right for pushing the nipper out in, chum," shouted one uncouth fellow, "but no blinkin' good as a car!"

Jack was sportsman enough to laugh, at which the crowd lost interest in us. They had no time for those who bore tribulation lightly. There was no room to turn, so we had no alternative but to follow the example of the other car. Had the fat driver not elected that afternoon to demonstrate his Car's hill-climbing merits, Bluebell would doubtless have survived the test; we would have driven on and not gone back to Cowhanger; we would not have witnessed the nearest approach to a nasty accident that I have ever seen: and I would not have been given much food for thought.

The driver of the other car was clearly far from expert. He seemed not to know which way to turn the wheel when travelling in reverse, and went down the hill in zig-zag fashion, jamming on his brakes at the end, as it were, of each zig. Our own descent, thanks to Jack, was much less like a music-hall turn. On the way down we almost caught the other car up. I had slewed round in my seat to see where we were going, and Jack was steering Bluebell with one hand. When we got to the bottom of the hill the fat man did not pause, but surged backwards into the main road. A horn hooted furiously and another car, driven at speed, swerved dangerously out of its course, missed the saloon by a couple of inches, nearly mounted the bank, righted itself—and went on its way without stopping. I had just time to identify the driver, whose left arm was round a girl who was snuggled up to him.

Jack drew a sharp breath, then sighed with relief.

"That was a near one!" I said. "Did you notice the driver?"

"Your friend Ridpath," said Jack.

"Who was that with him?" I asked incautiously.

"Greta Garbo," he grunted.

VI

Twice have the trumpets sounded.
Act IV, Sc. 6.

We stopped after two or three miles for a cigarette, for there was no pleasure in smoking behind Bluebell's flimsy windscreen at Jack's favourite speed, which was as fast as she would go. The afternoon was glorious, everything quiet and peaceful, and we said little for some time, each being busy with his thoughts. Finally, Jack, lying full length on the grass with his clasped hands behind his head, said casually:

"I've been wanting to talk to you for some time, Vaughan."

I was sitting against a tree with my hat pulled over my eyes.

"Oh?" I answered. "What about?"

"Myrna. . . . You've probably guessed how I feel over her. I've been following her about like a little dog for over two years. I know I look like one of the gargoyles over Notre Dame, and small children run screaming to their mothers when they catch sight of me, so I don't expect girls to tumble over each other to get at me. That's very likely why I never cared much for the species—until I met Myrna. ... I can't—think about anything else, Vaughan. . . . She makes me—oh, I know it's a damn' silly way of putting it, but she makes me physically hungry, as if I hadn't had a square meal for a week. . . . Yet, when I'm in the same room with her, I want to be somewhere, else—the same feeling as I get in an empty house or when I'm going to be sick."

He raised himself on an elbow to press his cigarette-end into the grass.

"I'm sorry for all this soul-searching," he went on, dropping back. "It must be uncomfortable for you, but you're by way of being a friend of mine and I badly need advice. . . . She wouldn't look at me at first, or only with fascinated horror, as if I was Dracula or a blasted crocodile. Then, a long time later, my winning little ways must have made her realise that I wasn't such a monster as I looked, because she got quite friendly, in an impersonal sort of way . . . I followed up my advantage by imitating a doormat, and she got accustomed to having me about the place; running little errands, changing her library books and killing spiders in the bath—which was all I asked, as a preliminary. She's an independent little devil, you know, and most of her remarks to me weren't particularly gracious; but she let me take her to the cinema now and again, and came out with me for runs in Bluebell."

I threw him across a cigarette and he sat up to light it.

"Then, last May, Ridpath arrived on the scene. I still had to run little errands and change the library books, but *he* got the fat part of killer of spiders in the bath. He was charming and handsome; Sir Lancelot, the model of chivalry and courage. I was something unpleasant brought in by the cat. She started going to the pictures with *him*. When he borrowed your car, it was to take her out. Bluebell wasn't good enough. She and I were a pair of plug-uglies and we got the bird.

"I made a damn fool of myself this morning, knocking that piano about. It put me right out of court. But I went completely fantods when he started looking at her in that— possessive way. After lunch to-day I cornered her in the hall, apologised humbly and asked her out to tea. She smiled very sweetly, but said she'd some letters to write—and then went and banged out that loathsome tune, until Ridpath was due to arrive with your car and a much more welcome invitation. Last night they were out in the garden. He'd got his arm round her. I wasn't spying. It was blatant."

He suddenly sat up.

"What am I going to do, Vaughan? Knuckle under or put up a fight? If it's the first, I shall have to leave Mrs. Doubleday's and pack up the LADS."

"I don't really know what to say," I admitted. "There are two kinds of love affair—I mean the respectable affair, without the 'e'—one that culminates in a wedding, the other that comes to an end when one of the parties realises that marriage would be a mistake. Don't be offended if I ask you,

Jack, but was that the case with you and Myrna?"

"No, it wasn't. We never got as far as a love affair. I couldn't find the courage to make the first move. If your friend, Ridpath, hadn't turned up, I should probably have proposed to her by this time."

"Then let me put it brutally, Jack. Your taking Myrna to the cinema and out in your car is not the modern idea of what used to be called an understanding. She was still a free agent. Tiddler Ridpath came into her scheme of things. She began going places with him instead of you. They were attracted by each other. ..." I paused for him to say something, but he was gazing across the sunlit Downs. "You see what I mean?" I finished lamely.

He turned towards me. "That I'm not wanted; that I never meant anything to Myrna; that those two may get married because they love each other; that all I can do is drift along to the wedding, throw confetti and get as tight as a newt at the reception. Is that it?"

"More or less," I agreed.

"Theoretically, Vaughan, you're perfectly right. I ought to accept my *congé* like a pukka sahib and go to Africa, to get myself mauled to death by a lion. But I don't feel like doing it. Myrna means more to me than anything else in the world —and it isn't calf-love, though I've told myself twenty thousand times that it is—yet I'm ready to admit that she's impetuous. She does things she regrets afterwards. More than once she's said damn' rotten things tome—and apologised later, with tears in her eyes. Why shouldn't this affair with Ridpath be just a —just an incident? I'm absolutely certain, Vaughan, that before he came to Mrs. Doubleday's, Myrna was beginning to change her attitude towards me. She laughed *with* me, not *at* me. We had little private jokes. She was getting into the habit of taking my arm when we came home from the cinema in the dark.... She was calling me 'Jack, dear.' "

I thought he had finished, but after a while he said:

"Vaughan, I appreciate that Ridpath is a friend of yours, but what do we know about him?"

"He and I went to school together."

"Most of the biggest blackguards in history went to school with someone or other."

I hastened to defend Tiddler. "He's a first-rate fellow. When I say we went to the same school, I mean we were friends there."

"And have you kept it up since?"

"No, not exactly. Until he turned up last May I hadn't seen him for a good many years."

"Then how can you know him? You've got to stick up for him, of course—I'd do the same in your place—but can I be sure that I'm doing the right thing by leaving him a clear field? Am I deserting Myrna, when I ought to be there to protect her? Ridpath has a way with women. How do I know that he's not just philandering with Myrna? Sir Lancelot wasn't the soul of chivalry, you know. He may have been king-pin in the diamond jousts and just the man for hunting down the Holy Grail, but he wasn't too fussy in his treatment of Guinevere, his best friend's wife."

"If you're still asking my advice," I told him, "I suggest that, for the time being, you leave things as they are. If they're sincerely attached to each other, they'll become engaged; but if it's only an infatuation, surely Myrna's clear-beaded enough to bring it to an end?"

Jack Gough got to his feet and looked down at me.

"Things can go too far," he said, and walked over to Bluebell.

I had no liking for the task, yet felt it my duty to have things out with Tiddler. When we were all on our way up to bed that night. I invited him into my room for a final cigarette. That afternoon it had been Jack who had had to start an awkward conversation. Now it was my turn; and I fumbled it.

"You're rather fond of Myrna, aren't you, Tiddler?" I managed to ask, after several false starts.

"I love her like a brother," he answered lightly and without hesitation.

"Isn't there more to it than that?"

"What makes you think so?"

"Oh, just—well, you're always together."

"What of it, Turtle? Certainly, we sometimes pair off, but there's nothing in that, surely? We're not so stuffy now as they were in Granny's young day. Does our engagement have to be announced in the *Telegraph* before I can take her to the flicks?"

"Look here, Tiddler," I said sharply, "I'm the last to interfere in your private affairs, but there's one thing that's got to be settled—"

He began to say something, but I disregarded him.

"You may say you haven't noticed it, but Myrna's head over heels in love with you. Do you feel the same about her? I'm not asking for an answer, but if it's No, you can't, in all decency, go on as you're going."

He gave me an affectionate smile.

"Dear, straitlaced old Turtle," he said.

"It isn't a question of being straitlaced. Myrna's a very sensitive girl, and if all you're doing is gallivanting with her, it's got to stop."

"And who's going to—" He pulled up short and altered the question to: "Who says I'm gallivanting with her?"

"Well, aren't you?"

"No. That's the worst of a country town. Merely because I sometimes take her to dances—"

"Don't be a damn' fool, Tiddler. It's gone further than that. You don't think everybody doesn't know, do you?"

"You mustn't believe all you hear, Turtle. Myrna and I are just good friends. All perfectly above board, old boy."

"You were noticed in the garden last night."

"So old Caliban's been spying, has he?"

"It was Mrs. Stoneham, if you want to know. She said this morning that you and Myrna were a perfect match."

"Very kind of the old lady."

"Irony won't help, Tiddler. Listen to me for a moment. Before you came to Mrs. Doubleday's, Myrna was going out with Jack Gough."

"Ill-mannered tough!"

"He's nothing of the sort—and you know it as well as I do. Before you arrived they were going out together. Whatever she felt about him, he was completely devoted to her—and still is. Now, then"—I leant towards him—"if you ask her to marry you, Myrna, in her present state of mind, will probably accept; and Jack, like the good fellow he is, won't interfere."

I wagged a finger at him, which made him grin.

"But if you're proposing to dilly-dally with her as long as it suits your convenience and then leave her flat, you're a cheap skate!"

"Dash it, Turtle! Does it have to be so infernally serious? You're making me out an absolute home-wrecker. I can't afford to think about marriage yet. You know that. I couldn't offer Myrna a comfortable home. Have I got to be a hermit till I'm earning five hundred a year?"

"Tiddler," I said, "answer this question: have you talked to Myrna about marriage?"

"We've touched on it once or twice in a general sort of way."

"Have you ever told her that, when you're getting a bit more money, you'll ask her to marry you?"

"Here!" he protested with a light laugh. "This hour of the night is hardly the time for an inquisition."

"Have you?" I persisted.

The answer was reluctant. "Yes, I suppose so."

"And do you intend to keep your word?"

Instantly he was on his feet.

"You mind your own bloody business!" he flared.

His handsome face was hard as he strode across the room. But he paused with his hand on the door-knob, turned and came slowly back.

"I'm sorry," he said quietly. "I shouldn't have spoken like that."

"It's all right," I told him.

It was a pleasure to have taken the grin off his face.

"I'm sorry," he repeated, sitting down again on the bed." I've too much cause to be grateful, to shout at you. Last spring you got me out of one of the worst—"

"Skip that," I cut him short.

"I know you're talking like a dear old Dutch uncle, to stop me making a fool of myself."

"I'm not considering you so much as Myrna and Jack Gough," I said roughly. "If you're not in earnest about Myrna, you're playing with a specially nasty kind of fire."

"Listen, Turtle. I'm going to be frank with you. Even though one of Nature's butterflies, I'm beginning to get worried. At first with Myrna and me, it was just the primrose path. Nothing very serious. Fresh faces and the moon in June. Then she started getting emotional—and one evening on the beach at Southmouth, with the lighted pier and the velvet sky making a backcloth for romance, I got the same. I said quite a lot of things to her—and still don't know whether I meant 'em or not. Since then we've drifted along. Often I've been— well, bored, if you like. Yet there have been other times when the moon was full—" He shifted his position uneasily.

"She acts on me like a recurring fever. So what am I to do?"

"At any rate, you can't leave things as they are. There's no doubt that Myrna's very fond of you; and there's no doubt either that she'd make you a darned good wife. You're getting too old for a butterfly. Why don't you settle down, Tiddler? The old-established business of W. V. Tudor could probably run to another pound or two a week."

"Turtle, you're a dear, generous old fellow and perfectly right to give me what Mrs. Doubleday calls 'a good talking to.' But let me have a little time. A man can't rush off and get married without giving a certain amount of thought to it first."

I remembered Jack Gough, ugly as a toad and loyal as a fox-terrier.

"The truth of the matter is," I said, "that you don't want to marry Myrna."

There was no denial. He sat on the bed, with his arms on his knees, staring miserably down at the carpet.

"And if you don't," I went on, "why don't you finish it?"

"*Because I can't.*"

He jumped up with an impatient ejaculation and his stride lacked its usual languid grace as, for the second time that evening, he made for the door. But now he opened it.

"I suppose," he said over his shoulder, "we all have our own particular hell." Then, smiling very faintly: "Good night, you old fairy godmother."

The door closed softly behind him.

It took me some time to take off my clothes and get into bed. These heart-to-heart talks somewhat disturbed the mind. Even after half an hour with my favourite bedside literature, joining in the adventures of that doughty hummer, Winnie-*ther*-Pooh, delightful little Piglet and Mr. Milne's supreme creation, the melancholy Eeyore, I could not sleep.

There was the problem of Myrna, Tiddler and Jack Gough to fret me. Which way were they going? Where would it end? Perhaps it was no business of mine, yet I was concerned for all three of them. For all his faults and weaknesses, I was very fond of Tiddler. He was like a merry puppy, who chews a hole in the carpet and then contritely licks his master's nose. I was fond, too, of Myrna, not as a man is fond of his sister, so much as of his cousin or his wife's younger sister. She was small and fresh. She looked well in her clothes and—for had I not seen her on Southmouth beach and what was a gossamery bathing costume more or less?—out of them. She had just the piquant little face and dark curls for those impudent fragments of hat that sell for five guineas in Bond Street. She was a bright conversationalist, silver-voiced and witty. And, like Jack Gough, she was loyal.

Yet sometimes she bored Tiddler Ridpath. It was like being bored by spring sunshine or a mountain brook. "Because I can't." What had he meant by that? Whatever he had meant, one thing was certain: he had no intention of marrying Myrna if it could be avoided. Then what about Jack? Even if Tiddler cut the Gordian knot, would Myrna once again laugh with Jack and not at him? have little private jokes with him? entrust him with the destruction of spiders in the bath?

It was all very difficult. If Myrna had been twins it would have simplified things. Then Jack could have married one and Tiddler could have—what? I turned over, but sleep still evaded me. . . . Elizabeth. . . . How different she was from Myrna! She was no dancing brook, but a smooth, deep river, mysterious and enchanting   Or a pool. . . "By laughing shallow and dreaming pool." . . . Myrna and Elizabeth.

Who was the world's most beautiful woman? Helen of Troy? No, she had no existence. She was the daughter of Zeus. . . . Cleopatra? "Age cannot wither her, nor custom stale her infinite variety." ... "If her nose had been shorter, the whole face of the earth would have been changed." Curious how all the best things had been said already. . . . Myrna's nose was short. Elizabeth's was—not exactly long, but sensitive. She was a trifle taller than I. Tall, dark and restful, yet with a may-fly mischievousness. A deep, slow voice with a hint of laughter. . . . Impudent hats were not for her. . . . Would she marry me if I asked her? Would it not be inviting a gentle rebuff? But one had to take risks sometimes. After all, there was no Tiddler Ridpath in the running. ... I must think it over.

Elizabeth would be splendid in "Measure for Measure." Isabella, with her "virginal strength and severity and beauty." Hard, unsympathetic and inflexible. What a part for a great actress! What a part for Elizabeth! . . . But there was the war. Probably "Measure for Measure" would have to be abandoned. . . . I should be called up. . . . The business would be closed and there would be no marriage with Elizabeth for a long time, even if she accepted me. . . . No marriage with Elizabeth. Life without her as a wife would be a dismal affair. . . . Winnie-*ther*-Pooh. . . . "Well, either a tail *is* here or it isn't there. You can't make a mistake about it. And yours isn't there." "That Accounts for a Good Deal," said Eeyore gloomily. "It Explains Everything. No Wonder. . . Somebody must have taken it. How Like Them." . . .I was running, running, running. . . They were coming after me. . . Thousands of them. . . Banshees with menace and danger and terror in their wailing. . . I was running. . . fell . . .

Suddenly, I was wide awake; and the tall new siren at the top of Beastmarket Hill was dragging us all from our beds.

We assembled in the lounge, all except Jack Gough and Mr. Garnett, both of whom announced in no measured terms that the Nazis could get on with it, as far as they were concerned. Our dishabille was varied. Of Mrs. Stoneham and Miss Tearle, it would be unchivalrous to mention anything here, except that they must have come down in a great hurry. Mr. Mortimer Robinson was dressing-gowned, but neat and well-groomed, as if he had not gone to bed. Tiddler, in a wrap gaudy with dragons and Chinese temples, was tousled-haired, but wideawake and cheerful. Myrna, sleepy-eyed, looked ravishing in her *négligé* and I was glad, for his own peace of mind, that Jack had kept to his room.

Mrs. Doubleday, fully dressed in her customary black, came in to ask if we wanted tea. We all agreed. Air-raid warnings are great provokers of a thirst for tea. Myrna and Tiddler joined in our small talk at first, but in a few minutes drifted over to the settee, where they chatted in undertones. An occasional merry laugh precluded any possibility that the Gordian knot was in danger of immediate severance.

The tea arrived and, after the first cup, conversation became less desultory. I need quote only a small part of it here. After we had all agreed, for about the sixth time, how quiet everything was outside, Mr. Mortimer Robinson said:

"I find it hard to credit that the war has really begun. Except for the siren, everything seems so very much as usual. I fully expected that the Germans would launch an instantaneous assault on this country—and that the sky would be full of enemy aircraft and bombs."

"They may be attacking London now," I reminded him. "Don't forget it's over fifty miles away."

"Yet I agree with Mr. Mortimer Robinson," said Mrs. Stoneham. "Everything seems too calm and still. Miss Tearle, Miss Ashwin and I spent the whole afternoon sewing and reading in the garden, as if our country were still at peace."

The whole afternoon in the garden. So it had *not* been Myrna in the car with Tiddler.

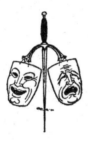

"Do you still side with Dr. Pangloss?" enquired Melpomene with something very like a sneer.

"Who's he?" asked Thalia, who was not very up in French Classics.

"Don't hedge!" snapped Melpomene, "admit that things aren't as good as they were."

"Well, perhaps not," conceded Thalia, "but it's always darkest—"

"I know the rest," flashed Melpomene, taking her revenge.

... he was ever precise in promise-keeping.
Act I, Sc. 2.

I had thought that, as Hitler had cried "Havock!" our lives would suffer a stern and radical change, but the war did not take the turn that we had all expected. Once slipped, the dogs of war held back, having no mind, it seemed, for famine, fire and sword. We in Lulverton valiantly manned the barricades, bandaged each other up and tried to keep it clear in our minds that it was phosgene and not B.B.C. that smelt like musty hay; but when the long-threatened assault did not mature, we began to relax our vigilance and turn our thoughts to less burdensome employment.

Six weeks after war was declared, bored stiff with nothing to do during the dark evenings, we held another meeting of the LADS. It was unanimously decided to go on with "Measure for Measure" and give the proceeds to the Red Cross.

Shakespeare borrowed the plot of "Measure for Measure" from Whetstone, who had stolen it from an Italian novelist named Cinthio. To whom Cinthio was indebted is not on record. Although straightforward enough in the main, Shakespeare's version is confused and contradictory in detail, as if the author re-wrote parts of it and did not afterwards bring the remainder into line.

"In the city of Vienna," begins Mary Lamb in the *Tales,* "there once reigned a duke of such mild and gentle temper that he suffered his subjects to neglect the laws with impunity; and there was in particular one law, the existence of which was almost forgotten, the duke never having put it in force during his whole reign. This was a law dooming any man to the punishment of death who should live with a woman who was not his wife; and this law, through the lenity of the duke, being utterly disregarded, the holy institution of marriage became neglected, and complaints were every day made to the duke by parents of the young ladies of Vienna, that their daughters had been seduced from their protection, and were living as the companions of single men."

The Duke, whose name is Vincentio, at length decides that this state of affairs can no longer continue, and that the old law shall be revived and strictly administered. But as, at the same time, he does not wish to lose favour with his people, he stages a visit to Poland, so that the responsibility shall rest on his deputy, Angelo, a man of most saintly reputation.

The first victim of the re-established law is a young gentleman called Claudio, who has anticipated his wedding with Juliet (or Julietta; the author does not seem to be sure which), his beloved. The now all-powerful Angelo sentences Claudio to execution. In his desperate plight, Claudio despatches his friend, Lucio (described in the *dramatis personae* as a Fantastic), to his sister, Isabella, who is about to enter the convent of St. Clare. Responsive to this appeal, Isabella hastens to Angelo, to beg for her brother's life. Angelo is unyielding, but, having cast an appraising eye over the supplicant, suggests that she calls again on the morrow.

Despite his published intention, Vincentio, the Duke, has not gone to Poland, but he crept back to Vienna dressed as a friar, in order not only to observe the results of the proclamation, but also to keep watch on the "outward-sainted" Angelo. In his disguise he visits Claudio in his prison cell.

Isabella goes again to see Angelo and he, after a night of torment and temptation, offers her the famous Alternative with which so many villains have confronted so many high-minded heroines: "Your brother will die unless ..." Isabella scorns the vile suggestion. With the ringing announcement, "More than our brother is our chastity," she hurries off to jail, to prepare Claudio's mind for death. "Lord Angelo, having affairs in heaven," she says, breaking it gently, "intends you for his swift ambassador."

If the modern phrase is permissible, Claudio can't take it. His view is that Isabella expressed her splendid sentiment the wrong way round. Death, he says, is a fearful thing, and any sin committed to save her brother from it would be almost a virtue. Isabella is scandalised and abuses him roundly. They are interrupted by the Duke, still dressed as a friar, who, after prevailing on Claudio to play the man, outlines a little plot to Isabella.

Angelo, he tells her, was once affianced to a girl called Mariana, but deserted her when her considerable dowry was lost at sea. Mariana still loves Angelo and it is the Duke's idea that Isabella shall agree to Angelo's outrageous proposal, but that Mariana shall keep the tryst; and so that Angelo shall be deceived into thinking her Isabella—

"Go to Angelo," says the Duke to Isabella, "answer his requiring with a plausible obedience, agree with his demands to the point; only refer yourself to this advantage; first, that your stay with him will not be long; that the time may have all shadow and silence in it; and the place answer to convenience."

Isabella is well pleased with the plan and proceeds, with the help of Mariana, to carry it out. But, in spite of the compliance with his demands, the rascally deputy gives orders for Claudio to be executed and for his head to be delivered to his own house. (Presumably, this sort of thing is quite usual in Vienna.) The Duke, luckily, is at the prison when the message is delivered and is able to arrange for the head of Ragozine, "a most notorious pirate," who had died that day in the prison, to be substituted for Claudio's.

When Isabella arrives next day at the prison to enquire whether her brother's pardon has yet arrived, she is met by the Duke, who, with that curious imperception that makes him so unconvincing a character, baldly informs her, without even first offering her a seat:

"His head is off, and sent to Angelo."

He has already despatched word to Angelo of his return from Poland, instructing him to meet him at the gates of the city. He now tells Isabella to be there and to behave as she would be later directed.

After Angelo and Escalus, an ancient lord, have welcomed their Duke at the gates, Isabella in the crowd cries out for justice, claiming that Lord Angelo has seduced her. Why the Duke has seen fit to require her to make so public and untrue an avowal is far from clear. Mariana, heavily veiled, then asserts that it was she, not Isabella, who went to Angelo the night before.

"This is strange abuse," says Angelo; then goes on with more sense of the dramatic than of prudence: "Let's see thy face."

Mariana unveils, to his swiftly repressed consternation. The Duke, feigning disbelief of both women, leaves Angelo and old Escalus to administer justice. He returns within a few minutes in his friar's habit and, when taxed by Escalus, who is acting in good faith, charges Angelo with his villainy. Escalus, of course, does not believe him.

"Away with him to prison!" he orders.

Lucio, the Fantastic, who has flitted in and out of the story, slandering the Duke from time to time, now takes a hand.

"Why," he cries, "you bald-pated, lying rascal, you must be hooded, must you? Show your knave's visage!"

He pulls off the hood and reveals the Duke. No more need be told, except that Claudio is produced with his head still on his shoulders (which is a pity, for he is a bit of a nincompoop) and marries Juliet (or Julietta); Angelo marries Mariana and is pardoned (which is also a pity); Lucio, after sentence to whipping and hanging, is married off to one of Vienna's frail sisterhood, presumably a girl called Kate Keepdown: and the Duke makes Isabella his Duchess.

There are other characters, of course: Mistress Overdone, who keeps a disorderly house; Pompey, her tapster and a diverting rogue; the Provost of the prison; Elbow, a foolish constable; Abhorson, the executioner; Francisca, a nun; and Froth, a half-witted gentleman.

After several adjournments and a good deal of heated discussion, the casting committee decided on the players.

Isabella, naturally, was to be taken by Elizabeth Faggott; Mariana, a very subordinate part, by Hilary Boyson; Juliet (or Julietta), an almost non-existent part, by Myrna Ashwin; Mistress Overdone, after horrible threats to resign if she didn't-get it, by Miss Lark; Pompey, the main comedy part by Paul Manhow; Elbow, the constable, by Jack Gough; Escalus, the ancient lord, by Mr. Mortimer Robinson; Francisca, the nun, by Mrs. Cheesewright ("How deliriously inappropriate," said Jack Gough); and the Provost, Vienna's chief police official, by myself.

All these have already been introduced. Of the others, there will be something to say later. It need only be added now that Vincentio, the Duke, was to be played by Geoffrey Cutner; Angelo by Franklin Duzest; Claudio by Boyd Gloster; and Lucio by Basil Northcott, who had done well as young Wilfred Kirby, but did not seem so promising as airy, graceful Lucio.

Messrs. Samuel French's do not publish a special acting edition of "Measure for Measure," so we had to do our own revision of the text. A small minority led by Mrs. Cheesewright urged wholesale expurgation, but we others had no such idea. As Paul said, had we cut out all the rude bits, he, as Pompey, would have been left with nothing to say. We were not out to purify Shakespeare, but to make him intelligible. "Woodman," "come Philip and Jacob," and "would all themselves laugh mortal," were doubtless fully comprehended in 1604, but a 1939 audience would better understand, "lady-killer," "come the first of May," and—not that we had the temerity to make such an alteration—"would all be tickled to death."

We groped our way to each other's houses for readings, through the blacked-out streets of Lulverton. We began to learn our parts. Lines from the play cropped up in our conversations. Following the disreputable example set by Jack Gough, we fell into the habit of calling Mrs. Doubleday (behind her back) Mistress Overdone, and Hobson (to his grinning face) Pompey.

Hobson, by that time, had reorganised our lighting system, installing a beautifully neat network of wires and an amazing control panel, on which he played with all the virtuosity of a cinema organist. It was he, too, who fitted the stage with sweetly sliding curtains and backcloth, by means of motor-car wheels and starting-handles. Where he obtained all this apparatus nobody dared to enquire. Paul Manhow was a great wangler, but he was a child to Pompey Hobson.

Elizabeth was soon word-perfect in the Isabella part. One could see, even during the readings, that she was going to be superb on "the night." The real character of Isabella is as great a mystery to the student as Hamlet's. My own opinion, for what it is worth, is that in neither case was Shakespeare able to make up his mind—and the effect is bi-focal. Is Isabella, one is forced to ask, a saint or a waspish prude? Take her denunciation of the unhappy Claudio:

> "O you beast,
> O faithless coward, O dishonest wretch,
> Wilt thou be made a man out of my vice?
> Is't not a kind of incest, to take life
> From thine own sister's shame? What should I think?
> Heaven shield my mother played my father fair!"

Does it show "virginal strength and severity and beauty"? Or is it just a meaty contribution to a vulgar slanging match? Elizabeth's interpretation did not suggest outraged modesty or spiteful prudery; but rather a frantic consciousness that she must not weaken; that she must crush her love for Claudio, even by a savage and over-coloured outburst, directed as much against herself as her brother. Even standing script in hand in Mrs. Doubleday's lounge, with none of the magical trappings of the drama, Elizabeth caught the desperate mood of Isabella.

Again, in the scene where Isabella first visits Angelo, Elizabeth's note of pleading would have touched the hardest heart in the dress circle.

"Could great men thunder
As Jove himself does, Jove would ne'er be quiet,
For every pelting, petty officer
Would use his heaven for thunder; nothing but thunder.
Merciful Heaven!
Thou rather with thy sharp and sulphurous bolt
Splitt'st the unwedgeable and gnarled oak,
Than the soft myrtle; but man, proud man,
Drest in a little brief authority,
Most ignorant of what he's most assured,
His glassy essence—like an angry ape,
Plays such fantastic tricks before high heaven,
As make the angels weep; who, with their spleens,
Would all themselves laugh mortal."

Had she been really Isabella and I Angelo she could have had anything she wanted: pardon and a generous pension for her brother; the head of my best friend delivered to her house before breakfast; my estates and riches; my life itself. It may sound a trifle sweeping, but that was how I felt. As Elizabeth, I loved her; but as Isabella, I was her adoring slave. Between rehearsals I waited with almost overmastering impatience for the next, when I should hear the deep, sweetly impassioned voice despairfully cry out:

"Merciful Heaven!"

Many times I tried to screw my courage to the sticking-place and make love to her, but my courage seemed to have no sticking-place. Jack Gough had said to me of Myrna that she made him physically hungry, as if he had eaten nothing for a week. I underwent the same torment. Worshipping from afar, like a star-struck youth in the back row of the gallery, I did not have the boldness even to ask her to a cinema—and as for a spin in the car, with a cosy *tête-à-tête* over tea and crumpets as our objective, it was the dream of a smock-faced coward.

Once I was within an ace of it. A protracted rehearsal had

kept her late at Mrs. Doubleday's and I had offered her my
escort home. When my electric torch had led us to her gate we
paused and chatted for a few minutes. The night was as black
as the pit. I could not see her, but she was very close to me. It
was difficult to talk casually about the evening's rehearsal; and
still more difficult to say the words that trembled on my lips.

"Well," she said at last, "I must go in. Thank you, Vaughan,
for seeing me home."

As she walked up the path, clamouring thoughts urged me
to call her back. Lily-hearted, I hesitated. Then:

"Elizabeth." .

She halted in the darkness.

"Yes, Vaughan?"

It was now or never. I took a deep breath.

"Oh, nothing," I said, and stumbled blindly along the road
until I fetched up sharply against a lamp-post.

Autumn gave place to winter. There seemed no change in
the relationship between Tiddler and Myrna. They were often
together, yet, with the watchfulness that had possessed me since
Mrs. Stoneham's unwitting revelation, I noticed that, from time
to time and with increasing frequency, Tiddler slipped away,
afterwards dropping no hint of where he had been. Sometimes
he borrowed my car; and, on two or three occasions, was away
the whole week-end. Jack Gough, from his manner, was also
aware of these mysterious excursions, but he made no direct
reference to them, except when once I asked him if he knew
where Tiddler was. He answered by quoting from "Measure for
Measure": " 'Groping for trouts in a peculiar river,' blast him!"
Jack seemed to have accepted his *congé* if only provisionally, and
was his old agreeable self when Myrna was about, so I thought
it best not to bring up the matter again. Let Jack bide his time,
let Myrna make her own discovery, let Tiddler make a fool of
himself—that became my Fabian strategy.

There was another matter that was giving me far more
concern.

One evening Mrs. Doubleday had taken me aside.

"Mr. Tudor," she had said, "I don't like to worry you, but it's about Mr. Ridpath."

"What's the trouble, Mrs. Doubleday?" I had asked rather apprehensively, for one never knew with Tiddler.

"I hope you won't mind me mentioning it, Mr. Tudor. I thought it would be better doing it this way."

"Of course," I had agreed, wishing she would get on with it.

"I suppose I should really have put it to him direct, but I didn't like to, somehow."

"Perhaps I can help you."

"He's such a nice, respectable young gentleman."

That had been a relief. Apparently, it was not what I had feared.

"I didn't want to have to say anything about it to you, Mr. Tudor, but he's three weeks in arrears with his account, and these things do mount up so."

I had promised to have a word with Tiddler. He had been penitent, had blamed an importunate tailor, and had been grateful when I had lent him the money to settle with Mrs. Doubleday.

That had not been the only instance. Although receiving an income quite sufficient for a single man, Tiddler seemed continually short of money; and when he borrowed from me, as he often did towards the middle of the week, he had to be gently reminded of his obligation when Friday came round.

There was an awkward incident in the office during the early part of November. I always kept ten pounds or so in ready money in a cash-box, of which Miss Jones held one key and I the other. When anything was needed to cover travelling expenses or other incidental payments, Miss Jones made an entry in a petty-cash ledger, which, at most infrequent intervals, I checked. One Thursday morning, when business happened to be slack, I asked for the cash-box and the ledger. On finding that the cash in hand was two pounds short, I had Miss Jones into my office and required an explanation. The poor girl was most distressed.

"I don't understand it at all, Mr. Tudor," she admitted.

"I see," I said, "that the last entry was made by Hindenburg yesterday. Paper-fasteners."

"I sent him out to buy them, Mr. Tudor. He was gone three-quarters of an hour."

"Blast that boy!" I muttered. "He's no better than the rest of them. Did he take the money from the box himself?"

"Oh, no, Mr. Tudor! I never allow him to touch the key. I gave him a shilling out of it and he brought back the change with the receipt. Then he wrote the details in the book. It couldn't be him, Mr. Tudor."

"There are no big items you haven't recorded?"

"Certainly not, Mr. Tudor."

"And you never let the key out of your possession?"

"Only to Mr. Ridpath, Mr. Tudor. He had it yesterday morning, just before we closed for the afternoon, for some fares to Paulsfield. You'll see the entry immediately above the paper-fasteners, Mr. Tudor."

"That very likely explains it," I said with an easiness that I did not feel. "I expect he's forgotten to enter something—probably to do with that Waghorn & Wheatley business. That'll do, thank you, Miss Jones. I'll have a word with Mr. Ridpath."

After she had returned to the outer office I glanced back through the pages of the petty-cash ledger. An estate agent's assistant has a fair amount of travelling about to do, but I could not think that the jobs I gave Tiddler took him as often to Paulsfield, Littleworth, Padging, Southmouth and Whit-chester as the entries in the book implied. Later in the day I had Tiddler in.

"Tiddler," I remarked in a casual tone, "we're a couple of pounds short in the petty cash. Any ideas?"

He answered quite readily. "Guilty, my lord! It was I who stole the money and murdered Dan Magrew."

"Well," I said with some impatience, "I wish you'd enter these things in the book. You've caused Miss Jones a lot of anxiety."

"Sorry, Turtle, old boy, but I drew it out yesterday in a hell of a hurry, just before early closing. Miss Jones was fidgeting to get away."

He stopped. I looked at him.

"You'll remember," he added, "that you wanted me to go up to London to see Fraser, Cook & Co. about those small-holdings at Burgeston."

"I also remember telling you that the transaction had fallen through."

"Of course you did! I'd forgotten. In any case, I was going to speak to you again before I went. I've been thinking that if only we can interest old Linklater in the freehold reversion—"

"Ten shillings would have covered your expenses to London."

"But I didn't want to get landed without a bean, Turtle. An air-raid might have kept me up there for the night."

It was difficult to be stern with him.

"All right," I smiled; "only do try to bear the office routine in mind. I very nearly had Hindenburg on the carpet, and Miss Jones is convinced I suspect her."

"Sorry, old boy. I'll see it doesn't happen again. Now, about old Linklater. For anyone with floating capital, those small-holdings are— What is it, Turtle?"

I was holding out my hand.

"Two pounds, please."

"That's the difficulty, Turtle. I haven't got it. Something cropped up yesterday afternoon, and, apart from that, I hadn't a penny. Do you mind holding it over until to-morrow and deducting it from my screw?"

It was time, I could see, for a show-down. I motioned him to the chair on the other side of my desk.

"Tiddler," I said, trying to make my voice sharp, "you and I have got to come to an understanding. I'm not a millionaire and can't go on getting you out of your money troubles. You've only yourself to keep. On your income you ought to live very comfortably. Yet you're always in debt. You suggest the two pounds should come off your salary to-morrow, but you've already had thirty bob from me on the same terms. If I deduct both amounts you won't have enough to pay Mrs. Doubleday on Saturday, let alone to see you through until to-morrow week."

"I've got myself rather in the mulligatawny, old boy. It's my own silly fault, I suppose, but money always slips through my fingers. A packet of cigarettes, a beer or two—and there seems nothing left. A fellow's got to maintain a certain position. Apart from that, I spend quite a lot making business contacts—and keeping 'em. It's surprising how small incidental expenses mount up."

"Yes," I agreed dryly. "I've been looking through the petty-cash book."

"So you see!" he took me up swiftly. "How can I consider marrying, with my affairs in such a sticky state?"

"We're not discussing marriage. What I want to know is, are you going to modify your way of living?"

"You told me, Turtle, that if I got engaged to Myrna, you'd increase my—"

"I said nothing of the sort. Leave Myrna out of this and answer my question: are you going to behave a bit less like a Mayfair play-boy?"

"I'm not behaving like a play-boy.. .. You always seem to be rowing me these days."

"Then what are you going to do? How do you propose to get out of this mess?"

"I don't know. It keeps me awake at night

I went on relentlessly; it was time he was taught a lesson.

"Have you been borrowing from anyone else?"

"No.... Well, yes. A pound or so here and there.

"How much altogether?"

"Three or four pounds."

"Which is it?"

"Five."

"And bills?"

"Only one, for a suit. Nine guineas."

"You can get a good suit for a good deal less than nine guineas. That's everything, is it?" He nodded. "Nine guineas plus five, say fourteen pounds ten, and three pounds ten makes eighteen pounds. What I propose to do is lend you fourteen pounds—on the understanding that you bring me the tailor's receipt to-morrow and give me your word that you'll use the rest of the money to pay off your other debts forthwith. Is that agreed?"

"Absolutely."

"You still owe me for the three weeks' board that I settled with Mrs. Doubleday, and one or two other small amounts. I'll write all that off. But the eighteen pounds I'm going to deduct from your salary by weekly instalments. But get this quite clear in your mind, Tiddler—I shan't lend you another penny, even if you're starving in the gutter."

His answering smile was wan. "That's very decent of you, Turtle," he said. "I don't deserve it.... Could you put it in round figures and make it twenty?"

"No. . . . All right, then. And one word of warning, young man: squiring too many dames can be an expensive hobby."

His pale face flushed.

"What do you mean by that?" he demanded.

"*You* know what I mean."

It was some seconds before he answered.

"Perhaps I do."

He got up and stood looking down at me quizzically across the desk.

"I told you," he said, "that you'd live to regret it."

VIII

Thou art not certain.
For thy complexion shifts to strange effects,
After the moon.
Act III, Sc. 1.

Saturday, November 25th, 1939, was a momentous day for me.

Paul Manhow was largely responsible. On the previous Monday evening, during a rehearsal at Mistress Overdone's—I beg her pardon!—Mrs. Doubleday's, he interrupted a scene between Escalus and the Provost (Mr. Mortimer Robinson and me) by the observation-:

"By the way, before I forget, they've got a Shakespeare season at the Prince Consort in London, and they're doing 'Measure for Measure' this week."

"Goody!" cried Myrna. "I'd love to go!"

"That's what I was getting at," explained Paul. "Couldn't we fix up a party? There's a matinee at half-past two on Saturday afternoon, and if we could catch the twelve-twenty-three . . ."

Elizabeth said: "How lovely! Who can arrange it?"

"Surely," smiled Mr. Mortimer Robinson, "such things come within the province of our secretary, good Master Provost?"

So it was left to me. If it can be avoided I shall never organise such an expedition again. Harassing is the precise word; and that thirteen of us caught the 12.23 to Waterloo and took our reserved seats at the Prince Consort three minutes before the curtain went up, I regard as my life's supreme achievement.

It would have delighted me to sit next to Elizabeth, but I was hemmed in by Mrs. Cheesewright and Hilary Boyson, while Elizabeth was in the row in front, between Mr. Mortimer Robinson and Franklin Duzest. I have made, as yet, only casual mention of Franklin Duzest, who was to play Angelo for us. He was a bachelor of independent means, in the early forties, not so tall as he appeared at first sight, with carefully brushed, dark hair, full, rather sensual lips and bags under his eyes. He lived at the Bunch of Grapes, which had first-class residential accommodation, and ran a Bugatti car. Tiddler Ridpath was a great favourite with the other sex; and so was Franklin Duzest, though not in the same way. His slightly dissipated appearance attracted them irresistibly. Had he entered a West End restaurant, every woman in the room would have turned to look at him, not because he was handsome or distinguished, but because he looked so captivatingly dangerous. Miss Lark's dictum was: "He gives the impression that he's *lived.*" That was probably why he did not quite succeed as Angelo, who was only a novice at dalliance.

I was far from comfortable with Mrs. Cheesewright on one side of me and Hilary Boyson on the other, for at every opportunity Mrs. Cheesewright resumed a conversation begun in the train. As far as I could gather, and putting it as coherently as possible, it was on the subject of some tomfool coat that Mrs. Cheesewright had bought in Southmouth in artificial light. It had been too long until she had had a bit cut off and then it had been too short; and anyway, when she'd got it home it hadn't gone with the hat that she had got at Higgins & Jones, which she wouldn't have bought, in any case, if it hadn't been the last day of the sale. She had been quite certain, at the time, that she wasn't going to like it, but it had been such a bargain that Miss Boyson or Miss Lark (who was on the other side of Hilary) would never guess how much she paid for it, and she wasn't even going to *hint* at the price, because they wouldn't believe her. Twenty-five and eleven! Now she'd given the secret away! But they'd hardly credit it, would they?

I certainly didn't. Mrs. Cheesewright never paid all that for a hat in her life. It was common knowledge that she got her clothes from shop-soiled stock. After a certain time, hats that had not attracted customers came out of the window in the Shambles and finished their undistinguished careers perched on the melancholy summit of Mrs. Cheesewright's untidy head.

From the hat, she went back to the coat, while Hilary and Miss Lark listened with that air of rapt attention that women can assume when an acquaintance is romancing about her wardrobe. I did suggest, during the second interval, that I should change places with Mrs. Cheesewright, but the motion was opposed: it would, without doubt, have spoilt her enjoyment.

Hilary Boyson, whom Elizabeth had succeeded as leading lady, was tall like Elizabeth, but as blonde as Elizabeth was brunette. She was what young women, older women, young men and older men all describe as "a nice girl"—for four different reasons. She was of the type (and the definition is not to be taken as a sneer) who, after being the most promising pupil at the High School, gaining diplomas for elocution and deportment, scoring successes at end-of-term performances in such parts as Captain Absolute in "The Rivals"—not for any masculine attributes, but because of her height—and finishing, in a blaze of glory, as head girl of the school and idol of the lower forms, usually lives quietly at home until she marries some medical practitioner fifteen years her senior and bears him two sons and a daughter. If she had beauty, it was the beauty of the daffodil. But she was a nice girl—a thoroughly nice girl.

We all enjoyed the show, yet it had a sobering effect on us—on me, at any rate. I had much the same feeling as an eighteen-handicap man, who, having hit the screamer of his dreams bang down the middle of the fairway, watches the professional effortlessly reach the green with a No. 1 iron.

Vincentio, the Duke, with his beneficent but rather foolish plotting, was not such a pompous exponent of parlour magic as Geoffrey Cutner made him out to be. The stage Duke conveyed the idea that he was enjoying his stealthy little antics: Cutner sounded like somebody reciting Shakespeare.

Franklin Duzest's Angelo was a congenital libertine—a snake in the grass, whose life had not been really blameless, whatever his high reputation in Vienna, and to whom Isabella was just another light o' love. The man we saw that Saturday afternoon on the Prince Consort stage was an austere anchorite, carried away on a surging flood of passion when Isabella first came pleading for her brother's life; struggling and fighting against his animal desires. "For I am that way going to temptation, where prayers cross." It was the despairing cry of defeated goodness. When Franklin Duzest delivered the line, one felt that no such tremendous surrender was involved.

I have previously expressed the opinion that Claudio is a bit of a nincompoop. Boyd Gloster had done nothing at rehearsals to make me alter my view. But this other Claudio got more out of the part than the author, who could be very slap-dash sometimes, ever put into it. He was not so spineless. Certainly, he put his own life before his sister's honour; but life was sweet, birds still sang—and there was Juliet (or Julietta), his darling, the girl he could marry if... It was so small a thing compared with death. "To lie in cold obstruction and to rot; this sensible warm motion to become a kneaded clod." Well might he cry: "The weariest and most loathed worldly life, that age, ache, penury, and imprisonment can lay on Nature, is a paradise to what we fear of death." Claudio was *young*—one seemed to realise it then for the first time.

Lucio is a Fantastic, for which, strangely enough, we, in our time, have no exact word. Previous generations would have called him a fop, a dandy, a Johnnie, a masher, a dude, or a knut with a k. P. G. Wodehouse approaches him most nearly with his Eggs and Crumpets. Pompey is the chief comedian in the play, but in the hands of a competent actor, Lucio can steal the honours. This one did. Pompey got his quota of laughs, but Lucio brought the house down. His airy gestures, his breezy references to a thoroughly disreputable past, his candid comments on matters that the best people never mention—all were beautifully done. "By my troth," said he to the Duke in his friar's habit, "I'll go with thee to the lane's end: if bawdy talk offend you, we'll have very little of it." Mrs. Cheesewright went *"tck-tck"* more than once, but she would have gone *"tck-tck"* at anything.

Basil Northcott was to play Lucio for the LADS. I shuddered. Basil was a nice enough boy and was useful in the first row of the scrum, but where was the light touch, the artless, thistledown indelicacy? The conversation in Act III, Scene 2, during which he tells the pseudo friar one or two unexpected things about the Duke's mode of living—if Basil plodded through that in his painstaking way, we should all be before the justices the next morning. It was thin ice and Basil, as a dramatic artist, was no featherweight.

The one Prince Consort player that I found little to my liking was Isabella. It was a technically faultless performance, but with the perfection of a circus dog jumping through a hoop or a seal balancing a ball on its nose. I might have been charmed by it, had I not first heard Elizabeth.

The Prince Consort is just off Piccadilly Circus. After the show I was the last of our party to come down the stairs and was cut off from them in the vestibule by a wave of people from the stalls. Outside in Shaftesbury Avenue it was black as pitch. There was a babel of voices: "Isn't it dark!" "I think she was marvellous!" "Are you there, darling? Take my arm." "A bit unconvincing as Angelo; he was better last week as Brutus." "*Star, News* or *Standard.*" "So I said, " 'Just you try it, that's all.' " "Mind the kerb!" "Well, I offered to change seats with you." "The papers say nineteen brought down."

I could recognise none of the voices. The others must have gone on to the Coventry Street Corner House, as had been previously arranged. As fast as the darkness allowed, I followed them. On the corner of Great Windmill Street I walked straight into somebody.

"I beg your pardon," I said, and a sweet, mocking voice replied:

"You really should be more careful, Vaughan."

I felt as pleased as Stanley at Ujiji.

"Elizabeth! You're going in the wrong direction."

"Am I? I thought you were all in front. Where were we

going to tea?"

A quick decision was to be made.

"Not the least idea. I was hoping to catch the others up."

"Which way do you think they went, Vaughan? I'm completely lost."

"Good—I mean good that we met like that. Let's try this way, shall we? You'd better take my arm, or we shall lose each other again."

And chattering gaily, I led her away from the Coventry Street Corner House.

We found a little underground place near the Strand where there were alcoves and subdued lights. At the doorway, Elizabeth looked round doubtfully.

"It's rather furtive, isn't it?" she said. "Have you been here before?"

"I used to bring my young sisters to tea. One thing I can promise you: there's no band, so you won't have to listen to the 'Blue Danube.' Let's go over there."

When she had settled in the corner of a deep, luxurious settee and the waitress had taken our order for tea and toast, Elizabeth asked:

"How many sisters have you, Vaughan?"

I felt mad, irresponsible. If this was a tide in my affairs, then, by heaven, I was going to take it at the flood!

"Seven," I told her. "There was another, of whom my family never speak. She was caught cheating at snakes-and ladders—went up a snake when she thought nobody was looking. I hope the others are enjoying their tea at the Coventry Street Corner House."

"Do you think that's where they went?"

"I know it was. We fixed it all up beforehand."

"But I thought you said—"

"Miss Faggott—may I call you Elizabeth?—I have a confession to make. I told you a thumping great fib. I am no better than my sister who went up the snake. By a subterfuge,

I dragged you into this hell's kitchen. Miss Faggott—Elizabeth, will you forgive me?"

" 'O, it is excellent,' " she said sadly, " 'to have a giant's strength; but it is tyrannous to use it like a giant,' "

"Shall I take you back to your friends?"

"Yes, but not till I've had a chocolate eclair."

After the orgy I said, as I held a match to her cigarette: "What did you think of Isabella?"

She blew out a cloud of smoke.

"*You* tell *me*" she smiled.

"She was good—and so she should be. She's one of our best actresses. A very polished and competent performance. No room for criticism anywhere. Word perfect. Very finely acted. I loathed it."

"Loathed it? Why?"

"Because I think she had a confounded cheek to play the part at all. Isabella is *your* part and nobody else's. You are . . ."

My courage failed me. I stopped.

"Flatterer!" she smiled. "I wish I could do as well as she did. It was a chastening experience, Vaughan. The difference between the amateur and the professional. She brought out a lot of points that I've never noticed, though I've studied the part inside out."

"Your Isabella," I maintained, "is a flesh-and-blood woman. Hers was a nicely adjusted clockwork automaton, who did the right things and said the right words just at the right time."

"That's unfair.. . . But it was sweet of you to say it.... You know, Vaughan, I'm absolutely wrapped up in Isabella. It's only going to be a little local show and all who'll see it will be a few ordinary Lulverton folk. Even if we get full houses and do three performances, that will only be two hundred and sixteen altogether. Three nights—and then it's all finished and forgotten. Yet I'm looking forward to it as the most exciting and important experience of my life. I've always wanted to be an actress—not just an ordinary actress, but a Shakespearian actress. Isabella is my chance. Supposing your friend comes down again from that evening paper and . . . likes me?"

"And Mr. C. B. Cochran reads the notice. . . "

She gave an answering smile.

"No but, Vaughan, it is really vital. It's happened to other people—why not to me?"

The conversation was not going the way I wanted, but I said:

"Why not, indeed?"

"To get away from stuffy old Lulverton, with its hundreds of Mrs. Cheesewrights. To come to London. . . . Small parts at first: Mariana—poor, sickly little thing!—Audrey in 'As You Like It,' Valeria in 'Coriolanus.' . . . Then Juliet, Desdemona, Cleopatra, Lady Macbeth." Her voice sank. "Lady Macbeth at His Majesty's. . . ."

"And Isabella."

"Yes, Isabella. I'm putting my very utmost into Isabella. She's a fearful ninny, but I've simply *got* to get her across the footlights."

"I think 'ninny' is rather unkind!"

"Well, I mean it. There's no comparison between Isabella and Lady Macbeth. Shakespeare lost his grip with Isabella, but Lady Macbeth is clean cut. Nothing must interfere with her ambitions. Duncan is King of Scotland. Macbeth must be king, so Duncan has got to be put out of the way. Banquo suspects, so he goes as well. Isabella is plain milk-and-water. She's not a saint—she's a half-wit. She knows that Angelo is crazy about her. Isn't that a trump card in the hand of an intelligent woman?"

"All this is academic, I suppose?" I laughed.

"What? Oh, yes. I'm talking from the stage point of view."

I had no particular wish to discuss the drama. It was difficult, though, to say what I wanted to say. My exalted mood had passed. I felt flat. Somehow the place seemed wrong. But I tried.

"You know," I said, "it's been great fun having tea together like this. Can't we do it again?"

"I should love to! We are both so keen on Shakespeare. We might even get two or three more people and have Shakespeare teas."

"I didn't mean quite that, Elizabeth. What I was really getting at was—oh, let's go to a news theatre, shall we, and then have some dinner somewhere?"

She looked dubious. "We shall be very late home."

"That doesn't matter. Why not be devils for once? I promise we'll not miss the last train."

"But we can't have dinner in these clothes."

"We can at Francois'."

Elizabeth smiled as she said: " 'For I am that way going to temptation....' "

"It wasn't the wine," murmured Mr. Snodgrass, in a broken voice. "It was the salmon."

In my own case, let it be freely admitted, it was the wine. In the basement tea-room, I had felt stifled. I had tried to remember what Jack Gough had said about Myrna: "When I'm in the same room with her, I want to be somewhere else." One should never make love, I had decided, at tea-time: it was like getting drunk at breakfast.

Undoubtedly it was the wine, a Montrachet 1906. Of course, the *Saumon fumé,* the *Consommé,* the *Filet de Sole Orly,* the *Poulet Poché au Riz,* the *Carre d'Agneau Roti* and the *Soufflé en Surprise Hélène* were all contributory, but it wasn't really the *Saumon fumi.* It was the Montrachet 1906.

We had a little table, just far enough away from the orchestra. The coffee was hot, black and fragrant, the brandy was 1865, the cigarettes were expensively Egyptian. The moment was right.

"Elizabeth," I said, across the table, "perhaps I was wrong about Isabella—I mean the one we saw this afternoon. Perhaps she wasn't a marionette. But she wasn't you, Elizabeth. I was unhappy. It was like having somebody wearing my slippers. For me, there's only one Isabella."

"The worst actress in the world loves flattery," she smiled, "especially after a marvellous dinner. Tell me some more."

"There's a great deal of it," I warned her. "It's my favourite subject, though I haven't had a chance to mention it to you before. You said this afternoon that when you play Isabella, it will be the most exciting and important experience of your life. You'll have to wait some weeks for that, but I have had my most exciting and important experience to-day."

"Yes, it was a wonderful opportunity to see how a professional company does it. It's quite changed some of my ideas about Isabella."

I was too exhilarated to bother whether she was being purposely dense.

"Blast Isabella!" I said with so much gusto that other diners looked across at us. I lowered my voice. "Can't you guess that I'm a tongue-tied lout—that I've never had the pluck to put it into words? Don't you know that"—even now I faltered—"that I'm crazy about you?"

Quietly she said: "Yes, Vaughan, I've known for a long time."

"You're all I can think about, the only thing I want to talk about or dream about. Shakespeare teas! There have always been too many people round us. To-day I've got you away from the others—had a chance to tell you what I've been aching to tell you for months."

I stopped short and, when she did not speak, appended lamely:

"Well, it's out now."

"Yes," she said softly, "it's out now. I've been unhappy about you, Vaughan. That—that night you took me home. When you tried to—say it, I nearly cried."

"Then it's. . . no good?"

"I don't know. I think you're one of the nicest and dearest men I've ever met, but—oh, Vaughan, I don't know."

"That's a pity"—I tried to make my tone light—"because I was going to ask you to marry me."

"Don't do that now, Vaughan," she begged me quickly, then added, with a shy glance of her lovely eyes: "There may be another Shakespeare tea."

"Then let's start a fresh topic. What shall it be?"

She took another cigarette from the box on the table.

"Vaughan," she said, "what's the name of your newspaper friend?"

"Philip Pearson."

"Do you think you can persuade him to publish a report on our show?"

"I don't see why not—unless he's joined up."

"It would be marvellous to get a notice in a London paper. Supposing he fixes up to go somewhere else?"

I put out my cigarette and got up.

"We Tudors," I told her, "are men of action. Don't stir more than a mile from this table. I shall be back within three hours."

From the call-box in the vestibule I telephoned Phil. Luckily, he was at home—and still more luckily, was very willing to come down for the Saturday performance.

"If she's worth it," he promised, "I'll see she gets a splash."

We chatted for a few minutes; then I went back to Elizabeth.

"I've just 'phoned him," I said. "It's in the bag." I wagged a menacing finger at her. "And you be careful, for if you're not nice to me, I'll cancel the date."

" 'Man, proud man,' " she taunted, " 'drest in a little brief authority.' Have you noticed the time?"

We took a cab to Waterloo and just caught the last train to Lulverton. We passed along the corridor, looking for an empty compartment, but the subdued lighting from single blue bulbs made it difficult. One can make oneself most unpopular by investigating every corner seat with a groping hand. Finally, we had to content ourselves with two places on the corridor side. I heard a man's voice mutter, "Damn and blast!" as I followed Elizabeth in. When my eyes became accustomed to the murk, I saw that one far corner was empty, but that two people were sitting together on the other side.

"By the skin of our teeth!" I laughed.

"What should we have done if we'd missed it?" asked Elizabeth.

"Chartered a special train," I asserted.

It was not a very good joke and I was gratified to hear a feminine titter come from one of our fellow travellers. I don't know why, but it is always pleasant to make complete strangers laugh at one's remarks to one's friends. But I was, in that respect, to be disappointed, for the titter had been not of amusement, but of embarrassed surprise. A familiar drawling voice came out of the gloom.

"A nice time to come home!"

Elizabeth cried: "Paul!"

"Pots and kettles," was my retort to him.

I could not identify his companion. She did not speak and I hardly liked to ask. Paul smoothed over the difficulty by filling his pipe and striking a match. The girl by his side was Hilary Boyson.

"We lost the rest of you in the black-out," she explained. "Where did you all get to?"

Paul grunted comically.

"Don't let's any of us ask questions," he said.

I took Elizabeth as far as her gate.

"You won't be cross," I asked, "if on some appropriate occasion in the future—when you're in the middle of a game of tennis or having your hair done—I ask you to marry me?"

"No, I shan't be cross. I'm sorry I was so cruel, Vaughan, dear, but I've a very important decision to make. Give me a little time to "

"Years, if you like."

"Not as long as that. Until after the show."

"That's a date," I agreed promptly. "And don't forget one thing: if peace puts an end to this black-out horror and it's a question of a name in lights across the front of the Prince Consort, Elizabeth Tudor is immeasurably more attractive than Elizabeth Faggott."

"It's certainly a point."

"I'll leave you with it. Good night, Elizabeth."

"Just a moment, Vaughan. You've been sweet to me to-day. Would it please you to—say good night properly?"

"Well," I observed judicially, "if we both muttered 'without prejudice' before the moment of impact, it could surely do no harm?"

I walked into the damned lamp-post again.

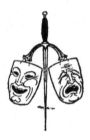

"She's very lovely," Thalia said wistfully.

Melpomene came nearer to a snort than was really becoming to a nicely brought up goddess.

"So was Delilah," she said.

IX

- . for he this very day receives letters of strange tenour.
Act IV, Sc. 3.

Another week passed before the bombshell was dropped, not by the Luftwaffe, but by a retired merchant from Wolverhampton. It has been said that Mr. Garnett was no socialite. His pipe, his *Hardware Journal* and his little note-book were his favourite companions. I was mildly surprised, then, on the morning of Sunday, the 3rd of December, when he said to me in the lounge:

"Any taste for liqueur brandy, Mr. Tudor?"

"When I can afford to buy it," I smiled. "I don't pretend to be a connoisseur."

"Nor I. Bought a bottle yesterday. Care to try a finger after mid-day dinner?"

"I shall be very pleased to.Where is the ritual to take place?"

"My room's best. No women. Can't enjoy a good brandy with gabbling women about. No need to tell Mortimer Robinson or the young chaps.You follow me up while they're clearing the dishes."

From which I gathered that Mr. Garnett sought a favour. Unfortunately, I was right.

His room was on the first floor opposite mine and I noticed several things when I joined him there. A cheerful fire burned in the grate, in front of which were two easy chairs brought up for the occasion from the lounge. On a table were set a bottle of brandy, two glasses and a new box of cigars that must have cost my host a lot of money. As we sat down a servant carried in coffee. Mr. Garnett, with an artistry that was unexpected, had set the stage.

Cigars were lighted and the brandy poured with proper reverence. I settled back in my chair. If I was to be panhandled, I might as well enjoy the accessory comforts. Mr. Garnett was out to make himself agreeable. For twenty minutes we talked nothing but generalities, then—still apparently avoiding the major issue—he got on to the subject of his hobby.

A collector of coins is not necessarily interested in exchange rates of currency inflation, and a man who accumulates match-boxes need not concern himself with pyrology; so it did not follow that Mr. Garnett was a dipsomaniac merely because he collected public-houses. Since I had been in the room I had noticed and speculated on, a large map of southern England, pasted on a sheet of three-ply that hung from the picture-rail. Stuck all over it, with a concentration in the neighbourhood of Lulverton were many little coloured flags, each numbered.

Mr. Garnett caught me staring at it.

"Wonder what it is?" he asked, with his nearest approach to a smile.

"It looks like a war map," I answered, "only I don't see the Maginot Line."

"All pubs. Make a bit of a hobby of it."

It seemed that Mr. Garnett was interested in tavern signs, and kept in his little red leather-covered note-book the names of all those he had encountered. Generally on his bicycle, but sometimes by train or bus, it was his habit to tour the country for new additions to his already considerable collection; and the day was not wasted if he found the Silent Woman or the House in the Clouds.

The record did not stop at curious names. In the red note-book, he told me, there were numerous classifications.

Each county had its own section. Under "Mermaid," "Griffin" or "Golden Fleece" were the towns and villages in which Mr. Garnett had encountered the sign. There were the Reds, the Whites, the Twos, the Threes, the Animals, the Birds, the Kings, the Queens. It was no wonder, from what he told me, that the little book was so thick.

I heard something, too, of the history of some of the signs: the Royal Oak, that derived from the tree in which Charles II hid after the battle of Worcester; the Saracen's Head, that had its origin in the family crests of the old crusaders; the Crossed Keys, the emblem of St. Peter: how most of the Kings were Henry VIII and most of the Queens his daughter, Elizabeth Tudor. (I jumped when Mr. Garnett said that!)

"And on the map," he pointed, "there's a different Coloured flag for each brewery: red for Charrington, blue for Ind Coope & Allsopp—and so forth."

All very interesting, but the homily lasted so long that I began to think it must be the only reason for the unprecedented invitation. After all, I told myself, what's the use of a hobby if you can't talk about it; and evidently Mr. Garnett had few friends.

Then suddenly, with an almost audible click, the tone of the conversation changed. The Tartar had been appeased with brandy and a half-crown cigar; he had been entertained with pleasant conversation: so now was the time. There was no transition period. One moment Mr. Garnett was talking about the Sun in the Sands; the next he embarked on an abrupt introduction.

"Women," he pronounced, "are worse than hell."

"They are difficult sometimes," I agreed.

"My eldest girl's as obstinate as her mother was before her. Got me down here from Wolverhampton not two months after her mother died, so that she could keep an eye on me. Didn't want me to live with *them*. Oh, no! But the bossing kind: likes things her own way. Sort that gives you no peace till they get what they're after. This is man to man, Mr. Tudor, so you'll understand it's her, not me, that's pressing the point. Me, I'm against it, but my girl won't let things lay."

I wondered where this was taking us.

"Her man, my son-in-law, is press-room manager up at the rubber-heel factory. The works manager'll be retiring in a week or so, and Tom—that's my son-in-law—fancies the job. But he's had word that they're more likely to give it to the chap who's now manager of the mixing department."

Was I to be asked to intercede for Tom?

"Tom is out to stop that—or I should say Elsie is. Tom wouldn't do anything off his own hook. And Elsie reckons the best way is to get into the good books of the boss. She's figured it out like this." He leant across and poured some more brandy into my glass. "The boss's daughter is keen on acting. It's Elsie's idea that if this lass can be got the leading part in the play you're going to do, and her dad gets to know who it was fixed it up, it'll be all the better for Tom's chances of getting the works managership."

I stifled a hearty guffaw.

"I'm afraid—" I began, but Mr. Garnett had his piece to say.

"Tom says the old man's set his heart on his girl getting the part, so I thought that you being secretary could very likely do something about it. Then besides helping Elsie and Tom, you'd be obliging me."

The matter needed tactful handling. I imagined that Mr. Garnett could be an ugly customer when roused.

"Of course I'm only too anxious to help you, Mr. Garnett. The difficulty is over the *leading* part. Now, if it were merely a question of getting this girl into the play, it could probably be arranged. All the speaking parts have already been decided on, but I've no doubt we could fit her into some of the crowds scenes. Has she any stage experience, do you know?"

His lower lip stuck out aggressively. "A small part's no good. It's got to be the lead."

"But really, Mr. Garnett, that's quite impossible! The first performance of the play is only a month from to-morrow, and we can't make any serious alteration now. Rehearsals are far advanced—and don't forget that Isabella is a long and difficult part to learn."

"The lass has already got it off by heart."

"That may be so, but there is more to it than just committing to memory. Miss Faggott, who is cast for the part, is a very competent actress. In the hands of a person less experienced, the result might be disastrous. Now, let me make a suggestion. Can this girl sing?"

"Yes."

"Well, there's an attendant in 'Measure for Measure' who sings a song called 'Take, O, Take Those Lips Away.' The committee haven't yet made a final selection for the part, and if she likes to come along for an audition . . ." |

It's got to be the lead," he repeated stubbornly.

I answered with some sharpness: "That's quite out of the question."

Mr. Garnett replaced the cork in the brandy bottle. The action seemed symbolical.

"Listen here, Mr. Tudor," he said. "I thought this wasn't going to be necessary, but seemingly it is. Cooper's Yard and the Bakehouse belong to me. I wasn't out to make a profit off you, so you had it rent free. There's a letter signed by you, young fellow, on behalf of the Society, asking the lawyers to thank me very much for my generosity and saying that if there was anything you could do at any time to repay my kindness, I'd only got to ask."

He paused before adding:

"I'm asking now."

It was for the committee to decide. An emergency meeting was called early that evening. When it was over I went round to the Bakehouse, where I kept my typewriter, slipped a sheet of the Society's letter-paper into the machine and wrote as follows:

"Dear Mr. Garnett,

"With reference to our conversation this afternoon, I have now been able to refer to my committee. They ask me to inform you of their pleasure in learning at last the identity of the Society's principal benefactor. We are indeed grateful. Without such excellent accommodation we should not be able to carry on.

"I am desired to express the committee's regret that they cannot consider any alteration in the cast of 'Measure for Measure.' I feel sure that, on consideration, you will appreciate the great difficulties that such a change at this late stage would involve. I shall be most happy, however, to arrange an audition for your friend, if she cares to get in touch with me.

"Yours very sincerely,
(signed) "W. V. Tudor,
"Hon. Secretary."

After taking the letter back to Mrs. Doubleday's and slipping it in the rack in the hall, I decided to go round and see Elizabeth. The story would interest her.

My ring was answered by Jill Geering.

Elizabeth was the only child of Dr. and Mrs. Faggott. Jill Geering had been adopted in infancy by them, when her widowed mother, who had been a patient of the doctor's, had committed suicide. At the time of which I write Jill was thirteen—a thin, sharp-featured, unusual child, with pigtailed black hair, spectacles and a flair for making inopportune remarks. I did not know her well myself, but, if rumour did not lie, she had asked, in her short existence, more awkward questions about the facts of life than an examiner at the Royal College of Surgeons. Some Frenchman must have had such a young person in mind when he coined the epithet, *l'enfant terrible.*

"Hullo, Jill," I greeted her. "Is Elizabeth in?"

She looked at me solemnly.

"Yes, Mr. Tudor," she said, "but I don't know whether she wants to see you. I s'pose you'd better come in, but wipe your feet, please."

She left me in the hall while she went upstairs. Elizabeth soon came down and took me into the empty drawing-room, where there was a fire. Jill followed us in, closed the door and plumped down on the music stool.

"Jill, dear," Elizabeth smiled at her, "don't you want to read your book?"

"Yes," answered Jill. "Margaret Montgomery has just been expelled. I'll get it."

"Don't do that, dear. There's a nice fire up in the morning-room."

Jill nodded towards me, as if I were some shameless debauchee. "Auntie doesn't know he's here," she said, and settled down more firmly on the stool, fixing her eyes on the ceiling with an expression of pious patience on her unattractive face.

"Stop being silly, Jill!" Elizabeth reproved her. "Run along like a good girl. I want to talk to Mr. Tudor."

When the door had closed not too gently behind Jill, I passed a hand across my brow.

"That child frightens my life out," I admitted. "You never know what she's going to say or do next. Doesn't she—"

I stopped, for, from the other side of the door, a monotonous young voice was declaiming in a high treble:

"'I got possession of Julietta's bed,
You know the lady, she is fast my wife,
Save that we do the denunciation lack
Of outward order....'"

Elizabeth gave a gesture of despair.

"She's uncontrollable. She got hold of my copy of 'Measure for Measure' and not only read the whole thing, but unerringly picked out the worst parts to learn by heart. Jill! Go back upstairs!"

Inexorably the shrill sing-song started on another speech.

"'O you beast,
O faithless coward, O dishonest wretch,
Wilt thou be made a man, out of my vice?
Is't not a kind—'"

'Jill!'

Elizabeth ran to the door and pulled it open, but, by that time, Jill was well on her way up to the morning-room.

When Elizabeth had come back to her chair I recounted the Garnett incident. She said she was glad we had been firm, for she would have certainly scratched the eyes out of Mr. Garnett's son-in-law's boss's daughter.

"What's her name?" she asked; and I had to admit that I had not enquired.

"You men!" she smiled. "Where does this son-in-law work?"

"He's a departmental manager at the rubber-heel factory."

Her eyes opened wide with amazement.

"Then don't you know who it is? It's Hilary Boyson!"

Up to that point it had been funny. Afterwards, it lost some of its humour. When I got back to Mrs. Doubleday's there was an envelope addressed to me in the rack. Inside was my note to Mr. Garnett. Across it had been scrawled with blue pencil: "All right, then. J. H. G."

By the first post on the Tuesday morning I received a letter addressed to the Hon. Secretary of the Amateur Dramatic Society. With a covering note from Dickson, Parrish, Willmott & Lister, there was a notice in duplicate that read:

"We the undersigned, as solicitors and agents for James Henry Garnett, hereby determine your interest and right of possession in all that upper part of the premises known as the Old Bakehouse in Cooper's Yard, Harpur Street, Lulverton, in the County of Downs, together with the staircases leading thereto, belonging to him and now in your occupation, and we require you forthwith to quit and deliver up possession of the same premises.

"Dated this fourth day of December, 1939.

"(signed) Dickson, Parrish, Willmott & Lister."

The second paragraph of the covering letter read:

"Our instructions are that if possession is not given up forthwith, an application will be made to the court for an order for possession."

That explained Mr. Garnett's cryptic, "All right, then."

I went straight round to Bank Chambers.

It is the custom among solicitors, symptomatic, perhaps, of their elusive craft, to do business under any names but their own: so it was not Mr. Dickson, Mr. Parrish, Mr. Willmott or even Mr. Lister, but Mr. Charles Howard, the senior partner, who received me. Besides being a professional acquaintance of some years standing, he was my own solicitor, a fellow-member of the golf club and father of Peggy Howard, who was a member of the LADS—one of those gallant many who never get more than a walking-on part, yet are the very life blood of an amateur dramatic society.

There was no hint in Mr. Howard's calm and dignified demeanour that he knew why I had called, although he was our most generous patron and enthusiastic supporter.

"It's about this notice," I exploded.

"Which notice, Mr. Tudor?"

"The notice to quit and deliver up possession of all that upper part—"

I looked at him, but he was still listening with attention, so I resumed:

"—of the premises known as the Old Bakehouse in Cooper's Yard, Harpur Street, Lulverton, in the County of Downs—do you want the bit about the staircases?"

Not by a flicker of an eyelid did he show anything but dawning comprehension.

"Thank you, Mr. Tudor. I can now identify the document. It is as well to avoid misunderstanding in these matters."

"It's unreasonable!" I protested hotly. "Here we are, with everything arranged for the new show, and then suddenly, without any warning, we get a notice to quit flourished in our faces!"

"Most unfortunate," Mr. Howard went so far as to concede, "but we are merely carrying out our client's wishes."

"Then he's a miserable old muckworm!"

"We received instructions—I may say very explicit instructions—from our client—"

"Aren't I also your client?" I demanded.

Came the dawn. Mr. Howard's austerity dropped from him like a cloak. He donned the friendly mantle of the sympathetic counsellor.

"This is an extremely regrettable situation, Mr. Tudor. It is not our practice to act for both parties in such a matter as this, but I see no reason why I should not advise you. The position, from your point of view, Mr. Tudor, is one of some difficulty. The notice is completely legal and binding on yourselves as tenants. It would be upheld by the court—of that I have not the slightest doubt. Your occupation is not residential. You are not protected by the Rent Acts. And you could not plead that dispossession would cause you real hardship. Now, Mr. Tudor, why should you not write a letter to my cli—to Mr. Garnett, asking for a waiver of the notice until after the performance of the society's forthcoming production?"

"Because it wouldn't be granted. He's not the kind of man to budge an inch. Isn't there any legal loophole? Can't we disclaim the notice?"

"I fear not, Mr. Tudor. Your only recourse is to persuade Mr. Garnett to withdraw the notice. That may be difficult, but perhaps it will not be impossible to come to terms."

"And I know the terms," I said bitterly, having in mind the purposeful aims of Mr. Garnett's eldest girl.

"For all that, Mr. Tudor, there can be no harm in writing such a letter. May I suggest that you offer to pay a small rental?"

"Useless!" I said. "He wouldn't take five hundred a year and rates. All right, Mr. Howard. Let's leave it at that. I'll have another word with Garnett."

He came with me along the passage as far as the street door.

"Good day, Mr. Tudor," he smiled; then leant forward and muttered urgently in my ear: "Give him a poke in the snoot for me!"

Perhaps that is why solicitors bide themselves behind many names, for within less than half an hour he had been the landlord's solicitor, the tenants' adviser and just plain Charley Howard.

My turn to go cap in hand to Mr. Garnett had come. I caught him on the landing just before lunch, and was curtly invited into his room. This time there were no cigars, brandy or fire; and the only chair was by the bed, with a pair of trousers hanging over the back of it. We stood up.

I tried to reason with him, but he was adamant. At our previous interview he had said that his daughter was the prime mover; but it was now obvious that, having been crossed, he was going to be mulish on his own account. The issue was quite clear, he said: if we agreed to give Hilary the Isabella part he would instruct Dickson, Parrish, Willmott & Lister to withdraw the notice to quit. On the other hand, if Hilary did not get the part, the notice would stand and we should be ejected from the premises, if necessary, by order of the court.

I protested that it was fantastic; that, in real life, people didn't do that sort of thing; that Hilary Boyson's getting the part would not influence her father's treatment of his employees.

"Do you mean to tell me," I railed, "that if your precious son-in-law goes to Mr. Boyson and claims that he's dragooned us into re-casting the play, Mr. Boyson will fall on his neck and give him half his kingdom?"

"That's what my girl reckons." He glowered at me ferociously. "And I'm not going against her."

"What about Miss Boyson's feelings? Do you imagine that, when she knows the circumstances, she'll accept the arrangement?"

"It's likely not, but you and your committee will do well not to tell her, for if she doesn't take the lead the notice to quit stands."

"And supposing Miss Faggott objects?"

"She can't. She wouldn't get the chance to play the big part even then, because the place would be closed down."

"This is blackmail!"

"Call it what you like, young fellow. My mind's made up. You know the terms. Take 'em or leave 'em. I'll give you till nine o'clock to-morrow morning. And mark my words: if you don't clear out, I'll have the law on you."

He lurched for the door like an angry gorilla and wrenched it open. I was not going to be stampeded. I strolled forward, but halted before the map on the wall.

"Interesting hobby," I remarked, after a leisured scrutiny. "Keeps you out of mischief."

He growled something under his breath.

I went on airily: "I'm sure you won't mind my mentioning

it, but I can definitely assure you that there's no pub in Westham St. Martin. . . . Allow me."

With a delicate touch I removed a flag from the map, stuck it somewhere in the Bristol Channel, and strolled nonchalantly past him out of the room. It was a pity that Mrs. Doubleday was just going by, for I collided with her and spoilt what would otherwise have been a most artistic exit.

One way and another, it was Black Tuesday. When I glanced at the letter-rack on my return from the office that evening there was another note for me, this time from Basil Northcott. He had enlisted in the Air Force, he wrote, and would therefore not be able to play Lucio. I breathed a weary sigh. It is said of Ludovico Sforza that his hair turned grey in a single night; and I have sometimes wondered whether he was honorary secretary of the Milan A.D.S.

Another emergency meeting of the committee had to be called for that evening. We met at Mrs. Doubleday's. In addition to myself, five members sat round the table: Mr. Mortimer Robinson, Pat Collingwood, Frederick Cheesewright, Myrna and Paul. Myrna was looking white and ill and not so band-boxy as usual, which made me wonder whether Tiddler had cut the knot.

Mr. Mortimer Robinson took the chair. The first item on the agenda was the resignation of Basil Northcott. The question was, who should replace him? There are sixteen male characters in "Measure for Measure." Six of these can be doubled, but even then one must find thirteen actors—and men are not so keen as women on making idiots of themselves on the stage. Our tally of acting male members was sixteen, which left us with three for the performance of such duties as lords, officers and the greater part of the population of Vienna. However miscast Basil Northcott might have been, not a single one of the sixteen (myself included) was half as suitable.

"Lucio," said Pat Collingwood, "should be slim and elegant able to strike a graceful attitude. There's nobody like that in our mob. Is there anyone we can co-opt in a hurry?"

The only suggestion came from Mr. Mortimer Robinson. "What about your friend Ridpath, Vaughan?"

My reply was doubtful. "I could ask him, of course."

"Oh, *dont!*"

We all looked at Myrna. There had been a desperate note in her voice. She glanced round at us and went on in haste:

"I mean, he wouldn't do. He's had no experience."

"No harm in asking him, though," said bald little Cheese-wright briskly. "No harm in asking him."

Myrna had no further comment to make, so the motion was carried, I being deputed to approach Tiddler. In my own mind, however, I debated the advisability of such a course: something had certainly happened between him and Myrna.

The second matter to discuss was Mr. Garnett's *coup de main.* I recounted the disastrous sequel to the committee's last decision. They heard me out in silence.

"But it's nothing less than blackmail!" burst out Cheese-wright when I had finished. "Nothing less than blackmail!"

"Morally, perhaps," I allowed, "but not legally. Garnett is acting quite within his rights. We shouldn't have a leg to stand on. We can't plead, you know, that our use of the Bakehouse is a contribution to the national war effort!"

There followed a baffled silence that was broken by the unhurried voice of Paul, who had been puffing stolidly at his pipe since the meeting began.

"It sounds so darned childish. Like Sir Jasper, the wicked landowner, foreclosing on the mortgage. Besides, I know old Boyson. He's one of the last-gentleman-in-Europe class. I can imagine his reactions if some scrubby little charge-hand came smirking with a yarn like that. Why can't you spike their guns, Vaughan, by getting your word in first with the old boy?"

"A wasted effort, Paul. Garnett was pushed into the business by his delightful daughter Elsie, who evidently possesses a sixpenny-novelette mentality, coupled with a spiteful temper. Do you remember the appalling creature with the blue slacks, high-heeled shoes and an over-developed inferiority complex, who was in here on the Sunday morning war was declared? Well, that type. Old man Garnett is frightened to death of Elsie. But her ridiculous ambitions are no longer the major issue. I realise now that if, last Sunday, I had instantly fallen in with Garnett's preposterous proposal, the son-in-law would, as Paul puts it, have gone smirking to Mr. Boyson and would have got the kick in the pants that he so richly deserves. But James Henry Garnett has all the characteristics of an army mule—and I crossed him. Poor Hilary is now only a symbol. Old Garnett's the sort of man to revel in litigation, and I warn you that if we tell Mr. Boyson—or even Hilary—or defy Garnett to carry his threats into effect, he'll let his son-in-law's job go by the board and hound us out of the Bakehouse with as much vigour as he ever sold pots and pans."

Pat Collingwood asked a question: "Could he get a court order before the beginning of January?"

"I don't know. But even if we manage to do 'Measure for Measure,' do we want to lose our theatre? We've done a lot of work to it."

"For all that," protested Pat, "we can't possibly ask Elizabeth to stand down. What we've done to the Bakehouse is nothing to what that girl's been putting into rehearsals. It'd be damnably unfair."

"We can't consider *her* feelings too much," Myrna said with unnatural acidity. "After all, it *is* Hilary's turn. . . ." Through his teeth our burly producer was whistling "Good King Wenceslas," but she took no heed of the danger signal. "... She stood down for Elizabeth in 'The Likes of Her'—and she's just as good an actress as Miss Elizabeth Faggott."

"There I differ," said Pat. "Elizabeth as Isabella is superb. In my considerable experience, I've never seen Isabella better or more understandingly played."

Paul said: "And it would place Hilary in a rotten position."

"That's the trouble with these amateur shows," persisted Myrna. "You always get one or two who are all take and no give. They think they've a divine right to stay at the top of the cast."

"Myrna!" I reproached her. "You're being a little unfair, aren't you?"

She turned on me like a small, neat tigress.

"Of course *you'd* stand up for her!" she flared. "And you're a damned fool!"

She pushed back her chair from the table. We waited without speaking until the door had slammed behind her.

"So much for that," remarked Pat evenly. "Would anyone else like an attack of temperament?"

Mr. Mortimer Robinson aligned his tie with the wings of his collar. The mild-mannered little man did not care for scenes.

"We must discuss this calmly," he said.

The decision, though long delayed, was inevitable. Hilary must play Isabella. Although I tried to avoid it, I was given the task of telling Elizabeth. I stipulated, however, that, though Hilary must necessarily be kept in ignorance, Elizabeth should be put in possession of all the facts; and that if she refused to relinquish her part to Hilary we should not pursue the matter, but should leave our sweet-natured landlord to do his worst. With this the committee concurred.

The evening was fairly well advanced, but Mr. Garnett wanted our decision first thing in the morning. I put a new battery in my torch and went round to see Elizabeth, far heavier hearted than on my last visit. My face must have told her that I came on a distasteful errand.

"What's the trouble, Vaughan?" she asked with concern, as soon as I arrived.

"I've a rather beastly job to do, Elizabeth.... I... That is, the committee want you to let Hilary do Isabella. . . . They've asked me to tell you that they ..."

My voice trailed off into miserable silence.

"Go on, Vaughan," she said in a low tone.

"It's that old devil Garnett!" I burst out. "He's got us by the short hairs! You know he wanted us to give the part to Hilary? Well, now he's put the screw on. He's suddenly produced himself as the landlord of the Bakehouse and given us notice to quit. He won't withdraw it unless we do as he wants. Will you—help us, Elizabeth? As soon as 'Measure for Measure' is finished we'll start on another Shakespeare play—'Macbeth,' if you like."

There were tears in her eyes.

"Vaughan," she said with a catch in her voice, "why do you so often make me want to cry?"

I stumbled on. "We discussed it for two hours this evening and found no other way out. He might not be able to get a court order in time to throw us in the street before 'Measure for Measure,' but sooner or later we'd lose the Bakehouse."

"Dear little Bakehouse. . . . And you and Paul and Pat Collingwood and Pompey Hobson have worked so hard. . ."

"Will you do it?" I said eagerly. "May I tell Hilary that you've decided not to carry on? Hell and damnation! The whole thing stinks!"

"I wouldn't like it to be different. . . Oh, Vaughan," her lovely voice broke—"please go now."

On my way back to Mrs. Doubleday's I called in at the Bakehouse and typed a note for Mr. Garnett.

"Dear Mr. Garnett," I began—and ripped the sheet out of the machine.

"Dear Sir" (I started again),

"I am able to tell you that my committee now agree to your proposal. You will no doubt arrange for the notice to quit that has been served on this society to be withdrawn forthwith by Messrs. Dickson, Parrish, Willmott & Lister.

"I feel I should mention that, although every effort will be made to comply with your wishes, circumstances such as illness or a definite refusal from a certain quarter may force us to amend our arrangements.

"Yours faithfully,

"(signed) W. V. Tudor,

"Hon. Secretary."

Fifteen minutes later I slipped it under his door, fetched *The House at Pooh Corner* from my own room and took it down to a comfortable chair in the lounge. But even the weighty question of Tigger's breakfast did not hold my attention long. My despondent thoughts were interrupted by the arrival of Jack Gough, looking the picture of misery.

"What's up with Myrna?" he asked.

I threw *The House at Pooh Corner* on the seat of the chair opposite and stood up.

"I don't know," I informed him recklessly, "and at the risk of a punch on the nose, I don't damn well care!"

I took his arm.

"Come on, Jack. We've both done enough wafting of sighs from Indus to the pole. Let's go along to the Blue Anchor and wrap ourselves round as much beer as possible between now and closing-time."

"I'm off beer," he confessed glumly.

He had six; and sang "Take, O, Take Those Lips Away" to a tune of his own all the way back along Friday Street.

When I opened the door of my room there were two letters on the floor. The first that I opened was short and much to the point: "Your word's good enough for me. J. H. G." It was scribbled on the back of a sheet covered with cabbalistic figures and notes. Mr. Garnett seemed not to believe in wasting paper.

The other was from Myrna:

"Vaughan, dear, I'm very, very sorry. Do please forgive me. I wouldn't hurt you for worlds."

I slipped them both away in a drawer; and it was in a happier frame of mind that I got into bed.

X

The baby beats the nurse, and quite athwart
Goes all decorum.
Act I, Sc. 3.

Tiddler, like Barkis, was willing. Supported by the presence of Mr. Mortimer Robinson, who nevertheless kept himself behind his *Telegraph,* I broached the matter at breakfast the next morning. To all appearances, Tiddler was his usual sprightly self; and, by jesting reference to the lateness down of Myrna, who, he suggested, would be keeping the kindergarten kicking their tiny heels, seemed not knowingly concerned with her state of mind on the previous evening.

"Lucio is a long part," I cautioned him, "and there's not much time. To-day's the 6th December. The show is to be on the 4th, 5th and 6th January, with the dress rehearsal on Wednesday, the 3rd. The costumes will be down from Wight's on the Monday or Tuesday, but there'll be a full rehearsal, with no costumes, but everybody word and action perfect, on the previous Saturday, which will be the 30th of this month. So you've got just over three weeks."

"You can depend on me," he affirmed.

"Now," I went on, "here are copies of the play and Lamb's 'Tales from Shakespeare.' Read the story first and then run through the play. You'd better take the day off and soak yourself in Lucio instead of real estate."

Before going to the office I rang up Hilary and asked her to take over Elizabeth's part. After a silence so prolonged that I began to think we had been cut off, she expressed herself very pleased, adding:

"But what about Elizabeth?"

"She's changed her mind."

"Oh… All right, Vaughan."

"Splendid! Rehearsal on Friday at seven sharp. Cheerio!"

Not quite easy in my mind, I replaced the receiver. Her tone had suggested that she suspected what we moderns call, with a picturesqueness rivalling Shakespeare's own, a phoney set-up.

Later in the morning Tiddler strolled into my office.

"Bit ripe, isn't it?" he grinned, throwing his hat on a chair. "No wonder you hold rehearsals behind closed doors! Who's playing Isabella—Betty Faggott?"

"We call her Elizabeth," I reproved him. "No, Hilary Boyson. Elizabeth is taking Mariana, the girl Angelo leaves in the waggon."

Or was she? I had omitted to ask. Would she want, I thought with a pang, to be in the play at all? . . . Dear Bakehouse. . . . Yes, she would do Mariana. Elizabeth was a trouper.

"Myrna told me some time ago," Tiddler was saying, "that she was Juliet, but it's not much of a part for a bright kid like that, is it? She's only put in to make things look tidy in the last scene."

"As a matter of fact," I told him, "there's no part really suitable for Myrna. Ariel in 'A Midsummer Night's Dream' is about her weight."

"Everybody," Tiddler complained, "gets paired off respectably but me. Can't I be fixed up with a happier ending? This Kate Keepdown's not at all my type. Couldn't there be some prettier way out for me?"

" 'Whipt first, sir, and hanged after,' " I sombrely decreed.

Tiddler struck an elegant attitude and minced with the disarming impudence of the true Lucio:

" 'Faith, my lord, I spoke it but according to the trick. If you will hang me for it, you may; but I had rather it would please you I might be whipt.' "

"You'll do," I approved.

Mr. Garnett accosted me in the hall after lunch.

"I've told the lawyers to cancel the notice to quit."

I nodded; thanks were out of place.

"And I've said to my girl that if her Tom tries to make capital out of what's happened, they'll neither of 'em get a farthing from me when the times comes. If he's fit to be works manager, he'll get the job." His dour features relaxed a little. "It was a good tussle, young fellow."

Hope began to rise in me.

"Then this new arrangement—" I blurted.

He banged a fist on the other palm.

"That stands."

Turning without a word, I made for the stairs. He called me back, clumsily pushed an envelope into my hand and lumbered into the lounge. Inside the envelope was a cheque. It was payable to the Lulverton Amateur Dramatic Society and was for twenty pounds.

Elizabeth and Hilary changed roles so naturally and with so little fuss that it passed almost without comment from the other members of the company. Hilary had been Elizabeth's understudy and was already well acquainted with the lines. Within a short time she was word perfect. Tiddler learnt his part with amazing rapidity, and frequently I came upon him in the office declaiming to a rapt and appreciative audience in the persons of Miss Jones and Hindenburg. Whether their moral fibre was weakened by the burden of his song, I may never know, for Hindenburg had to be replaced soon afterwards and was never heard by me to greet Tiddler's performances with more than an awed "Good-oh"; and it was my practice to discuss only business with Miss Jones.

My impression at the second emergency meeting of the committee was later confirmed. There was a definite break between Myrna and Tiddler. They were civil enough to pass the cruet to each other at mealtimes, but the association went little further. I got the idea that it had been left to Tiddler to put an end to the affair, for he behaved as if a weight had been taken off his mind, while, for a fortnight, Myrna moped most drearily.

The first war-time Christmas came and Mrs. Doubleday rose, in her culinary majesty, so magnificently to the occasion that, when Myrna returned on the Wednesday, after spending the holiday with her parents in Whitchester, we others, bloated with food, declared her so under-nourished that she must immediately place herself in the hands of Mrs. Doubleday. This was pleasant exaggeration, for Myrna looked better and brighter than she had done since the night she had lost her temper with me.

Tiddler went off early in the morning of Boxing Day and arrived at the office an hour late on the Wednesday. His manner was abstracted for the rest of the day. When I ventured to ask him the reason, he admitted having whooped it up rather lavishly the night before.

In the evening of the Wednesday—that is, the 27th December —there was nearly a serious accident at the Bakehouse. With a company of some thirty-five strong there was frequent congestion in so limited a space, particularly in the passage leading from the foyer to the auditorium. That evening, when Pat Collingwood had called a few minutes' break and there was a general adjournment for coffee, Elizabeth caught her foot in the rather ragged strip of carpet in the passage, fell forward against Hilary and sent her pitching down the staircase. Hilary's scream was followed by the sound of splintering wood, as she crashed through a rotten stair-tread. Paul and I hurried to help her and managed to get her extricated. With considerable relief we found that, except for a grazed shin and a bad shaking, she was uninjured. Miss Lark, who was always splendid in an emergency, took charge, administered first-aid and went home with Hilary in a car driven by Paul. There was a good deal of speculation when they had gone on whether the accident would prevent Hilary from taking part in the play; but the next day she was reported none the worse for her misadventure, save for the grazed shin and one or two minor bruises.

Saturday, the 30th December, was the day for the full rehearsal without costumes.

There are some mornings when one's first feeling, on waking, is of foreboding. The shadow of coming events seems to be over the not quite conscious mind. The sensation is largely illusory and a cup of tea will normally dispel it. Such was the beginning of the 30th December with me, except that even two cups of tea were unavailing. I felt that something unpleasant was going to happen at any moment.

But I had to wait until the evening before it did.

A business appointment kept me overlong in Paulsfield, and I arrived at the Bakehouse fifteen minutes late for the rehearsal, which had been fixed for half-past seven. I hurried along Harpur Street and shot round into Cooper's Yard with such velocity that a warning grunt did not stop me from cannoning into someone standing there.

Breathlessly I apologised and a voice enquiringly mentioned my name. I admitted identity and the voice said: "This is Garnett."

"Oh, hullo, Mr. Garnett," I greeted him agreeably.

We had decided that he was not really such a bad old stick. Elizabeth had not seemed so put out as I, for one, had expected her to be; and the twenty pounds had come in useful, though it *had* smelt rather of hush-money. We had spent most of it on a fresh coat of paint and new appointments for the Bakehouse, which looked all the better for it. As is the way with house decorating, the work had been delayed, and even then was not quite finished.

"What are you doing in this part of the world?" I asked.

"Having a look round. A man can inspect his own property."

The words were blunt, but the tone was friendly.

"You won't see much in Cooper's Yard to-night!" I laughed, adding, on an impulse: "Will you come inside the theatre and see how we spent your money ?"

The answering grunt implied agreement.

Everyone was waiting for me and derisive shouts went up as I entered the foyer. They ceased abruptly when the ungainly figure of Mr. Garnett followed me in. I took a chance.

"Ladies and gentlemen," I shouted, "for a long time we've had the free use of the Bakehouse and recently, with the help of a handsome contribution to our funds, we've been able to rig the dear old thing out in a new dress. Our thanks for both are due to this gentleman—Mr. Garnett!"

It went down well. Even the object of my encomiums, astraddle our new carpet, with his bowler hat solidly set on his head and both thickly gloved hands on the handle of his unrolled umbrella, allowed his craggy features to relax into what, by a stretch of the imagination, might be described as a smile. The ceremony was brought to an end by a voice raised to a yell of lugubrious complaint from the auditorium.

"Mr. Collingwood, sir, if you're not all thinking about going home just yet, sir, I got the lights all fixed for Act-One-Scene-One-the-Juke's-Palace."

Pompey Hobson was fretting at the controls. It was not really necessary to have stage lighting for this rehearsal, but Pompey wanted, as he put it, "to get the feel of the switches."

We trooped along the passage into the auditorium. I found a seat for Mr. Garnett and then, as I should be wanted for the second scene, went to take instructions from Pat Collingwood. The members of the cast not immediately needed on the stage were sitting about in the auditorium. Among them was Elizabeth, who, as Mariana, did not appear until the beginning of the fourth act. I noticed that with her was the terrible child, Jill Geering, and shuddered.

The first short scene, in which the Duke deputes his authority to Angelo, with old Escalus as secondary, and then leaves, ostensibly, for Poland, went through with only one interruption from Pat, who was sitting, script and pencil in hand, in the middle of the front row. Geoffrey Cutner as the Duke was stately, in spite of his grey flannel trousers. Franklin Duzest as Angelo held a proper balance between dignity and obedience to his master's will. Mr. Mortimer Robinson as Escalus, though in manner sufficiently venerable and full of years, looked, in his scrupulous workaday attire, no more like an ancient lord than could be expected of the chief clerk of the valuation and rating department. Patriarchal robes and a wig would make all the difference.

The street in the next scene was, like beauty, in the eye of the beholder, being little different in outward appearance from the Duke's palace. Our backcloths were curtains, which served, with slight adjustments, for palace, street, prison, moated grange and fields outside the city. For the rest, it was left to Pompey Hobson to weave his spells with floats, battens, deep ambers and pinks. But in Act-One-Scene-Two-a-Street, Hobson temporarily lost his grip. Tiddler as Lucio was ready to enter with Ralph Freshwater as First Gentleman and Stewart McIver as Second Gentleman. The front curtains were not being used for this rehearsal and it was merely a question of waiting for the lights to be changed from the subdued richness of the palace apartment to the sharper definition of the open street.

After a minute of complete darkness the stage was flooded with a rich red glow, as if the whole of Vienna was in flames. This went out and another Stygian period was followed by illumination of an eerie blue, which prevailed until, after the sound of somebody breaking up a packing-case for firewood, the face of Hobson entered between the curtains. It was the first time I had ever seen a livid, disembodied ghost wearing a cloth cap.

"Sorry, Mr. Collingwood," he said, "but there's an 'itch."

So I imagined," replied Pat dryly.

The piercing voice of Jill Geering was then to be heard demanding: "Elizabeth, is that the man they call the flesh-monger?"

Hobson's 'itch was soon put right and there was no more trouble with the lighting.

Lucio entered with the two Gentlemen. They got through the opening lines about the King of Hungary's peace, which was a topical enough allusion in November, 1606, but obscure to a modern audience. Then, the Second Gentleman having said, "Amen," Lucio replied:

" 'Thou concludest like the Sanctimonious Pirate, that

went to sea with the Ten Commandments, but scraped one out of the table.'"

The Second Gentleman was going to speak again, but Pat stopped him.

"Just a moment, Mac," he said. "Peter"—I was the only one to call him Tiddler—"that was too serious. Try it again and make it lighter. And you forgot the business with the dagger. Although you're not wearing it now, pretend to draw it out of the scabbard. Vaughan, did you ask Wight's to send a dagger?"

"Yes, Pat," I answered. "I wrote specially for it. It's coming with the other stuff on Monday or Tuesday."

"Good. Right, Peter, carry on."

Tiddler repeated the lines. Pat made no comment and the scene proceeded rather insipidly until the entry of Miss Lark as Mistress Overdone and Paul Manhow as Pompey, who played their scurrilous parts with such relish that I forgot the others.

The play went on. I as the Provost carried Claudio off to jail. Lucio visited Isabella and more than once forgot his lines. Pompey and Froth, the foolish gentleman, were brought by Elbow, the constable (Jack Gough) before Escalus and allowed to go free—and Paul carried the long comedy scene through triumphantly. I had never seen him in better form. Isabella (Hilary Boyson) visited Angelo and pleaded charmingly for her brother's life. The Duke, in the character of a friar, but still wearing his flannel trousers, had a short scene with Myrna in the part of the hapless Juliet, who was then, though Myrna was a long way from giving that impression, "very near her hour."

Angelo and Isabella had their second meeting. He offered her the immemorial alternative. She very prettily refused. At the beginning of Act III she had her scene with Claudio and even during the recriminatory speech, made the gentle breeding of Isabella apparent.

In Act III, Sc. 2, Elbow had his revenge on Pompey and dragged him away to prison. The second part of this scene is Lucio's big moment. The actor at the Prince Consort had made it so. He had flitted through it like a naughty butterfly through a field of forbidden flowers. Basil Northcott had blundered through it like the bull of unthinking vulgarity through the china shop of public susceptibilities. It is the scene in which Lucio gives the counterfeit friar the low-down on the private lives and morals of his grace the Duke and the deputy, Lord Angelo. As the much aggrieved Duke plaintively remarks to himself afterwards in impeccable blank verse, "... backwounding calumny the whitest virtue strikes." In the manner that Tiddler delivered it, it *was* backwounding calumny—and nothing pleasanter.

Lucio attacks Angelo first.

" 'Some report a sea-maid spawned him,' " said Tiddler; " 'some that he was begot between two stock-fishes. But it is certain that—' "

"Just a moment, Peter." It was our producer's habitual interjection. "That's not airy enough—and put more life into the gestures."

Tiddler went through it again and I caught something of the Lucio that had strutted in front of Hindenburg and Miss Jones.

After dealing with Angelo, Lucio turns his attention to the Duke.

" ' ... He would be drunk too, that let me inform you.' "

"Just a moment," Pat again interrupted. "Not 'that let me *inform* you,' but '*that* let me inform you.' Throw your head back. You're passing on a tit-bit that you hope is going to surprise and shock him."

It had to be repeated twice before Pat was satisfied. Nine lines later there was another check. Tiddler had just said:

" 'A very superficial, ignorant, unweighing fellow.' "

"Just a moment, Peter. You don't want those great pauses between the adjectives. It sounds like a conscientious young porter calling out stations. Rattle it off quickly, but casually, as if you're finally disposing of the Duke as a subject of conversation."

"I forgot the order they went in,"Tiddler lamely explained.

"What's the matter with you?" demanded Pat—"You were first rate on Wednesday. This evening you're not much better than"—I think he was going to mention Basil Northcott, for he hesitated before saying—"a clumsy schoolboy."

"I'm sorry, Pat" answered Tiddler. "I think I'm going a bit stale."

"*Stale*? You wait till you've played the same part every night for two years! Now go on, and for Pete's sake put more friskiness into it!"

I was somewhat disturbed about Tiddler. His mind was not on the play. If he had received a blow, I conjectured, it had left him more worried than grieved.

At the end of Act III we broke off for a quarter of an hour. Pat called Hilary, the Duke, Claudio and me over to him, while most of the company drifted out into the foyer, where two of the girls were pouring coffee. Elizabeth and Jill went with them. Mr. Garnett remained in his seat smoking his pipe.

Pat wanted to talk to us about the scene at the beginning of Act IV, in which the four of us appeared. It was nearly ten minutes before we were permitted to follow the others into the foyer. Going along the passage I was immediately behind Hilary. As we got to the doorway I heard someone speaking in the foyer—and had she not been just in front of me I would have sworn that it was Hilary. Instinctively, she stopped and we others halted too.

" 'Heaven shield my mother played my father fair!
For such a warped slip of wilderness
Ne'er issued from his blood. Take my defiance,
Die, perish! Might but my bending down
Reprieve thee from thy fate, it should proceed.' "

It was Hilary's voice. There was the same deep-rooted refinement, the same ladylike quality about it. There was the same hint of the head prefect of the High School and paragon of the lower forms, the same suggestion of a thoroughly nice girl making allowance—for Shakespeare. It was beautifully done, going far deeper than mere mimicry.

" 'I'll pray a thousand prayers for thy death,
No word to save thee.' "

A pause; then:

" 'O, fie, fie, fie!' "

A shout of laughter greeted this last genteel reproof, Hilary stepped forward into the foyer and I followed.

"Don't stop for me, Elizabeth," she said. "I only came out for some coffee."

It was difficult to tell whether she was annoyed.

Elizabeth was in the middle of the crowded little foyer with her back to us. She may, not have heard Hilary's remark, because, almost without a break, she raised her voice so that the words were clipped and the manner perky.

" 'Thus, what with war, what with the sweat, what with the gallows, and what with poverty, I am custom shrunk.' "

Miss Lark, by the buffet, hopped about like a sparrow.

"You little beast, Elizabeth!" she cried above the general hilarity. "I'm quite sure I don't sound like that!"

Like an echo, the words came again:

"You little beast, Elizabeth! I'm quite sure I don't sound like that!"

It was uncanny.

The voice changed. It was deeper, but with the whining twang of the Londoner and the suggestion of adenoids and bronchial catarrh.

"Mr. Collingwood, sir, if you're not all thinking about going home just yet, sir, I got the lights all fixed for Act-One-Scene-One-the-Juke's-Palace."

From behind me in the passage the real Pompey Hobson bawled out:

"Now do me doin' 'The Charge of the Light Brigade,' Miss Faggott!"

The divertissement ended there. General talk was resumed. I got some coffee for Hilary and stood chatting with her until Mrs. Cheesewright arrived with Jill Geering and carried her off. Thus freed, I edged my way through the crowd towards Elizabeth, who was talking to Franklin Duzest. As I reached them he was saying in a low voice:

"But you're different, more sympathetic, more—oh, hullo, Vaughan."

"And how," I asked with a smile, "are the villainous deputy and his forsaken betrothed?"

"We've settled it out of court," laughed Duzest. "I've promised to be a good deputy in future and not to stay out playing darts all the evening." His smile faded. "I was just saying to Elizabeth that I can't understand why she threw in her hand. Hilary's a nice girl"—there it was again!—"but she's not forceful enough for Isabella or—and Elizabeth won't mind if I say it—vulgar enough. If she thought more about the part and less about the purity of her vowel sounds, perhaps she'd come to life."

He jerked his head over his shoulder. \ (

"That old boy," he added inconsequentially, "looks more like a broker's man than a *deus ex machina*. Does that hat come off or is it part of his head?"

Turning, I saw Mr. Garnett in the entrance from the auditorium. Jill came dragging Mrs. Cheesewright by one hand and Miss Lark by the other.

"Show them it, Elizabeth," she ordered.

Elizabeth looked blank. Jill stamped her foot with childish impatience.

"The present," she said.

"Something tells me," said Melpomene, "that things are working up to some sort of unpleasantness."

"Do you think they're going to scratch each other's eyes out?" asked Thalia hopefully.

"I'm not worrying about those two girls. The trouble lies far deeper and"—her voice dropped with foreboding—"the cauldron is beginning to bubble."

XI

The maid will I frame . . .
Act III Sc. 1.

E lizabeth laughed.

"They won't want to see that, Jill."

"Show them it!"

With a tolerant shrug of her shoulders, Elizabeth opened her handbag and produced a piece of paper, which she unfolded. It was a ten-pound note.

"Daddy gave it me for a birthday present," she explained. "It fascinates Jill."

A ten-pound note is something of a curio in these times. Other people crowded round us and the note was passed from hand to hand with much laughter and all the dear old jokes. Mr. Mortimer Robinson affected to slip it away in his wallet, to Jill's genuine concern. The jolly interlude was ended by Pat Collingwood, who summoned us for Act IV.

It happened that I went to the cloak-room. I was there only a couple of minutes and was on the point of crossing the foyer to join the others in the auditorium, when I heard Hilary's voice. It was quick and tense.

"... only took the part because they wanted me to. Yet you've been horrible about it ever since. Oh, I know you haven't said a word when I was there. That beastly impersonation—you wouldn't have done it in front of me. Everybody was giggling. Why must you make things harder for me?"

Elizabeth's tone was soothing.

"It was only a joke, Hilary. And you're imagining things. I know I wanted to do Isabella, but when the committee—"

"So it wasn't you? Vaughan told me you'd asked for me to take it over. Well, now I understand and I know what to do."

This was outrageous eavesdropping. I reached behind me, slammed the door of the cloak-room and then went into the foyer, humming gently to myself.

"Why, hullo, you two!" I exclaimed. "What about Act IV, Sc. 1? Shouldn't you be on, Elizabeth?"

Pat Collingwood was of the same mind, for just at that moment he shouted for her from the auditorium.

"Just coming, Pat!" she called back and ran along the passage.

"Vaughan . . ." began Hilary.

I stopped her. "He'll be yelling for you in a moment," I told her. "Come along!"

Leaving her to follow, I beat a hasty retreat, to avoid an uncomfortable discussion.

It will be recalled that I had told Mr. Garnett of our difficulty in finding a "boy" to sing the song, "Take, O, Take Those Lips Away," with which the scene opens. But musical talent was limited in the company and so Elizabeth had to sing the song herself. This was easily arranged by cutting out the line, "Break off thy song and haste thee quick away," that gets the attendant off the stage before the entry of the Duke. When I got into the auditorium Elizabeth was sitting alone on the stage, singing. She had no accompaniment, yet her soft contralto held me fascinated.

Act IV, Sc. 1, is between Mariana, the Duke and Isabella. At the end of the song the Duke, still disguised, joins Mariana and has a short conversation with her. Then Isabella enters and Mariana goes off. Isabella tells the Duke that she has fixed the appointment with Angelo. Mariana comes back and the Duke introduces her to Isabella. The two girls exit, so that Isabella can explain the idea to Mariana. When they return, Isabella says to the Duke, "She'll take the enterprise upon her, father, if you advise it." The Duke replies, "It is not my consent, but my entreaty too."

To save this scene from degenerating into a popping-in-and-out competition, Pat had arranged that when Elizabeth as Mariana said, "Will't please you to walk aside," they did not leave the stage, but retired to the back of it, while Geoffrey Cutner came forward and delivered a soliloquy. It was not intended that Isabella should take more than a few moments to persuade Mariana or that either of them should do more than make a show of talking, but their conversation, though low-pitched, was real and spirited, and they were so long over it that the Duke finished the covering speech and stood waiting for them to rejoin him.

"Come along, you two!" Pat called out. "This is a play, not a social."

Hilary turned and answered him.

"I want her to do Isabella."

"This isn't the time for that," said Pat sharply. "Please get on with the scene."

Hilary was flushed and her lip was quivering.

"Only if I have the Mariana part back."

Elizabeth said abruptly: "Very well, then."

She went towards the Duke.

" 'She'll take the enterprise upon her, father, if you advise it.' "

Solemn Geoffrey Cutner then made the only joke I ever

heard him utter.

"It is not *my* consent, "but Pat Collingwood's that matters. The answering laughter was a little forced. Though I was not near enough to hear, I felt sure that our producer was busy with his carol.

"Let's stop this nonsense," he said. "Elizabeth, you'll carry on as Mariana."

Hilary cried out: "She won't! I'm sick of all this sneering and ridicule! If she wants the Isabella part, let her have it!"

"You shouldn't be put out by a bit of leg-pulling," Pat told her. "Elizabeth only meant it in fun."

"Fun?" flashed Hilary. "If only you knew her idea of fun!" Swiftly she stepped across the stage. "I'm going home," she said, and disappeared through the curtains.

I watched Paul Manhow rise from his seat, murmur to Pat and leave the auditorium.

"Don't go yet, any of you," Pat requested. "Elizabeth and Geoff, you'd better come and sit down for a few minutes."

Although Cutner came straight round to the front, it was several minutes before Elizabeth followed. She looked about, saw me sitting by myself, and came and dropped into the next seat.

"Very unpleasant," I murmured.

"Never mind that," she said urgently. "Vaughan, that ten-pound note has been stolen from my bag."

"Surely not!"

"When Pat called out to me, I rushed off in such a hurry that I left my bag on the centre table in the foyer. When I went back just now it was still there, but the note was missing."

"Have another look," I suggested.

She opened the bag on her lap and carefully went through the contents. The note was certainly not there.

I announced the loss to the others and ordered a general search of the Bakehouse. This proved fruitless. With all the company reassembled in the auditorium, I said:

"Is this somebody's funny joke, because it's gone far enough."

Everyone protested innocence. I asked Elizabeth to go through her purse again, then made her get her overcoat from the girls' dressing-room.

"What do we do now?" I asked rather desperately.

"Turn out our pockets," was Frederick Cheesewright's prompt rejoinder. "Turn out our pockets."

Several people began to speak, but Jill Geering's high treble was the most audible.

"Miss Boyson can't turn out hers, 'cause, she's gone home."

A child will make such a statement with no other implication than the fact itself. For all that, the others suddenly stopped talking. The difficult silence that ensued was broken by Pat Collingwood.

"Paul went with her," he told us. "Why not wait till he comes back?"

It was not a very intelligent suggestion, but, by deferring an awkward necessity, was more acceptable than Cheesewright's. Cigarettes were lighted and the company broke into groups, in the fond hope that a few words from Paul were going to clear the whole thing up. He, however, was longer gone than we had anticipated. The girls made some more coffee and we were standing drinking it in the foyer when the door below was slammed to and we heard footsteps on the uncarpeted stairs. Jill ran out on to the landing, but returned alone with a momentous expression on her face.

"It's a policeman," she announced importantly.

"Lights!" said everyone with dismay, and went round examining the curtains.

"Ask him to come in, Jill," I instructed her.

I expected him to be in uniform, but he was in plain clothes: a big grey-overcoated man of about fifty, in a black Homberg hat, which he took off when Jill led him into the foyer.

"Good evening," he said in a deep, pleasant voice. "I'm a police inspector. I understand you've had some trouble here."

Jack Gough at my elbow muttered tensely in my ear:

"It's Charlton!"

I smiled to myself; we could soon dispose of *him*.

"Good Lord, no!" I said easily. "There's absolutely no need to bother you people. I'm sorry you were troubled to come round. Can we offer you a cup of coffee before you go?"

He ignored my invitation.

"What exactly is the trouble?"

We were all standing round like a lot of criminals, as if we had been caught running a gambling-den or selling cigarettes after time.

"Absolutely nothing to worry you with," I assured him. "Somebody's unfortunately mislaid some money. As a matter of fact, just as you arrived we realised what had happened to it. Give the inspector some coffee, Peggy."

The police had to be kept out of this, if I paid the money out of my own pocket.

"No coffee for me, thank you, Mr. Tudor." I jumped when he addressed me by name. "What *had* happened to it?"

"Pardon? Oh, you mean what had happened to this money? Well, the facts are these, Inspector: one of our ladies was given a ten-pound note by—"

"Is she here now?"

"Yes." I waved towards Elizabeth. "Her father gave this note as a birthday present, and she brought it along here this evening to show to us. A ten-pound note is something of a rarity these days! We're rehearsing, you know, for our new show, 'Measure for Measure' and—"

I paused at the look of courteous enquiry on his rather fine face.

"You were going to tell me," he reminded me, "what happened to the note."

Down in the courtyard the door slammed again. Paul, I thought.

"Excuse me a moment," I said, and was out on the landing and half-way down the stairs before the detective could stop me.

"Is that you, Paul?" I whispered in the gloom, and he

grunted agreement. "Have you seen anything of Elizabeth's note?"

"I've got it here."

"Well, for God's sake get rid of it! We've got the police in." I did some quick thinking. "Screw it up and drop it on the floor in the cloak-room before you come in the foyer."

"Right," he muttered.

I went back to the others.

"Only one of the company," I explained to the inspector with a bright smile. "He's just been seeing one of our ladies home. Now, I was explaining about this banknote. A moment or two before you got here we were on the point of organising a thorough search of the theatre, which you'll see is old and full of odd corners." Paul came in. "Your arrival interrupted us. So come along, everybody!"

Some of them must have decided that the business was decidedly fishy, but all joined eagerly in the hunt through foyer, dressing-rooms, stage, auditorium, prop-room, kitchen, box-office and cloak-room. It was Franklin Duzest who discovered the tightly folded note in a corner of the cloakroom.

"Well, that's that!" I said, displaying great relief. "Once again let me apologise, Inspector, for dragging you out at this time of the night."

The answering smile, like the heathen Chinee's, was childlike and bland—and just as open to doubt.

"Not at all, Mr. Tudor. I happened to be working late at the station, and when the telephone-call came through—"

"Telephone-call?" I interrupted in astonishment. "But nobody 'phoned from here."

"The message was that something very serious had taken place, and would we send round at once."

I scanned the ring of faces.

"Who was it rang up the police station?" I demanded.

"I did," replied Jill Geering. "Elizabeth told me to."

"*Jill!*" protested Elizabeth, aghast. "I said nothing of the sort!"

"Well, I thought you did," said the dreadful child serenely. "Anyway, the police are always called in if anything is stolen. Mr. Grainger rang up when his house was burgled."

"Nothing was stolen, Jill," I said sternly, "and you shouldn't have done it." I turned towards the detective with an apologetic smile. "That explains it, Inspector. Now, I don't think we can let you go without a couple of tickets for next week's show. When shall it be—Thursday, Friday or Saturday?"

"Friday would do very well," he smiled, and Myrna, the ticket secretary, wrote out special tickets for two seats already allocated to somebody else.

We prevailed upon him to have some coffee and a cigarette; and found, to our surprise, that he knew as much about "Measure for Measure," as we did.

"It's full of contradictions," he said, "as if Shakespeare dashed it off in a hurry after a bout with Ben Jonson. And the timing is all wrong. I wonder you didn't choose 'Twelfth Night,' which is one of the finest comedies ever written."

His coffee finished. I escorted him down the stairs. He halted in the courtyard.

"Thank you, Mr. Tudor," he said, "for an entertaining half-hour. I hadn't imagined that amateur dramatics could be so—illuminating."

He disappeared into the dark, leaving me to wonder what he had meant.

With Hilary absent, the rest of the rehearsal had to be abandoned. While everyone else was getting ready to leave, Paul asked me to stop behind, as he had something important to say to me. When the others had gone, we sat in the box-office, which was the only corner of the Bakehouse free from draughts.

"Now," I demanded of Paul, "what was the little game?"

"Very simple," he answered grimly. "That banknote was planted on Hilary. She found it in her overcoat pocket when we got to her home."

"But who the devil would do that?"

"Ask yourself that, Vaughan. But the precious little plot went wrong. Somebody hadn't bargained for Hilary leaving here so early. At the right moment—that is, when Hilary had put on her overcoat at the end of the rehearsal—the loss of the note was to be made public. The Bakehouse would be ransacked and afterwards we would all be searched—and there, in Hilary's pocket of all places, would be the stolen money! Nobody could prove she'd pinched it, nobody would even try; but imagine the beautiful scandal, the delightful things that could be said behind her back! Think of the splendid time Frau Cheesewright would have, the old *Klatschbasel.*" He embarked on an imitation that made up in malice what it lacked in accuracy. 'My *dear,* I was there when it happened and although there wasn't an atom of proof, one can't avoid the tiny suspicion that everything wasn't quite as it should be. There were well over thirty people here this evening, Vaughan. Would they all keep from lying gossip? Would they, hell! Innocent or guilty, Hilary would have got drummed out of the society. Which would have met with great approval in certain quarters."

I looked at him steadily. "I don't understand what you mean," I said.

"Vaughan, since we first got mixed up in this Bakehouse business together, we've got to know each other. Some things we don't agree about and never will; but, for all that, we're pretty good friends, aren't we?" I nodded. "Well, what I'm going to say is likely to strain our relations. I'm ready to risk that, not only because it's high time somebody told you, but also because—putting it bluntly—Hilary means more to me than you do. Shall I go on?"

"I suppose you'd better, now you've started."

"I made a few enquiries after that detective fellow had gone this evening, and collected these facts. Stop me if they're not correct. At the end of the coffee interval between Acts III and IV, the company trooped back into the auditorium, leaving

Hilary and Elizabeth Faggott together in the foyer. It was not a coincidence. One of them deliberately detained the other."

"That was Hilary," I said, and Paul raised his eyebrows. "She held Elizabeth back in order to air a grievance. I was coming out of the cloak-room and heard her complaining bitterly about one thing and another, particularly that impersonation."

"Did you hear her stop Elizabeth from going after the others?"

"No," I was forced to admit.

"Right, then. Suddenly Elizabeth ran off, leaving her handbag on the table."

"She had to go. Pat called her."

"As it was to be presumed he would, if they stopped behind long enough."

"Hilary was doing all the talking. And in any case, I was there as well. I stayed in the foyer with Hilary for a moment or two and then followed Elizabeth. I don't know what happened to Hilary."

"She was alone in the foyer quite long enough to take the note from the handbag on the table and slip it in the pocket of her overcoat in the girls' dressing-room. The moment was well chosen—by somebody. Let's go a bit further. As soon as Isabella comes on the stage in that first scene in Act IV, Mariana exits and is off for thirty-two lines—again quite long enough to transfer the note from the bag to Hilary's overcoat. When did Elizabeth Faggott tell you that the note was missing?"

"Immediately you and Hilary had left here. As soon as Hilary rushed off in a huff, Pat told Elizabeth to come down off the stage—and the first thing she did was, very naturally, to collect her bag from the foyer. She came straight to tell me."

"That's where the plan miscarried, as I said before. The balloon wasn't scheduled to go up until Hilary had put on her overcoat and could be caught with the swag actually on her. The next best thing was to publish the news at the earliest possible moment, so that Hilary shouldn't find the note in her pocket and get a chance to clear herself. As it was, it was only by the merest accident that she noticed it—and I came rushing back here, to find the police had been called in.... We both know who was responsible for that."

"Young Jill Geering."

"And Elizabeth Faggott put her up to it. Oh, I know she disclaimed it, but who wouldn't? Why should a child like Jill do such a thing without being prompted?"

"Because she's an interfering, unpleasant little brat."

"Which is no real answer. Look here, Vaughan, most impersonations are a bit unkind to the victim, but will you deny that Elizabeth Faggott's solo performance this evening was so distorted that it must have been prompted only by personal spite?"

"Miss Lark and Hobson took theirs in good part."

"I'm not talking about them. Aping Hilary was a deliberate attempt to make her a laughing-stock, just as the banknote trick was intended to stir up little suspicions and poison the minds of the company and all the friends they prattled to afterwards. You'd better understand now, Vaughan, that I'm not putting up with any more nonsense from that young woman. Do you know anything about her real character? Do you know that nothing must stand in the way of her ambitions and that she'd go to any lengths to hurt Hilary? Didn't she deliberately push Hilary down the stairs? You're nuts on her. Perhaps you love her. Perhaps you want to marry her. She's probably been telling you the old, old story, but when she's got all she can out of you, she'll throw you away like a sucked orange. She might even marry you if you've got enough money. Do you know that you're not the only string to her bow?"

"*Stop that!*"

"Do you know she's carrying on with another man and that she goes away with him for week-ends? Just a minute! Let me tell you who he is and then you can ask *him*. It's your pretty young friend, Ridpath!"

"That's a lie!"

We were both standing now.

"Ask him! Ask him where they both spent Boxing Night! Ask him to tell you about a Mr. and Mrs. Matthew Shaw, who stayed at a hotel in Guildford last September! Why do you think Myrna called you a damned fool at the last committee meeting? Because she'd just found out about their goings-on. The poor little devil is madly in love with Ridpath. He dangled her on a string, at the same time running after the Faggott. Now *he's* got the bullet, if his asinine behaviour this evening is anything to go by. Very likely she's decided that you're a more remunerative proposition. She's nothing more than a common—"

With all my strength, I drove my fist into his flabby white face.

(At that point, save for one more page, Vaughan Tudor's manuscript ends. The body found by Mrs. Mudge was his.)

Part Two

SCARECROW OF THE LAW

We must not make a scarecrow of the law,
Setting it up to fear the birds of prey,
And let it keep one shape, till custom make
Their perch, and not their terror.
Act II, Sc. 1.

XII

For that's the utmost of his pilgrimage.
Act II, Sc. 1.

In Inspector Charlton's room in the Lulverton Divisional Headquarters of the County Police, only two sounds broke the early morning silence: the gentle purr of the gas-fire, and the occasional mutterings of Detective-Sergeant Martin, who, with his feet on his chief's desk, lay back in a chair, casting and re-casting the figures in his expenses book and arriving at a different total every time. He was half-way up the shillings column in his fifth attempt when the telephone bell rang.

"One moment, please," he murmured politely, and just as civilly, the bell stopped. "Eight, nine, twelve, thirteen, fifteen...."The bell rang again rather pointedly, but Martin was getting near the top. "Sixteen and two's eighteen, nineteen. ..." A sustained peal demanded instant attention. "Nineteen—or was it eighteen? Oh, Pete take the thing!"

He took his feet off the desk and reached across for the instrument.

"Inspector Charlton's room. Yes, Harrison. . . . Suffering cats!... All right, I'll come downstairs and see 'er."

The station-sergeant had found Mrs. Mudge a chair and given her a glass of water. She was white and shaken, but garrulous.

"'Ullo, Mrs. Mudge," Martin greeted her. "What's this Sergeant Harrison's been telling me?"

"Oh, Mr. Martin, it's Mr. Tudor. I've just found 'im murdered to death in the Little Theatre. Lying across the desk 'e was, with a knife through 'is back. It did give me a turn, you'd never credit. And as nice a gentleman as ever walked, I always say. I'd done out the foyer and went into the box-office to run the cleaner round it—and there 'e was, with 'is poor arms 'anging down something 'orrible and 'is 'ead laying on the typewriter. The biggest shock I ever 'ad in me born days, I tell you! There was a real gentleman, if ever there was one. Only yesterday, 'e says to me, 'Mrs. Mudge,' 'e says with that pleasant smile of 'is, ' Mrs. Mudge, 'e says, 'it's a better day to-day,' 'e says. No nonsense there wasn't about Mr. Tudor. As nice a gentleman as—"

"No doubt about it," Martin agreed. "I'll go straight there. You'd better stay in the station for the time being, Mrs. Mudge. Jim, be a good chap and get in touch with the Super, will you? 'E'll probably tell you to get the D.I. along, not 'aving a childlike faith in an ordinary dick such as meself."

"Just think of 'im being taken," said Mrs. Mudge, nodding her head up and down. "Such a nice gentleman."

"So you was saying," said Martin.

The preliminary routine was over. On the instructions of Supt. Kingsley, Charlton had been called away from his breakfast at Southmouth-by-the-Sea. A uniformed constable had been posted in Cooper's Yard. The police photographer had taken a dozen flashlight pictures of the box-office and foyer. Dr. Lorimer, the police surgeon, had expressed the opinion to Charlton that Tudor had been dead between ten and twelve hours. The contents of the pockets had been carefully listed and checked by Charlton and Martin. The coroner had been notified and the body removed to the mortuary.

"Now, Martin," said Charlton briskly, "let slip the blood-hounds of the law."

"You wouldn't be thinking of a nice hot cup of coffee first?" said Martin tentatively, with an expression of innocent enquiry on his round red face.

His chief looked at him severely.

"Is this the time for coffee, Sergeant?" he asked. "Where do you suggest we go?"

They were back within fifteen minutes, to find a constable waiting with Mrs. Mudge, who was thoroughly enjoying herself in a befitting sorrowful manner.

At Charlton's dictation, Sergeant Martin took down these notes:

THEATRE

Forms whole of upper storey of two-storey building in Cooper's Yard, turning off Harpur Street. Cooper's Yard (a *cul de sac*) is sole means of access to building, which bounds left-hand side of Yard. Far end bounded by high wall and right-hand side by wall of garden attached to property belonging to pawnbroker (Aaron Sugarman), whose side gate opens on to Yard. Old bakehouse building's central archway cuts ground floor into two and leads into walled courtyard at rear of premises. Access from archway by two staircases. Theatre entirely self-contained.

WINDOWS

All windows found fastened inside. No evidence of unlawful entry.

FOOTPRINTS

Cooper's Yard, archway and back courtyard all cobbled. No footprints found.

ENTRANCES

Door right-front of archway marked "Stage Door" over. Sheet of L.A.D.S. note-paper drawing-pinned to outside. Reads: "Danger. This staircase is not to be used until further notice." Dated 27. 12. 39 and signed "W. V. Tudor, Hon. Sec." Similar sheet at top of staircase. Both notices typed in black.

Length of white tape drawing-pinned waist-high at top of staircase, but one end hanging loose with signs of having been torn away from drawing-pin found attached to left-hand jamb. Staircase match-boarded on left-hand side and fastened to archway wall. Third tread from top broken through. Evidence of rot, but builder to examine. Stage-door recently painted inside and out. Paint not wet but tacky. Fitted with panic latch, opened by pushing bar from inside. Cannot be opened from outside. Door found shut. Panic latch and bar also painted. Particles of woollen or other material found adhering to bar, as if bar gripped by two gloved hands. Fingerprints also discernible ("a-b-l-e?" asked Martin) on surface nearest the door. Panic latch removed from door for Peters to examine. Particles of woollen or other material also found adhering to outside of door. Samples scraped off. No fingerprints on door.

Door left-rear of archway marked "Entrance" over. Sheet of L.A.D.S. note-paper drawing-pinned to it. Reads: "No further advance booking can be accepted for any of the Society's performances of 'Measure for Measure.' A few seats may be available immediately before each performance." Dated to-day 4. 1. 40, and signed "W. V. Tudor, Hon. Sec." Typed in red. Door of heavier construction than stage-door. Also newly painted, but not as recently as stage-door. Yale lock and separate rim-latch with oxydized bronze knobs. Door found locked on Yale. Witness, Agnes Mudge, confirms finding it locked on her arrival this morning. Key on bunch belonging to deceased. Witness, Agnes Mudge, also holds key. Letter-box with cage inside and oxydized bronze furniture outside. No discernible fingerprints on knobs, but removed for Peters to examine.

Black-out curtains at foot of each staircase.

25-amp., blue-washed, shaded lamp on each staircase, controlled from top and bottom. Main staircase light found switched on, other switched off. Witness, Agnes Mudge, asserts main staircase light was on when she arrived this morning.

OTHER LIGHTS

Points found switched on in cloak-room, kitchen, foyer and box-office. Witness, Agnes Mudge, asserts finding all lights out except main staircase light

INTERIOR GENERALLY

No suspicious marks or stains, except in box-office.

CLOAK-ROOM

Dark grey double-breasted overcoat and brown felt hat found on peg. Tab inside inner breast-pocket of coat marking-inked "W. V. Tudor, Esq., 19. 11. 38." Metal letters inside hat, "W. V. T." Pair of wash-leather gloves in right-hand pocket of overcoat. Witness, Agnes Mudge, asserts finding hat and coat on glass-topped table in foyer and removing them to cloak-room.

BOX-OFFICE

Formed by partitioning off corner of foyer. Door opens inwards, hinged on right as looked at from foyer. Ticket-window in other partition wall. Furniture: small mahogany table, two bentwood chairs, tallboy, typist's desk and chair.

TABLE.

Below ticket-window with a bentwood chair in front of it. Single drawer found half-open, with key in lock and remainder of keys of deceased attached by a ring. Fingerprints on drawer (Peters to examine). Two piles of "Measure for Measure" programmes on table. Large pile on left, as from printers, but smaller pile on right with four amendments in ink. Single programme between the piles, opened at centre page, with two amendments made. Not blotted like right-hand pile. Blotting-paper and ink-bottle on table, with nib of pen resting on lip of uncorked bottle. Drawer contained nothing but a cash-book relating to LADS transactions. (Peters to examine.) Telephone on table.

("That reminds me," said the sergeant, seizing the oppor-

tunity of a few moments' break. "I was asked to tell you there
was a 'phone call through to the station for you last night.
Chap didn't leave 'is name. Said 'e'd ring you some other
time. Funny thing always about 'phone calls is—"

"Tallboy," said Charlton implacably. "Against wall opposite
door."

Martin sighed and licked the point of his pencil.)

Tallboy. Against wall opposite door. Unfinished
white-wood. Used as filing-cabinet, with labels pasted on
drawers. No locks. Papers in drawers showed signs of disturbance. Three drawers found half-open. (Peters to examine.)

Typist's desk. Against wall opposite ticket-window, with
typewriter on it. Two unlocked drawers, one containing
L.A.D.S. notepaper, the other, plain quarto and box of carbons.
(Peters to examine desk.)

Chair. Metal Tansad with revolving leather-covered seat,
on which deceased was found.

TYPEWRITER

Corona 4-bank portable, with two-colour ribbon. Sheet
of paper with thin cardboard backing-sheet, as supplied
with boxes of carbons, found in machine. Sheet quarto and
identical with plain paper in drawer of desk. Numbered 229
in top right-hand corner. Reads thus, beginning quarter-way
down sheet:

"Chapter XII

"Paul stumbled backwards with both hands to his face.

" 'Do you want any more?' I said between my teeth.

"He did not answer. I stood in front of him for a moment,
then went to get my overcoat and hat from the cloak-room.
He was still in the box-office when I left the Bakehouse.

"Black thoughts raced through my mind as I strode
through the dark streets to Mrs. Doubleday's. . . .   Tiddler's
absences. . . .His reckless spending. . . . Lady Macbeth. . . .The
banknote. . . .The impersonation of Hilary. . . .The accident on

the staircase. . . . Lady Macbeth . . . Duncan is king of Scotland. Macbeth must be king, so Duncan has got to be put out of the way. . . *Had she really meant that?* Oh, God!

"It was getting late, but Tiddler was in the lounge when I arrived.

" 'Come up to my room,' I told him abruptly. I want to talk to you.' "

Red ink mark on backing-sheet to denote arrival at last line on page. Typing in machine had reached that point. Machine set at quotes following word "you." Careful examination of alignment revealed no inaccuracy. Sheet typed in black. When machine examined, two-colour movement to left of keyboard set at red. Close inspection of platen-knobs revealed minute strands of woollen or other material. (Laboratory to compare with fragments from stage-door and panic latch.)

Deceased

Found sitting on Tansad at typist's desk. Fallen forward with arms hanging down and right cheek resting on keyboard of typewriter. Dagger driven up to hilt between shoulder-blades. Double-breasted blue lounge suit, unbuttoned. Blue soft collar and dark red tie. Black shoes. Silver wrist-watch (still going) with leather strap. Dark hair tidy. Leather note-case containing five one-pound notes, one ten-shilling note and other papers of apparently minor importance. Silver Dunhill cigarette-lighter in top right-hand pocket of waistcoat, gold Ever-sharp pencil in top left. No fountain-pen. Identity card No. AHCBIW/46/3. Driving licence.

Body not visible from doorway, unless door at considerably more than right-angles to frame. Door at slightly less than right-angles when found. Witness, Agnes Mudge, confirms door thus on her arrival this morning.

Blood Marks

Floor of box-office covered with lino. A number of stains,

cracked and flaky, believed to be dried blood in immediate vicinity of deceased. Section of lino cut out for laboratory tests. No other blood traces in box-office.

The Weapon

Dagger as used in dramatic performances. No evidence of having been specially sharpened. Eight-inch blade. Ornamented electro-plated pommel and cross-guard. Wooden hilt wound with wire. Particles of woollen or other material adhering to hilt. (Laboratory tests.) Position found suggests driven downwards into bent back of deceased by some person standing behind him.

Scabbard found on floor in middle of box-office attached to Elizabethan sword-belt of black velvet piped with silver braid, with white metal buckles and ornaments. Tab sewn inside belt reads: "Wight & Sons, Theatrical Costumiers, Gray's Inn Road, London, W.C.I" and, in marking-ink, "Mary Queen of Scots— William Maitland." Scabbard of brown leather finished at ends with white metal. (Peters to examine.)

Costumes for "Measure for Measure" found in disorder on chairs and pegs in dressing-rooms. Brocaded dresses, tunics, black hooded gown, etc. No daggers or other arms. Large basket trunks from Wight & Son in props room.

First query: Is dagger required for any character in "Measure for Measure?"

Second query: Is dagger normally supplied with costumes for that play?

Third query: If not, who arranged for it to be sent by Wight & Son?

Fourth query: Where were belt and dagger left at end of rehearsal last night?

"Right," said Charlton, "that's all for the moment."

The sergeant closed his note-book with a thankful sigh. He often wished he knew shorthand.

Mrs. Mudge was dismissed, after being warned against careless gossip, and sailed off under full spread of canvas to tell the neighbours. She had not been gone a couple of minutes before the constable called up from the foot of the main staircase that a Mr. Smart had arrived. Followed by Martin, Charlton went downstairs.

Mr. Smart was a house-decorator in business for himself and, like most house-decorators in business for themselves, he suffered from asthma and always wore cycle-clips. His appearance was careworn and he had a tobacco-stained moustache. His overcoat was unbuttoned and from the side pockets of it protruded untidy bundles of papers and from the breast-pocket, a folding boxwood rule. Behind his ear was a stump of pencil, in his mouth a charred cigarette of his own unskilful manufacture; and his habitual manner, though civil, suggested that he was late for an urgent appointment elsewhere.

"Yes," he replied to Charlton's first question, "I done the decorating for them. I've just come round to have a look at a staircase that needs attention. They want it finished by this evening."

"Do you know how the tread got broken?"

"Yes, one of the young ladies taking part in the theatricals put her foot through. Nearly a nasty accident, so Mr. Tudor was telling me. But as I said to him, the whole place is a couple of hundred years old, if it's a day, and woodwork don't last for ever, it don't. Seeing you police here put it into my head that somebody had broken their neck on them stairs. What's the trouble?"

"When did this accident happen?"

"To the young lady? Wednesday of last week."

"And when did you finish the decorations?"

"Last Friday, except for the stage-door."

"When was that done?"

"Day before yesterday."

"Why was it left?"

"Here, Mr. Charlton! I don't like the sound of all this! If somebody killed themself on that staircase, it ain't any concern of mine. I can't get the labour these days and what with all the A.R.P. on hand, there's been no chance of—"

"You don't have to answer my questions unless you want to, Mr. Smart. These enquiries are only of a general nature."

"You tell me the facts and then I'll think about answering."

"Mr. Tudor was found dead in the theatre this morning. There is no evidence to show that he fell down the staircase."

"Mr. Tudor? Why, he was one of the best gentlemen I ever done work for. I've got no time for estate agents as a class—cheeseparers, the whole lot of 'em—but Mr. Tudor was different. Well, you do surprise me. What was it—heart?"

"That needn't concern us, Mr. Smart. I'm looking into the matter. Will you tell me why the painting of the stage-door was delayed?"

"Yes, now I know where I stand, I will. You've been attached to Lulverton Division long enough for it to get round that you're not the tricky sort."

Mr. Smart was not the first, or the last, to cherish such an illusion.

"I'll tell you," he said, "why the door wasn't done. We'd given the first coat to all the outside woodwork and was going to do the second coat on the Thursday; but as I say, the young lady took a fall on the Wednesday evening and as I hadn't a carpenter to put the staircase to rights, the stage-door was held over till I could get a man along, so as what the new paintwork wouldn't get knocked about. Then things turned out so that I couldn't take my carpenters off other urgent jobs and, wanting to get the painters out of the place, I had the stage-door finished off Tuesday. Yesterday morning, Mr. Tudor was on the 'phone to me, saying the stair-tread 'ad got to be made good by this evening, because of the first night of the theatricals, and I promised him to have it done to-day without fail. So if it's all the same to you, Mr. Charlton, I'll go and measure up."

"Thank you, Mr. Smart, but things must be left as they are for the time being. I'd like you to come back this afternoon, if you will, and then let me have a report on the present condition of the staircase. I'm interested to know your opinion of the cause of the tread breaking away."

It seemed a relief to Mr. Smart, who wished them good-morning and hurried off, pausing only for a moment in Cooper's Yard to try to light his disreputable cigarette-end with a petrol-lighter that refused to work. "Not a bad start, Martin," said the inspector, as they went back up the stairs. "The stage-door was painted the day before yesterday. Since then, the panic latch has been touched by two bare hands and—if we may deduce from the scraps of material—by somebody wearing woollen gloves. Tudor's gloves are wash-leather. There are notices at top and bottom of the staircase and, in addition, the whole of the company must have known that it was dangerous. The tape across the top of the flight has been torn away from the drawing-pin. So since the day before yesterday, the staircase has been used by someone in a great hurry—someone wearing woollen gloves, who either didn't know about the broken tread, or did know, but was forced to take the risk. If we can match up the woollen fragments on the floor and panic latch with those on the typewriter and the dagger-hilt, we shall have achieved something."

"The romance of crime detection," said Martin in an awed voice.

"Which doesn't really depend on the microscope and the test-tube, so much as on asking innumerable questions and weeding out the answers."

"And when this bloke 'ad rushed down the staircase, after stabbing Tudor and doin' a bit of typing, did 'e make a point of taking off 'is gloves, so that we got 'is fingerprints as well?"

"That," replied the inspector, "remains to be seen."

Miss Muriel Jones was in the outer room when they called later at Tudor's office at the foot of Beastmarket Hill, the centre of the town's commercial life. Charlton introduced himself and gently broke the news, saying no more than that

Tudor had been found dead. It was clearly a great shock to her, although she was able to answer his questions.

"He usually comes in soon after nine o'clock," she said, "and I waited till eleven before I rang up his boarding-house. Mrs. Doubleday, who runs it, told me he went round to the Little Theatre yesterday evening, but didn't come home and she hadn't seen him since. It's terrible, really terrible ... I don't know what I'm going to do...."

Her voice trailed off drearily.

"Who are his nearest relations?"

"His mother and father. They live in London; 40, Westcroft Road, Lee, S.E.12."

"Are they on the phone?"

She gave him a number on the Lee Green exchange.

"And his solicitors?"

"Dickson, Parrish, Willmott & Lister."

"Is there someone to carry on the business for the time being?"

"Only me. It wouldn't have been so difficult if Mr. Ridpath hadn't left us. Oh, it's terrible! Mr. Tudor was always so kind. In my last place, they——"

"Who is Mr. Ridpath?"

"He was Mr. Tudor's assistant, but he left at the end of last week. Mr. Tudor told me that Mr. Ridpath had decided to give up his employment here and that we had to find someone to take his place."

"Did Mr. Tudor give any reason?"

"No, just that Mr. Ridpath had gone."

"Can *you* think why, Miss Jones?"

"Well, I hardly like to say. Mr. Ridpath was a nice young man and ever so good-looking. He knew how to behave and never took liberties. But he was so awfully happy-go-lucky. Not a careful business man like poor Mr. Tudor. If Mr. Tudor gave him something to do and he remembered to do it, he did it quite well; but most often, he forgot all about it. I was always reminding rum about jobs he hadn't done. But it was nice to have him in the office, although he was so careless, especially about money. He had such a sense of humour and was always up to something. With him gone and now poor Mr. Tudor—"

"You say he was careless over money, Miss Jones. Were you speaking in general terms?"

"Oh, yes! I didn't for a moment mean you to think Mr. Ridpath was dishonest! He simply had no idea of responsibility and caused us a lot of anxiety by not obeying Mr. Tudor's instructions."

"You mean instructions about money?"

"Yes. He'd take money out of the petty-cash box to cover expenses and forget to enter it up in the book. Then when Mr. Tudor came to check the balance, it was short. Don't think I'm suggesting Mr. Ridpath wasn't to be trusted. An honester young man never walked. But he hasn't really grown up. You couldn't get him to work to any kind of system. His papers were always in a mess. If you were to ask what I think, I'd say he ought never to have been in business. He'd have done better as an artist." She looked at Charlton with great earnestness as she added: "He was under the influence of Jupiter in conjunction with Venus. Cheerful, truthful, a lover of life and a lover of spending."

"How long was he employed here?"

"He came to us at the beginning of last June. It was very extraordinary, really. He and Mr. Tudor were at school together and great friends. After they left, they didn't see each other for years. Then last May Mr. Tudor advertised in the *Estates Gazette* for an assistant—and the very first answer was from Mr. Ridpath. Very peaked and ill he looked when he started here, but good food and country air soon put him right. I never knew all the facts, but it wouldn't surprise me to hear that Mr. Tudor saved Mr. Ridpath from the gutter."

"Have you a note of Mr. Ridpath's present address?"

"Yes. Just a minute."

She went into the other office and returned with a letter,

which she handed to Charlton.

"Dear Miss Jones (it read), If it is necessary to get in touch with me, the above address will find me. Will you please ask Mrs. Doubleday to forward any letters. Yours sincerely, Peter Ridpath."

The letter was dated Monday, 1st January, 1940 and the address at the head of it was 54, Back Eldon Street, Whitchester. Whitchester was the county town of Downshire and some ten miles to the north-west of Lulverton. Charlton grunted. If any part of Whitchester could be called a slum, it was Back Eldon Street.

"I'll keep this, if you don't mind," he said, and when Miss Jones nodded, slipped it carefully into its envelope.

He changed the subject.

"Mr. Tudor was writing a book, wasn't he?"

Miss Jones looked blank. "Not so far as I know."

"Curious. I understood that he was. There's no typescript— two hundred pages or so—locked away in the office here?"

'Oh, no! I've keys of everything, including the safe, and I should have been sure to have noticed it. Mr. Tudor did buy a typewriter, but he used it round at the theatre on LADS. work. I think Mr. Tudor was far too busy to spend time writing stories."

"So much for that," he smiled. "Had Mr. Tudor a friend whose Christian name was Paul?"

'That would be Mr. Manhow. He's in the dramatic society, too, and has sometimes been in here to see Mr. Tudor. A rather heavily made young gentleman with a big white face and a drowsy way of talking, as if he's half asleep. I believe he's an architect." Miss Jones sniffed with genteel disapproval. "I suppose he's all right."

"And who is Tiddler?"

"Mr. Ridpath. It's Mr. Tudor's nickname for him. It goes back to their schooldays. Mr. Ridpath's name for Mr. Tudor was Turtle, because he was born on Lord Mayor's Show day."

"Was Mr. Ridpath a member of the LADS?"

"Yes. He only joined a few weeks ago and was given ever such a good part in 'Measure for Measure.' Shakespeare, you know. I suppose that'll all be cancelled now. I was going to-morrow evening with my mother, and we were both so looking forward to it. Poor Mr. Tudor gave up a lot of his time to the LADS. It does seem such a dreadful tragedy. I know it's easy to be wise after the event, but I could see it coming."

"What exactly do you mean by that, Miss Jones?"

His tone was so sharp that she took fright.

"Oh, nothing really. Only there always seemed to be a dark cloud hanging over Mr. Tudor. He was under the influence of Mars—and that means an early and violent death." She stared at Charlton fixedly. "And his line of life was broken on both hands, which always spells mortal danger."

This was not the time for fortune-telling.

"Perhaps you can be a little more specific, Miss Jones. Have you any reason to think that Mr. Tudor's safety was threatened? Had he made any enemies?"

"Oh, no! Mr. Tudor hadn't an enemy in the world. I've never heard a word said against him, even by people in competition with us. He was so kind and considerate—but ever so manly with it. If he thought anything was wrong or unfair, he said so at the top of his voice. He wasn't roused easily, yet he had a real temper." She dropped her voice to a confidential murmur. "He doesn't—didn't know that I know—and I've never told a soul—but there's a sort of odd-job man at Mrs. Doubleday's, whose name is Hobson. He's got a wife who's insane and for a long time Mr. Tudor's been paying to have her properly looked after. They believe she can be cured. Then there's a widow called Mrs. Mudge, whose son went into consumption. Mr. Tudor paid for him to be sent to a sanatorium. And he—gave me ten pounds for the funeral when my—my . . . father died. . . . Oh, dear!"

She burst into tears and Charlton signalled to Martin for them to leave her.

"Well," said the sergeant, as, with his toes well out, he

marched spryly along beside his tall superior on their way to Eagle House, "did you notice one very funny thing? She didn't ask what had happened to 'im."

"She didn't have to," grunted Charlton. "He was under the influence of Mars, so sudden death was to be expected."

Martin glanced up at the clock over Benshaws', the jewellers. There was a thirsty glint in his eye.

"I'd sooner be under the influence of bitter in conjunction with Burton," he said.

By the mysterious channels through which news travels, Mrs. Doubleday already knew of Tudor's death. Although it was a point of honour with her to fuss over her guests, what happened to them when not under her roof did not greatly disturb her; and it seemed to Charlton that her only real concern was the effect that the tragedy might have on the fair name of her establishment. She answered Charlton's first questions without visible emotion.

"Yes, dinner is served as a rule at half-past seven, but they asked for it early last night, because of the rehearsal. Mr. Tudor left here with the others soon after quarter-past seven."

"Who were these others?"

"Miss Ashwin, Mr. Mortimer Robinson and young Mr. Gough. They're all members of the dramatic society."

"Where and when can I speak to them?"

"They'll all be in to lunch very shortly."

"Can you tell me what time they got back here last night?"

"Just after eleven o'clock. I waited up for Mr. Tudor until one o'clock, in case he wanted something hot when he came in, and then, as he didn't arrive, went to bed, leaving the front door unbolted."

"You weren't uneasy about him?"

"No. He frequently stayed late at the theatre."

"Did the other three make any reference to him?"

"Not to me."

"Then amongst themselves?"

Mrs, Doubleday pursed disapproving lips.

"I never heavesdrop on my guests."

"But you may have caught some casual remark?"

"Well"—she hesitated—"I did happen to hear Mr. Gough say that *he*—he didn't mention any name—was probably working on . . . what was it he called it? . . . The secret opus."

"What was their reply to that?"

She bridled slightly. "I don't remember."

"Are you sure?"

Again she hesitated before saying: "Miss Ashwin said *he* probably wouldn't be in the best mood or humour or frame of mind—I'm not sure of the exact phrase—for writing." She added in a tone that was final, "I don't remember another word."

"What did the three of them do when they arrived back?"

"They were here in the lounge for ten minutes or so, then Mr. Mortimer Robinson went up to bed. I got the other two some coffee and they sat talking until about quarter to twelve, when Mr. Gough went out. Miss Ashwin sat here until he came in again, which was just turned midnight. A minute or two afterwards, they went up to their rooms."

"Did you get any idea of where Mr. Gough had been?" Mrs. Doubleday shook her curiously shaped head. "You're sure it was he who went out?"

"Well, I didn't actually see him go, but I heard him say that he wouldn't be long; then the front door was opened and closed. I was in my bed-sitting-room at the other end of the hall. I caught the sound of the front door when he came back, just after the church clocks had struck midnight. Miss Ashwin came out to meet him in the hall and they both went back into the lounge."

"Was anything said in the hall?"

"I didn't listen. It was no concern of mine. Ten minutes or a quarter of an hour later, they went up to their rooms."

"So everyone except Mr. Tudor was in by a minute or two after twelve o'clock?" She nodded. "Whom had you staying here last night?"

"Mrs. Stoneham, Miss Tearle and Mr. Garnett, who are regular guests, and a young couple, who were here just the one night and left immediately after breakfast this morning. Their names are in the visitors' book, if you want to look at it."

"Don't bother, thank you. How many of your staff sleep on the premises, Mrs. Doubleday?"

"Three girls and Hobson, the odd-job man. I ought to have told you that he was at the rehearsal last night. He helps them with the scene-shifting."

From the way she said it, Charlton gathered that she did not entirely agree with the arrangement.

"Do you know if he returned here with the others?"

"I think not, although I saw him at about twenty-past eleven. He was on his way up the back staircase, after having stoked up the boiler for the night."

"I want a word with him and the servants before I leave, but first of all, Mrs. Doubleday, I must take up a little more of your time. What is Miss Ashwin's christian name?"

"Myrna. She is a junior mistress at the Girls' High School."

"A high-spirited young lady?"

"Oh, yes—a bright little thing."

"But rather sharp-tempered on occasions?"

"Oh, no! I wouldn't say that, Mr. Charlton."

"Have any of your regular lodgers recently left you?"

There was a certain furtiveness about the sharp little eyes that glanced at him through steel-framed spectacles.

"The last *guest*"—evidently Mrs. Doubleday did not much care for his word—"was a Mr. Ridpath, who packed his bag and went last Sunday morning."

"Is there anything you can tell me about him?"

"He's a good-looking young man with fair, curly hair—and a very old friend of Mr. Tudor's. He came to stay here at the beginning of last June and Mr. Tudor found a post for him in his office. Early on Sunday morning, he came to tell me that he was leaving at once, without even waiting for breakfast."

"Did he supply any reason?"

"He told me that he'd been offered a better position in Whitchester and had to take it up at once. He had already packed his bag and went within a few minutes."

"How about the rest of them? Did anyone go to see him off at the station?"

She shook her head. "And I'm not even sure that he went to the station. He just walked down the drive with his case in his hand—and that was the last I saw of him."

"How would you describe his manner that morning?"

"Sad and subdued. He was always so bright and cheerful. He hadn't been his usual self for some days. A letter came for him last Saturday morning, and it may have contained bad news."

"Have there been any for him since?"

"Yes, there was another on Tuesday morning. I had his address in Whitchester, so I forwarded it to him."

"Were both letters addressed in the same handwriting?"

"I should say yes."

"What were the postmarks?"

"Really, Mr. Charlton!" Mrs. Doubleday was deeply insulted. "It is certainly not my habit to pry into my guests' private affairs."

He smiled reassuringly—and had Mrs. Doubleday known him as well as Martin did, she would have taken heed of that smile. "It's quite a natural failing to look at the postmark on other people's correspondence, Mrs. Doubleday. I'm afraid I do it myself! Did the letters come from the same place?"

"Yes—Guildford."

"Was the handwriting feminine?" She nodded assent. "An educated hand?"

"Not very. The addresses were neatly written, but without much character. The kind of stuff they teach in helementary schools."

The tone implied the slight patronage of Roedean and Girton.

"Were there any letters from the same source previous to

last Saturday?"

"I don't recall any."

"What sort of quality was the stationery?"

"Not really cheap, but a long way from being good."

"If other letters come for him, Mrs. Doubleday, I should like you to let me know before you send them on. Did Mr. Ridpath pay his bill regularly?"

Bill was no more to her taste than lodger.

"His account was always settled promptly. He left without owing a penny."

"It was he and not Mr. Tudor who made you the payments?"

"Yes."

"Thank you, Mrs. Doubleday. And now, if you'll allow me, I'd like to have a chat with Hobson."

When she left them alone in the lounge, Sergeant Martin hissed:

"She knows more than she'll say!"

The inspector grinned at him as he answered:

"It's what a woman doesn't say that matters."

XIII

... if you live to see this come to pass,
say Pompey told you so.
Act II, Sc. 1.

Hobson paused at the door and looked down at the carpet, as if in search of somewhere to wipe his feet. He was fidgeting with his stained cap, as he shuffled nervously into the room. His jocular manner had deserted him.

"Did you want to see me, sir?" he asked with a hesitant smile that displayed teeth of the inartistic regularity and white brilliance that are the hallmarks of commercial science's ascendancy over Nature.

"Yes. Sit down . . . Your name's Hobson, isn't it?"

"Yessir. Archibald Hobson."

"And you once got sent away for three months for working the buses at Southmouth?"

Hobson gulped so suddenly that his teeth clicked.

"Yessir, but that was a long time ago. I bin clean ever since, God's honour! How did you come to know that I used to be at the whiz?"

"Just a part of my job. I hope you decided that dipping pockets didn't pay?"

"Gone straight as a dart ever since, sir."

"Good. I'm not bringing it up against you, but wanted to get you placed. Now, I'm told that you were at the 'Measure for Measure' rehearsal yesterday evening."

"That's right, sir. I'm kind of electrician and stage-carpenter for the society. I've always bin pretty clever with me "ands."

"So they tell me," murmured Charlton, and the wiry little man gave an awkward smirk. "What time did you leave the theatre?"

"With most of the others, as soon as the re'earsal was over. Say eleven o'clock."

"And you came straight here?" Hobson agreed. "Did you walk back alone?"

"Well, sir, we were all sort of together most of the way, but I wasn't side by side or in company with anybody, though as you couldn't see your 'and in front of your face, I might 'ave bin right on the 'eels of the Archhishop of Canterbury and not known it. Everyone was talking and walking into things and falling off the kerb, but they gradually thinned out and, coming along Friday Street, there was only four of us, three of the lodgers 'ere and me, fifteen or twenty yards be'ind 'em. They came in through the front door and I went round the back, stoked the boiler, did one or two other little jobs and then went up to bed."

"After you got in, did you hear anyone enter or leave Eagle House?"

"No, sir, but that's not to say they didn't. It's a regular

'oneycomb, this place. There's 'alf a dozen ways in and out and all the German spies in the country"—he gave the detective a swift, cunning glance—"could come and go without you being any the wiser, specially in the black-out."

"Was Mr. Tudor left alone in the theatre?"

"I couldn't swear to that, sir. There was such an 'urly-burly down the stairs, that you couldn't tell who'd gone and who was left. I 'eard Mr. Tudor say that 'e was going to stop be'ind, but whether 'e did or not, and whether anybody stayed with 'im, I shouldn't like to say."

Charlton's tone became more conversational, and the sergeant, reading the signs, straightened himself expectantly in his chair.

"How did the rehearsal go off?"

"As well as could be 'oped, sir, which isn't saying much. There's bin a tidy bit of trouble over this show, sir, one way and another. Too much jockeying for positions—too many underground manewvres. It all started when the principal girl lost 'er stripes and they gave the part to another piece—to another young lady. If you was to ask me my opinion, sir, I'd say there was some monkey-business. Miss Faggott was so set on the part that she wouldn't 'ave turned it in without somebody first put the screw on."

"Miss Faggott is tall, isn't she?"

"Tall and dark, sir, with a voice you'd call rich and fruity. A really nice young lady, with no la-di-da and none of your 'igh-and-mighty nonsense. The other one, Miss Boyson, is just as tall, but fair. Pretty enough, I suppose, if you don't mind 'em watered down. Speaking for meself, sir, when it comes to blondes, I'm no gentleman!"

"Is either of them called Hilary?"

"Miss Boyson, sir. Miss Faggott is Elizabeth."

"Was it Miss Boyson who went home early last Saturday?'

"That's right. She 'ad a sharp attack of la-di-da."

"And is Miss Faggott clever at impersonations?"

"You bet she is! Takes off everyone a treat, including the

writer. The pity is that she lost the big part. Miss Boyson's not in the same street. She don't seem to get the *feel* of it"

"Was Mr. Ridpath there last night?"

"Mr. Ridpath, sir? No. 'E was to 'ave bin in the show, but left 'ere rather hurried last Sunday morning."

"Any idea why?"

"Nothing definite, sir. Only by putting two and two together and p'raps getting the sum wrong."

Charlton smiled. "Care to tell me your answer?"

The other fiddled with the cap on his knees and hesitated. Then he burst out:

"Look 'ere, Inspector, this ain't just tale-bearing, 'cause I've got no time for tittle-tattle, see? But Mr. Tudor, 'e meant a lot to me. Best friend a bloke ever had! All the rest you can keep—'cep' p'raps Miss Faggott—but nobody's going to say nothing to me against Mr. Tudor. And if I can't bring 'im back, I can do me best to send the other chap after 'im. . . . Maybe you've met Mr. perishing Ridpath? 'E's a masher—a proper push-specialist, if ever there was one. Takes up with all and sundry. A quick worker *and* thorough with it. To *my* knowledge, there was Miss Collingwood—Felicity, that is, the younger one—Peggy Howard, the solicitor's daughter, and the girl in the cigarette-kiosk at the station—Molly Wyant or Wyatt or some such name. Then for a time, 'e knocked around with our Miss Ashwin, till she got a line on 'im and dropped 'im like a hot potato. Mr. Tudor never made a show of 'is feelings, 'cept when 'e lost 'is temper and then not without reason. But for a long time past, you could've seen with 'alf an eye that 'e had a pash on Miss Faggott. All open and above board, mind you. A real nice couple—and they'd 'ave made a do of it. But not content with all 'is other shenanachida, Mr. Ridpath 'ad to make a pass at Miss Faggott as well. She'd got no time for 'is lordship, but 'e's the go-getting sort, didn't know when 'e wasn't wanted, and began to make a blinking nuisance of 'isself."

Charlton stirred in his chair.

"Just a minute, sir," begged Hobson. "Let me say this out. Last Sat'dy night, I was on me way up to bed, which took me past Mr. Ridpath's room on the second floor. Inside, there was a pretty average dust-up in progress. I didn't catch the first part of it, but just as I was passing the door, Mr. Ridpath was saying: 'And if I *did* sleep with 'er, what the flaming 'ell are *you* going to do about it?' Then there was a sort of shout, probably from Mr. Tudor, and *crack* went one on the kisser. 'Would you like to say that again?' says Mr. Tudor sweet and low; and it sounded as if Mr. Ridpath was blubbin' like a six-year-old. Couldn't take 'is medicine, see? That sort. I 'ear Mr. Tudor say:' I've 'ad quite enough of you. To-morrow out you go.' I just 'ad time to nip out of sight before 'e lugged the door open. First thing next morning—the Sunday—I saw young Ridpath. 'Is top lip was all puffed up lovely and one of 'is front teeth 'adn't reported for duty."

He leant forward with a grimy hand on each knee.

"Nah, then," he said, "what more likely than that Ridpath, knowing Mr. Tudor was in the 'abit of stopping late at the theatre, didn't slip back to Lulverton last night and murder Mr. Tudor from be'ind, the treacherous little bar—"

"Who told you it was from behind?" asked Charlton quietly.

"Who what? Well, it was, wasn't it?"

"Where did you get that information?"

"Nowhere particular. It's all round the town. Things like that can't be kept dark for long."

"Who was it told you?"

"Nobody actually said it was from be'ind, but stabbing's usually done in the back, ain't it?"

"Who told you Mr. Tudor was stabbed?"

Hobson shook himself impatiently.

"Cor dammit? If you must know, it was Mrs. Doubleday, just before you came. And if you want to know 'ow *she* knew, Miss Jones rang up from Mr. Tudor's office. And if you want to know 'ow Miss Jones knew, you told 'er yourself. And if you want to know how I know you told Miss Jones, Miss Jones told Mrs. Doubleday you'd told 'er, and Mrs. Doubleday told me." He sat back in his chair, slipped his hands inside his belted trousers and added with a complacent smile: "And that's 'ow news gets round."

The sergeant adroitly turned a guffaw into a cough and stroked his mouth with the back of his hand.

"I see" said Charlton evenly. "Your only informant was Mrs Doubleday, her only informant was Miss Jones and her only informant was myself. Is that it?"

"That's about the size of it," Hobson agreed, still smiling.

"Yet all I said to Miss Jones was that Mr. Tudor had been found dead so what makes you imagine"—the tone was of kindly enquiry—"that Mr. Tudor was stabbed through the back?"

"Wasn't he, then?

"*Answer my question!*" There was a sharp note now.

"I …Well …I don't know that 'e was. I'll tell you the way I figure it out, sir. The—"

"So when you said that Mrs. Doubleday told you that Mr. Tudor had been stabbed through the back, you were lying?"

"That's putting it too strong," complained Hobson. "It wasn't exactly the truth, but the remark was made 'asty. You got me on the run with all your questions. I'll admit nobody told me and even now I'm not sure Mr. Tudor wasn't shot or poisoned or blown up by the I.R.A. It's only what they call intelligent conjecture." His voice changed to appeal, "Was I right, sir? 'E's bin that down–in–the–mouth these last few days, that 'e might 'ave taken lysol and I shouldn't like to think 'e suffered. Stabbing's a clean quick death. … I was very fond of Mr. Tudor, sir. 'E was the sort of man I'd like to be serving under now out in France."

"Yes" nodded Charlton, "he was stabbed through the back. And now I want you to tell me precisely why you were so certain about it."

"Definite first-and evidence, sir. The costumes for 'Measure for Measure' was—"

"Before we go any further, Hobson, I'd better tell you that your statement will be written down by the sergeant here and that I shall afterwards ask you to sign it. I warn you that it may be used in evidence."

Hobson scratched his head.

"'Aven't I 'eard that before somewhere? he asked. "Well, sir, the costumes for 'Measure for Measure' was ordered some weeks ago and arrived at the theatre Tuesday, day before yesterday. With them came a dagger with a fancy belt to wear with it. I'm going to ask you, why was it sent? Not 'cause it was needed for the play, but by reason of Mr. Ridpath 'aving partic'ly asked for it. And 'ow do I know that? 'Cause I 'eard 'im!" He assumed an air of superiority. "You wouldn't know, but there's a character in 'Measure for Measure' going by the name of Lucio. It's a proper pansy part and was taken first of all by a Mr. Northcott. When 'e joined up in the R.A.F., they looked round for another Lucio and fixed on Mr. Ridpath. Though you'd never find so much as a postcard from me in Mr. Ridpath's fan-mail, I've got to hand it to 'im that 'e made a better go at Lucio than young Mr. Northcott. 'E'd not only got all the airs and graces off pat, but was clever with it— introduced little bits of business which was very comical. One evening at re'earsal, when they was doing Act-One-Scene-Two-a-Street, Mr. Ridpath—"

"Just a moment. Can you remember the date?"

Hobson pondered. "Not to a day. Just before Christmas, anyway. May 'ave bin the Tuesday or Wednesday."

"Thank you. Please go on."

"At the beginning of the scene, Ridpath 'ad to make mention of a two-faced old pirate that took the orders of the day from the ten commandmants, till 'e found that 'Thou shalt not steal' 'ad a cramping effect on trade, and cut it out of the agenda. Mr. Ridpath's idea was for 'im to 'ave a dagger and at the right moment whip it out and go through the movements of scraping out the words. Mr. Collingwood, the producer, 'e thought it no great shakes, but Mr. Ridpath was so set on it and swore 'e could get laughs out of the dagger in other parts of the play, that Mr. Collingwood agreed. So Mr. Tudor wrote to the costume people, asking them to throw in a dagger and belt with the rest of the duds."

He bent towards Charlton.

"Ask yourself, Inspector, why did Ridpath press for the dagger? Was it for a bit of stage business that wasn't worth the trouble of getting a dagger specially for? Or was it to 'ave a weapon 'andy to use on Mr. Tudor? If it came down from Wight's, nobody would 'ave 'ad very much to say about it laying about the Bakehouse, and anybody might 'ave snatched it up and stabbed Mr. Tudor. That'd be the way 'e'd look at it. Where was young Ridpath all last evening? Find 'im and ask 'im, Inspector! In Back Eldon Street, a bloke can get a cast-iron alibi for the price of a pint, but if you catch Ridpath quick, 'e might not 'ave 'ad time to fix it. And don't say I didn't tell you!"

"Let's leave that for the moment, Hobson. You gave me the impression just now that things didn't go too well at the theatre last night. What happened?"

Hobson wagged his head up and down and clicked his tongue.

"It was a proper Fred Karno, I tell you! The 'ole company seemed to go to pieces. On Sat'dy night, the general atmosphere wasn't what you might call chummy, but it was a picnic to last night. On Sat'dy, there was a set-to between Miss Faggott and Miss Boyson, who couldn't think of any better answer than sweeping off 'ome, like Josephine after the battle of Waterloo. She's as full of tantrums as a sick camel, is that young woman! But last night she came along to the Bakehouse early, all simpers and as pleasant as you please. 'Good evening, Hobson,' she says, 'and how are—' "

"Were you the first to arrive?"

"No, Mr. Duzest was there before me. 'E come along to me in the afternoon and borrowed my key, because 'e wanted to get there well in front of the others, to try on 'is costume. There'd bin no chance for 'im to do it before. Well, as I was telling you, Miss Boyson was as nice as pie. It was, 'I do 'ope the play's going to be a success, don't you, Hobson?' and 'You poor man, to be cooped up in that stuffy little 'utch with them switches all the evening.' "

His lip curled.

"The smile on the face of the tiger! When she'd finished her fine lady act, she went into the dressing-room. They'd got all the costumes sorted out the night before, so it wasn't long before she was out again, all rigged out in a red velvet dress and a bit of nonsense fixed round 'er head. By that time, the rest of the company was beginning to drift in, and Mrs. Cheesewright, 'oo's an interfering old crab at the best of times, catches sight of 'er and says, 'Why, Hilary, dear, you've got the wrong dress on. There's a white robe and veil for Isabella.' Miss Boyson smiles sweetly and says, 'Miss Faggott is playing Isabella.' Oh dear, oh lor, I says to meself, 'ave we got to go through that all over again? Miss Faggott, 'oo turned up just then, seemed to think the same, for she shrugged 'er shoulders and sighed 'eavy. Mr. Collingwood, 'oo's had some experience of temperamental belladonnas, then says very businesslike, 'Miss Boyson, Miss Faggott, Mr. Tudor and Mr. Mortimer Robinson, 'ave the goodness to step with me into the box-office.' They closed the door behind 'em, so I didn't catch what was said, but after five or six minutes, Mr. Tudor raises 'is voice so much that we all 'eard 'im say, 'What you need, 'Ilary's a damn good thrashing! You're be'aving like some silly schoolgirl!' With that, the door was snatched open and out comes Miss Boyson, as red as a beetroot. She prances along to the girls' dressing-room and before you could wink, was out again ready for the street. She left the theatre in 'igh dudgeon."

"By which door?"

"The main one. Everybody in the foyer pretended to be doing something else as she swep' past 'em, like Josephine retreating from Moscow. After a minute or so, Miss Faggott comes out of the box-office, with the others follering. Mr. Collingwood was looking worried. 'Miss Boyson 'as withdrawn from the cast,' 'e tells us. 'Will anybody take over Mariana?' Nobody says nothing, so 'e says to Miss 'Oward, 'What about you, Peggy?' 'If you really want me to,' she says. 'Then everybody get changed,' shouts Mr. Collingwood, 'and make it snappy!' "

"Who took Mr. Ridpath's place as Lucio?" asked the inspector.

"A Mr. Leslie Nash. 'E'd been regular to re'earsals and 'ad a working idea of the part, but was as much like Lucio ought to be as my old Aunt Maggie."

"Was he wearing the dagger last night?"

Hobson looked at him shrewdly.

"So that *was* the one it was done with, eh? Yes, Mr. Nash wore it—and a first class mess 'e made of the ten commandments business with it! Finished up by dropping it on 'is toe."

"Did you notice what happened to it at the end of the rehearsal?"

"Can't say I did, sir."

"Were there any other awkward developments?"

"Well, everybody was on edge. Miss Faggott didn't seem 'erself, and 'er acting was a long way off the bull. Mr. Collingwood 'ad a terrible job to keep 'is temper and was working overtime on 'Good King Wenceslas,' which is 'is favourite whistling solo when things aren't going quite the way 'e wants 'em to. Mr. Cheesewright, the stage-manager, nearly came right off the 'ook. To give you some idea of the general feelings, I'll tell you another thing. Mr. Mortimer Robinson— and nobody could call 'im anything but even-tempered—'ad got 'isself all togged up in 'is gown and white wig, but 'ad forgotten to take 'is glasses off. Mr. Gough, 'oo likes 'is little joke, starts pulling 'is leg and Mr. Tudor makes it worse by saying a bit sarcastic, 'I think Mr. Mortimer Robinson always looks magnificent in fancy dress.' Me, I 'ad to laugh, 'cause when it comes to magnificent, Mr. Mortimer Robinson looked anything but. 'E was genuinely put out, though, and when Mr. Gough asks whether 'e'd brought any of the animals along, meaning that Mr. Mortimer Robinson looked like Nor, 'e went quite white. As a matter of fack, the only 'appy smile last night was Mr. Gough's. 'E was like a boy let out of school—and for why? 'Cause Miss Ashwin 'ad decided to be friendly."

"Was Mr. Manhow at the rehearsal?"

"Funny you should say that, sir. I was just going to mention Mr. Manhow. 'E takes the part of Pompey in the piece and a real scream 'e is, too, though a bit near the knuckle. But 'e was no better than the others last night. E's sweet on Miss Boyson, so it couldn't 'ave bin much to 'is taste when she made an exhibition of 'erself with 'er bella donna tricks. 'E always reminds me of John Tilley with a dash of Charles Laughton, does Mr. Manhow. When Miss Boyson ups and outs, 'e makes as if to foller, then stops where 'e is and lights 'is pipe with more than the usual amount of varlent puffing. Soon as Mr. Tudor comes out of the box-office, 'e steps up to 'im and says none too quietly, '*She* ain't the one what'll git the thrashing.' 'Oh?' says Mr. Tudor, calm, but pale, 'and 'oo's the other, might I ask!' 'You should know,' snaps Mr. Manhow. 'Try it any time you like,' says Mr. Tudor, as cool as a twopenny Snofrute, then goes on with as near to a sneer as 'e ever got, "Ow now, noble Pompey? What, at the wheels of Caesar? Art thou led in triumph?' That's out of the play and was mean sardonical. Mr. Manhow turns on 'is heel and goes off to the dressing-room without another word. Oh, it was a gala night, I tell you! I've bin in some pretty mix-ups in my time, but never one like that. Though I remember once—"

"How did that ten-pound note get lost, Hobson?"

The softly uttered question cut right across the course of Hobson's reminiscences and left him with his mouth open.

"Eh?" he said at length.

"The ten-pound note. How did it stray out of Miss Faggott's

bag last Saturday evening?"

"So that's your line, is it? Trying to suggest I cabbaged it? Well, it wasn't nothing to do with me, see? Just 'cause a bloke's bin over the wall, you—"

"I'm not hinting at anything," the inspector said. "All I'm asking is do you know how or why the banknote got mislaid and how it came to be found on the floor of the cloakroom?"

"No, I don't"

"Thank you." Now, one last question. Mr. Tudor spent much of his spare time at his typewriter. Do you know what he was working on?"

"Not the foggiest."

"Have you ever seen a thick wad of typescript that might, have belonged to him: in the theatre or perhaps up in his room?"

"No, sir."

"Then that's all, thanks."

When the substance of Hobson's discursive evidence had been written down and the statement laboriously signed with the sergeant's fountain-pen, the handyman was dismissed. Left by themselves, Charlton and Martin looked at each other reflectively.

"Stimulatin'," observed the sergeant at last,

"Very," the inspector agreed.

XIV

Who Called here of late?
Act IV, Sc. 2.

The other two servants had nothing to tell, but Edith Timms, the chambermaid, gave Charlton food for thought.

"At half-past six yesterday evening," she told him, "I was up in Miss Tearle's room. . . ."

But before her evidence is reported, it will be as well to

describe Eagle House in some detail, for it has considerable bearing on Charlton's investigation. The main building, which faced north, was quite conventional in design. On the ground floor, to the right (or west) of the central staircase, was the dining-room, and to the left (or east), the lounge, with Mrs. Doubleday's private apartment behind it. On each of the first and second floors were four rooms, divided by two passages that hisected each other, so that the rooms stood like the corner buildings at cross-roads. The top floor was devoted to servants' quarters and store-rooms.

The interior complications and the exterior disharmony arose from the two-storeyed wings that some predecessor of Mrs. Doubleday had caused to be built over the garages at the sides of the house. On each floor of these wings were three rooms connected by a passage running from north to south, with a lavatory at the northern end and a short flight of stairs at the southern end. Access to the wings was gained from the main building through doorways cut in the original flank walls; and, for some reason best known to the designer, doors from the four chief bedrooms on both floors also led into the wings, so that each of these rooms had two doors. At the end of the central passage there was a back staircase extending from the basement to the top floor.

The four principal bedrooms on the first floor were used by Mr. Garnett (front left), Mrs. Stoneham (front right), Tudor (back left) and Miss Tearle (back right). Jack Gough had the southernmost room in the left-hand wing and Myrna Ashwin, the middle room in the other wing.

So: "At half-past six yesterday evening," Edith Timms told Charlton, "I was up in Miss Tearle's room. The door was open and I heard somebody shout in a very angry way. 'Get out!' "

"Did you recognise the voice?"

"No, sir. I couldn't say it was anybody in particular, only that it was a man."

"Where do you think he was?"

"I wouldn't like to say, sir. It sounded like from the annexe on the other side. As I say, the door was open and the door of Mr. Tudor's room just opposite was open, too; and a little while after the shout, Mr. Tudor 'imself came through from the annexe by the door on the farther side of his room."

"Had that door been previously closed?"

"Yes, sir. Mr. Tudor was looking very put out. 'E absolutely strode across the room, throwing his hat and overcoat on the bed as he went, and slammed the door, so as I didn't see no more."

"Had you previously been in any of the other rooms?"

"No, sir. Miss Tearle was feeling poorly and was going to bed immediately after dinner, so Madam told me to light the gas-fire in the room and put some hot-water bottles in the bed. Soon as I'd done it, I went downstairs again."

"You're quite certain you couldn't identify the man's voice?"

Edith shook her head with decision. "It was too muffled, though it sounded close. It might not 'ave been 'Get out!' but it was more like that than anythink else."

"That'll do, then, thank you. Please ask Mrs. Doubleday to come back."

At his request, Mrs. Doubleday took them up to Tudor's room. There was nothing elaborate about the furnishing, yet it was cosy: a good carpet, an easy chair, a divan bedstead, a compactum full of clothes, a graceful writing-table with cut-glass inkwells and a row of jacketed novels between book-ends, a dressing-table by the window, which overlooked the terraced back garden of Eagle House. A pedestal hand-basin, with spotless chromium-plated taps, stood in a corner, with a mirror and glass shelf fitted above it. On the bedside table was a reading lamp, and on the walls a few good etchings.

"A charming room," approved Charlton.

"Yes," answered the gratified proprietress, "I like to make my guests as comfortable as possible, though Mr. Tudor's spent some money on it himself. He was quite well-to-do, you know."

She and the sergeant stood just inside the doorway, while Charlton roamed and ferreted about, opening drawers and peering behind furniture. Martin conjectured that he was searching for the missing typescript, and was disappointed at his lack of success with the dressing-table, the writing-table and a built-in cupboard.

Within the compactum, down one side, were six drawers. Charlton pulled them out one by one.

"Not a very tidy young man," he murmured.

"Oh, you shouldn't say that!" protested Mrs. Doubleday. "Mr. Tudor was most horderly in his ways."

She waddled across, with Martin following, and looked in the last drawer the inspector had examined.

"Good heavens!" she exclaimed. "Mr. Tudor never left his collars and handkerchiefs in a mess like that! Let me see the others."

In considerable agitation, she shouldered the big detective out of the way and he grimaced over the top of her head at the grinning sergeant while she peered into the other drawers.

"What *can* have happened?" she asked.

"Mice," was Martin's suggestion.

"These dress-shirts," wailed Mrs. Doubleday. "I laid them carefully in this drawer myself only last night and now look at them! Just as if they'd been crumpled into a ball. I shall have to send them back to the laundry again."

Charlton stepped round behind her and muttered into the sergeant's ear: "Somebody's been here before us." To Mrs. Doubleday he said: "What time did you put the shirts away, Mrs. Doubleday?"

She stopped crooning a dirge over the garments, which were not nearly so dilapidated as she had implied.

"About half-past ten. It's such a pity people aren't more careful. These starched fronts show every mark."

"They certainly do," Charlton cordially agreed, and, turning to Martin, uttered the single word: "Peters."

Charlton opened the door that led into the wing—or annexe, as Mrs. Doubleday and her staff preferred to call it. The floor was below the level of the main building and two steps led down to it from Tudor's room. By looking along to the left, he could see the steps at the end of the principal passage; further along, the entrance to Mr. Garnett's room: and past that, across the end of the passage, the door of a lavatory.

Mrs. Doubleday came up and stood beside him.

"That's Mr. Gough's," she explained, pointing to the right at a door numbered "7" on the opposite side of the passage, just by the curtains that hid the staircase to the upper floor.

"Which was Mr. Ridpath's room?" asked the inspector.

"Oh, that's upstairs. Do you want to see it?"

"Yes, in a moment."

He stepped down into the passage and walked along to pull back the curtains. Because the house was built on a slope, the back of the house was almost at ground-floor level, and down a single step from where he stood was the door leading into the back garden. The staircase formed a convenient way for the residents in the wing to pass in and out of Eagle House without using the main entrance and stairs.

He allowed the curtains to fall and went back to Mrs. Doubleday.

"Was it Mr. Tudor's practice," he asked, "to use that door?"

She shook her head. "Not very often, I should think. He kept his car in the garage on the other side, which made it quicker for him to come round the front. In the summer time, he might have done."

"Your other guests last night, Mrs. Doubleday—which room did they occupy?"

She pointed to the left.

"Numbers five and six over there. Three of the big rooms upstairs were free, but these are cheaper because they're not so large and with no wash-basins."

"I think you said they were a young married couple?"

"No, only engaged—and very hengrossed with each other

. . . They arrived in a car and were here just the one night. According to the visitors' book, they came from London. A Miss Brown and a Mr. Smith."

Sergeant Martin's noisy cough was fraught with wicked meaning. Charlton frowned at him.

"What time did they get here?"

"In time for lunch."

"Were they in their rooms at six-thirty?"

"They went out in the afternoon and came back soon after six, so it's very likely. But I won't be sure."

"If you hear any further from either of them will you let me know?" She nodded from the waist. "Now, if we may, we'd like to see Mr. Ridpath's old room, please."

It was characteristic of Mrs. Doubleday that she did not conduct them by the back stairway, but by the longer and more impressive route up the main flight. The room that Ridpath had used was similar to Miss Tearle's immediately below. Next to it, but divided, of course, by the passage, was Mr. Mortimer Robinson's apartment, which was over Tudor's. Ridpath's room was less handsomely furnished than Tudor's. The suite was of heavy, over-ornamented mahogany, and the whole effect was of complete impersonality, heightened—but, somehow, not entirely—by the removal of the bedclothes and Ridpath's private belongings.

The inspector asked: "He left nothing behind, I suppose?"

"Nothing at all. Not that the unfortunate young man possessed very much in the way of this world's goods. Even what he had was all due to Mr. Tudor, who was a real friend to him. When Mr. Ridpath came here last June, he was nothing but skin and bone. And shabby, you wouldn't believe it. He's sure to be very grieved when he hears about Mr. Tudor."

Just as he had explored Tudor's room, Charlton now went scouting round again. The search was so thorough that Martin began to get bored, but his attention was suddenly recaptured when Charlton gave a satisfied grunt. The prize was no more than a safety-razor blade that had been lying on the glass shelf above the wash-basin, but it was handled most tenderly until it was put away in an envelope that the sergeant suitably inscribed.

After that, Charlton lost interest in the room.

"Mrs. Doubleday," he said, "you told me earlier that, when he left here, Mr. Ridpath's manner was sad and subdued. Did you notice anything else about him?"

"No, I don't think so."

He looked puzzled. "That's very curious, Mrs. Doubleday. Did you not observe that his mouth was swollen and that one of his front teeth was missing?"

"Oh, yes," she hurriedly conceded. "I thought you meant —the way he behaved. He walked into his wardrobe in the dark."

"Were you there when he did it?"

"No, but that's what he told me."

"And you accepted the explanation?"

"I had no reason to do otherwise."

"Mrs. Doubleday," he said rather grimly, "you're not being very frank with me. Mr. Ridpath may have told you he was leaving Lulverton, to take up a better position at Whitchester, but that was not necessarily the truth. I am given to believe that last Saturday night there was between Mr. Ridpath and Mr. Tudor a serious dispute that led to Mr. Ridpath's early departure on Sunday morning. Can you disprove that?"

"Everyone's entitled to their own opinions, Mr. Charlton, and just as entitled to keep those opinions to themselves. Mr. Tudor and Mr. Ridpath were two very nice, well-behaved young gentlemen and I'm not going to say a word against either of them. If they didn't quite see eye to eye sometimes, I'm sure there was a good deal to be said for both sides."

"Are you prepared to say that, to your knowledge, they had no quarrel on Saturday night, Mrs. Doubleday?"

Beady little eyes stared hard at him through ugly spectacles.

"If you think Mr. Ridpath killed Mr. Tudor," she said, "you're wrong."

"You haven't answered my question," was his courteous reminder. "I'm not implying that, because they quarrelled, Mr. Ridpath killed Mr. Tudor."

"You police are not to be trusted," she declared. "You twist people's words round to mean what you want them to mean. . . . But if you must have a straight answer, I have never heard them quarrel."

"Did Hobson tell you what *he* heard on Saturday night?"

"He considered it his duty to report the hoccurrence to me," replied Mrs. Doubleday with tremendous dignity.

"Which way does he normally go up to bed?"

"By the back stairs. My staff are forbidden to use the main flight, unless their duties take them that way."

"Would Hobson have had any such duties after eleven o'clock last Saturday?"

"No, his last task was to stoke the boiler. But don't you make any mistake, Mr. Charlton: Mr. Ridpath didn't kill Mr. Tudor. If it had been the other way round, I shouldn't like to be so positive."

"Why do you say that, Mrs. Doubleday?"

"Because, for all his pleasant manners, Mr. Tudor had a very hot temper. I once saw him knock a man down with very small excuse. The man scrambled to his feet and attacked him, and Mr. Tudor knocked him down again. It happened outside here and I saw it all from the window."

"How had the man offended him?"

"He'd been ill-treating an 'orse" she was overcome by a ladylike cough—"a *h*orse."

"So you meant nothing more by your remark than that Mr. Tudor was more headstrong than Mr. Ridpath?"

"That's it. Mr. Ridpath is too easy-going to kill anybody. You've got to be firm-willed to commit murder."

The inspector went off at a tangent.

"I enjoyed my little chat with Hobson. A very amusing talker. Has he been with you long?"

"Nearly three years."

"You're lucky to keep the services of such an obliging, respectable man."

Mrs. Doubleday seemed not over-keen to discuss her employee, and merely nodded.

"Is he married?"

"Yes, but his poor wife suffers from some mental disorder and has to be kept under restraint. A hopeless case, yet Hobson manages to keep cheerful."

"Very sad," he agreed. "Now, can you tell me if, at six-thirty yesterday evening, you heard somebody on the first floor shout 'Get out!'?"

She looked aggrieved. Vulgar vociferation was out of place in Eagle House.

"Definitely not. I was down in the kitchen, superintending the preparation of dinner."

"In the same way," he smiled, "as you should now be seeing about lunch! I mustn't detain you any longer. If we may, my sergeant and I will wait downstairs until Miss Ashwin and the others arrive."

Her relief at this dismissal was manifest; and she left them to follow at their leisure.

There was an alert brain beneath Bert Martin's sandy poll. As they reached the first-floor landing, he laid a restraining hand on Charlton's arm.

"Sometimes," he said, "when there's a session in the House of Commons, the door says 'Vacant' when it ought to say 'Engaged' and very often those inside don't fancy being intruded on."

"There are times, Sergeant," answered Charlton, changing his direction, "when I discern in you some faint glimmerings of intelligence."

"It's all the fish I eat," explained Martin.

Nothing was wrong with the lock on the door at the end of the passage in the east wing.

"But they might 'ave forgotten to fasten it," was the sergeant's suggestion. "And if you don't think that's enough reason for yelling 'Get out!' how about Miss Brown and Mr. Smith, that took care to book separate rooms? Mightn't Miss Brown 'ave invited Mr. Smith in to see 'er collection of fag-pictures?"

The inspector looked at him sadly.

"You think of all the worst things," he complained.

Martin was sent off with a list of instructions that included getting Miss Jones's fingerprints, arranging for Tudor's parents to be informed of his death, obtaining the co-operation of Sergeant Peters, the fingerprint man at Whitchester headquarters, sending the fragments of wool and the strip of linoleum to the police laboratory in London, checking the previous night's movements of all vagrants in the neighbourhood of Lulverton, and persuading Peter Ridpath to leave the disreputable purlieus of Back Eldon Street and return to Lulverton for a fireside chat with Inspector Charlton.

"'Ow would you like me to spend my spare time?" he asked before he left.

"Questioning witnesses," Charlton told him sweetly. "There are about forty."

"Blimey!" said Martin. "What do you take me for—a perishing 'orse?" He coughed falsetto, then came down with a thump on the aspirate: "Horse?"

With which, with his bowler hat set at a jaunty angle, he went off to find Detective-Constables Bradfield, Emerson and Hartley, who were unobtrusively playing odd-man-out for a penny a time in a quiet corner of Lulverton police station.

Jack Gough was the first to arrive for lunch. He and Charlton were already acquainted, having met each other professionally in the course of the detective's enquiries in the matter of some forged banknotes. Gough talked freely, as if to an old friend.

"Poor old Vaughan," he said. "I'd like to catch the swine who did it. Is there any definite clue?"

"Tell me about last night," Charlton invited him. "Who was in the theatre when you left it?"

"That I can't say. I came away with Myrna—Miss Ashwin and Mr. Mortimer Robinson, our treasurer. There was a general stampede home round about eleven o'clock and I didn't really notice who went where. I do know that Vaughan was intending to stop behind."

"To get on with his secret opus, I suppose?" Jack looked at him sharply, but Charlton's handsome face displayed only polite interest.

"Some little bird's been busy," said Jack. "Yes, I expect that was his idea."

"What was the secret opus?"

"Nobody really knows, though the popular guess is that he was writing a book. We pulled his leg about it, but all he did was grin. He used to work late on it at the Bakehouse, but I've never seen the manuscript."

"What was the state of affairs at the rehearsal last night?"
"Oh, it was a fearful mess-up! I won't give you the whole grim story, but they were all at each other's throats. Nerves, chiefly. Even dear old Mortimer Robinson, who wouldn't normally say Boo! to a goose, jumped on me for a little bit of leg-pulling."

"You noticed nothing that might have had some bearing on what followed?"

"Good Lord, no! It's always the same at dress rehearsals.

Everyone's convinced that the show's going to be a complete flop—and, in consequence, is thoroughly unpleasant to everyone else. But as for it leading to murder ..."

One of the weapons in Charlton's armoury was the unexpected question.

"Do you think," he now asked, "that Miss Faggott would have made Tudor a good wife?"

Jack looked startled, then his ugly young face grew stern.

"No, I don't," he said abruptly.

"Why not? Because she wanted to play Lady Macbeth?"

"That was clever of you, Inspector. Yes, ambition may be the main trouble with her. She wants to become a famous actress and doesn't much mind whose toes she treads on in the process. And I wouldn't mind betting she succeeds. She's darned attractive, you know. For anyone looking for a combination of La Gioconda, Helen of Troy and Lucrezia Borgia, she's the very thing. Poor old Vaughan was flat out after her—and she led him right up the garden."

"Why?"

"Well, for one thing, he was secretary of the dramatic society—and a famous actress has got to start somewhere, even if it is only in the LADS. Then he had a friend called Philip Pearson, who's something of a somebody in Fleet Street. He could always be persuaded by Vaughan to splash half a column, in a paper that really matters, on that brilliant young amateur, Elizabeth Faggott, whom discerning critics have already, etc. etc. And money. Vaughan was fairly well off—and hard cash always comes in useful."

"Somebody was telling me that Tudor had to share her favours with a man called Ridpath."

There was a subtle change in Jack's manner. Charlton never missed a thing like that.

"Are all these random remarks of mine going to be repeated in a sing-song voice in court?" Jack asked casually. " 'The witness then deposed'—and so forth?"

"I can't promise they won't be," was as far as the inspector was ready to go. "You needn't say another word if you don't want to, although"—he smiled—"I'm very interested in the events leading up to last night."

"I'll spill it, then. Mind you, Inspector, I'm accusing nobody. I can give you no direct evidence at all. But dear old Vaughan was the salt of the earth"—his wide mouth quivered and he went on with a brittle flippancy—"and if a few remarks from Our Special Correspondent will be welcomed, you shall have them. Ridpath, in my opinion, is a species of beautiful fungus. He's a very pretty young gentleman and irresistible to women when he revs up the charm. But he poisons everything he touches—and it sometimes needs a fairly powerful antidote. Now, your business is to ask questions, and one of the things you're certain to be told, if you don't know already, is that—is that. .."

He floundered and Charlton helped him out.

"I do know," he said.

"Then we won't pursue it. I want you to understand, though, that this is not just sour grapes."

"Please go on," Charlton suggested.

"We in the society have known for some time that Vaughan was in love with *La* Faggott, yet I don't think he realised it himself until quite recently. Dumb adoration describes his attitude, but as Elizabeth Faggott gave him every shy encouragement, he wasn't likely to be tongue-tied for ever—and we were all looking forward quite happily to wedding bells. At the beginning of last summer, Ridpath turned up from nowhere, very down-at-heel and—dangerously furtive, like those fellows who step up to you in the Strand with, 'I say, old man, I'm in a dreadful hole.' With money borrowed from Vaughan, who was always too generous, he soon turned himself into the glass of fashion and the mould of form; and began to preen himself and cast a speculative eye over the female population of Lulverton. We won't discuss his other cheap conquests, but keep to Elizabeth. She fell under the hammer some time in August. Where they first met, I don't know, because he wasn't then a member of the LADS.

"They thought they were keeping it a dead secret, but everyone knew except Vaughan and—one other person. Nobody was very pleased, for it would hurt Vaughan, probably the most popular fellow in the LADS, and because Ridpath was already deeply involved with—this other person."

"The girl in the cigarette-kiosk at the station?" asked Charlton as if he meant it.

Jack looked surprised.

"What, Molly, the old men's darling? I didn't know he'd

staked a claim there. He gets about, doesn't he? No, it wasn't Molly. Let's say he was already deeply involved with a girl called—Mary Smith. The new intrigue with Elizabeth didn't put an end to the old association with Mary Smith, which continued on a semi-official basis, while simultaneously he was meeting Elizabeth under the cover of night or any other suitable concealment."

"Did Miss Faggott know about Mary Smith?"

"Of course!" answered Jack, adding bitterly: "Everyone did. Yet, for all that, she carried on a clandestine affair with Ridpath."

"Can you suggest why?"

"She couldn't resist a pretty face, I suppose. Or perhaps she thought she could use him to further her career as a great actress. One thing's certain: Ridpath fell for her in a big way. It was probably the only genuine sentiment he ever felt for a girl. She can do that to a man, you know. I'll admit, in confidence, that even though I'm permanently fixed up elsewhere, she sometimes plays merry hell with my better judgment. She manages to give the idea, without actually putting it into words, that you're the Big Shot and she doesn't know what she'd do without you. I think she must have discovered the secret of perpetual emotion. She's a glad hand specialist. Sympathy, sweet reasonableness, and appreciation of manly virtues may be only a part of her stock-in-trade, but Golly she knows how to dress the window!"

Charlton smiled. In a world of humdrum talk, Jack's conversation was a sparkling tonic. . . . "Which, like the toad . . . wears a precious jewel in his head." There were some words in between that he could not remember—"ugly and something or other." His smile died at Jack's next words.

"Last Saturday afternoon, the Faggott gave Ridpath his marching orders."

"Did she? Are you sure?"

"Well, I wasn't on the spot when it happened, but he was bright and cheerful enough in the morning and Public

Misery No. 1 in the evening."

"So you consider that Miss Faggott had finally chosen between Ridpath and Tudor?"

"No, I wouldn't go as far as that, Inspector. I certainly think Ridpath got the ancient order of the boot, but on Sunday afternoon Vaughan took Elizabeth for a spin in his car—and he wasn't looking too happy when he got back. Mind you, it's only conjecture. ... I believe she'd a third string to her bow— quite a new addition."

"Will you tell me his name?"

Jack gave an awkward laugh.

"I don't much fancy playing squeaker like this," he admitted. "His name is Duzest—Franklin Duzest, and he was to play one of the leading parts in 'Measure for Measure.'"

"Angleo?"

"Yes. It isn't my custom to snoop, but lately at rehearsals, I've noticed a tendency for the two of them to gravitate towards each other. On Saturday evening, I saw them having a real heart-to-hearter that was broken up by Vaughan, as soon as he became aware of it. But you mustn't attach too much importance to this, Inspector, for I may be mistaken. Their parts in the play threw them together a lot."

Charlton pulled out his note-book.

"I've got to get a full list," he explained, "of everyone at the theatre last night. Will you give me all the names and addresses you can remember?"

The details took some time to write down. As Charlton put the book away, he said:

"Now, there are two more points—and then I've finished with you. The first: where were you at half-past six yesterday evening?"

Jack thought for a moment. "In my room. Dinner was timed for a quarter to seven—early because of the rehearsal —and I was finishing off a letter to the aged parents that I started a fortnight ago, so that I could post it on the way to the Bakehouse."

"Did anyone interrupt you while you were writing it?"
Jack shook his head.

"Then did you hear someone shout, 'Get out!'?"

The question was met by a crooked smile.

"What you're trying to get at is whether I had a row with
Vaughan and finished by ejecting him on his ear. Isn't that it?
No, nothing of the sort happened. Vaughan was a very good
friend of mine. If anyone told him to get out, it wasn't me—
and I didn't hear it."

"Nobody walked past your door at about six-thirty?"

"They may have done. I didn't notice. Letter-writing is not
my strong point and I was in the throes of composition."

"Right. That's the first point. Now for the second. Just
after eleven o'clock last night, you came back from the Little
Theatre with Miss Ashwin and Mr. Mortimer Robinson. At
a quarter to twelve, you went out again. Where did you go?"

"If I may say so, Inspector, you haven't wasted any time! I
went back to the Bakehouse."

"Why?"

"Myrna and I were anxious about Vaughan. The old fellow
had been pretty depressed for the last few days and we didn't
like the idea of him brooding by himself in the Bakehouse
half the night. So Myrna suggested that I should pop round
and persuade him to come home."

"You saw him?"

"No. When I got to the Bakehouse, the door was locked,
from which I gathered that Vaughan had already left. But
to make absolutely sure, I knocked several times and then
shouted through the letter-box. I must have kicked up a bit
of a row, because somebody jerked up a window and rather
testily invited me to make a little less noise, so that respectable
people could get some sleep."

"That was from a window overlooking Cooper's Yard, I
take it?"

"Yes, a back window over the pawnbroker's shop. I
expect you know it? The peevish gentleman's name is Aaron

Sugarman and he and I do business of a strictly confidential nature from time to time, especially towards the end of the month. So when I got a chance to interrupt the lamentations of Judah and apologise for the disturbance, he recognised my voice. I told him that I'd come back to find Mr. Tudor and he said that, a minute or so before I arrived, he'd heard someone close the door of the Bakehouse and walk out through the Yard into Harpur Street. I reckoned it must have been Vaughan, apologised again to old Sugarman, and came back here. If you're interested in times, the clocks were striking midnight, one after the other, while I was on my way."

"Was the staircase lighted when you looked through the letter-box?"

"It's impossible to say. There's only a low-powered blue lamp—and, of course, the black-out curtains."

"And when you reached here?"

"Miss Ashwin was waiting for me. I asked her whether she'd heard Vaughan come in. She said she hadn't and we decided that he must have gone for a walk. About a quarter of an hour later, we both went up to bed."

"Not bothering any more about Mr. Tudor?"

"Well, we did knock on his door, but of course he wasn't there."

"You didn't go in?"

"No. I opened the door, found the switch and poked my nose in the room . . . To be absolutely candid with you, Inspector, although earlier on I'd been concerned about Vaughan, at that particular moment he didn't seem very important, ... As a matter of fact, I'd . . . made the pleasant discovery that, after starting at something like 100 to 6 and then being badly away, I'd sailed past the judge's box with three lengths to spare, so, as I say, at that particular moment. . . "

Charlton, who liked Jack Gough, offered sincere congratulations, then asked when Myrna Ashwin would be in for lunch.

"Soon after one o'clock," Jack told him. "I have to take

mine early."

Charlton felt for his watch, remembered he had left it at home and glanced at the clock on the mantelpiece.

"That's five or six minutes fast," Jack said.

"Then I'll come back in about half an hour. Perhaps you'll tell Miss Ashwin and Mr. Mortimer Robinson to expect me."

He got to his feet and looked down at Jack.

"Was Miss Boyson deliberately pushed down the stairs?" he asked carelessly.

"It was an accident," was the quick reply. "There were a lot of people there at the time and she got jostled."

"Who was nearest to her?"

"I wasn't there, so I can't tell you."

"And how far is the ten-pound note concerned in the death of Mr. Tudor?"

"The what? Oh, that. Very little, I imagine, but somebody was out to make trouble."

"Who?"

Jack rose from his chair.

"If you don't mind, I'd rather not say."

"Has Mr. Manhow recovered from his injury?"

"Yes, his nose has gone back to more or less its normal shape."

"How did it happen?"

"His version is that he bumped into the sideboard."

"Curiously enough, Mr. Ridpath fell foul of his wardrobe on the same evening. I wonder whether the two pieces of furniture were of the same period?"

Jack looked blank for a moment, then caught the inspector's meaning.

"Shall we call it Queen Anne?" he suggested.

There is an inelegant type of crudely coloured picture-postcard that can be obtained in sea-side towns and sent to less leisured, but equally broadminded, friends at home. Apart from the fat woman in the small rowing-boat, the intoxicated gentleman with a beer bottle sticking from his pocket, and the girl who has been provided by the artist with an excuse for falling backwards, perhaps the most familiar figure on these cards is the elderly Jewish pawnbroker with an enormous waistcoat, standing beneath the sign of the three brass balls. One has only to remember this representation—and who can deny having paused in the Arcade, between the sun-hats and the shrimping-nets, and given a stealthy turn to the revolving stand?—to get an instant picture of Mr. Aaron Sugarman.

When he found that the tall, distinguished stranger who faced him across the glass-topped counter did not come as a customer, most of Mr. Sugarman's first enthusiasm cooled, but he answered the inspector's questions readily enough, though with an abstraction that suggested he had not entirely given up hope of interesting his well-dressed visitor in his extensive range of unredeemed pledges.

"You know Mr. Gough?" Charlton began.

"Vy, yes. He is a good customer of mine."

"Did you speak to him last night?"

"Yes, from my bedroom vindow."

"At what time?"

"Midnight almost. Vit his hangings and shoutings, he vas keeping respectable peoples avake."

"You told him, I believe, that somebody had left the theatre just before he arrived?"

"That vas so."

"How long before?"

"Perhaps a minute. I do not know for a certainty. All the evening, they had made noises enough to vake the dead, and me and my poor vife ve get no vink of sleeps till the amateur dramaticals vas finished and they all go home. Then for a little vile, there vas peacefulness and qviet; and my vife at my side she drops off into sleeps, vit me, vot had done a hard day's vork by the shop, vide avake and turning in the bed from this vay to the other. After a little vile, I hear footprints coming into Cooper's Yard. They go along and under the archvay. I listen to the door, vich vas loose by its lock, shaken vit the owner of the footprints; then the jingle of keys on a ring. Then the door vas closed vit a bang."

"What time was that?"

Mr. Sugarman threw out his jewelled hands.

"By my life!" he wailed. "It is alvays the same vit the police! Alvays, 'Vat time is it?' An honest man can bear vitnesses that he vas there, on the spot, vatching vit all his eyes open, ven the robbery by the safe or the murderous crime vas taking place, and he knows the name of the man vat he saw did it; and vat does he get for his troubles? Does he get vun vord of t'anks? Oh, no, no! All the police say to him is, '*Vat time is it?*' "

"I'm sorry," smiled Charlton, "but it's sometimes important."

The little pawnbroker went off the boil.

"Then I'll tell you ven it was. Now, it vas tvelve o'clock nearly ven Mr. Gough arrives. These utter footprints vas about a little vile under a qvarter of an hour before. There vas utter comings and goings that I listen to in between."

By no sign did Charlton show his quickened interest. "Oh? Please tell me about them." "A little vile after—"

"How long?" asked Charlton patiently; and Mr. Sugarman again bubbled over.

"Ven, ven, ven! I am a business man, not a stop-vatch! A little vile—some times later—two or free minutes, some body slams a door, not shut, but like it goes back and hits the vail or somet'ings. I t'ink it is the stage-door, somehow. Then a man's voice yells out, 'Murder!' and the—"

"Yelled out *what!*"

" 'Murder!' It vas murder that vas done, ain't it?"

"How would you describe this shout? Did it suggest terror or anger or that it was meant as a joke?"

"It vas no joke by me, I tell you! It did not suggest anyt'ings to me but that a man yells out, 'Murder!' and ven a man yells out 'Murder!' he don't mean it as a joke. Oh, no!"

Charlton left it at that; it was too much like hard work.

"What did you do when you heard the shout?"

Mr. Sugarman looked surprised and laid thick fingers on his chest.

"Me? Vat did *I* do? Vy, not'ings. If it vas trouble in my own house, I send my vife for the police, but outside, it ain't no businesses of mine. How do I know they don't yell 'Murder!' to get me out in the Yard and steal from me? Oh, no, no! I done not'ings but stop vere I vas. After a vile"—he looked quickly at Charlton—"a qvarter of a minute later, the door was closed shut."

"Which door?"

"The small stage-door. It is nearer to me than the utter door and not made of such heavy, t'ick voods."

"After it slammed open, did you hear anyone leave the Yard—I mean immediately after?"

"No, there vas no footprints just then, unless they valk very qvietly. For five—maybe six more minutes, all is peace, and I am just dropping off into sleeps like an innocent little child, ven suddenly I listen to more footprints coming into the Yard from the street. I do not hear if they go under the archvay. I vait for a door to be opened, but if it is, I don't hear it and anutter minute goes past before the foot prints come back and out into the street. I call it four minutes aftervards ven I *do* hear the big door pulled to, but not so loud as formerly. Then the utter fellow follows the first fellow into the street. And a minute later, I am listening to Mr. Gough's arriving footprints. Ven he starts into his shoutings, I jump out of bed and open the vindow in order for some complaints. 'On my son's life! I say by him. Vit your hangings and shoutings, you're — "

"I don't think you need repeat the whole conversation, Mr. Sugarman."

"Veil, Mr. Gough he apologises and after ve say good night, I pull down the vindow, go back into bed by the side of my vife, and am sound asleep in the tvinkling of a trice."

"That," concluded Mr. Sugarman, with a sweeping gesture of finality, "vas all the comings and goings I listened to."

"Would you say from the footsteps, Mr. Sugarman, that any

of these visitors were women?"

Again the spread fingers on the chest.

"Me? How should *I* know?"

"Well, a woman has usually a lighter tread than a man and often she walks more quickly."

Mr. Sugarman waved his arms about.

"You come to me vit too many qvestions," he cried. "I hear the footprints. I vant to help the police all I can, so I tell you vit the footprints. By my life, you ask too many qvestions. How can tell if a footprint is muscular or effeminate. A footprint is a footprint and ven I listen to footprints, I—"

"Then I won't worry you any further, Mr. Sugarman. Fm much obliged to you for your help."

He slipped his fingers in his waistcoat pocket, then recalled that he was without his watch.

"Can you tell me the time, please?" he asked politely.

The reply was high-pitched and plaintive.

"Vat, *again!*"

The first person he met when he got back to the Guest House was Sergeant Martin, whose face was fraught with news.

"When we went to the office to take Miss Jones's finger-prints," he said, "she told me that five minutes after you and me left, a bloke she didn't know from Adam called in a car and asked to 'ave a decker through Tudor's papers."

"Naturally she didn't let him."

"Oh, yes, she did! He was all dolled up like a Cabinet Minister and said 'e represented Messrs. Golightly & Farthingale, the executors' solicitors, and the Jones girl gave him the freedom of the city."

"What on earth made her do that?"

"She said it was Thursday, the fourth, a day for quick decisions against the dictates of prudence; and she added that I was born under the influence of Saturn in the third decanus of Sagittarius, which means a glutton for work, but showing too much servility to superiors."

"I haven't noticed it," growled Charlton. "This chap nosed around for five minutes or so and then asked Miss Jones what she knew about a thick wad of typescript. Remembering that you'd put 'er the selfsame question, she at once got suspicious. The chap saw the red light, wished 'er an 'asty good-morning and was outside and off in the car before she could do anything. She didn't get the number of the car, or even the make, but we've put through a general call, in the hope of picking him up."

"Very curious, Martin, and a bit disturbing. I'd formed the impression that this was one of those tidy little crimes, with everybody neatly labelled. But now strange men start dashing about in cars, it's going to make things more difficult."

"P'raps 'e was acting as agent for young Ridpath, who hired 'im to get hold of the typescript, because there was something in it Ridpath didn't want us to know."

"I hope you're right."

XV

I hope here be truths,
Act II, Sc. 1.

Inspector Charlton has said that real crime detection lies not in the microscope and test-tube, but in asking innumerable questions and weeding out the answers. It follows, therefore, that in compiling a faithful record of a murder case in which many persons play a part, it is possible to become "compassed about with so great a cloud of witnesses," that each fresh interrogation is, in the main, a reiteration of those that have gone before. For all that, the student must be given full opportunity to sift the evidence for himself; and it is not for the biographer to exclude facts and conversations, on the plea of avoiding tedious repetition.

To get round this difficulty, the questioning by Charlton

and his assistants of the remaining witnesses has been reduced to tabloid dimensions. It must be taken for granted that the talks took place in various homes and offices; that some witnesses were frank, while others were reserved; that some were grieved at Tudor's death and some indifferent; that all were asked about the secret opus, where they had last seen the dagger and whether they had returned to the Bakehouse; that all were invited to establish alibis; and that two of them lied, one foolishly and unnecessarily, and a third did not tell the whole truth.

Every story was checked and tested against another, until Charlton had a complete account of the dress rehearsal and an accurate list of all the persons present. Nothing of any consequence has been omitted, the answers having been merely partially sorted out; and when Charlton had completed the analysis, hunted down the secret opus, read it once—and then again more thoroughly—and had carried out a search in a certain place, he had a complete case to lay before the director of public prosecutions.

Here, then, are the depositions:—

Miss Myrna Ashwin

"I came home with Mr. Gough and Mr. Mortimer Robinson. We left Mr. Tudor behind. He said he would be coming along later. When Mr. Mortimer Robinson had gone up to bed, Mr. Gough and I sat talking till quarter to twelve. Then Mr. Gough said he was rather anxious about Mr. Tudor and I suggested that he went round to the theatre to fetch him home. Mr. Gough came back alone at about five past twelve. The theatre had been all locked up and we decided that Mr. Tudor had gone for a walk."

"Yes, Mr. Gough switched on the light and put his bead round the door. Afterwards, we stood talking on the landing for about ten minutes, then said good night and went along to our rooms."

"The banknote? No, the only thing I know is that when Mr. Tudor told us it had been lost, we all had a look for it; and Mr. Cheesewright and I searched every inch of the cloakroom without finding it. Yet later on, Mr. Duzest discovered it there."

"How did it happen, Miss Ashwin, that Miss Faggott gave up the principal part in favour of Miss Boyson?"

"Well, it was very curious, really. One of the people living here is a Mr. Garnett, whose daughter is married to one of the departmental managers at the rubber-heel factory. I expect you know that Mr. Boyson, Hilary Boyson's father, is managing director of the company. Mr. Garnett is the owner of the Bakehouse and, so as to get his son-in-law in the good books of Mr. Boyson, he forced us, by threatening to throw us out, to take the Isabella part away from Elizabeth Faggott and give it to Hilary Boyson. This son-in-law of Mr. Garnett—I believe his name's Saunderson—is very keen to be made works manager. The present works manager is on the point of retiring and the idea was that if the Saunderson man went to Mr. Boyson and said, 'I'm glad to tell you, sir, that I've been able to get Miss Hilary put at the top of the cast,' Mr. Boyson would be so delighted that he would make him works manager there and then."

"Rather an optimist, wasn't he?"

"That's what we said and we refused Mr. Garnett at first, but he immediately gave us notice to quit, so then we had to do what he wanted. He did agree that, if Hilary Boyson fell ill or refused to take the part, it wouldn't be our fault."

"So if she'd seriously injured herself on the staircase, the notice would not have been enforced and Miss Faggott would have been able to regain the lead?"

She gave him a quick glance.

"Yes," she agreed, and it was left at that.

"No, at six-thirty, I was out. I got back just in time for dinner at quarter to seven."

"Were you on friendly terms with Mr. Ridpath?"

"Yes, I liked him very much."

"You were once engaged to him, weren't you?"

"Oh, no! I used to go out with him a good deal, but we were never engaged."

"Why did you stop going out with him, Miss Ashwin?"

"Because it was decided to break off the—friendship."

"Who made the decision?"

"I did."

"Why?"

"Because we were unsuited."

"Was that the only reason? ... I said, was that the only reason?"

"No; there was another."

"May I know it, please?"

"Really, Mr. Charlton, I don't see what this has got to do with the murder!"

"Let me be the best judge of that, Miss Ashwin. Why did you dismiss Mr. Ridpath?"

Her pretty little face went very red.

"I absolutely refuse to tell you! If you really want to know, ask Mrs. Cheesewright."

Hubert Mortimer Robinson

"Noticing that I was somewhat *de trop,* I left the young people in the lounge and went up to bed. I understand from Mr. Gough that later on he returned to the theatre; and I can quite appreciate the anxiety felt by him and Miss Ashwin.

Poor young Tudor was in a very dejected frame of mind yesterday. They say the onlooker sees most of the game, Inspector, and I have been following his courtship of Miss Faggott with great interest. Unfortunately, there seems little doubt that last week-end they had a disagreement. Mr. Tudor has not since been his usual pleasant self, and I noticed yesterday evening that nothing more than conventional remarks passed between them."

"Do you know of any reason for this disagreement?"

"No, Inspector, it came as a surprise to me. I can only think that it was a lovers' quarrel."

"Would you have been pleased to hear of their engagement?"

"I should have been delighted, just as I was this morning, when Miss Ashwin told me that she had accepted Mr. Gough. Miss Faggott is a very charming young lady. If I were a younger man ..."

His grey eyes twinkled.

"Do you know if she had other attachments?"

"There have been certain malicious rumours, but I ask you not to believe them. A girl of Miss Faggott's attractions is always the victim of slander, especially in a small country town like Lulverton. She has only to pause in the street to chat with a casual male acquaintance, for their names to be linked by the busybodies."

"What is your opinion of Mr. Ridpath?"

"He is an extremely pleasant young fellow, but has, I fear, too great a fondness of the other sex. There is no serious intention behind his trifling, yet it causes considerable distress to the objects of his attention, who assume him to be more earnest than he really is."

"You imagine he's never had a—well, the French call it *grande passion.*"

Mr. Mortimer Robinson shook his head with decision.

"I am certain not, Inspector. All his love-making was completely superficial."

"Why was Tudor murdered?"

"The only theory I can advance is that the unfortunate young man was surprised by some wandering tramp, who had slipped into the theatre to see what he could steal. The door would have been open until Mr. Tudor finally locked up for the night."

"I understand that you are the society's treasurer, Mr. Robinson."

"*Mortimer* Robinson," was the gentle amendment, "without

a hyphen. There are so many plain Robinsons. Yes, I am treasurer. The society has an account with the Southern Counties Bank, though not a very large one, I'm afraid."

"Was any cash held in the theatre?"

"A small amount—a couple of pounds, at the most."

"Where was it kept?"

"In a cigarette tin in a locked drawer of a table in the box-office. Had it been tampered with?"

"Who holds keys of the drawer?"

"Mr. Tudor, Miss Ashwin, who is ticket secretary and myself. If I remember rightly, when I checked the balance on Tuesday evening, there was a pound note and eighteen shillings and sixpence in silver in the tin. Was it intact when you examined it?"

Charlton's disregard of other people's questions would have seemed uncivil had it not been so genial.

"And keys of the theatre—who holds those?"

"I am not sure. There were several cut. Mr. Tudor, I know, had one; Mr. Manhow another; and Mrs. Mudge, the cleaner, a third. I have one myself, but who holds the others, I don't know. I can, of course, find out for you, if you wish?"

"Please do."

"Where were you at half-past six yesterday evening?"

"To the best of my recollection, in my bedroom."

"I suppose you didn't shout, 'Get out!' at anybody?"

"That doesn't sound very polite! No, I certainly didn't."

"You heard nobody else say it?"

The neat little man shook his head.

PATRICK COLLINGWOOD

"I understand," said Charlton, "that, in the ordinary way, daggers are not supplied with the costumes for 'Measure for Measure.' Was this one specially ordered?"

"Yes. Peter Ridpath, who was going to take the Lucio part, suggested having it for a few bits of humorous by-play."

"Did they justify the trouble of getting it down from London?"

Pat Collingwood shrugged his broad shoulders.

"Not really, but Ridpath was set on it, so I agreed."

"But he left Lulverton before it arrived from the costumiers."

"Yes, he went on Sunday morning and the costumes didn't reach here until Tuesday."

"Can you tell me what happened to the dagger last night?"

"'Fraid I didn't notice. Ridpath's successor, a man called Nash, used it for the rehearsal, so I suppose he left it on his peg in the men's dressing-room."

"Who still remained in the theatre when you left?"

"I was one of the last to go. My daughter, Felicity, who's in the cast, and a fellow called Duzest, were with me. The three of us had got into a heated argument about Hamlet—whether he was a clever schemer or just a silly idiot—and we hadn't noticed that everybody else had gone home. Tudor had shut himself in the box-office and was busy with his typewriter. By ten-past eleven we still hadn't reached agreement about Hamlet, so I called off the fight. I went across to the box-office and pushed my head round the door to say good night to Tudor. He looked rather—well, not exactly guilty, but as if he didn't want us to see what he was up to. Felicity and Duzest had come up behind me and I got jostled into the box-office, though Tudor was obviously not very pleased to have us. He pulled the sheet on which he was working out of the machine and laid it face downwards on the desk."

"Was the sheet ready to come out—that is, had he reached the bottom of it?"

"I should say yes. It only seemed to need a flick to free it from the typewriter. We chatted with him on this and that for a couple of minutes, then I asked him if we were sold out for all performances. 'Yes,' he said, 'and that reminds me. I must do it before I forget.' He took a sheet of LADS letter-paper from the drawer of the desk and slipped it into the machine."

"Did he use the backing-sheet?"

"No, that was left with the other page. Tudor typed a notice to the effect that we were sold out, removed it from the machine and signed it."

"With a fountain-pen?"

"No, he got up and took the notice across to the table, on which there was an ordinary pen and a bottle of ink."

"He typed the notice in red, didn't he?"

Collingwood looked at him with an expression of humorous admiration.

"Great one for detail, aren't you?" he said. "Yes, Tudor switched the little gadget on the machine across, just before he started typing, saying that people might take the trouble to read it, if it was written in red. My daughter asked where he was going to display the notice. 'Downstairs on the door,' he said; and she offered to pin it up on our way out. Just in case you want to know"—there was a smile on his big, good-natured face—"the drawing-pin was supplied by Tudor from a small box that he produced from the desk. My daughter fixed the notice in position when we left very shortly afterwards."

"Did Tudor give you the impression that he was going to stay at the theatre for some time?"

"Yes. I urged him to go home and get some sleep, as we'd a heavy day in front of us, but he said he'd some arrears of work to make up."

"What kind of work?"

"He didn't say."

"Had he any typescript—about two hundred pages— either loose or in a binder, with him?"

"If he had, it was tucked away somewhere. I didn't see it."

"And you left him sitting at the typewriter?"

"No. The last I saw of him was in the chair at the table. We've had several changes in the cast during the last day or so, and he was going to alter the programmes. Felicity and I offered to stay and help, but he appeared only too anxious to get rid of us. So we went."

"And Mr. Duzest accompanied you?"

"Yes."

"Elizabeth Faggott, Inspector, is one of the most promising young actresses I have ever seen. I've been mixed up with the stage for twenty-five years, and reckon I can pick out the winners. Given an opportunity, she'll go a long way."

"And Miss Boyson?"

"A very nice girl, but . . ."

He shook his head regretfully and, like Humpty Dumpty, left it at that.

(Felicity Collingwood confirmed her father's evidence.)

FRANKLIN DUZEST

"I'm sure there was no one except Tudor in the Bakehouse, when I left with Collingwood and his daughter."

"Did you walk home with them?"

"Only as far as the end of Friday Street; then they went one way and I the other."

"Where did you go after leaving them?"

"Straight home, then, after a quick night-cap, to bed."

"Miss Faggott, I take it, had gone earlier?"

"Yes, I think she went off with Miss Lark. They live quite close to each other."

"You arrived for the rehearsal some time before the others, didn't you?"

Duzest tapped a cigarette on his expensive case.

"Who told you that?"

"A man called Hobson. You borrowed his key."

"Quite right. I was out of Lulverton on Tuesday, which didn't give me an opportunity to see if my costume fitted properly. So I got a key from Hobson and went along early."

MICHAEL KELSO (to P.C. Bradfield)

(Michael Kelso. Cast for the parts of Friar Thomas and Barnardine, the drunken prisoner. Freelance journalist and book-reviewer. "Amicus Curiae" of the *Daily Post*. Tall, young and untidy, with horn-rimmed glasses mended across the bridge with adhesive cellophane. A voracious reader, a keen student of international diplomacy, a mobile information bureau and a redhot Socialist.)

"Only one thing strikes me as strange. During a lull in the proceedings last night, Tudor got chatting with me, and casually brought up the subject of the fifth column. He asked, first of all, whether I thought we ran the same danger here as they did in Poland. I told him I didn't think so, as we've no German minority, which is only a prettier name for a subversive element. Then Tudor said he expected we had a special government department to keep an eye on such matters. I said, 'You bet we have!' and told him all I knew about the Intelligence boys who call themselves M.I.5. He said he supposed they were fairly inaccessible. I laughed and said you wouldn't find them listed in the telephone directory, but that if he'd caught a fifth columnist in *flagrante delicto,* as it were, he'd better have a quiet word with somebody in authority at the nearest police station.

"This didn't seem to be all he wanted to know, for he said he'd heard that fifth columnists had been found in all sorts of disguises. I said, 'Naturally—that's a part of the game: army officers, railway officials, A.R.P. wardens—any sort of get-up is to be anticipated.' I told him that the ordinary civilian diversionist usually keeps a brassard or armlet ready for emergency use, so as to avoid getting shot when the Hun contingents arrive. If invasion is imminent, I said, they wear them underneath their overcoats or mackintoshes.

"I asked him jokingly if he'd unmasked one of the species and he hastily denied that his questions were prompted by anything more than idle curiosity; and as we were interrupted just then by Franklin Duzest, who'd been standing near us, talking to Mortimer Robinson and Stewart McIver, the conversation turned to other things."

FREDERICK CHEESEWRIGHT (to Sergeant Martin)

"I am fully prepared to state on oath in the witness-box, Sergeant, that when I examined it with Miss Ashwin, there was no bank-note on the cloak-room floor. No bank-note on the floor. We went over every inch of it. Every inch of it."

"The whole floor?" Martin asked, just to make sure.

"The whole floor. Yes, the whole floor."

Martin debated whether to enquire about the ceiling, but decided against it.

MRS. CHEESEWRIGHT

"Yesterday mornng, I was in the Post Office at the same time as Mr. Tudor. He was sending off a registered letter. What it contained, of course, I don't know, but the envelope was of quarto size and fairly thick."

"Did you see the address on it?"

"No, I wasn't able—that is to say, I didn't notice."

"It is hardly my place to tell you, Mr. Charlton, but I feel it my duty to say that this Faggott girl's personal conduct has not been beyond reproach. Men—especially handsome ones—have a great attraction for her. It is common knowledge that she has been in the habit of going away for weekends with a young friend of Mr. Tudor's named Peter Ridpath—a dangerously good-looking young man, who receives letters regularly from Italy and is probably a Fascist supporter, which is most unpatriotic, with that country already virtually at war with us. It is most significant that both disappeared on Boxing Day and were not seen again in Lulverton until the following morning. Mr. Tudor seemed very attached to this Faggott girl and I was very sorry to see such a nice young man throwing himself away on a"—she paused before adding defiantly—"woman of easy virtue."

"That is a serious charge against Miss Faggott," Charlton said. "Can you support it?"

"With the most conclusive proof. A Mrs. Manderville, with whom I play bridge every Tuesday, went to stay last September with some friends in Guildford—(Guildford again, thought Charlton)—and she happened to catch sight of the Faggott girl going with this Ridpath into a hotel. He was carrying two suit-cases, and when Mrs. Manderville caused enquiries to be made at the reception desk, it was found that they had signed the visitors' book as man and wife."

"May I have Mrs. Manderville's address?" he asked.

This sounded like something more than idle gossip.

MRS. MANDERVILLE (to Sergeant Martin)

"Yes, that is quite correct. They signed the visitors book as Mr. and Mrs. Matthew Shaw of Birmingham. The name of the hotel was the Chandos."

CHANDOS HOTEL, GUILDFORD (to P.C. Emerson) "A Mr. and Mrs. Matthew Shaw were visitors here on the 9th September last. They stayed one night and came from Birmingham."

NORAH PARSONS, Clerk at Lulverton Post Office (to P.C. Emerson)

"It was directed to 'John Tudor, Esq., 40, Westcroft Road, Lee, London, S.E.12.' "

LESLIE NASH (to P.C. Hartley)

"Two or three of us were playing about with the dagger after the rehearsal. I left it hanging from the back of a chair in the foyer. It was in the scabbard attached to the belt."

HILARY BOYSON

"I left the theatre at about a quarter to eight and went straight home."

"How did you come to fall down the stairs, Miss Boyson?" asked the inspector.

"There was a crowd of us going from the foyer into the auditorium. The passage isn't very wide and just as I got to the top of the stairs, Miss Faggott lurched forward into me. She said she tripped over a mat, but whatever the real cause, I was sent pitching down the stairs. My foot went right through one of the treads and I got badly grazed and bruised. It's a miracle I wasn't killed or, at any rate, seriously hurt."

"You say, 'whatever the real cause.' Are you implying that there was a deliberate attempt to injure you?"

"Yes, but as I can't prove it, I'm not going to say any more about it."

"Mr. Manhow came home with me. I found the banknote in my coat pocket, when I was getting out the key of the front door. Mr. Manhow at once took it back to the theatre."

"How do you imagine it came into your pocket. Miss Boyson?"

"It was put there by somebody who wanted to get me into trouble. My coat was in the girls' dressing-room—and one person had plenty of opportunity to slip the note into the pocket."

"Who was that?"

"Miss Faggott. I'm not accusing her of doing it, because, once again, there's no proof; but why did she tell little Jill Geering to ring you up, as soon as I had left the theatre? When anything unpleasant like the losing of money happens, no ordinary person rushes at once to telephone the police.

That girl, Inspector, has a very malicious disposition. Since they took the leading part in 'Measure for Measure' away from her and gave it to me, she's behaved in a horrible manner towards me. She doesn't like it when she can't have things all her own way."

"How did the cast come to be re-arranged, Miss Boyson?"

"The committee told me first of all that Miss Faggott wanted to give up the part; then I found out afterwards that she was desperately keen to do it, but that the committee had decided I was more suitable. With the support of Mr. Tudor, she made herself so objectionable that yesterday evening I was forced to resign from the society. And now that she's got the part," concluded Hilary with a certain amount of relish, "she won't be able to play it, because the show will be cancelled."

GEORGE BOYSON (father of Hilary)

"Yes, a man whose name is Saunderson. I've just made him works manager. A very competent fellow."

"When the new appointment was first considered, was there any question of his being passed over in favour of someone else?"

"Certainly not. I've always made it clear to Saunderson that as soon as Hill, the former works manager, retired, he would get the job. Saunderson's the best man I have. He's had more than one tempting offer from other firms in our line of business, and I can't afford to lose him. He knows it, confound him!"

THOMAS SAUNDERSON

"What, put another man over me? I'd like to see 'em try! As it is, I'm only stopping on to please the old man."

JAMES HENRY GARNETT

The meeting took place in the lounge of Eagle House.

"Where were you, Mr. Garnett, at half-past six yesterday evening?"

"Sitting in this same chair."

"You heard no disturbance?"

"There's always a disturbance in this place and damned glad I was to have the lounge to myself for ten minutes. Yes, they were all running up and down, getting ready for a rehearsal or some such foolery."

"But nobody troubled you in the lounge? You didn't order somebody to get out?"

Mr. Garnett allowed a smile to flash across his craggy features.

"I've often been tempted, but I've not done it yet. That's not to say that if I get much more of Widow Stoneham's buck, I shan't—"

"You heard nobody shout 'Get out!' at six-thirty?"

The old manufacturer shook his head.

"Your bedroom is opposite the late Mr. Tudor's. Did you, at any time after half-past ten last night, hear anybody go into it?"

"Yes, Miss Ashwin and young Gough. I was reading in bed when they came upstairs talking. They went along to Tudor's room and knocked on the door. Then they opened it and I heard Gough say, 'He's not there,' and shut the door again. The two of them came back and began billing and cooing on the landing. Not that I greatly minded. I did a fair bit of it myself, when I was a young chap."

"And before they came upstairs, you heard nothing?"

"Not a sound."

(It would possibly have embarrassed Myrna and Jack had they learned that both Mrs. Stoneham and Miss Tearle also caught what happened on the landing. In addition, the two ladies confirmed that they had heard no one else in Tudor's room.)

"There is another question, Mr. Garnett, that I want to discuss with you. I believe I'm right in saying that you played some part in the re-casting of 'Measure for Measure.' Is that true?"

The big chin jerked menacingly forward.

"What of it?"

"I should like to know, please, why you considered it necessary to cause confusion and discontent in the amateur dramatic society, by compelling Miss Faggott to surrender the principal part to Miss Boyson."

"That's got nothing to do with you, Mr. Detective-Inspector! Your business is looking into a murder case—not interfering in other folks' private affairs."

"Are you not going to answer my question?"

"I'll see you in hell first!"

"It has come to my knowledge that you wanted Miss Boyson to take the lead, in order that your mediation might afterwards become known to Miss Boyson's father and so influence him in favour of your son-in-law. Am I right, Mr. Garnett?"

The only reply was a challenging grunt.

"Yet my enquiries tend to show," Charlton went on serenely, "that Mr. Saunderson was never in any danger of failing to get the new appointment. He himself laughed at me when I suggested such a possibility."

From beneath heavy frowning brows, the old man's hard grey eyes glared at the detective.

"Have you been talking to my girl?" he demanded.

"Do you mean Mrs. Saunderson? No, not yet."

"Then we'll go round and see her now."

MRS. SAUNDERSON

Almost before Mrs. Saunderson had opened the front door of the little house in London Road, Garnett said:

"I want a word with you, Elsie, my girl."

"What's the matter, Dad?" she asked, and her tone was full of apprehension.

He pushed her roughly into the front room and Charlton followed.

"Now, then! Didn't you tell me Tom stood a chance of being made works manager if the Boyson girl got the big part in the play?"

"Yes, Dad." The reply was nearly inaudible.

"And didn't you persuade me."

Charlton began to speak, but the old man, who had omitted

to remove his hat, swung round at him and growled:

"Leave this to me. Didn't you persuade me, Elsie, against my better judgment, to turn the screw on young Tudor? Didn't you? Come on, girl!"

"Yes, Dad."

"But you didn't tell me, did you, that Tom would've got the job in any case, whether I made a damned old fool of myself or not? You didn't mention a little thing like that, did you?"

"Dad! Please don't shout at me! You've got me so as I don't know what I'm saying. Who is this gentleman?"

Garnett dismissed the subject of Charlton with an ungainly sweep of both arms.

"You've been playing some kind of game with me, young woman, and I'm going to get the truth out of you. Why did you pitch me a string of lies?"

"It wasn't lies, Dad. Tom got very worried when he heard Mr. Hill was going to retire, because Mr. Hill was a very easy man to get on with, and Mr. Etheridge, manager of the mixing department, who might have got the job instead of Tom, was —"

"Etheridge was out of it!" roared her father. "You knew it—and so did Tom."

"He didn't say anything about his worries to me, Dad, but I could see he was anxious, so I thought—"

"You *thought!* God knows what you thought, you cunning little slut, but you'd got some other reason. What was it? Come on, out with it!"

But Elsie Saunderson lapsed limply into tears and could not be prevailed upon to say another word. As the two men walked back together along London Road, Garnett grunted:

"That girl of mine's like an obstinate jellyfish that comes floating back as soon as you've scared it off."

The simile appealed to Charlton, who nevertheless promised himself another, and less stormy, interview with Mrs. Saunderson.

CHARLES HOWARD (of Dickson, Parrish, Willmott & Lister)

"Yes, we acted for the late Mr. Tudor and have already taken over the administration of his estate, pending the arrival of his personal representatives."

"Did he leave a will?"

"Yes. The executors are his father, Mr. John Tudor, and an uncle on his mother's side, Mr. Percival Fox-Hammond. I am expecting Mr. and Mrs. Tudor to arrive this afternoon."

"Do you know the provisions of the will?"

"It was I who drew it up, but at this stage, of course, I cannot divulge its contents."

"Where is it lodged?"

"In the Southern Bank strongroom, underneath these offices."

"Thank you. I can arrange with Mr. Scott-Brown to inspect it."

"In that case, Inspector, I must insist on being present. It is my duty to safeguard the interests of the parties concerned."

MAURICE SCOTT-BROWN

"Always find me ready to help, Charlton, but this will have to go through Scotland Yard and my Chief Inspector in London."

A sigh of resignation came from Charlton.

"Have all my munificent subscriptions to the Bank Clerks Orphanage been in vain?" he asked sadly.

The manager swung his massive body round in his revolving chair and reached for the telephone with a rumbling chuckle.

"Far from it," he said. "Even those few coppers were put to good use."

"Dr. Faggott came in last Friday, so one of my cashiers tells me, and drew a ten-pound note over the counter."

The key of Tudor's security box in the strongroom of the Southern Counties Bank was on the ring held, for the time being, by Charlton. Mr. Scott-Brown opened the box, while Charlton and Mr. Howard hovered in the background.

Besides a miscellaneous collection of old cheque-book counterfoils, a fire insurance policy, premium renewal receipts and other personal documents and papers, the box contained the lease of the premises in Beastmarket Hill, a life assurance policy and the will.

Of the secret opus, there was no trace.

The residuary beneficiary under the will was Tudor's mother, the legacies being: Fifty pounds each to Myrna Ashwin, Jack Gough, Muriel Jones and Peter Ridpath; and an annuity of ten shillings a week to Archibald Hobson, towards the care of his wife, Florence Hobson, with the proviso that the payments should cease at her death, and that no allowance should be made in the event of her being discharged from the institution in which she was detained, before the death of the testator. There was also a proviso as to the payment of the allowance for Mrs. Hobson's benefit, should her husband predecease her.

Charlton turned to Mr. Howard.

"What will be the position," he enquired, "if Mrs. Hobson is cured in, say, a year's time? Will the allowance to her husband continue after that?"

"On the phrasing of the document, yes. I remember raising the point with the late Mr. Tudor, at the time the will was drawn up. He appreciated my argument, but expressed the wish that the clause should remain as be had originally drafted it. I recollect his remarking that the unfortunate woman would probably die a long time before he did." Mr. Howard shook his head ruefully. "Now, if she recovers next week and goes on to enjoy the residue of a normal span of life, there will be a call on the deceased's estate for many years to come."

ALFRED SMART, house decorator (to Sergeant Martin)

"I've had a good look at that staircase, Sergeant. There's no doubt at all it was rot was the cause of it. The whole flight's affected and, to my way of thinking, should be pulled down and rebuilt with new."

MISS MAUD LARK

"I'm sure you won't be offended, Mr. Charlton," said the perky little woman with the audacious red feather in her hat, "if I tell you that you're barking up the wrong tree. I've known all these young people for some time and have grown very fond of them; and although they're far from perfect— thank heaven!—I simply will not believe that any of them killed poor Vaughan Tudor, least of all Peter Ridpath, who owes everything he has to Vaughan—and, in any case, hasn't the guts. Elizabeth Faggott is a sweet girl and has confided in me. I'm not going to abuse her confidence, Mr. Charlton, but take it from me that she'd nothing to do with it and neither had Peter Ridpath. It's clear which way your mind's working, but have you forgotten we're at war with Germany? For all we know, the country may be full of enemy agents. I do urge you, Mr. Charlton, to widen the scope of your enquiries."

"Then," he smiled pleasantly, "may I know what you did after leaving Miss Faggott last night?"

XVI

Who will believe thee, Isabel?
Act II, Sc. 4.

PAUL MANHOW

"I left the theatre about eleven o'clock and walked round to Miss Boyson's house; but by that time, she'd gone to bed, so I went home and did the same."

"Yes, Vaughan Tudor met me on the stairs, said you'd arrived on the scene, and told me to get rid of the bank-note p.d.q. I dropped it in the cloak-room. Highly immoral, of course, but we didn't want to make a police-court case of the affair."

"Though apparently someone else did?"

"You must draw your own conclusions on that point."

"Who knew that the note was found in her pocket by Miss Boyson?"

"Only she and I—and Tudor. None of us had any cause to tell the world about it."

"What were your associations with Mr. Tudor?"

"He and I were very good friends. The dramatic society threw us together a lot."

"You were very good friends," repeated Charlton slowly. "It's curious, then, that last Saturday evening, he punched you on the nose."

Manhow's big white face did not readily register strong emotion and his thick, weary voice seldom quickened in tempo, but now in both there was startled alarm.

"It's a lie!" he protested.

"And after he'd hit you, he asked if you wanted any more. Your nose began to bleed. Then Mr. Tudor went off, leaving you alone in the theatre. Did it happen like that, Mr. Manhow?"

"Who told you?"

"I got it from Mr. Tudor himself."

"Then he came to the police before he was mur—"

"Perhaps you'll agree now that it isn't a lie?"

"Yes, it's true enough. I spoke without thinking. Tudor lost his temper and went for me."

"Why?"

"Oh, we had a battle of words—and Tudor was always liable to get on his hind-legs."

His voice had gone back to its unhurried monotone, and he had relighted his large pipe.

"What was the argument about, Mr. Manhow?"

"The old trouble—women. I'd just as soon not talk about it, if you don't mind."

"I'm afraid I do mind. I can't compel you to say anything, but a little frankness from you will make this conversation

much more—agreeable. Mr. Tudor was brutally and treach-
erously stabbed in the back—and if *you* didn't do it, Mr.
Manhow, it's up to you to help me find out who did."

Manhow puffed stolidly at his pipe.

"I'd rather not discuss this particular matter," he said. "It
was quite private and has nothing at all to do with the murder."

"Then if you won't tell *me*" said the inspector, sharply for
him, "let me tell *you*. Tudor was in love with Miss Faggott and
you yourself were interested in Miss Boyson. You believed that
Miss Faggott was making things unpleasant for Miss Boyson,
because of a change in the cast of 'Measure for Measure'; and
last Saturday evening, you warned him that the alleged persecution had got to stop. In support of your arguments, you
made a charge against Miss Faggott of such a kind that Tudor
hit you. Am I right?"

"If you insist on an answer, yes. And I should very much
like to know how you found out. Did Tudor report me to
the police?"

"From all the evidence I have collected, Mr. Manhow, one
definite fact emerges: Mr. Tudor lost his temper only when
he was in the right. If I am to believe what I hear from many
sources, he had a great sense of justice and equity, and was
violently against any kind of unfairness. He was, in fact, a very
honourable man."

These deliberately ponderous observations made Manhow
say from behind a cloud of smoke:

"That's absolutely correct. Tudor was one of the best fellows
I ever met."

"Then maybe he did right to punch you on the nose."

"So I'm being trapped into admission, am I?"
drawled Manhow. "Well, I'll repeat that Tudor was one of
the best fellows I ever met. But like many another good
fellow, he was misled by a woman. The lady in question is
a tornado. She wanted the Isabella part and, when it was
taken away from her, stopped at nothing to get it back. She
hounded Miss Boyson out—that's the only way to put it. First

of all, she pushed her down the stairs, then——"

"Can you prove that?"

"I saw it happen. We were all going along the passage to the foyer, when suddenly, for no real reason, Miss Faggott lunged sideways at Miss Boyson and sent her down the stairs. She was full of regrets, of course, and said she'd caught her foot on the edge of a mat, but I'm not so sure. Then there was that bank-note business. . . ."

Here Manhow repeated the arguments he had used to Tudor on the previous Saturday evening.

"The following day," he then continued, "I went round to make it up with him. I told him I was ready to admit that I shouldn't have spoken as I had, but that I didn't want to see any friend of mine make a fool of himself."

The inspector almost smiled: he could picture Tudor's reactions to this complacent patronage.

"I offered my apologies for poking my nose into something that didn't really concern me, and he said he was prepared to accept them, provided I withdrew everything I had said against Miss Faggott. I told him plainly that it had been the truth and therefore I wasn't going to eat my words. If somebody hadn't come in just then, there would have been another brawl."

"And last night you threatened to thrash him."

"You seem well-informed, Inspector."

There was a hint of a sneer.

"Yes, last night I threatened to thrash him; and I suppose the theory now is that I went back to the Bakehouse, after everyone else had left, and drove a knife into his heart?"

"I'm inviting you to convince me that you didn't, Mr. Manhow."

"Nothing would please me better, but there's no evidence for me to advance. My mother was asleep when I got home. The servant who answered the door to me at the Boysons' house was the last person I saw until breakfast-time this morning. That's the trouble with an alibi; you don't know you're going to need it until it's too late to arrange one. But quite honestly, Inspector, do you really think that an ordinary fellow like me is likely to go round sticking knives into his friends, even though he *has* had a row with them? In my opinion, there's something far more serious than minor squabbling behind this murder. There's an old tag—but do you want me to go on?"

"Yes, please."

"There's an old tag to the effect that dead men tell no tales, so isn't it possible that Tudor found something out and had to be silenced? You know as well as I do that nothing less than death would have kept his mouth shut if he considered it should be opened. Apart from any peace-time troubles, what about the war? I believe that, even in the best run countries, there are enemy agents who don't much care for publicity."

Charlton smiled slightly. "Have you been exchanging views with Miss Lark?" he asked.

"As a matter of fact, I have. Miss Lark is a very shrewd and observant little woman. She put it to me quite bluntly that, because of the recent strained relations between Tudor and me, I was bound to be suspected, and that I'd better polish up some sort of alibi. She added that she didn't imagine I'd killed Tudor any more than she suspected Peter Ridpath—but perhaps you haven't heard of him?"

"His name has cropped up once or twice," Charlton admitted dryly.

"Then Miss Lark made the bright suggestion that Tudor might have been killed by one of those spy fellows. Don't think I'm throwing mud at Tudor, but there's another thing. It's worth remembering that he hadn't been very many years in Lulverton. All we knew about him was that he came from London. Could he have been mixed up in some sort of subversive organisation! Far-fetched, perhaps, but not by any means impossible, is it? He was always tapping away secretly at his typewriter and nobody was ever allowed to see what he wrote. He might very well have been one of those—what-do-you-call-'ems, the fellows who helped to spread chaos in Poland."

"Diversionists, whose job, Mr. Manhow, is to confuse the main issue."

He got up from his chair.

"And," he added, "they are not confined to Poland."

HUBERT MORTIMER ROBINSON (2nd interview)

"I have prepared a list of keyholders for you, Mr. Charlton. The names are: Mr. Tudor, Mr. Manhow, Mr. Collingwood, Mr. Cheesewright, Miss Ashwin, Hobson, Mr. Ridpath and myself."

"Did Mr. Ridpath surrender his, when he left Lulverton?"

"No, he took it with him."

ELIZABETH FAGGOTT

"I said good night to Miss Lark at the corner of our road and went home to bed. I didn't go out again."

"Why did you give up the principal part in the play, Miss Faggott?"

"Because I was specially asked to by the committee."

"I expect it was a great disappointment to you?"

"A terrible disappointment, but in the theatre world, you've got to take your medicine. I've always hoped to take up acting as a career, and I suppose that little incident was a valuable experience."

"So you were quite ready to take a smaller part for the benefit of the society?"

"Yes—and it *was* for the general benefit, for if I hadn't agreed, we should have lost the theatre. You see, the building belongs to a dreadful old man called Garnett, who's got a daughter. I've never seen her, but she must be one of those large, domineering women. Her husband is—"

"I know the circumstances, Miss Faggott; and I am under the impression that, although Mr. Garnett was anxious for Miss Boyson to play the lead, he agreed not to enforce the notice to quit should Miss Boyson have fallen ill or refused to take the part. That was so, wasn't it?"

Her beautiful eyes looked at him steadily.

"I can see," she said in a low tone, "that the usual number of malicious tongues have been busy. They've tried to persuade you, I suppose, that I did all I could to make things difficult for her, so that she would eventually resign and I'd get the part back; and some of them have probably told you that I pushed her down the stairs on purpose, to break her leg or something. They have, haven't they?"

"I'm sure, Miss Faggott," was his easy evasion, "that none of your friends would make such serious accusations."

"None of my *friends,* but during these last few weeks, Mr. Charlton, I've discovered how very few friends I have. I'll say to you now, on my word of honour, that the staircase affair was entirely accidental and the very last thing I wanted to happen. I could kick myself for being so clumsy. Hilary Boyson and I have never been very fond of each other, but I'm sure she'd never say that I did it deliberately."

"What can you tell me about the bank-note, Miss Faggott?"

"The note? But surely that doesn't come into it?"

"Even if it doesn't, will you please tell me all you know?"

Elizabeth looked perplexed, and watching her, Charlton was captivated by her dark, fascinating loveliness. No wonder, he thought, that frothy, light-minded Peter Ridpath, straight-forward, English-of-the-English Vaughan Tudor, and sophisti-cated, man-about-town Franklin Duzest had surrendered to her, and Jack Gough had admitted her attractions. Whether she was good or bad, she had that magnetism that could draw all men and turn them, as if by a random throw of the dice, into heroes or villains. Even he, Inspector Charlton of the C.I.D., the relentless bloodhound, had to remind himself firmly that he was there not to be wooed by the magic of her voice and presence, but to induce her to tell him more than she intended. For he was certain, in his own mind, that if there was one person around whom the story of Vaughan Tudor's life and death revolved, it was lovely Elizabeth Faggott.

"There's so very little to it," she said after a pause. "Last Saturday was my birthday and although the old darling can't afford it, my father gave me the note as a present. I slipped it in my bag. Jill, my little adopted sister, was so wildly excited about so much money being concentrated in one small piece of paper, that she insisted on me showing it round at the rehearsal that evening."

"Was Miss Jill at the dress rehearsal last night?"

"No. I had to take her with me on Saturday, because my parents went to a dinner-party and it was the maid's evening out. Coming back to the bank-note, everybody was politely interested in it, and afterwards I put it back in my bag."

"Which you then left on the table in the foyer."

"Yes, and when I went back to fetch it, the note had gone. I told Vaughan—Mr. Tudor, and he organised a search. Then you arrived and, as you'll remember, we had another look for it and Mr. Duzest found it in the cloakroom, where it must have slipped out of my bag."

"You didn't tell Miss Jill to ring up the police?"

"Of course I didn't! The wicked little wretch made it up on the spur of the moment. I forced her to admit it when we got home."

"Then why did she 'phone?"

"You probably don't know my adopted sister, Mr. Charlton, but she's a public nuisance and sometimes I'm absolutely ashamed of her. We've done what we can to teach her to behave properly, but she's incorrigible. She rang you up just to make things a little more difficult than they were already."

"And you're satisfied, Miss Faggott, that you dropped the note in the cloak-room?"

"Oh, yes. The fastening on my bag wasn't at all secure. I had it seen to on Monday."

"When did you go to the cloak-room?"

"After I'd picked up my bag in the foyer."

"And when did you find that the note was missing?"

"On my way through the foyer to the stage."

"It didn't occur to you to go back to the cloak-room?"

"No; I'm afraid my first thought was that somebody had stolen the note, and I went straight to Mr. Tudor."

"You didn't go into the ladies' dressing-room?"

She shook her head. "I was very relieved," she said, "when it was found."

"I am sure you were."

"Now, there is one other matter, Miss Faggott, and I am sorry I must mention it so soon after Mr. Tudor's death. Was there any understanding between you two?"

Elizabeth was silent for some moments, then asked:

"Do we have to talk about it?"

"My task is to find out who killed him—and why."

"Then I shall have to tell you, because"—there was a note of suppressed passion in her voice—"I want whoever murdered him to be hanged. On Saturday, the 25th November of last year, at Francois', just off Leicester Square, he asked me to marry him. I didn't give him a definite answer, as I—wasn't certain of my own feelings; and he said he would wait until after we'd finished 'Measure for Measure.' Ten days later, on Tuesday, the 5th December, he had to come round here to tell me that I must give up the Isabella part. It was then that I... Mr. Charlton, must I go on?"

"Yes, please."

"Did he—suffer?"

"No, death was instantaneous. He probably didn't realise what had happened."

"Thank God," she murmured; and Charlton thought that, if this was play-acting, it was consummately done.

"You were telling me about his visit."

"Yes, he was so—oh, I can't think of the word! He was so like a little Scottie, who's expecting to be spanked for something he hasn't done that it seemed to ... gush up inside and choke me. I didn't mind about not playing Isabella. I'd have scrubbed the floors, if he'd asked me to."

"Did you tell Mr. Tudor of your decision?"

"No. We'd agreed to leave it till after the show. Yet if he'd asked me again that evening, everything might have been different and happier, for now the show is abandoned and Vaughan is—oh, God! Why did it have to happen?"

"Mr. Tudor didn't mention the subject on any later occasion?"

"No, he stuck to his side of the bargain—and I thought it would be nicer to wait. We were so busy with rehearsals and things, that there was no real opportunity."

"Not even during your car-ride together last Sunday afternoon?"

To a man trained to observe, every change of mood is apparent; and Charlton now noticed a sudden tenseness in Elizabeth.

"Oh, that was just a little run," she said with a careless gesture. "I asked Vaughan to take me. As a matter of fact, I'd been responsible for a small piece of unpleasantness the previous evening, by giving an imitation of Hilary Boyson doing my old Isabella part. It was a catty thing to do, and feeling thoroughly ashamed of myself afterwards, I wanted Vaughan to know how sorry I was."

"How did he take it?"

"He was cross with me at first, but finished up by laughing."

"Nothing was said about the—other matter?"

"No ... not exactly."

He leant forward. "Miss Faggott, since early this morning, I have been asking hundred of questions, and I've received many interesting answers. One of them was that, when he returned from his drive with you, Mr. Tudor was in a very dejected frame of mind. Before coming along to see you, I concluded that you had refused his offer of marriage; but from what you have told me of your intention to accept when next he asked, I am wondering what actually took place while you were out together."

Elizabeth looked round desperately.

"Nothing!" she declared. "Nothing, I tell you!"

He tried shock tactics.

" 'Duncan,' " he murmured, " 'is king of Scotland. Macbeth must be king, so Duncan—' "

"*Don't*".

Her hands went to her head. When she took them away, there was an expression of bewilderment on her face.

"How did you know that?" she almost whispered.

It was not the moment to disclose how useful the sheet of paper in Tudor's typewriter had turned out to be.

"Why don't you tell me the truth, Miss Faggott?" he suggested gently. "It was not you, but Mr. Tudor, who brought the association to an end, wasn't it?"

She bit her lip and turned her head away.

"Yes," she said very softly.

"Why?"

"He was in a strange mood that afternoon. After we'd gone some distance, I. . . reminded him of our talk in Francois' and said that if he . . . still felt the same, he might like to ask me the question again. His only answer was that he was sorry, but he didn't feel the same. When I'd asked him several times what was the matter, he blurted out about my being . . . friendly with another man. This man had been pestering me for a long time, but I'd never encouraged him; and, after a tremendous struggle, I managed to convince Vaughan that his suspicions were groundless. He saw that it wasn't my fault that the other man was always hanging round me, and, when he'd threatened horrible things if he caught the man doing it again, he became much brighter. We stopped at a little place for tea and I had to swear to him that I had never . . ." She stopped and looked appealingly at Charlton, but he made no move to help her out. "That I had never . . . slept with this other man. Afterwards, he was his old charming self, and while we were smoking a cigarette before starting off for home, asked me to marry him. I accepted."

He waited for her next words and was just about to speak

himself, when she continued, he thought at first, at a tangent.

"You know the top of Cowhanger, where the lane leads off to the hill-climb. We had got just there, on the way back to Lulverton, both feeling very happy; and I told him to drive carefully, because I had once been nearly involved in a nasty smash, when a car had shot out of the lane and just missed the car I was in by inches. Vaughan had been humming gaily to himself as he drove along, but when I said that, he suddenly became silent. After the trouble I'd had with him already, I quickly explained that it had happened some years ago and that a girl friend of mine had been driving. He didn't take any notice, but brought me right back here without saying another word.

"When we pulled up outside, he jumped out and opened the door for me ... I tried to soften him, but the only thing he said as he got back into the car was, 'You've fooled me long enough.' I think he must have been so worked up about the other man I mentioned just now, that as soon as he heard I'd been out in a car, all his suspicions broke out again. I wrote him a letter, but he took no notice of it—and he cut me off when I 'phoned him. The dress rehearsal last night was a terrible ordeal, but I had to go through with it."

"Was this other man Mr. Ridpath?"

He thought she was going to refute it, but after a moment's hesitation, she nodded.

"And—forgive my asking—you were never intimate with him?"

"No, never."

"Do you remember a Mr. and Mrs. Matthew Shaw of Birmingham?"

The quiet question brought her to her feet.

"You heartless beast!" she blazed at him. "Why don't you leave me alone? He's dead—*dead* and you come here to torment me! For God's sake go away!"

"Please sit down, Miss Faggott. A C.I.D. man very often has to be callous, but"—a stern note came into his voice—"he's not such a heartless beast as one who stabs an unsuspecting fellow creature in the back. As soon as you've told me the truth about Mr. Ridpath, I'll go. And please don't imagine you can mislead me—I know considerably more than you think. I know, for example, that on the 9th September of last year, you and Mr. Ridpath spent the night at the Chandos Hotel at Guildford, and that you signed the visitors' book as Mr. and Mrs. Matthew Shaw. I urge you not to deny it, for I can produce witnesses."

"I don't deny it, but I do deny that... anything happened. He persuaded me to go away with him. I thought I was wildly in love with him and, like a silly little fool, agreed. But when it was almost too late, I got scared and locked myself in the bathroom attached to our room. . . . That was the farthest I ever went with Peter Ridpath, but what was the good of confessing even that to Vaughan?"

"The narrow escape on Cowhanger Hill—I take it you were with Mr. Ridpath?"

"Yes. . . It was on the Sunday that war was declared, at about which time my infatuation for him was at its height. The persuasion he used was that he would soon have to go off to fight and would probably get killed, so why not make the—and I was crazy enough to listen. I scarcely realised the existence of Vaughan Tudor then. . . . Only four months ago!. . . . He was just a quiet, pleasant, good-looking acquaintance—a typical well-bred Englishman—who seemed to retire into his shell whenever I spoke to him. He called me Elizabeth and I called him Vaughan, but everybody uses christian names in an amateur dramatic society. I knew that he championed me and overcame a great deal of opposition when he got me the lead in 'The Likes of Her,' but it was some time before I guessed that he was too tongue-tied to say what he wanted to say.

"The Guildford incident was the turning-point in my affair with Peter Ridpath. Not at once, but slowly, I took less interest in him and more in Vaughan Tudor. Peter seemed to think that Guildford was only a temporary setback and was always pressing me to go away with him again. I flatly refused and, by the 25th November, when Vaughan took me to Francois', I was heartily sick of pretty Peter Ridpath."

"Why didn't you accept Mr. Tudor in November, Miss Faggott?"

"I know it sounds dreadfully selfish, but it was my career as an actress. Marriage with Vaughan would have finished it. . . . There would have been no 'Elizabeth Tudor' in lights over the Prince Consort. I should have stayed in Lulverton and . . . had babies."

"Where did you spend the night of Boxing Day?" he asked curtly.

"I went up to stay with an aunt of mine, who lives in Streatham. Why?"

"Did you have any conversation with Mr. Ridpath last Saturday?"

"I believe we did exchange a few casual words."

"You didn't finally give him his dismissal?"

"Oh, no. He got that weeks ago—and accepted it, too, after a while."

"Then what was the matter with him in the evening? I've been told by various people that he was in a most dispirited state."

Elizabeth shook her head. "I can't tell you. In any case, I had nothing to do with it. He'd had plenty of time to get over his disappointment with me. Perhaps he'd met with a similar rebuff from someone else." The letters from Guildford. . . . "Perhaps he had," said Charlton.

•   •   •   •   •

Miss Jill Geering

"I rang you up because I didn't want Elizabeth to lose her birthday present. She was going to buy a new dress with some of the money; and I knew that the police always get back anything that's stolen and put the thief in prison. It was a fib when I said that Elizabeth told me to ring up the police."

" Late last night, Mr. Ridpath came here to see Elizabeth."

XVII

This will last out a night in Russia,
When nights are longest there.
Act II, Sc. 1.

The iron tongue of midnight had long since tolled twelve and it was Friday, the 5th January, 1940.

Four men sat smoking in Charlton's room in Lulverton police station, three of them exhausted, the fourth wide awake and hungry for news. The three were Inspector Charlton, Sergeant Martin and P.C. Bradfield; the fourth was Superintendent Kingsley, who, though nominally in authority over the C.I.D. men posted to his Division, usually gave them a free hand. He was a breezy, out-spoken Southmouth man and the size of him can be gathered from the fact that all his friends called him "Tiny" and all the local law-breakers, "the Carthorse." When the fancy took him, he wore uniform: that evening, the fancy took him.

"Now," he said, with a briskness that the other three were far from imitating, "give me the facts. No flummery, just the bare facts."

Charlton drew at his cigarette and exhaled the smoke with a deep, weary breath.

"I'm fed up with the sound of my own voice," he complained, "but if you must have a report at this ungodly hour, Tiny, here it is."

"Quick as you like," said the Super. "Vaughan Tudor was stabbed through the heart from behind with a dagger that was to be used in a performance of 'Measure for Measure' by the LADS"

228

"The wife and I were going on Saturday."

"Lorimer examined the body at 9.30 this morning and expressed the opinion that death occurred from ten to twelve hours previously—that is, between 9.30 and 11.30 last night. Unless thirty-two witnesses were telling lies—and even I must accept such crushing weight of proof—Tudor was alive at eleven o'clock last night, and on the evidence of three witnesses, he was still alive at 11.15. So taking Lorimer's evidence into account, he was killed between 11.15 and 11.30. But the time-of-death diagnosis is always a bit uncertain—as Lorimer is the first to agree—and I've therefore allowed a margin of error and assumed that the murder took place between 11.15 and 12.30.

"Yesterday evening, they held the dress rehearsal for 'Measure for Measure' at the Little Theatre. Forty-three persons were present, one of them, of course, being Tudor. I found some programmes in the theatre, but have made my own list of the cast, officials and visitors. This is it." He passed a sheet of paper across to the Super.

MEASURE FOR MEASURE
Characters in the Play

Vincentio	Geoffrey Cutner
Angelo	Franklin Duzest
Escalus	Hubert Mortimer Robinson
Claudio	Boyd Gloster
Lucio	Leslie Nash
First Gentleman and Froth	Ralph Freshwater
Second Gentleman and Friar Peter.	Stewart McIver
Provost	Vaughan Tudor
Friar Thomas and Barnardine	Michael Kelso
Justice	James Quin
Elbow.	Jack Gough
Pompey	Paul Manhow
Abhorson, the Executioner	Roy Chittenden
Isabella	Elizabeth Faggott

Mariana	Peggy Howard
Juliet	Myrna Ashwin
Francisca, a Nun	Alice Cheesewright
Mistress Overdone	Maud Lark
Attendant at the Palace.	Doris Belcher

Lords, Officers, Attendants, Harlots, Nuns, Citizens, etc.:—
Alexander Anscomb, Victoria Fox, Pamela Wargrave,
Kathleen Newton, Susan Haydon, Joyce Sinclair,
Felicity Collingwood, Marjorie Scott-Brown, Eileen
Smith, Hilda Cotton, Richard Penn.

Officials

Producer.	Patrick Collingwood
Stage manager.	Frederick Cheesewright
Stage Carpenter.	Archibald Hobson
President.	Maurice Scott-Brown
Steward.	Edgar Boothroyd
Programme seller.	Ursula Wheatly

Visitors

Mr. and Mrs. J. H. Upjohn, Mr. and Mrs. R. L. Grainger,
Miss Grace Marshall, Miss Ruth Marshall,
Mr. Leopold Mears, MA.
Performers, 30; Officials, 6; Visitors, 7—Total, 43.

The Super muttered a running commentary, as he studied the details.

"Geoffrey Cutner. Pompous ass. . . . Franklin Duzest. Duzest? Isn't he the chap living at the Bunch of Grapes? Runs a Bugatti. Nothing to do and all day to do it in. . . . Ah, that very charming old lady, Mortimer Robinson. . . . Boyd Gloster . . . Leslie Nash . . . Ralph Freshwater . . . Stewart McIver. Always losing his bicycle. Accent too Scotch to be true. . . . Provost, Vaughan Tudor. Sort of chief of police, wasn't he? . . . Michael Kelso, 'Amicus Curios'. . . . James Quin. Better educated than his father and with a tenth of the old man's brains . . . Jack Gough. One of these days, that young Adonis will get himself into trouble with that travelling death-box of his... Paul Manhow. Blue bow-tie with white spots. Always reminds me of a sleepy slug ... Roy Chittenden ... Elizabeth Faggott. What a peach! What a snorter! 'A something or other beyond the reach of art.' You know, Harry, if I had my time over again—"

"Quick as you like," replied Charlton. "Just the bare facts." The Super coughed.

"P'raps you're right," he conceded, and returned to the list in his hand. "Peggy Howard, Charley Howard's girl—and very nice, too. Charley holed out in one on Boxing Day. Cost him twenty-seven bob . . .Myrna Ashwin. . . Alice Cheesewright, the old gumboil. . . . Maud Lark. Trim little party. Brave as a lion. Remember how she rallied round during that typhoid scare? She told me one the other day about a doctor who was called out in the middle of the night by a couple of newly—but some other time will do for that. . . . Attendant at the Palace, Doris Belcher. Dressed as an Elizabethan boy, I suppose. Sorry we shan't be seeing the show—she's got a fine pair of legs for tights."

Thus, with pithy and sometimes slanderous annotations, he worked his way through to Mr. Leopold Mears, M.A., "author of 'Francis, Lord Verulam' and the biggest bore since."

He handed the sheet back to Charlton, who then resumed: "Martin, the Three Musketeers and I have worn ourselves to unsubstantial shadows to-day, going round to see all those forty-two and a good many others. All their fingerprints have been taken. As far as possible, we've checked the movements of every one of them between 11.15 and 12.30; and as most of them seem to have left the theatre round about eleven o'clock and gone straight home to bed, there's not much to go on. The last to depart were Collingwood, his daughter and Duzest, who all confirm leaving Tudor sitting at a table in the box-office. The one exception to the home-and-bed contingent was young Jack Gough, who returned to the theatre just before midnight."

Whereupon, Charlton had the chastening experience of having to reply to his own favourite question.

"Why?"

"Because he was worried about Tudor, who was very much in the doldrums, and wanted to bring him home. But the entrance door was locked, so, getting no reply, he went back to Eagle House in Friday Street, where he lives. He produced a witness, Aaron Sugarman—"

"What, that far too prosperous old Semite? You know, I wouldn't take much persuading to believe that Aaron is a fence."

I've had the same idea, but I've never been able to catch him at it. Anyway, he vouches for the fact that Gough came round to the theatre, knocked at the door and called through the letter-box with such vigour that he, Sugarman, protested from his bedroom window, which overlooks Cooper's Yard. Sugarman had other interesting things to tell me. According to him, Gough was not the only one to call at the theatre between 11.30 and midnight. From the old gentleman's spate of words, I have compiled a little timetable, which isn't at all likely to be exactly right, but will have to do. Besides Gough, whom I've called No. 3, two other people, Nos. 1 and 2, are involved."

"You know I'm no good at figures," grumbled the Super. "Couldn't you have made them A, B and C?"

"It would have been too complicated," Charlton explained.

He handed the Super a slip, which read:

11.42   No. 1 arrived. Jingle of keys. Main door closed noisily.

11.44   Stage-door slammed back against wall, followed by man's voice shouting "Murder!" Nobody heard to leave Yard. Stage-door closed.

11.50   No. 2 arrived. No evidence that he (or she) entered theatre.

11.51   Someone left Yard. Probably No. 2, but possibly No. 1 or some other person in theatre beforehand.

11.55   Someone closed main door quietly and left Yard. Probably No. 1, but possibly No. 2 or some other person in theatre beforehand.

11.56   No. 3 arrived.

11.59   No. 3 left Yard.

Kingsley threw the slip back on Charlton's desk.

"Reads like the plot of a French farce to me," he admitted. "What's that about somebody shouting 'Murder!'?"

"Sugarman said it sounded like that, but it seems unlikely. The first assumption is that Tudor was stabbed at the bottom of the stairs leading down to the stage-door, after having had just enough time to push at the panic latch and send the door slamming back, and then shout 'Murder!' But such a man as Tudor seems to have been would surely stop short of melodrama? The second assumption is that some third party saw the murderer kill Tudor in the box-office, ran down the stairs, burst open the stage-door and yelled 'Murder!' Yet nothing happened afterwards. Anyone hysterical enough to shout 'Murder!' is going to follow it up with 'Help!' or 'Police!' if he doesn't get any response to the original appeal. But Sugarman heard no more excitement until Gough turned up. My own opinion is that the cry was not 'Murder!' but 'Tudor!' "

Sergeant Martin stirred in his chair.

"Or 'Turtle!' " he suggested dryly.

"That's an idea, Martin! There was only one person called him 'Turtle'—and that was young Ridpath."

"And who might he be?" was the Super's query.

"An old school friend of Tudor's who's been working for him and staying at Eagle House since the beginning of last June. He and Tudor had a row over Elizabeth Faggott last Saturday night, and he cleared out of Lulverton first thing on Sunday morning."

"Where is he now?"

"Bradfield looked into that. I've only had a rough outline

of his day's doings, so he'd better tell you himself."

After Sergeant Martin, Detective-Constable Peter Bradfield was Charlton's most valued and trusted helper. The son of a London solicitor, he had scorned the Police College at Hendon, which would have enabled him to begin his career as a junior station inspector, and had elected to start "on the beat." By the time of this investigation, he was out of uniform: a sunny-tempered, energetic young man, wearing his clothes with an air and his hat at a rakehelly angle; smooth-haired, with a wide, flat nose, and the darling of the other sex. As the inspector was accustomed to say, Peter Bradfield maintained the social contacts of the C.I.D. in Lulverton, and could obtain more useful information by taking a girl to a cinema than could the most wily K.C. by putting her into the witness-box.

"The D.I. was informed this morning, sir," he now told the Super, "that when Ridpath left here on Sunday morning, he went to Whitchester and put up at 54, Back Eldon Street. I called there and got these facts from the landlady, Mrs. Raffety. Ridpath went out last night at quarter to ten, telling her that he was going to visit friends and might not be back for a couple of hours. He didn't return until getting on for half-past three in the morning. Mrs. Raffety heard him come in and then dropped off to sleep. This morning, there was no sign of him—he'd packed his bag and hopped the dolly. As he'd paid for a week's lodgings in advance, and Mrs. Raffety's clientele have a habit of going and coming at unconventional hours, she didn't worry very much about him. I made some enquiries at the railway station, where I was told that he had caught the 10.3 down, which stops at Lulverton. A ticket-collector at Lulverton confirmed that a man answering Ridpath's description left the train, but is quite definite that Ridpath was not on any train going back to Whitchester. The last from here to Whitchester was the 11.52. I reported to the D.I. before proceeding further, and his instructions were to go after Ridpath to-morrow."

"And I can depend on my pet bloodhound to find him," smiled Charlton. "Apart from that, we've sent out an all-stations call and notified the *Gazette*. There's other evidence to show that—"

The telephone on his desk was ringing. He lifted the receiver.

"Inspector Charlton. . . . Yes, Peters? Do you usually stay up all night? . . . Yes, but I'm a busy man . . . That's fine! Is it too late to send them straight along? . . . Good. Nice work, Peters!"

He pushed the instrument aside and turned to the Superintendent.

"Who said the County Constabulary was the dormouse at the tea-party?" he asked. "Peters has developed all those fingerprints and wanted to know if we'd like to see them before they go up to the Bureau. He's sending them here straight away by motor-cyclist, with a provisional classification. Now, where was I? Oh, yes—Ridpath. Some time after eleven o'clock last night, somebody rang Dr. Faggott's house. Miss Faggott, who'd only just got back from the rehearsal, and was still in her outdoor clothes, answered the call; and a few minutes afterwards went and stood by the front gate, where she was joined almost at once by a man. My informant, who is the adopted sister of Miss Faggott—a child of thirteen or so—couldn't see the man, of course, but the front garden of the doctor's house is short and, by cautiously opening her bedroom window a crack, the detestable child heard Miss Faggott call him Peter several times."

"Peter?" said the Super with a chuckle. "Bradfield, what were you doing last night?"

"Fretwork, sir. It's a fine hobby for the long, dark evenings."

"Does Miss Molly Winterton share your enthusiasm?"

Bradfield had the grace to blush.

"I didn't know you'd heard about her, sir."

"I hear about everything—and if you want to know who told me, it was Mrs. Cheesewright."

"The old battle-axe!" said Bradfield with venom.

That was the curious thing about Mrs. Cheesewright;

everyone describing her began: "The old . . ." the last word varying according to individual preference. Mrs. Cheese-wright was inevitable; as much an ineradicable part of an English country town as the chromium-plated shopfronts in the High Street.

"Bradfield's not guilty this time," Charlton told the Super, with a grin at his assistant's discomfiture, "because this young pest, Jill Geering, identified Ridpath's voice, though she couldn't catch more than a word here and there. At the end of five minutes' conversation, Miss Faggott came back indoors and Ridpath walked off in the direction of the Little Theatre.

"Miss Faggott had previously told me that she hadn't seen Ridpath since last Saturday, but when I tried to have another word with her, she flatly refused to see me. Dr. Faggott, who was in the house at the time, informed me sharply that his daughter was suffering from serious shock and was not to be disturbed any further. I'll make another attempt to-morrow."

"Is there anything to prove that this Ridpath fellow actually went to the theatre?"

"Not yet, though I'm hoping that Peters' work on the fingerprints will produce something. But your question brings us back to my time-table. I've been told by Robinson —*Mortimer* Robinson; I beg his pardon!—who's treasurer of the dramatic society, that Ridpath holds a key of the entrance door. Gough doesn't, but Miss Ashwin, his fiancee, does. So Ridpath might very well have been No. 1 on the time-table.

"Let's assume that Tudor, to ensure a certain amount of privacy, goes down and releases the catch on the Yale after all the others have left; so that when Ridpath arrives, he has to use his key to get in. Ridpath goes upstairs, to find Tudor sitting just inside the box-office, correcting programmes with pen and ink. Hanging from the back of a chair in the foyer is the sword-belt with the dagger in its scabbard. Rather frigid greetings are exchanged. Perhaps Ridpath apologises. He takes up the belt from the chair, with the remark, 'Sethis is the dagger,' and saunters across towards Tudor, who is still sitting at the table. Still casually chatting, Ridpath gets behind Tudor, whips out the dagger and stabs him through the back."

"Having done which," added the Super brightly, "he goes down the back staircase, pushes open the door with a crash and bellows out, 'Murder!' or 'Tudor!' or 'Turtle!' or 'Any old iron!' Is that the way your mind's working?"

"With deadly precision," allowed Charlton, "you hit on the weak point. I'll try it another way. When Ridpath gets upstairs, Tudor isn't visible. He may be in the men's dressing-room, on the other side of the stage. Ridpath thinks he hears a noise at the foot of the staircase, goes down and—"

"Breaks 'is neck," threw in Martin.

"I hadn't forgotten the damaged tread, Sergeant, but, for anyone who knew of it, it wouldn't have been very difficult to step over. Ridpath gets to the foot of the stairs. The door comes open rather too easily and slams against the wall. Ridpath calls out, 'Turtle!' gets no answer, pulls the door closed and goes back upstairs, to find Tudor waiting for him on the landing. Then, when he's got Tudor nicely in position in the box-office, things proceed more or less as suggested in my first hypothesis. This second theory's far more likely than the first, because, on Sugarman's testimony, the entry of No. 1 with the key took place only two minutes before the shout.

"Six minutes after the shout, No. 2 turns up, tries the door, finds it locked and goes away again or—and this is an interesting alternative—the stage-door was not properly closed by Ridpath and, having no key of the other door, No. 2 first tries the stage-door, without making any noise, discovers it open, and slips upstairs. Ridpath hears him coming, takes a quick look round and beats a hasty retreat down and out through the main door, which he cautiously unlatches and leaves open, to avoid noise. That makes him the person who left the Yard at 11.51. At 11.55, No. 2 follows him and nearly bumps into Gough, who arrives at 11.56.

"Now, as No. 2 was in the theatre for four minutes after Ridpath had gone, surely he would have had time to look round the theatre and come across Tudor's body? It was an accepted thing with the LADS that Tudor worked late at the theatre, and No. 2's probable intention was to have a private chat with him. In that case, he surely wouldn't leave the theatre without having a look in the box-office, where he knew Tudor was almost certain to be? Why couldn't No. 2 have murdered Tudor? Assume that Ridpath and Tudor were talking in the box-office, when they caught the sound of No. 2 coming up the staircase. Ridpath had his own particular reasons for not being found there, so wished Tudor a hasty good night and quietly vanished, leaving No 2 with four useful minutes in which to dispose of Tudor. How does that strike you, Tiny?"

"Too damned involved," grunted that matter-of-fact man. "If you'll take my advice, Harry, you'll find young Ridpath, tell him you've proof he did it, and get him to sign a confession. It's so much less fatiguing than your farthing-candle gropings."

"Thank you," murmured Charlton with gratitude. "If I may butt in, sir," said Bradfield, who had been listening with close attention, "we're still left with one important question: who *was* No. 2?"

"Precisely so," agreed Charlton promptly, "and I've a shrewd idea who it was; but after the remarks by the voice of authority, I'm going to keep it to myself. So let's leave that for the moment, Tiny, and come to something else— the typewriter. As one enters the box-office, there is a small mahogany table on the left, just below the ticket-window. Tudor was sitting at it when Collingwood and the others left him. When Martin and I examined it, Tudor's key of the drawer was in the lock, with the rest of his keys attached by a ring. The drawer was half open. I'm told by Mortimer Robinson that a sum of money amounting to one pound, eighteen shillings and sixpence was in a cigarette tin in the drawer. We found no trace of tin or money.

"On the table, in addition to the telephone, was a pile—or

rather two piles—of programmes, one to the left, the other to the right. Those in the left-hand and larger pile were just as they had come from the printers, while those to the right had the names of some of the players altered in ink. The programmes were eight-page affairs—that is, two sheets folded down the middle and joined by staples. Local advertisers monopolised most of the space, but they had conceded the double centre page to the cast. Between the piles was one programme opened at the centre page. There were four amendments to be made on each programme: Leslie Nash for Peter Ridpath as Lucio, Elizabeth Faggott for Hilary Boyson as Isabella, Peggy Howard for Elizabeth Faggott as Mariana, and Peggy Howard to be removed from the ranks of the harlots and nuns. This open programme had had only the first two alterations made to it, and, unlike the others, the ink had dried, instead of being blotted. There was a piece of blotting-paper to one side of it and an uncorked bottle of ink towards the back of the table, with a pen resting by its nib on the lip of it. The general impression one got was that Tudor (I've confirmed that the handwriting was his) had been sitting working at the programmes and had paused, for a moment, to light a cigarette or give his fingers a rest.

"So much for the table.

"To the right as one went in, against the wall opposite the ticket-window and partially screened by the opened door, which was hinged on the right, was a typist's desk carrying a portable Corona machine. In front of it was a Tansad chair—and it was on this chair that we found Tudor, bent forward so that his head rested on the keyboard of the typewriter. Spattered about on the lino in the immediate neighbourhood of the body were drops of dried blood."

He smiled an apology at the Superintendent.

"Sorry for all these halting details, but I've got to present the facts in their right order. When Martin-and I had a look at the machine, there was a sheet of paper in it. I'll tell you, in a minute, what was typed on it. What concerns us now is that the sheet was finished and ready to be removed. Our interest lies in the fact that it *had* been removed—and put back again."

"Nothing in that, surely? It's not unusual to re-insert a page and carry on from where you left off."

"But it is when you reached the bottom of the page in the first instance. Listen, Tiny. Tudor was disturbed at his typing by the Collingwoods and Duzest. When they came into the box-office, he pulled the sheet out. It may have been only to prevent them from casting an inquisitive eye over it, but Collingwood got the impression that, in any case, the sheet was ready for removal. Tudor laid it face downwards on the desk.

"Just before they left him, he typed off a 'House Full' notice and, to make it more striking, did it in red. When we gave the Corona the once-over this morning, the two-colour movement was *still* set at red. Doesn't that indicate that the announcement was the last thing Tudor tapped out last night—and that the other sheet was put back afterwards?"

"P'raps Tudor did it himself and was called away before he could change the colour?"

"I've just told you," said Charlton patiently, "that the sheet was already full."

"I see what you mean—some other fellow put it back." He thought for a moment, then added craftily: "Was it straight?"

"The alignment was perfect enough to bear the closest inspection. The final word on the page was 'you' followed by a full-stop and double-quotes. The double-quotes key was therefore the last to be struck to finish the page. The machine was set exactly at the double-quotes."

"Then if you don't mind my saying so, Harry, I find your colour theories a bit far-fetched. That's the trouble with you—you don't keep your feet on the ground. Now, I could think of a thousand and one reasons for—"

"Perhaps you could," Charlton coolly cut him short, "but can you think of one single reason why the machine was set at the double-quotes, when, if that key was the last to be struck, the machine should have been set at the next space?"

The Super's mouth fell open.

"To make it perfectly clear," Charlton went on with a complacency that he knew would rile the big policeman, "when one has struck a typewriter key, the carriage jumps into position for the next letter as soon as the pressure is taken off the key. So I hope you'll now agree, Tiny, that the sheet was removed by Tudor and replaced either by the murderer or an accomplice."

"Yes," said the Super, without noticeable warmth.

"Why, then, was it replaced? Surely to give the impression that Tudor was busy on it when the knife got him through the heart: to make us believe that he was sitting at the desk: to prevent us from discovering that he was not at the desk when the blow was struck, but at the table, just where Collingwood had left him a short while before."

"Why?" demanded Kingsley; and this time Charlton welcomed the question.

"Tudor was stabbed plumb-squarely through the back. Sitting at the table, he was sideways on to the doorway. He couldn't have been taken unawares. Nobody would have been able to get into a suitable position to stab him, without him knowing it. But with him sitting at the typewriter, it would have been a different matter. The doorway would have been well behind him to the right; and with the door open, as he might well have left it, any light-footed person could have crept in and pounced on him before he had a chance even to turn round."

"Wouldn't that have suited the murderer better?"

"Not if he was sufficiently well-known to Tudor to arouse no suspicions by strolling across the foyer, nonchalantly swinging the dagger-belt. He didn't want us to know that Tudor was wiped out by one of his own familiar circle, but rather to assume the existence of some marauding stranger, who dropped in on the off-chance, disposed of any opposition, rifled the cash-drawer, and then made a quick get-away."

"A point well made," approved the Super.

Sergeant Martin coughed.

"Which reminds me to tell you, Inspector," he said, "that we've checked up on all the rogues and vagabonds round about here last night, and gave 'em all a clean bill."

"One thing occurs to me," the Super said. "How do you account for the bloodstains on the lino round the desk?"

"The dagger was driven into Tudor right up to the hilt, which, as you know, leads to practically no loss of blood. Most of the bleeding is internal. I've found out that last Saturday Tudor punched a man on the nose, while he was standing just by that desk. The blood marks on the lino were cracked and flaky when I examined them, which means a much longer lapse of time than a few hours. I've cut out a strip of the lino and sent it up to the Home Office with a sample of Tudor's blood and some from the recipient of the poke in the snoot. If the first and third are in the same blood-group and the second in a different blood-group, that will clinch it."

Superintendent Kingsley gazed at him with wonder.

"How have you found time to get through all this to-day?"

"It's done with mirrors," Charlton told him, and yawned.

"Have I heard everything now?"

The Super was not so bright himself.

"Not quite. The theatre has recently been redecorated. The last thing to be done was the stage-door, which was painted on Tuesday. By reason of the damaged tread, there were 'Not To Be Used' notices at the top and bottom of the staircase, yet on the bar of the panic latch on the door there were clear and definite prints, as if it had been pulled shut by two sets of hooked fingers. This is in support of Sugarman's evidence. Peters will be able to say for certain, of course, but as far as Martin and I could ascertain, there were no other fingerprints on the door; on the face of it, the person who left the prints merely closed the door and did not previously open it.

"We found some more prints on the drawer of the table in the box-office, but they might have been made by any member of the LADS The only other prints that have entered so far into this most diverting case were found by me on some dress-shirts in Tudor's compactum at Eagle House. We won't go into details now: I'll just say that after half-past ten last night, some unknown person was rummaging round in Tudor's room, apparently in search of something."

He lighted another cigarette.

"Next there's the question of the gloves. It's not definite yet, but all the evidence indicates that the murderer wore gloves—not rubber, but honest-to-goodness wool. This suggests a certain haste; that he knew of the conventional necessity to wear gloves, but didn't get time to slip round to Marks & Spencer's. The Sergeant and I detected fragments of presumably woollen material on the dagger-hilt, the platen-knobs of the typewriter—for turning up the paper, you know—on the bar of the panic latch and also on the outside paintwork of the stage-door. Samples from each were sent up to Metropolitan Police Laboratory this morning."

"I purposely said nothing about gloves to any of the witnesses, but when they arrived here to-day for their finger-prints to be taken, they were all asked to confirm that they were wearing the same gloves as they did last night. There were no exceptions to the general affirmative answer; and specimen strands were taken from all those of woollen manufacture. There weren't really a great number, as a good many wore leather or kid. This second lot of samples followed the others up to London; and it will probably be some days before we get the report."

"What colour was the wool?"

"It's difficult to say without a very powerful lens. On the typewriter and dagger, the fragments were almost micro-scopic; and by the time we'd scraped the others off the dark brown paintwork, they were a bit messy. I think we'll wait for the verdict of the experts."

He stifled another yawn.

"For some time past," he resumed, "Tudor has been

engaged—not exactly secretly, but in private—on typewriting work. The page you heard about a few minutes ago was numbered 229 at the top and headed 'Chapter twelve.' It described the end of a scrap between Tudor and Manhow, your sleepy slug. From this, one gathers that Tudor was writing a book—a sort of autobiography in the form of a novel. But I haven't been able to lay my hands on the first eleven chapters. I wish I could; they might help a lot. The only clue I've so far obtained was from—you'll never guess! . . . Mrs. Cheesewright. (The other three were too drowsy even to murmur 'The old gentlewoman. . . .') She claims that on Wednesday morning she was in the post office while Tudor was registering a thick envelope large enough to contain quarto sheets. The G.P.O. afterwards verified that it was addressed to Tudor's father. His parents arrived in Lulverton this afternoon, and, apart from the formal identification of the body, we haven't troubled them yet; but by Friday, at the latest, I hope to get hold of the secret opus, to repeat young Gough's description of it."

The Super put his hand across his mouth and mumbled sleepily:

"Is that the lot?"

"No, Tiny, it isn't. You asked for it and you're going to get it, if it takes all night! . . . There's one rather queer feature about this case: although it has all the hallmarks of a personal crime—call it a crime of passion—there's been a curious persistent undercurrent throughout the enquiries. Bradfield hasn't handed in his report yet, but Martin, Hartley, Emerson and I all noticed it: a hint here and there of a motive that had nothing to do with love, jealousy, robbery with violence, or gain through wills or life assurance."

He leant his elbows on the desk in front of him and placed his spread fingers together. The sleepier the Superintendent grew, the more was he himself inclined towards discourse.

"During the Spanish Civil War of 1936-39," he declaimed with unction, "when General Franco attacked Republican

Madrid, his troops advanced on the capital from four different directions. But they might not have succeeded in capturing the city, had it not been for their supporters within the gates, who did their best to cause civil disturbances and the spread of panic. And just as the army was divided into four columns, so could these subversive agents well be described as—"

The Superintendent's interjection was firm.

"Cut it!"

Charlton looked pained and surprised.

"Don't you want to be told the origin of the fifth column?" he asked.

"I do not. Neither do I wish to learn the facts of life or the truth about Father Christmas."

Peter Bradfield tittered.

"All I want," the Super went on, with the plaintiveness of an exhausted child, "is to go to bed."

Sergeant Martin's sandy poll had fallen forward and he was snoring very softly, so as not to hinder the conversation.

"Then what I was working round to," explained the inspector, "is that it seems an accepted belief among certain members of the dramatic society that Tudor was murdered by a fifth columnist because of something he had found out, or even that he himself was an enemy agent. Martin, Hartley and Emerson were all told the same thing; and I had it from Manhow and Miss Lark. Even Hobson, Mrs. Doubleday's odd-job man, referred to German spies with a crafty expression on his face. So it's just poss—"

Bradfield stopped him.

"Excuse me, sir, but there's something I ought to tell you at once. One of the witnesses I interviewed this afternoon was Michael Kelso, the journalist. He told me that, during the dress rehearsal, Tudor began asking him indirect questions— quite in a casual way—about fifth columnists. He said he'd heard that fifth columnists had been discovered in Poland in all sorts of disguises. Kelso said, 'Of course—that's part of the game: army officers, railway officials, A.R.P. wardens—any sort of get-up is to be anticipated.' Tudor also wanted to know who was keeping an eye on fifth column activities in this country. Kelso gave him a few details about M.I.5. Tudor said he supposed M.I.5 men were pretty inaccessible, and Kelso suggested that someone in authority at the nearest police station was the best man to go to with any information. When Kelso asked him jokingly if he'd found a fifth columnist, he quickly denied that—"

"Martin!" rapped out Charlton.

The sergeant jerked his head upright.

"Yes, dear?" he asked; blinked and coughed an apology.

"That 'phone-call, Martin."

"Which one would that be, sir?"

"Didn't somebody ring me here last night?

"Very probably, sir."

"Don't be damn silly! The call you told me about this morning, man!"

"Oh, that one, sir. Yes, of course, *that* one. This chap wanted to speak to you. Nobody else would do. When the officer on duty told 'im you'd gone home—getting on for eleven-thirty it was by that time—and that you'd be in soon after nine this morning, 'e said 'e'd ring again then."

"And did he?"

"Not as far as I know, sir."

"Right. Follow it up, first thing in the morning. See if the exchange can trace the call and tell you whether it was put through from the Little Theatre." He turned to the Super-intendent. "Rather interesting, Tiny. Tudor's chat with Kelso explains why the fifth column cropped up such a lot during our questioning of witnesses to-day. The crowded theatre wasn't the best spot for such a conversation and they were probably overheard. Doesn't it strike you as a possibility that Tudor was silenced before he got a chance to spill the beans?" The Super leant towards him.

"Take my tip, Harry," he said, "and concentrate on Ridpath. Leave this fifth column stuff to the Sunday papers. Somebody's trying to sidetrack you, but you know as well as I do that the most obvious motive for a crime nearly always turns out to be the correct one. Stick to Ridpath and you—"

He stopped short and cocked his ear. The quietness of Lulverton's empty streets had been broken by an approaching motor-cycle. Two minutes later, a gaitered constable entered the room, saluted the Superintendent and handed Charlton a packet.

"We haven't Ridpath's prints, of course," Charlton said, as he got busy with his paper-knife, "but I supplied Peters with two articles he'd handled: a razor-blade from his old bedroom at Eagle House, and a letter he'd written to Tudor's girl secretary, whose prints we took as well."

Besides the photographs, the packet contained a report from Sergeant Peters. Amongst other things, it stated, to the considerable satisfaction of the Super, that prints found on the razor-blade and letter coincided with those on the bar of the stage-door panic latch.

"There you are, Harry!" he exulted. "Your case is complete."

Charlton grunted without listening, and then read out from the report:

" 'The prints on the dress-shirt removed from Eagle House and the prints on the table-drawer in the box-office are identical with No. 16 on the attached list of members of the LADS' "

"And who's No. 16?" demanded Kingsley.

He and Bradfield looked at Charlton eagerly. Even the sergeant woke up again. Charlton ran his finger down the names, stopped—and whistled.

"Franklin Duzest," he told them.

XVIII

Call hither,
I say, bid come before us, Angelo.
Act I, Sc. 1.

Mr. and Mrs. Tudor called on Charlton at the police station early in the morning.

"He's seemed so happy recently," Mrs. Tudor told him. "Last Saturday we had a letter from him. He told us all about the Shakespeare play they were going to give this week and then said that he hoped very soon to have some interesting news for us." Her mouth trembled. "The dear boy said, 'Wish me luck!' so we thought that he was going to get engaged. And now he's . . ."

"Have you any clues, Inspector?" asked Mr. Tudor in a man-of-the-world tone that brought a lump into the case-hardened detective's throat.

"My enquiries are proceeding, Mr. Tudor." He chatted with them for a while before raising the question that bulked large in his mind: the missing typescript. Mr. Tudor soon reassured him.

"Yes," he nodded, "my son has been sending it to me by instalments, as he hardly liked to leave it lying about in his office or the boarding-house. We have at home six unopened envelopes, the last of which did not arrive until yesterday morning. It was my son's express wish that we should not read the manuscript at present; and, of course, we did as he asked. He told us what it was—a literary experiment in the shape of a diary written as a novel. Whether he proposed, when it was finished—if such a work can ever be considered finished—to alter all the names and try to find a publisher, I cannot tell you."

"May I be allowed to read it, Mr. Tudor?"

The old gentleman looked doubtful, but Mrs. Tudor said:

"If it will assist the inspector, dear, I think he ought to have it. Vaughan may have written something in it that will help to find his—murderer. My husband and I are trying not to be vindictive, Mr. Charlton, but we want whoever killed our dear boy to be discovered and punished."

"Are you on the telephone at home?"

"Yes. The maid will be there to answer it."

"Then, if you don't mind, I'll put through a call now, so that you can ask her to hand over the envelopes to the man I propose to send up to London at once."

"As you wish," answered Mr. Tudor with resignation.

The call was made, Mr. Tudor signed a note for the messenger to take, and the interview came to an end. Alone in his office, Charlton went to the window and watched his visitors walk slowly away, Mrs. Tudor clinging to her husband's arm. As they turned the corner and passed out of sight, the thought came to him that if the murderer had foreseen the grief of that forlorn old couple, the blade might have been checked, even on the point of descent, before it could slide through Vaughan Tudor's defenceless back.

He was discussing the programme for the day with Martin and the Three Musketeers, when the 'phone bell rang. The caller was Mrs. Doubleday.

"You remember," she said in the slow, distinct, pidginny tone of one who imagines that the telephone is not very familiar with the English tongue, "that you asked me to bear in mind a Miss Brown and a Mr. Smith, who stayed here on Wednesday night? Well, this morning I have received a letter from Miss Brown, who has lost a brooch and wonders whether we have since found it in Heagle—in Eagle House. The address she gives is"—her voice went up an octave—"94, Beechwood Road, Sutton, Surrey."

"Any telephone number?"

" No. Just a stamped envelope for a reply."

"What do you say her name is?" Charlton asked, having in mind a possibility first suggested by Sergeant Martin.

"Brown. Miss Faith Brown."

He thanked Mrs. Doubleday, rang off and turned to P.C. Emerson.

Ring up and arrange for an inspector to go round and see this young woman," were his instructions, "and get her answers to these questions."

Emerson took them down at his chief's dictation. He was a brawny young giant, who could crumple a tobacco-tin in his hand, as if it were a paper-bag, and a very useful man in a rough-house.

"And don't stray far from here," Charlton told him, "until we get the report back. Sergeant, you follow up that telephone-call; and you, Bradfield, get your nose down on Ridpath's trail—and if you don't find him to-day, consider yourself back on the beat. I shall not be in again until round about half-past four."

Elizabeth Faggott consented to see him when he called. She was looking white and ill, as if she had not slept all night.

"Miss Faggott," he said gravely, "I need not impress on you the seriousness of misleading the police. Yesterday you told me that you had not seen Mr. Ridpath since last Saturday. I have since learned that he visited you here on Wednesday night. Was that so?"

"Yes," she admitted in a low tone. "I talked to him at the front gate."

"Why did he come?"

"He was very worried over what had happened. You see, he hadn't known that Vaughan wanted to marry me; and when Vaughan found out last Saturday about the Guildford blunder—oh, how bitterly I regret that!—he went straight back to Mrs. Doubleday's and had a furious row with Peter. Peter was dumbfounded and didn't know what to say. When Vaughan told him to get out and not show his face in Lulverton again, he thought he'd better go until the storm blew over. But even a few days away were too uncomfortable for him, so he crept back here to ask me what his chances were of making it up with Vaughan."

"And what did you advise?"

"I told him that my position was no better than his; that Vaughan flatly refused to have anything more to do with me. 'If Vaughan,' I said to Peter, 'could only be made to understand that Guildford was only a silly indiscretion that took place before I looked on him as any more than a casual acquaintance, and that since then, I have refused to have anything to do with you, it might make things easier for all three of us.' Then Peter asked whether I thought it would do any good for him to see Vaughan. I said it wasn't at all likely, but was worth trying; and that if he went round to the Bakehouse immediately, he would find Vaughan alone there. So Peter went."

"Have you seen him since?"

"No. Do, *please,* believe me, Mr. Charlton! I didn't tell you the truth yesterday, because I was badly frightened. Peter Ridpath means nothing to me now, but he seemed so *helpless* that I simply couldn't put him in a worse position by telling you that he was at the Bakehouse on Wednesday evening. . . . It's funny about Peter. Even after I'd sent him away last September, I couldn't get rid of the feeling that I ought to look after him. I had a curious sort of protective instinct, as if he was a little boy and had to be stopped from running into the road."

"Do you think, Miss Faggott, that on Wednesday night he—did run into the road?"

"No!" she said quickly. "No, I don't. Peter would never kill anybody. He's too soft, too—effeminate. All he wants—I see it now—is an easy life, good clothes, money in his pocket, and a succession of not too intelligent girl friends. He's a butterfly— and butterflies aren't dangerous, are they?"

"I don't know," he replied, not entirely in jest. "I have never seen one roused."

He was on his way along the road, when a shrill cry from behind made him pause and turn round. Jill Geering was

251

running towards him with her pigtails flying.

"Well, young lady," he smiled with forced geniality, as she pulled up panting, "what's all the excitement?"

"Do you still want to know," she asked, "who took that note from Elizabeth's bag?"

"Yes."

"And put it in Hilary Boyson's coat pocket, so that everybody would think she'd stolen it and then she'd be sent to prison and Elizabeth would get her part back? Do you still want to know who it was did it?"

"Yes, I do."

"Well, it was me.

There was Mrs. Saunderson, old Garnett's daughter, to be visited again. He failed to see what part she could have played, however indirect, in the death of Tudor, yet somehow he felt that further investigation was called for. Whoever it had been and whatever reason had prompted it, somebody had been anxious for Hilary Boyson to supplant Elizabeth Faggott. Wishy-washy little Mrs. Saunderson, the obstinate jellyfish that kept floating back, had admitted her instrumentality in the affair, but the excuse she had given had been an obvious lie; and when it was a question of murder, liars called for special attention.

Had the front room curtains not moved slightly as he opened the front gate, be would have gone away when his first two rings were not answered. As it was, he rang a third time with peremptory insistence, and after a pause, Mrs. Saunderson opened the door a crack.

"Good morning," he smiled. "I am a police inspector. You'll remember that I called with your father yesterday. May I trouble you to give me a few more minutes please?"

"Yes," she replied insipidly. "Will you come in?"

She pulled open the door and led him into the room where her father had upbraided her on the previous day. She invited him to take a seat and sat on the edge of her own chair, playing nervously with a tea-cloth that she had been too disturbed to think of laying aside.

"When I was here yesterday, Mrs. Saunderson," he began, "your father got you to confirm that your reason for asking him to arrange for Miss Faggott to be superseded by Miss Boyson was that it might influence Mr. Boyson in his choice of a new works manager. Do you still stick to that, Mrs. Saunderson?"

"Yes. I did it for Mr. Saunderson's sake."

He objected on principle to wives calling their husbands "Mr.", which may have accounted for the very sharp tone that gave an added menace to the conventional warning:

"I'll tell you first that I am enquiring into a murder and that anything you say will be written down and may be used in evidence. Now I'll ask you once again, Mrs. Saunderson, whether you still adhere to your remarks to your father in my presence yesterday?"

She had twisted the tea-cloth into a knot. Now it fell to the floor. She picked it up and unravelled it before answering.

"Dad frightened me. I didn't know what I was saying, especially with you there. I thought you came from the factory—that Mr. Boyson had sent you. Dad gets so angry sometimes that he scares me out of my wits."

"You haven't answered my question, Mrs. Saunderson."

Suddenly, like a too-quickly revolving gramophone-record started in the middle, she said in a sing-song voice:

"I wasn't telling Dad the truth. Mr. Saunderson would have got the job, whatever happened. I wanted Miss Boyson to get the part, so that Miss Faggott shouldn't have it. I had a grievance against Miss Faggott and wanted to pay her out."

"What had she done to offend you?"

"She was giving some impersonations at a charity concert and one of them was meant for a dig at me. Everybody laughed and started turning round and Mr. Saunderson said to me, 'She's got you off a treat, Elsie.' I wasn't going to let her get away with that—standing up there on the platform all smiles and bowing when they clapped."

"How did you first come to meet Miss Faggott?"

This very ordinary question seemed to disconcert Mrs. Saunderson, as if she had not been prepared for it. When she spoke again, her tone, though still flavourless, was slower and hesitant.

"I don't really remember. Everybody knows everybody else in Lulverton. I'm always seeing her about."

"But does she know *you*?"

"She must do, or she wouldn't have ridiculed me on the stage. Even Mr. Saunderson noticed it, so it wasn't my imagination."

That was as far as he could get with her. The jellyfish had reversed its tactics, for now every time he tried to detain it, it drifted away.

He called at the Bunch of Grapes, but was informed that Franklin Duzest had gone to Southmouth in his car and was not expected back until sometime after lunch. He left a message for Duzest to ring him at the police station on his return; and then, as the Tudor case was far from having the only claim on his time, turned his attention to other matters.

At 3.5 Emerson took a call from the Surrey police.

"I got in touch with Miss Brown," the inspector at the other end told him. "She herself heard nothing, but the Smith fellow was a bit more helpful. I had to trace him to his office in the City, or I could have rung you earlier. He says that a few minutes before half-past six on Wednesday evening, he went out the back way to cover up his car in the garage. He was just coming in again, when somebody up on the first floor shouted, 'Get out!' in a very angry way. It was a man's voice and was followed by another man's voice saying, 'Sorry!' Then Smith heard a door being closed, not too gently. He didn't recognise either of the voices. Will that do?"

Emerson thanked him and rang off.

At 3.15 the messenger arrived back from London with a brown-paper parcel containing Tudor's typescript.

At 3.20 Sergeant Martin joined Emerson.

At 3.25 Scotland Yard rang up to pass on a report from the Home Office on the bloodstains found by Inspector Charlton in the box-office.

At 3.35 Franklin Duzest put through a call from the Bunch of Grapes and was told that the inspector was expected back at 4.30. He told Martin he would call at the police station at 4.45.

At 4.5 Charlton strolled into the office—to the embarrassment of the sergeant, who could never be entirely comfortable without his feet up on something—threw his hat on a filing-cabinet (a system he always neglected in favour of a pile of papers on a chair), slipped out of his overcoat, slumped into a seat, lighted a cigarette and gave vent to a long-drawn, "Ah!"

Martin allowed a decent interval to elapse before mentioning business, then said:

"One or two little things, sir. Mr. Duzest will look in at a quarter to five. That 'phone-call for you on Wednesday night was put through from the Little Theatre at 11.25. The operator says it was a gentlemanly sounding voice."

"Martin," said his chief, "this case is beginning to take shape."

"The Yard 'ave been on the blower about them bloodstains. They say the Home Office people's report is that the stains on the lino were Group 1, but Tudor's blood fell in Group 2. The Manhow sample puts him in Group 1, same as the lino stains."

When he stopped, Charlton said nothing, so he went on:

"Emerson's taken a call from the Surrey police about Miss Brown and the man called Smith. Emerson, say your lines...."

"Smith, sir," said Emerson to the inspector, "confirms that a man somewhere on the first floor shouted, 'Get out!' It was followed by another man saying, 'Sorry!' and a door being closed with a certain amount of vigour."

"Looks to me, Inspector," threw in the sergeant, "as if it wasn't the last few words of a row, but that someone 'ad intruded on someone else, without due notice, 'oo was probably changing into 'is other trousers."

"Yes," said Charlton absently, "changing into his other trousers." Suddenly, his eyes opened wide and he stared at the startled sergeant. "That's what he was doing, Martin. He was changing into his other trousers."

Martin turned towards the door.

"I'd better get you a nice cup of tea," he said in a soothing tone.

Restored by three cups from the pot that Martin brought, he untied the parcel from Lee, S.E. Inside were six sealed, registered envelopes, all bearing the Lulverton postmark. The first was dated the 18th September, 1939 and the last, the 3rd January, 1940. He slit them open with his paper-knife and, keeping each section separate, began to glance through the sheets.

He was interrupted at 4.45 by the punctual arrival of Franklin Duzest, whose appearance was, if anything, even more suggestive than usual of the fleshpots of Egypt. Charlton slipped the typescript away in a drawer of his desk as Duzest was shown in by Emerson, who then left the two men alone.

"I wanted to see you again," Charlton explained, "so as to be quite sure I got your story right yesterday. You said then that you walked with Mr. Collingwood and his daughter as far as the end of Friday Street, where you left them and went home. When you arrived home, you had a drink and then went to bed. Do you want to add to that?"

"No, I don't think so. It just about hits the thing off."

"I'm quite correct in assuming that, after saying good night to the Collingwoods, you went straight on to the Bunch of Grapes and retired for the night?"

Duzest smiled wearily. "Where's all this leading us, Charlton? Am I on your little list? The answer to your question is, yes."

"For all that," said Charlton agreeably, "I'm going to put it to you that you did *not* go to bed, but went round to Eagle House and slipped up to the late Mr. Tudor's room."

The other man stroked his sleek dark hair.

"I did no such thing," he said.

"You searched the room, failed to find what you were after, and left quietly by the back way."

"You seem very sure of all this, Charlton!"

"I *am* sure. Your fingerprints were found on some dress-shirts that were not put in Tudor's compactum until 10.30 on Wednesday night."

Franklin Duzest threw back his head and laughed merrily.

"Trapped by the Yard! I didn't think you were so thorough. Well, I'm not going to waste any more of your time, so I'll admit that, for private reasons, I had a little snoop round Tudor's room."

"What were those private reasons, Mr. Duzest?"

"I prefer not to tell you any more than that I hoped to find certain papers."

"In other words, the manuscript that Mr. Tudor has been working on for some months past."

"So you've got wind of it, have you? Yes, that's what I was after."

"Why?"

"Because I wanted to read it."

"Why?"

"What an insistent fellow you are, to be sure! The fact is that everything points to Tudor's *magnum opus* being a chronicle of events in the history of the Little Theatre. Tudor himself threw out a hint of it from time to time. Frankly, I've never been a white-headed boy and I wanted to make certain that details of some of my little escapades hadn't found their way into the script. It was tough luck on me that, on the very same evening, somebody decided to dispose of Tudor. If I'd known that such big conclusions were being tried elsewhere, I'd have been rather more careful how I scattered fingerprints about."

"Miss Faggott—" began the inspector, but Duzest pulled him up with a jerk.

"Please keep her out of this."

"That's not possible. Miss Faggott is deeply concerned in the affair; and I should like you to tell me now the exact extent of your own relations with her."

Duzest sat back in his chair and threw one leg over the other.

"She means nothing to me," he said with studied unconcern.

"I'm not suggesting otherwise," was the acid rejoinder. "You've just said that you don't claim to be a white-headed boy; and what I'm asking is, how far did you go with Miss Faggott?"

"No distance at all, I assure you. It takes two to make an *affaire de coeur*. Miss Faggott and I are just good friends."

"Then why were you so concerned over what Tudor may have written."

"Oh, that was another business entirely."

"Mr. Duzest, I don't think you realise the serious position you're in. I'm not suggesting, at this stage, that you were implicated in the murder of Vaughan Tudor, but I *am* suggesting that it's steadily getting more difficult for you to prove your innocence. Tudor was killed for some very good reason—and there is at least one that occurs to me. Murderers, Mr. Duzest, are almost always convicted on circumstantial evidence alone."

Duzest got up and, with his hands in the pockets of his heavy overcoat, strolled round the room for some minutes. Charlton watched him in silence. Then Duzest returned to his seat, pulled his valuable case from an inner pocket and extracted a cigarette, which he tapped on the case and lighted without haste.

"I hadn't intended to tell you," he said, leaning forward to drop the spent match in the ash-tray on the desk, "but you've got me in a corner. The answer to all your questions is very brief."

"And it is ...?"

"M.I.5."

Sneak not away, sir.
Act V, Sc. 1.

"**B**y my order and for the good of the State, the bearer of this will do what he is about to do."

Such is reputed to have been the burden of the *lettres de cachet* held by the emissaries of the great Cardinal Richelieu; and in similar, if not quite such sweeping, terms was couched the authority that Major Duzest exhibited to Charlton, who whistled when he saw the signature at the foot.

"You forced my hand," smiled Duzest. "You were too damn smart over those fingerprints of mine. Certain eminent persons wouldn't be too delighted if I got myself mixed up in a local murder case. I'd better tell you the whole story, so that you can return to your investigations and leave me to get back to mine.

"The deadliest weapon in the hands of the Nazis," he went on in a style that reminded Charlton of his own discourse to his irritated Superintendent, "is their elaborate network of agents, who, as well as carrying out valuable espionage work, also prepare the way for the main *putsch*. Ever since 1919, these conspirators have been busy—these so-called minorities, whose members form part of what Admiral von Hintze prettily described as a nation of ninety million Germans joining hearts and hands across the political frontiers and whose only task is to abuse the hospitality they enjoy and afterwards betray their good-natured, easygoing hosts.

"Take the case of Poland. The *Verein für das Deutschtum im Auslande*—that is, The Society for Germans Abroad—the *Auslandsinstitut,* which was ostensibly a scientific institution; the German Teachers' Union, the Western Poland Agricultural Society—they all took their instructions from the Second Bureau, and were paid by the German War Office through a Dutch Bank. Hundreds and hundreds of young German Poles went on holiday trips to Dantzig and were sent on from there to Berlin by the German Consul-General, for an intensive training course in espionage and fifth column work.

"When the time for the *putsch* arrived, the minorities were ready. They spread rumours, provoked panic, destroyed means of communication and started fires—in fact, stirred up so much confusion that the invading troops had not much more to do than goose-step into the cosy billets that were all prepared for them."

He flicked the ash from his cigarette.

"Besides these German Poles, of whom it can, in fairness, be said that they did what they did in the service of their Fatherland, there were, among these diversionists, a considerable number of true-born Poles—poisonous swine, prepared to sell their services to the highest bidder and betray their country, either for cash or for the assurance of a nice little post in the new administration.

"All these things happened in Poland. You'll probably say that they can't happen here. But they can. Certainly, we have no minorities like the Sudetan Germans in Czechoslovakia or the Bydgoszcz Germans in Poland; but there are Germans everywhere and each one of them is, in himself, a minority, joining hearts and hands, etc. etc. We've done what we can to round up Nazis and Nazi sympathisers in this country, but between you and me, there are far too many still at large. A frightening number of these pathetic refugees who come streaming across the Channel with their pitiful little bundles are nothing more than fifth columnists, ready to make contact with underground organisations already in existence—and to help lose us the war.

"As you've probably guessed by now, it's my present job to smoke out one of those organisations. It's been a headache to our people for some time. We know it exists and we know some of its members, who'll be gathered in when the time is ripe. But it's the men at the top we're after—the Senator Wiesners and the Pastor Zocklers; the big-timers, who may, for all we know at the moment, he preaching from pulpits, sitting on charitable committees or serving behind the bacon counter. I know all this Master-Mind-in-the-Background stuff sounds like a Secret Service novel; but that's the trouble with Intelligence work—it so very much resembles a seven-and-sixpenny thriller, except that the Master Mind is not dear old Professor Fiddlefaddle, but a most efficient and highly organised General Staff in Berlin, under the genial and inspiring patronage of Adolf H., Esq.

"We've been working on it for some little time and have narrowed things down to the neighbourhood of Southmouth, where, apart from the rather important docks that everyone knows about, there are also other things that it is preferred should remain in discreet obscurity. No hint of them has, as yet, leaked out of this country through the Eire mails, but we've every reason to believe that, besides arranging to receive their invading friends in due season, the fraternity known as No. 23 (because of the place this district occupies on the divisioned map of England in the sumptuous offices of the Second Bureau) have been collecting information about the 'other things' at Southmouth, and are ready to smuggle the complete report to their Nazi bosses, who'll undoubtedly make use of it in a manner that will prove most uncomfortable for us.

"D'you see, then, why I was so interested in Tudor? My immediate predecessor on this consignment had the misfortune to meet with what the papers described as a 'Fatal Black-out Car Smash,' so it was with some diffidence that I answered the stirring call of duty, tore myself away from my dear little wife and kids, and insinuated myself gracefully into the social whirl of Lulverton, where carefully fostered rumours soon transformed me into the town's most fascinating chartered libertine, which, for a man interested only in gardening and first editions, is a damn difficult character to sustain, but which gave me the *entrée* into all the best homes in Lulverton. As a part of my campaign, I joined the LADS and had some quite good incidental fun.

"Tudor first attracted my attention when I discovered,

quite by accident, that he was in Germany just before the September Crisis in 1938. Admittedly, he wasn't the only foolhardy holiday-maker in the Bavarian Alps at that time, but it was a pointer, and Tudor was just the type of inconspicuous English gentlemen who make the most useful fifth columnists. Anyway, while pursuing my other lines of enquiry, I kept a wary eye on him, and became particularly intrigued when his secret midnight candle-burning got to my ears. A man doesn't lock himself up and work busily at a typewriter until all hours of the night, without some very good reason—and the only one to occur to my pre-occupied mind was that he was documenting the data obtained on the subject of the 'other things' at Southmouth.

"The day before yesterday—and God knows I choose the wrong day for it!—I decided to get a line on what he was really up to. A code message that we'd intercepted on Tuesday read, 'Full report within a few days,' so there was not much time to be lost.

"There were three places where Tudor might have kept the papers: his office, the theatre and Eagle House. A few infinitely tactful enquiries elicited the information that Tudor's secretary, moustachioed Miss Muriel Jones, had access to everything in the office, including the safe, so I ruled that out. Early on Wednesday evening, I borrowed a key of the theatre from Hobson, on the excuse of trying on my costume, and frisked every inch of the place."

"Including the cash-drawer in the box-office," murmured Charlton.

"Yes—a very elementary lock. Did I leave fingerprints?"

"All over the box-office! It was a Herschel's playground! Would you like to see photographs?"

"No, thanks! I must remember in future that I'm not the only clever fellow in the world. I didn't find a thing in the Bakehouse and Tudor brought nothing with him to the rehearsal in the way of a portfolio or attache case, so when I'd made dead sure he was going to stay put for an hour or so, I—"

"Before we go any further, Major: was there a cigarette-tin in the table-drawer, with cash in it?"

"Yes, a Player's fifty. I didn't count the cash, but there was a pound note and some silver."

"Did you leave any of the tallboy drawers open?"

"Oh, no. I left everything as tidy as possible. Then I popped along to Mrs. Doubleday's, slid in the back way—the door was still unlocked—and gave Tudor's room a combing. Luckily, I wasn't disturbed."

"And yesterday morning, you arranged for a representative of Messrs. Golightly & Farthingale to call on Miss Jones?"

"You got on to that, did you?" grinned Duzest. "A pretty piece of impromptu nomenclature, don't you think?"

"A Frogbaskett in the middle would have lent it distinction," replied Charlton judicially.

"The only thing left for me to explain, then, is that my interest in Elizabeth Faggott was entirely professional. I cultivated her society because I hoped, through her, to find out more about Tudor. And I should like to add, quite privately, that she's a very delightful young person."

"So you're still not sure whether Tudor was an enemy agent?"

"No, mainly because of my failure to find the papers I was after."

Charlton opened his drawer and pulled out the envelopes.

"You may be interested in those," he said, pushing them across the desk.

Duzest pounced on the top one and extracted the sheets, which he began to glance eagerly through.

"I don't think you'll find much to interest you there," the inspector told him, "except references to an actor who did not quite succeed as Angelo, because Angelo was only a novice at dalliance."

"What a reputation for a respectable married man!" said Duzest with a rueful smile. "May I take this stuff away?"

Charlton looked doubtful before agreeing.

"It may help us to solve our two conundrums," suggested the Major.

"Perhaps," added Charlton, "the same answer will do for both."

An hour later, Bradfield came into the room.

"There's a man downstairs to see you, sir," he announced with satisfaction.

"Who is it?" asked Charlton, looking up from his work.

"A Mr. P. Ridpath."

"Where did you find him?"

"London."

"A big place."

"When a man arrives in London, sir, with very little money and nowhere to go, he always drifts into one of the parks—and that's where I picked him up, sitting on a seat in Kensington Gardens, looking as miserable as sin. He didn't try any funny stuff, but came like a lamb."

"Good work, Bradfield. Show him up, will you."

Ridpath's delicately handsome features wore a hunted expression as he took the seat Charlton offered him.

"I'm sorry to bring you all the way from London, Mr. Ridpath, but as you've possibly heard, your friend Mr. Tudor was killed on Wednesday evening, and I'm hoping that you can give us some information."

"I'll tell you all I can," Ridpath answered in a subdued tone. "You probably won't believe me, because it doesn't sound very convincing to me. Do you mind if I smoke?"

"Not at all. Have one of these."

They lighted cigarettes and Ridpath went on:

"Last Saturday evening, Tudor and I had a terrific brawl over a girl, and in consequence, I cleared out of Lulverton on Sunday morning and went to stay in Whitchester. By Wednesday, I got thoroughly fed up with it and in the evening came back here, with the idea of patching up the quarrel. As soon as I reached Lulverton, I went to see the girl "

"Miss Faggott?"

"Yes. I wanted to find out from her how things stood. She told me that Tudor followed up his row with me by break ing with her. He'd found something out about the two of us. There wasn't a word of truth in it, of—"

"Are you quite sure, Mr. Ridpath?"

"Well, when I say not a word of truth, I mean not in the way he thought. Miss Faggott and I certainly went to a hotel together last September, but spend the night very respectably in different rooms, although"—he smiled wanly—"one of them was a bathroom. You see, Inspector, the trouble was that, up to a few days ago, I'd no idea Tudor was really keen on her. It's a nasty jolt to find yourself accused by your best friend of mucking about with a girl he's practically engaged to. Tudor was such a straight-laced old devil that I always got a good deal of quiet fun out of shocking him, but last Saturday I went a bit too far and said a lot of silly things that I was damned sorry about afterwards. Those were my principal reasons for wanting to see him again: to apologise for talking like a cad, and to try to clear up the misunderstanding between him and Elizabeth Faggott."

"And when you left her on Wednesday night . . .?"

"I went straight round to the theatre—and found the door locked. I had a key on my bunch and let myself in. The light was on in the foyer and Tudor's coat was lying on the table. The box-office door was open, but the light switched off. I was just going to look round for Turt—for Tudor, when I heard a noise coming from along the passage leading to the stage."

"What sort of noise?"

"A clatter, as if someone had fallen over something. I went along the passage and felt a hefty gust of air coming up the staircase. I switched on the blue light and saw that the curtain at the bottom was blowing in. I went down the stairs and—"

"One of them was broken. Did the clatter you heard sound

like somebody falling foul of it?"

"Yes, I suppose it did, although, when I went down the stairs to investigate, I decided that it must have been the stage-door, because it was swinging backwards and forwards and, just as I got to the bottom of the stairs, slammed back against the wall. Thinking that Tudor had gone out into the Yard, I called to him."

"What did you say?"

"Oh, just 'Turtle,' an old school nickname I used for him. I got no reply, so, assuming that the door had been blown open by the wind, I closed it and went back upstairs, very perplexed."

"Did you close the door properly?"

"I think so. It's got one of those push-bar-to-open arrangements on it and I believe I worked it correctly. Back upstairs, I wandered round looking for Tudor, then switched on the light in the box-office and went in. He was lying across the typewriter with the hilt of a dagger sticking out of his back. I didn't touch him, but stood there petrified with horror—until slowly a thought came into my mind: how was I going to prove I hadn't murdered him? You can guess my feelings, I expect?"

The answering grunt was non-committal.

"When I'd pulled myself together," Ridpath went on, "I decided the best thing to do was to get away without being seen. I had a quick look round and then left by the main door."

"Did you close it behind you?"

"Yes, I left it locked on the Yale. By that time, it was getting late and I had to walk back to Whitchester. I got there well after three o'clock and, though absolutely dead tired, packed my things and hopped the first lorry going towards London."

"What time had you got to the theatre?"

Ridpath shook his head. "I really don't know. Round about quarter to twelve, I should think."

"And how long were you inside?"

"Something like ten minutes."

"Apart from the noises you've mentioned, did you hear anything else?"

"Not a sound. That's what put the breeze up me—the dreadful silence."

Charlton pointed to Ridpath's brown leather gloves.

"Were you wearing those last night?"

"Yes. They're the only pair I have."

"Did you call at Eagle House on Wednesday, either late at night or earlier in the day?"

"No, I didn't go near the place."

"You took employment with Mr. Tudor last June as a result of a newspaper advertisement. Did you know, when you applied for the position, that the notice had been inserted by your old school friend?"

"Oh, yes. If I hadn't recognised the name, I shouldn't have bothered to follow the thing up. I had no qualifications, you see. Yes, somebody had previously told me that Tudor had set up business in Lulverton."

"Who is your Italian correspondent, Mr. Ridpath?"

"Oh, a little Neapolitan girl I got friendly with some years ago. We write to each other occasionally."

"Why did you leave the service of Mrs. Salveter?"

"Mrs. Salveter?"

"Yes, the American widow with the good-looking niece."

"You seem to know a great deal about my private affairs," Ridpath said in an injured tone. "What's Mrs. Salveter got to do with the matter in hand?"

"Why did she dismiss you?"

"Because I got too matey with the niece. Anyway, it was years ago."

"During the rehearsal on Saturday evening, Mr. Ridpath, you had something on your mind. What was it?"

Ridpath looked distressed. "I was worried."

"Will you tell me why?"

"I'd. .. had bad news."

"Perhaps you'll give me some details?"

"I'd received a blackmailing letter."

"From whom?"

"Does that really matter?" asked Ridpath desperately.

"Yes; I want to know."

"Then it was from a girl. I was fool enough to tell her my address. She threatened me with a breach of promise case if I didn't marry her. Her old cow of a mother put her up to it."

"Was there any urgent reason why you should marry her?"

Ridpath gulped and said: "Yes."

"Did she offer an alternative to marriage?"

"She hinted, without putting it into words, that I could buy her off."

"But you hadn't the money?"

"Not a bean."

"So on Wednesday, you came back to Lulverton to borrow it from Mr. Tudor. That was the primary motive for your visit, wasn't it?"

"Yes." The admission was made with reluctance.

"And what did you propose to do if Mr. Tudor refused to lend you the money?"

"I didn't anticipate he *would* refuse, after I'd told him the truth about Elizabeth Faggott and me."

"Who's this latest light o' love at Guildford?"

"How do you know she's at Guildford?"

"What's her name?"

"Sheila Watkins. She's one of the chambermaids at the Chandos. I got chatting with her after Elizabeth Faggott had locked herself in the bathroom."

The inspector got to his feet.

"If you'd told the police as soon as you found Tudor," he said, "we might have caught his murderer by now. You'd better take your bag to Eagle House—and I advise you to stop there till you hear further from me."

Ridpath was looking down at the floor.

"I'm afraid I'm not showing up very well in this business,"

he said. "But it's a disease with me—the terrible eternal itch for something fresh."

Charlton looked down at the bent curly head with distaste.

"You spineless little rat," he said without anger.

It was refreshing to look on the healthy ugliness of Jack Gough, who came round later, in response to a telephone message.

"Gough," he said (and it was something of a compliment that he dropped the prefix), "I want another word with you about Wednesday. Between half-past eleven and midnight, three people called at the theatre. You were the third, and the first—though please keep it to yourself—was Ridpath. The question now is, who was the second?"

"I was," said Jack promptly.

"So I imagined. I was afraid you were going to deny it."

"The first time I went," Jack told him, "I pushed at the door and finding it locked, decided that Vaughan must have gone home. I hadn't met him on the way, but, as I expect you know, there are two routes between Mrs. Doubleday's and the Bakehouse. I was half-way home again before I suddenly thought that Vaughan might have been in the Bakehouse all the time, and had locked himself in for privacy. So I went back and snouted through the letter-box until old Sugarman stopped me."

"I wish you'd told me that yesterday, Gough."

"Sorry, Inspector, but it didn't seem sufficiently important."

The next question caused Jack to look astonished.

"Is your uniform a good fit?"

"My what? My *uniform!* I don't understand you."

"Somebody told me you'd got a commission."

"Good Lord, no! I've been toying with the idea of joining up, but I haven't actually taken the plunge yet. As for a commission, I probably shan't get much higher than the ranks. But coming back to the murder, it's rather curious isn't it, that Ridpath and I were the only two to call at the theatre?"

"Very curious indeed, Gough. There's only one explanation."

"And that is?"

"Rubber soles."

Just before Charlton went home to Southmouth, a constable brought him up a packet. Inside it was Tudor's manuscript, with a covering note from Major Duzest.

"There seems a good deal in here for you," it read, "but very little for me. There is one thing, however, that invites investigation. I must discuss it with you very soon."

Tired though he was, Charlton took the manuscript to bed with him and attentively read every word. Then he laid it on the bedside table, turned out the light and settled down between the sheets. But his brain was too active for sleep and it was an hour before he ceased pondering over Tudor's story. Then, at the moment when wakefulness was merging into slumber, a single thought shot into his brain.

"Good God!" he said aloud—and sat up.

He switched on the light, reached for the manuscript and flicked through it until he found the page he sought.

XX

Act V, Sc. 1.
Show your knave's visage ...
Show your sheep-biting face!

It was with a strange tale that Amos Miles, an old shepherd, came to the police station early on the Saturday morning. At break of day, he told Charlton, he had been up on the Downs. As he had made his slow way along the ridge, Amos's aged, but hawklike, eyes had caught sight of a figure away in a field to the south. In the ordinary way, Amos would not have paid much attention, but the figure had been behaving so oddly that even the unimaginative old countryman had paused in his strides.

"Round and round that there field 'e were going," said Amos, "for all the world like an old ram at the end of a tether. Then after a while, 'e tires of it and starts going across the field from side to side, till I were thinking 'e never would be done walking backwards and forwards. Why, the ploughed up ground were that trampled afore 'e were finished that—"

"Would you be able to recognise this man again?"

"No, 'e were too far away, but I figured I'd best come and tell the police, for all that. There's no knowing what devil's business 'e might 'ave bin up to, with 'is walking round and round and across and back."

Charlton looked at Martin with raised eyebrows, and Martin scratched his sandy head.

"Better go and take a look round, sir?" he suggested.

"Where is this field?" Charlton asked Amos.

"Way out past Sheep, alongside Farmer Gamble's big meadow."

They were just setting out in the black Vauxhall, when the thickly overcoated and dazzlingly old-school-scarfed figure of Major Duzest strolled towards them from the direction of the Bunch of Grapes.

"Going places?" he enquired. "I was on my way to see you."

"Yes. It's something that may be more in your line than ours. Care to come along with us?"

Duzest got in beside him, while Martin and old Amos fraternised in the back. As they drove along, Duzest mentioned Tudor's manuscript and told Charlton, in an undertone, of his suspicions.

"With all respect," was the detective's reply, "I think you're wrong—in fact, I'm certain you are. I read those eleven chapters very carefully last night and found one tiny incident that provides, if not the final, at any rate, a most important piece in my jig-saw puzzle." He paused a moment before adding: "And in yours."

He went on to confide in Duzest, who whistled.

"He couldn't possibly have known anything about it, as

long ago as that," said the Major. "Funny she should have been there."

"Just one of those little coincidences; and such women *are* dangerous, you know."

They travelled some distance before Duzest spoke again.

"Did you notice," he asked, "the grimly ironic touch on the first page of Tudor's manuscript? 'A plain man's doings and sudden death.' How the gods must have laughed, when he put it that way round!"

"He was obviously referring," replied Charlton, "to the motor-cycle accident with the friend who was killed. But, as you say, the gods must have laughed and nudged each other, as they peered over his shoulder in the quiet little box-office."

Directed by Amos, he pulled up the car by a gate in a lonely lane. They all got out and went into the field, which was ploughed and, as Amos had said, lay beside a large meadow, on which one solitary and unhappy-looking cow was grazing. While Martin and the old shepherd stayed by the gate, Charlton and Duzest went round the field, tracing out the pattern left by the early-rising pedestrian.

"You know what this is, I take it?" asked Duzest, as they followed the outer circle of tracks.

"A signal to a Nazi airman?"

"That's it; and when we've got the whole pattern clear, I may be able to tell you the message it conveys. If we were up in a plane, we could see it all at once. It shows up very clearly from above. The blighters did a lot of this sort of thing in Poland. Specially arranged trusses of hay was another of their little capers."

It took them ten minutes to follow all the tracks. Then:

"Got it!" said the Major.

The inspector looked at him enquiringly.

" 'Pick me up here at dawn to-morrow.' "

During the afternoon, the report on the fragments of wool came through from the Home Office. It was to the effect that the fragments found by Charlton on the dagger, typewriter and stage-door were identical; but that there was no similarity between them and the samples taken from the gloves of the LADS members. Although this report was only provisional and was subject to the confirmation of an expert adviser in Nottingham, the Home Office chemists had been sufficiently sure of their conclusions to add that the character of the fibre and its unusual shade of dark green identified it (but not beyond all question) with a London firm of glove manufacturers, whose sole agent in Lulverton was a Mr. Frederick Cheesewright.

Charlton, of course, went round to the Shambles, but obtained no more information than that from the dozen-box that had been in Mr. Cheesewright's stock for some months, one pair of green woollen gloves had been sold. All the assistants were asked three times whether they remembered by whom the gloves had been bought, but they shook their heads and said, "No, Mr. Cheesewright," with a unanimity that infuriated that plump, officious little man.

The last act of the drama was staged in the wet grey twilight of a January dawn. Messages had passed between police headquarters, the military authorities and Fighter Command; and all was ready to receive the visitor from overseas.

Charlton and Duzest lurked in a very damp ditch with Martin, Bradfield, Emerson and the officer commanding the operations. The field was in the form of a parallelogram, with the lane running along its northern side, in the middle of which was its only gateway. Charlton and the others were in the south-west corner. In the hedges and ditches on the southern and western sides, Bren gunners and infantry with tommy guns and rifles were concealed.

"We don't often get a chance like this," smiled the C.O., "and we want to capture the plane intact, if we can. He'll skim over our heads and land against the wind, which is in the north-east, and, as this field isn't any too big for landing a plane roomy enough to take a passenger, he'll have to taxi back to this corner of the field and then turn into the wind again for the take-off. As soon as he begins to taxi round, the infantry will advance. He'll only have fixed machine-guns forward, so if they keep in front of him he won't be able to bring his free rear gun to bear. If the navigator starts any nonsense with the forward cannon, the men will chuck themselves on the ground and leave the fellows with the Brens to polish him off.

"I'm gambling that the man you're after will do the natural thing and come into the field through the gateway. I don't want to lose any men, if I can help it, and have kept them away from that side of the field and out of range of the plane's rear gun. So your man's suspicions won't be roused as he comes along the lane."

For fifteen more minutes they lay still.

" 'Ope they won't be much longer," muttered Martin to Charlton. "This isn't doing my lumbago any good. The missis was 'orrified when she knew what we was thinking of getting up to."

"You shouldn't have come," Charlton murmured back.

The sergeant was scandalised. *"Me* not come? I'd rather miss me bacon ration than this little turn-out. I only wish I 'ad me mitts on one of them bondooks."

The CO. had his field-glasses trained on the other side of the meadow.

"Don't make too much row," he whispered. "Your man's turned up. He's waiting by the gate with a suit-case that looks pretty heavy and he's wearing a raincoat and cap. Keep quiet, or he'll hear us."

A whispered order for absolute silence was passed down the lines of men.

They did not hear the plane approaching, for it glided inland from a great height. As it circled round, the CO. raised his glasses.

"It's a Messerschmitt 'Jaguar' reconnaissance-bomber," he said.

They saw the crosses on the wingtips, as it skimmed over their heads. It landed towards the further corner of the field, then, as the CO. had forecast, swung round and taxied back in their direction. The man by the gate started off after it. He had gone some distance when another figure appeared in the gateway and set out in pursuit.

"Who's the second fellow?" asked Duzest.

"I can't see in this rotten light," Charlton answered impatiently, and almost snatched the field-glasses from the CO. Then, "It's young Ridpath," he said shortly.

The Messerschmitt was coming towards them. Ridpath shouted. The man with the suitcase turned his head, then broke into an awkward run. Ridpath sprinted after him. The CO. gave a sharp word of command. The infantry left the cover of the hedges and closed in on the plane from two directions. Martin began to scramble out of the ditch and Charlton dragged him back. Ridpath was catching the other man up. The other man waved his hand, stopped and crouched. The machine-gun in the aft cockpit chattered for a brief moment. Ridpath threw up his arms like a runner breasting the tape, fell and lay still.

Through the Messerschmitt's transparent nose, the pilot saw the infantry coming at them. He weighed up the chances, turned and spoke a few quick words to the navigator, who swung the forward cannon—and got a .303 rifle bullet through the brain.

The pilot switched off his engine. He and the rear gunner clambered out of the machine and put up their hands.

The man in the raincoat stood in the middle of the field with his suit-case on the grass by his side. He did not move as Charlton and Duzest left the ditch and walked over to him. As they stopped in front of him, he said without a tremor in his quiet voice:

"Good morning, gentlemen."

It was Charlton who answered him.

"Good morning, Mr. *Mortimer* Robinson," he said.

Major Duzest picked up the suit-case.

XXI

The quietness of Sunday morning pervaded Eagle House when they called. The news of the morning's affairs had not yet reached it. Charlton, Duzest, Martin and the two young detectives went up to Mortimer Robinson's room. Under the bed was a cabin-trunk, in which they found some interesting things, those chiefly concerning Charlton being a Player's cigarette-tin (containing one pound, eighteen shillings and sixpence in cash), a pair of green woollen gloves and the complete uniform, including greatcoat and gold-braided cap, of a staff captain in the British Army.

"That's why Tudor died," he said, holding up the jacket. "It was Mortimer Robinson who shouted, 'Get out!' at six-thirty on Wednesday evening. This room is identical with Tudor's on the floor below, with a similar door leading into the annexe. Tudor wasn't in the habit of coming in the back way, but on Wednesday evening he did—or so we must assume. His mind was on other things and he forgot that, by coming through the back door, he was already on his own floor. He came up the staircase to this floor, walked along the annexe passage and took Mortimer Robinson completely by surprise by suddenly appearing in the doorway. Mortimer Robinson had very likely locked the main door of his room, but had overlooked that one. This is only theory, of course, but it does explain why somebody shouted, 'Get out!' and somebody else said, 'Sorry.' In whatever way it happened, there's no doubt that Tudor accidentally burst in on Mortimer Robinson."

"But what was 'e caught doing?" asked Martin.

"You suggested it yourself on Friday, Martin. He was changing into his other trousers. In other words, he was trying on his uniform. It had to fit him nicely, you see, so that when the invasion of this country began, he could strut about in it, issuing misleading orders, giving false information

276

and generally causing as much confusion as possible. One can imagine his feelings at being discovered in it by Tudor, who didn't have to be very intelligent to draw the right conclusions—and it's obvious that he did, judging from his questioning of Kelso later in the evening. You heard part of their conversation, didn't you, Major?"

"Yes," Duzest agreed. "I was talking to Mortimer Robinson and a man called McIver, only a yard or so away from them. I caught one or two of their remarks, and it's very likely Mortimer Robinson did as well."

"And he must have felt even more uncomfortable when Tudor said, on seeing him in his Escalus costume, that he always looked magnificent in fancy dress. I'm told that he went quite white. So there was only one thing for him to do—close Tudor's mouth. He was just in time. If I'd been at the station when Tudor rang at eleven-twenty-five, his life might have been saved.

"Mortimer Robinson went home to Eagle House with Miss Ashwin and Gough, said good night to them, went up to his room, waited until—well, we don't know exactly, but more or less the same time as Tudor was on the telephone— slipped out of one of the back doors of Eagle House and returned to the theatre. There was no time to get a pair of rubber gloves, so he had to use the next best thing—a woollen pair, very probably bought, at some time, from Cheesewright. The main entrance door to the theatre was unlocked, but he released the catch and closed the door against other callers. We don't know for certain yet, but let's assume that Tudor was sitting at the table, with the door of the box-office open. He heard Mortimer Robinson coming up the stairs and saw him enter the lighted foyer. Mortimer Robinson had thought up some sort of story—perhaps an explanation for the uniform incident—something, at any rate, to allay Tudor's suspicions for a minute or two. The sword-belt was hanging from the back of a chair, with the dagger in its scabbard. Very convenient for Mortimer Robinson, but if it had been somewhere else, he had only to fetch it. He knew it was in the theatre. He strolled across the foyer, casually picked it up and went with it into the box-office. Tudor may have been satisfied with his story about the uniform, or didn't expect a murderous attack from such a quiet harmless little man, for he didn't get up, or even turn round, when Mortimer Robinson came in behind him.

"Whether the trick with the typewriter was impromptu or thought out beforehand, we can't say, but he could only have had just enough time to fiddle with the machine, transfer Tudor's body to the other chair, derange the papers in the tallboy, open the drawer of the table with Tudor's keys and take out the cash-box, before the arrival of Ridpath. He heard the key in the door and Ridpath's footsteps on the stairs. He took a last look round, switched off the light in the box-office, ran along the dark passage and walked into the tape across the top of the stage-door staircase, dragging one of the drawing-pins out of the wall.

"By that time, Ridpath was in the foyer. He tells me that he heard a clattering sound, which was probably Mortimer Robinson falling foul of the damaged tread. Mortimer Robinson managed to get the stage-door open without noise, but dared not close it behind him. With no further ado, he slipped back to Eagle House—if he was wearing rubber-soles, old Sugarman wouldn't have heard him go—and, I should imagine, narrowly escaped bumping into young Gough, who was then on his way to the theatre. There are, of course, two routes.

"Kelso's evidence, coupled with the disturbance at Eagle House at six-thirty, persuaded me that one of Mrs. Doubleday's lodgers—guests rather—was responsible for Tudor's death. What I still don't quite understand is why that Smith man said the 'Get out!' shout was uttered on the first floor, while actually it was up here on the second."

Emerson coughed. "He was quite definite about it, sir. He was on his way in from covering up his car in the garage and was just coming through the back door when he heard the shout upstairs on the next floor."

"That explains it!" Charlton laughed. "You weren't to know, Emerson, but because this place is built on a slope, when you come in from the garden you're already on the first floor, so that the next floor up is the second. I ought to have made the point clearer when I gave you the job—and I certainly ought to have seen the implications when you gave me the Surrey inspector's message."

"How did you first get on to Mortimer Robinson, sir?" asked Bradfield.

"Well, as I said just now, I believed that one of the residents here killed Tudor, so when I read his manuscript a second time, I paid particular attention to the actions and sayings of Gough, Mortimer Robinson and Garnett."

Major Duzest interrupted him.

"As I told you yesterday, I was much intrigued by Tudor's description of the map with the little coloured flags in old Garnett's room," he said. "Granted that fifth columnists don't usually hang their operational charts on the walls of board-ing-houses, but the flags might very well have indicated the positions of stocks of petrol, rifles and ammunition, instead of the Green Man or the Gardener's Arms. As Tudor told Garnett, there *is* no pub at Westham St. Martin, but there might have been a case of hand-grenades or a couple of machine-guns."

"Everything Tudor had written about those three," Charlton resumed, "I read with great care. There was one incident whose significance escaped me at first, but suddenly came to me afterwards. It took place on the day war was declared, when the guests here were assembled in the lounge, to hear the Prime Minister's speech. In his manuscript, Tudor mentioned that a casual visitor, who'd stayed here with her husband for just the one night, was there with them, while the husband was out in the drive, trying to get his motor-cycle to start.

"Just before Mr. Chamberlain's speech, Tudor leant across

to Manhow, who was also there, and asked him how he would have liked to be married to this woman, who was evidently a bit of a vixen. Mortimer Robinson was sitting with them and said with a smile that she reminded him of a magnetic mine—attractive but very dangerous."

"I don't see where that took you, sir," admitted Bradfield.

"As far back as 1918," Charlton said, "experiments were being made with magnetically controlled devices known as bubble mines; but it wasn't until towards the end of last November that Hitler sprang on us his much discussed 'secret weapon'—the magnetic mine. Did you ever hear anyone talk about magnetic mines before they were mentioned in the Press last November? Our Naval experts must have known of them, but the man in the street, the butcher, the baker, the candlestick maker were ignorant of their very existence. Why, then, should the chief clerk of the L.U.D.C. valuation and rating department have knowledge of them over two months before? Surely because he was aware of the advance plans of the unprincipled swine who were going to use them against all shipping, neutral or otherwise.

"How Mortimer Robinson became a German agent, we shall find out in due course. He probably did it because he was well paid—or because he'd been promised the job of Downshire *gauleiter,* when the conquest of this country was complete."

"I've had a quick look through the contents of the suitcase," the Major told them, "and there's enough evidence there to round up the whole of Section 23. Mortimer Robinson seems to have been in control of it. You know those 'other things' I was telling you about, Charlton? Well, in the suit-case there's a comprehensive report about them—and if that had got into the hands of the German Higher Command, it wouldn't have been at all funny. If we hadn't forestalled Mortimer Robinson to-day, he'd have been on his way to Berlin with it by now."

"And young Ridpath would still be alive," added Charlton. "When we dragged him back from London, I sent him to live here until the matter was cleared up. I suppose he noticed Mortimer Robinson creeping out the back way, became suspicious and followed him. I had some men watching the place, with orders to keep Mortimer Robinson under observation, but they had no instructions to stop Ridpath from leaving.

He closed his note-book.

"We'd better get back to the station," he said.

As they went down the stairs, somebody was picking out the tune of "One Day When We Were Young" on the piano in the lounge, while a most unmelodious masculine voice endeavoured to follow with the words.

Myrna and Jack, at any rate, were happy.

Melpomene bent her fingers and examined her well-manicured nails.

"I knew it was going to be him," she said airily, "right from the very beginning."

"Oh, yes?" said Thalia, with the merest pretty trace of an American accent.